NASHVILLE NIGHTS COLLECTON

TEMPTATION, SALVATION AND REDEMPTION

ROBIN COVINGTON

TEMPTATION

TEMPTATION
A Robin Covington New Adult Romance

Giving in never felt so good.

She needs to be good.

At sixteen, Kit ditched her crappy life and moved to Nashville with only $200, her guitar, and a notebook full of songs. She hit it big, but five years of living like a rock star plus a stint in rehab has killed any good will she had with her label. The suits have ordered Kit to shape up or ship out of the limelight. The last thing she needs is a hot, sexy distraction with a sinful smile.

He doesn't know the meaning of the word.

Max Butler is as far from a celebrity as you can get and he likes it that way. A Nashville firefighter, he's living the single life with a revolving door of parties, friends, and a different woman in his bed every night. When his normal life suddenly collides with the girl on his favorite Rolling Stone cover, he sees the perfect chance to fulfill his ultimate fantasy and see just how bad Kit can be.

Sometimes bad is so very good.

With three weeks until Kit leaves for her big tour, Max promises to give her a break from being the good girl--no strings attached. But when hot days lead to sultry nights, the lines get blurred and suddenly three weeks of bad might not be good enough.

What others are saying about TEMPTATION

"Fresh and fun- I enjoyed every second of this tempting read!" – *New York Times and USA Today Bestselling Author Cora Carmack*

"Meet your new book boyfriend. Protective, strong and multi-layered, Max Butler delivers. This book will sweep you off your feet. Right into the arms of a sexy fireman." – *Tessa Bailey, New York Times and USA Today Bestselling Author.*

TEMPTATION

BY

ROBIN COVINGTON

Giving In Never Felt So Good

COPYRIGHT PAGE

Burning Up the Sheets, LLC
23139 Laurel Way
Hollywood, MD 20636

Visit my website at
www.robincovingtonromance.com.
Edited by Kristin Anders, The Romantic Editor
Copy edited by Kim VanDerwerker,

Wordsmith Proofreading Services and Nicole Bailey at Proof Before You Publish, Inc.

Cover design by Babski Creative Studios.

Cover Photo Credit: Jenn LeBlanc/Illustrated Romance

Formatting by Anessa Books

Manufactured in the United States of America

First Edition August 2014

For my father, who gave me the gift of music at an early age and taught me the power of a great lyric delivered with heart. I love you.

ONE

Kit

I WAS GOING to die in a bathroom.

Just like Elvis.

The thought that I might end up as one half of a morbid trivia question—I'll take "name the music stars who died in the bathroom" for $400, Alex"—did not stop the panic from rising in my throat as I struggled to focus my thoughts over the God–awful shrieking of the fire alarms. In the restroom of my record label's rehearsal studio, the emergency lights gave off just enough light to let me see the smoke creeping under the edge of the door. I was no expert on the ideal smoke–to–actual–fire ratio before you died of smoke inhalation, but I knew I had to get out of here and make it to safety. Now.

Physically shaking off my dark thoughts, I stumbled over to the row of sinks, grabbed several lengths of paper towels, ran them under water and squeezed out the excess just like they'd taught me in school many years ago. *Hey, Mrs. Midkiff, I really was paying attention!*

I caught my dim reflection in the mirror and it wasn't pretty. Terror was not a good look for me. My long curly hair was in snarls and sticking to my face and neck with sweat, the crimson streaks that were my trademark looked Halloween–costume creepy when paired with my runny mascara and eyeliner and the smeared red of my lip gloss. I hadn't looked this bad since I'd checked my ass into rehab.

Coughing at the smoke irritating my throat, I slapped the towels over my nose and mouth, my hands shaking as I desperately tried to get my nerves under control.

I didn't want to die. I was only twenty–one years old.

Succumbing to panic was not an option.

I took another look at the smoke creeping under the door.

And neither was staying here any longer.

The smoke was definitely getting thicker now and I had to force my wobbly legs to take me to the door. I reached out with the back of my hand and touched the metal door to see if it was hot and I almost wept when it wasn't. I might have a clear path to safety once I got out of the restroom.

Dropping to my knees, I covered my mouth and eased the door open with my free hand. The alarm was even louder in the hallway and the smoke so heavy the emergency lighting was useless out here. I was now virtually blind and deaf because of the noise. Not a good combination.

I picked the direction that I thought led to the stairwell, briefly considering going back to the studio for my beloved Martin guitar, Jolene. I loved that instrument more than anything in the world but I couldn't risk trying to find my way back through the twisty hallways of the One More

Song Entertainment studios. The thought of never holding it again made me want to lie down on the floor and bawl like a baby, but I couldn't do it. I'd worked too hard to get clean and bounce back from all the stupid decisions I'd made eighteen months ago. I was just starting to see the future that I could have—one where I called the shots and where I figured just who the hell Kit Landry really was in and out of the spotlight.

It wasn't going to be easy—there were so many people who didn't want me to rock the successful, money-making boat that they'd all ridden on for years. They wanted me to be the same girl—America's country-music sweetheart— and I was just figuring out that I was more; that I *could* be more. More than the image I'd hidden behind for the last five years. I was determined to have the chance to find a balance between the old and new Kit and that desire kept me crawling on this floor. It kept me from lying down and giving in to the exhaustion that was weighing me down.

The top of my head hit an immobile object with a brain-scrambling thud and I reached up, feeling the emergency door under my fingertips. *Thank you, baby Jesus!* With the excitement of potentially avoiding death giving me an extra jolt of energy, I lifted up and pushed on the release bar.

It wouldn't budge.

Shit.

Overcome with the urge to take a deep breath, I dropped to the ground and re-covered my mouth with the cloth. Panic hovered on the edge of reason as I frantically searched my brain for what to do next. I was running out of all the stuff I'd learned in the few years I'd attended school regularly.

Okay... just staying here sounds like a bad idea, but I

can't see down the hall...maybe I should just stay here... the fire department will see me signed in on this floor... the smoke is getting really thick... don't cough... makes it worse... damn, I really don't want to die like this... this will be on one of those awful "How did they die?" documentary shows... I'm just getting my life back...

Huddled closer to the ground, I tried to breathe in shallow bursts but the smoke was so thick I couldn't stop coughing, and inhaled more and more smoke. I couldn't go forward. I couldn't see enough to go back.

I was so screwed.

Paralyzed with fear and only shitty options, I re–covered my face with the towels and listened for any sounds of rescue.

I was dizzy and disoriented, a heaviness settling in my arms and legs—making it hard to keep my mouth covered. I tried to focus, but my mind was drifting, memories moving through like the way sunlight skated across my eyelids when I was a kid lying on the soft grass near my house—my Daddy and Mama, being on my own way too soon, coming to Nashville alone and broke at sixteen, selling my first record... touring... Jake when he was my first love and the first one to break my heart... my months at Spring Ridge Rehab... the fans... performing....

Fuck; they were right. It really does pass before your eyes...

But what killed me were the things I didn't see. A normal life. A real date with a guy I hadn't met through my publicists. An end to all the lying and secrets. A family. Marriage. Kids. A home.

Hell, yeah, to the minivan. Bring it on—at least some-day. I wasn't going to judge something I'd never had.

And if someone didn't find me quick... I never would.

I heard noises in the distance, relief kicking up the adrenaline again and giving me enough energy to raise myself up on my knees. I tried to see if anyone was coming down the hall but the smoke had thickened, the smell of burning plastic, commercial carpet, and electronics getting stronger by the second. Hot tears fell from my burning eyes and down my face, and I knew I was about three seconds from losing my shit. I was a tough girl. Life had knocked me around, but this blow had come from left field and I zigged when I should have zagged.

Too fucking bad.

I removed the towels from my mouth and yelled as loudly as I could. Which wasn't loud at all.

I sucked in another breath through the towel filter and coughed before trying again. "Help!"

Oh, shit. That took it all out of me and I collapsed on the floor, ignoring the pain that shot through my chin when my head landed with a THUNK! on the nasty commercial carpet. I hoped to God that someone heard me because I had just blown my entire wad with that stunt. My eyes were sliding shut and there wasn't a damn thing I could do about it.

A voice, distant and muffled, filtered into my consciousness. "Hey, Dean! I found someone over here!"

Through the fog in my brain, I registered a pair of rough gloves yanking on my arms and hauling me close to a large body. A mask was placed over my mouth and I sucked in big gulps of smoke–free air. It was delicious. Better than chocolate, I swear.

"Hang on. I've got you. Just hang on." The smooth, deep voice of my rescuer rushed over me, calming me until I suddenly remembered Isaac, the security guard on duty.

Pushing off the mask, I croaked, "You've got to get..." I

wasn't able to finish the warning because I started coughing, so much that I expected to see my toenails go flying across the room with the next big hack.

"Is there someone else in the building?" He looked down at me, up close and definitely space–invading because of the thick smoke, but he was able to see me nod. He pressed a button on his uniform and spoke into a walkie–talkie mounted on his shoulder. "Dean, we've got a second vic in the building."

"Get yours outta here. I'm on it."

"My guitar." I knew it was stupid and selfish to mention an object, but she was like a person to me.

"Your guitar?" he asked and when I nodded he immediately shook his head. "Sorry, I'm not going back for a guitar. My captain would have my ass in a sling for that one."

My rescuer lifted me up, murmuring into my ear as he moved down the hallway, "Let's get you safe and checked out. Just hang on, ma'am."

Shifting his hold on me, he shoved against the emergency door several times. It still wouldn't budge even with his ginormous body ramming against it. That fucking door was really messing with my need to get out of the blazing inferno. Mr. Rescue wasn't happy either.

He let out a creative curse and spoke into the walkie–talkie again. "Unit Three. I have a female victim on the third floor. Emergency exit blocked. I'm headed to the windows on the northeast side of the building. Going to the fire escape. Over."

Fire escape. Heights. Rickety stairs.

I pushed down the panic that surged up from my stomach and threatened to splatter all over his nice fire-man's uniform. I hated heights. When my team had suggested my adding some of that Cirque Du Soleil stuff that P!nk did in her shows to my concert, I told them that I was all for it as long as they issued raincoats to all the seats under me. I would hurl. Everywhere. I've seen me do it.

But now, I could do nothing but cling to him as he carried me into an office, shut the door, and walked over to the expanse of windows.

Placing me on the floor, he eyeballed me through the safety glass of his mask. "I have to break out this window." He positioned my mask more firmly on my face. "Stay here and keep this on."

I started to nod my head in agreement but moving made me feel sick all over again, so I slumped against the wall and waited for him. Glass shattered and a clean rush of evening air cooled my cheeks. My rescuer knelt down, lifted me up, and propped me up close to the new opening.

"Let's get you outside for a little fresh air."

Let's not. Let's get out of the building in a way that doesn't require me to suspend myself three stories above the very hard concrete on nothing but a rusty metal staircase.

I kept my death grip on the wall as he stepped onto the escape and kicked at the ladder release with a booted foot several times. It shuddered and squealed and made noises that did not assure me of its stability. If he suggested that we jump, I would kill him.

He swore and turned on his walkie–talkie. "Unit Three. Fire escape on northeast side is broken. We need a bucket."

Oh, great. I've seen this on TV. I've watched "Back-draft". We were going to leave the fire escape and get into a container suspended on top of the fire ladder. Why was I here on a Friday night?

That's right; I was being a good girl these days.

After confirmation squawked back into his device, he reached inside and lifted me through the open window and over the windowsill. I had shut my eyes tightly the minute it looked like he was going to take me out on the suspended death trap, but when he stopped I couldn't help myself. I opened my eyes and immediately, involuntarily, looked down. On instinct, I jumped back away from the ledge, grabbing the fireman standing next to me.

"Whoa, whoa. You okay?"

Heart pounding, I hid my face against his chest like a little kid. "I'm afraid of heights."

He chuckled. "Well, we could go back inside..." When I grabbed him and lurched towards the opening that led back inside, he held me tighter and stroked my back soothingly. "Hey, we can't go back in there. Sorry. Fireman humor."

I whimpered. Honest-to-God whined like a puppy but I couldn't stop it. I now understood the whole "rock and a hard place" thing. I knew in my head that I couldn't go back inside, but standing out on this tiny fire escape with smoke around us and the wind blowing was like someone had reached inside my head and arranged my worst–case scenario. But when I rubbed two of my oxygen–deprived brain cells together, I knew this was better.

Still clinging to him with one hand, I moved the mask off my face. "I really didn't want to die in the bathroom."

His chest rumbled with low laughter. "Most people aren't real particular about the location. Just the *not dying* part."

I peered up at him in the dark but couldn't clearly see his face with all the safety gear on. "Are you making fun of me?"

"No, ma'am; just trying to distract you."

"Oh..." I huddled closer to him, shaking uncontrollably. "I can't stop sh–sh–aking."

He chafed my arms with his hands, the rough texture of

the gloves causing enough friction to warm me up a little bit. He grabbed the oxygen mask and put it back over my nose and mouth, tightening the strap to make sure it stayed on. "It's shock. They'll fix you up once we get you to the bus. Just hang on."

Nodding, I took a deep, shuddering breath to steady my nerves. *Don't cry. Don't you dare cry.*

His voice broke across the silence. "What were you doing here on a Friday night? No hot date?"

I coughed again and shook my head, moving the mask to the side in order to overshare. I babbled when I was nervous. Not a good trait when you had to give interviews to rapid–fire, story–hungry reporters all the time.

"I haven't had a date in over a year."

"The men you know must be stupid or blind."

My head was starting to do that swimmy–thing again, but I squinted up at him. "Are you hitting on me?"

He shrugged, placing the mask back on my face. It was becoming a game. Yay.

"Maybe. Is it working?"

"Oh... you're distracting me again." I leaned against him as the coughing resumed. The lights from the fire truck that had pulled in below us hurt my eyes as he spoke to his co–workers on the walkie–talkie. My head felt like it was floating—I couldn't focus. Bone–deep exhaustion was seeping into my muscles. *I just want to go to sleep.*

"Hey!" He shook me gently and spoke into my ear, "Stay with me; your ride's here. Don't pass out on me now—you haven't agreed to go out with me yet."

I tried to laugh, but the heaviness was pressing down again and it took all of my effort to stay awake. Through the fog in my brain, I was aware of my fireman securing a belt around my waist and moving me into the metal cage at the top of the ladder. I thought about going into a full–blown panic attack at this new level of craptastic fun, but I just couldn't muster the energy. The rollercoaster lurch in my stomach as we made our way to the ground was minimized by my epic level of tiredness.

Once it landed on the ground, I was instantly surrounded by a mob of people tugging on me, putting me on a stretcher, and checking my vital signs. I forced my eyes open and looked up into the face of the man who had saved my life.

His mask was pushed completely off his face now and I could see his features clearly. His skin was smudged with black soot that emphasized his strong, angular jaw. His eyes were a deep topaz fringed by thick, black eyelashes.

He was fucking gorgeous. Not movie–star or prettied–up male model good–looking, but real man, works–for–a–living, has–women–falling–all–over–him at the grocery store smokin' hot. If I could have custom–ordered a man, this is what he would look like.

I slumped against him and groaned. "Oh, no. I'm dead."

Concern clouded his perfect features as he leaned down to me. "No, ma'am; you're okay. You'll be fine."

"Nope. I'm dead." I pointed at him with a shaky finger. "Because anybody as beautiful as you must be an angel."

I thought I heard laughter as everything went black.

TWO

Max

LET'S BE CLEAR. I'm no angel.

I've been called many things. Some of the people I rescue call me a hero but I hate that word. I'm just doing my job, but it did make me feel like all my hard work and the risking–my–life thing was appreciated by those I serve. The women in my life called me the name of the Almighty when they were under me and then a son–of–a–bitch when I left —but those were both exaggerations made in the heat of the moment. In truth, I was somewhere in between.

But I have *never* been called an angel.

When the tiny brunette had uttered those words at the scene, it was cool. But, when Bobby Lane, the firefighter manning the bucket, told the other guys on the A–Shift team, the warm glow of the moment turned into burning irritation.

In the face of the ration of shit they gave me, I wore an expression of nonchalance—as my mom always said, "Don't give that dog something to chase." But two weeks of finding little halos and wings in my locker had grated on my last fucking nerve. Add to that the almost constant "411" commentary from the assholes on my celebrity victim and I was about to go out of my ever–lovin' mind.

I didn't need the "411" anyway.

I was Kit's biggest fan.

Now two weeks later, I'm trying to hide my six–foot–three–inch frame behind a fake plant in a random munic-ipal conference room, still unable to believe that I'm going to meet her again. In fact, I'm going to be seeing a lot more of her since her label and my boss decided that the joint–positive PR from a few events was a good idea.

I wasn't complaining.

In less than an hour, I would walk over to the makeshift stage situated on the other end of the room and receive a letter of commendation—delivered by Kit Landry herself. She was probably one of the few things that could have enticed me to get decked out in my dress uniform and endure the formal ceremony. I love the job, but I can't stand the press–the–flesh crap that comes with the territory since we got our new director—Paul Bates. He never passed up an opportunity to rub shoulders with the celebrities in Music City, especially if it got him a photo op and some good press for the department.

He was totally in love with me right now. Saving the "Sweetheart of Country Music" had saved my bacon with the brass. According to my captain, they were prepared to overlook some of my less–than–stellar off–duty activities—specifically my "chasing tail, drinking and fighting".

And I got to spend some quality time with my favorite fantasy girl.

"I can't believe you didn't recognize her."

I glanced over at Dean, my best friend, and shrugged. "Man, it was smoky and my mind was on the job."

"Uh-huh." Dean rubbed his lower back. "My back is still out of whack. How did I get stuck with the security guard built like a linebacker and you got the hottie who weighs about a buck ten?"

"Righteous living, my friend."

Laughing, as Dean gave me the one-finger salute, we both turned as Bobby Lane sidled up to us. Bobby is an okay firefighter. So far, he's managed not to get my ass killed at a scene but he's also the world's biggest douchebag.

He fucks anything that moves and brags about it even though none of us wants to hear it. Don't get me wrong; I'm all about getting laid as often as possible but I don't have to brag about it. The fact that my partners usually end up coming back for seconds and thirds says it all for me. Truth be told, a third date is about the limit for the women I typically meet. Once they realize that moving in and buying a new comforter and throw pillows isn't ever going to be on the agenda with me, they move on, unless they like to keep it hot and casual.

"Is she here yet?" Bobby smoothed a hand over his short blonde hair. "I can't believe you had the balls to ask her out."

I groaned. "I told you, I was just trying..."

"Yeah, yeah; you were just trying to distract her." Bobby waved me off. "Just let me know if you actually plan to follow through with nailing your dream-girl, because if you don't..." He leaned in a little closer and I took a step back. Did I mention that he's a douchebag and a close talker? "...I plan to."

Dean choked out a laugh and Bobby looked like he wanted to knock him on his ass. "Why do you think she'd go out with you? If she's gonna go out with anyone, it would be Max. He's the one who saved her life."

"I know." Bobby placed his hand over his heart and flashed a leering smile. "God bless women at the scene—they're always *so* grateful."

"Bobby, you need help," I said.

"Hey! Don't act like you've never done it." Bobby was offended and then accusatory. "You've done your share of cashing in on badge–bunny adoration."

Okay, he was right. I wasn't one to pass up the best perk from the job—appreciative hot women who wanted to deliver their thanks up close and personally. I just didn't want to talk about it with Bobby. And I definitely wasn't talking about Kit with him.

Dean was the first to speak. "Kit Landry is no badge–bunny."

"And, I'm not *you*," I said. And, this was Kit Landry we were talking about. Famous people were a whole other species in this town and I wasn't interested in dipping my dick or anything else into that gene pool. I'd grown up in Nashville and the celebrity around here was served with a side of fake and a dab of crazy. No thanks.

But for Kit, I would make an exception. At least one night; one *very long* night.

"Yeah, I know." Bobby snorted. "You think because you don't talk about all the fucking you do that it makes you better than me. How many times have I had to deal with one of your women who didn't get the memo about how quickly you turn them in for the next model?" He had the balls to lean over and poke me in the chest. "And you're going to do the same thing with your favorite jerk–off fantasy girl, so save the angel act."

His comment pissed me off and only Dean's hand on

my arm kept me from taking a swing. It wouldn't surprise anyone around here if I got into a fight—just another one of the things they overlooked because I was good at my job. "Shut the fuck up."

Bobby had apparently eaten his Wheaties this morning, because he barely glanced down to where my fist was clenched at my side before he kept talking. "Look, we all know you have a thing for her. You have *all* of her music."

I shrugged. "So do lots of people."

Bobby wiggled his eyebrows. "Yeah, but everyone doesn't have that issue of *Rolling Stone* with her centerfold in those little Daisy Duke's and halter top stashed under their bunk."

I bit back a curse and looked away. Crap. He wasn't wrong.

I looked around the room, wondering when this was ever going to get started so I could get out of this uniform and away from Bobby. I hate being trussed up like a turkey on Thanksgiving even more than I hate Bobby and his childish attitude, which on a good day puts him on the same level of maturity as a fourteen–year–old.

I needed to walk away before I also acted like a high–schooler and gave him a swirlie in the bathroom.

But still, Bobby kept talking. "I'll bet you a hundred bucks you can't hook up with her."

Okay, make that a twelve–year–old.

I turned my gaze towards Bobby as Dean mumbled something that sounded a lot like "what an ass".

"Are you kidding me? I'm not going to bet that I can fuck a woman—Kit Landry or anyone else. Were you born a dick? In what universe is that cool?"

"Since your dream girl can't get you motivated, I'll throw in a little money to sweeten the pot."

I rounded on Bobby, the effort to keep my voice down in this crowd of bigwigs making my throat hurt. "I'm not crazy enough to take your sucker bet. Kit Landry is a world–famous country music star. She dates movie stars, football players, rock stars—do you see a pattern here?"

"We all know she's got a bad girl inside who loves to come out and play, and I'm betting that even rehab didn't calm down Miss Kitty."

I would never admit it, but I think he's right. Until a year and a half ago, she'd been the poster child for the kind of girl you took home to your parents and then put a ring on it. But then, she'd taken a turn—a sexy, bad girl turn—and then a nosedive. I hadn't liked watching her spiral into rehab but I hoped that the new, improved Kit kept some of the edge from her walk on the wild side. While she hadn't been hitting the party scene lately, she'd kept the crimson red streaks in her long brown hair, added a new tattoo on her arm and the bootleg versions of her new music circulating the local scene showed an entirely different sound. They weren't the carefully executed songs that stayed with the good girl image, but raw and honest—with maybe a glimpse at the real girl behind the guitar.

And that was a girl I would love to meet up close and personal, and preferably naked.

Bobby moved my finger off his chest and flashed a smile that didn't quite reach his eyes. That's the thing about Bobby—deep down he had a streak of mean and I wanted no part of it. "I'll make it five hundred."

The crowd behind us started getting loud, the buzz of excitement rumbling through the small space. I turned around just in time to see Kit come through the door. Flashbulbs were going off all around her, but they were completely unnecessary—she lit up the room all by herself.

Today she was dressed in a modest black dress instead of her usual jeans, sexy top and boots. With her glossy black curls trailing down her back and her petite frame, she was the living and breathing version of my dream girl. And, as usual, my dreams were definitely drifting into the X–rated section of the mental video store.

Bobby leaned over to me and stuck out his hand. "Five hundred. Are you in?"

"Fuck off."

"Gentlemen."

I turned to look down at the man who'd slipped up behind us without our noticing. The press pass hanging around his neck was the last thing I wanted to see. *Fuck me. What had he heard?*

The newcomer glanced around the group, but his eyes finally settled on me. His eyes were hard and assessing and, although I didn't know exactly what the guy was selling, I knew I wasn't buying.

"Firefighter Butler." His lips pulled back in a smile but it didn't quite reach his eyes. "Congratulations on your commendation."

"Thanks." I crossed my arms over my chest and waited him out.

The stranger chuckled softly, reached into his pocket, and fished out a business card which he held out to me. I didn't take it, didn't even look at it. This dude was the worst judge of body language, otherwise he'd be long gone.

"I'm Earle Foster with the Daily Scoop and I'm prepared to offer you one thousand dollars for an exclusive interview with you about Kit Landry."

"It isn't much of a story. Everyone knows I rescued her from the fire. No big deal."

I was done. I turned my back on him. The reporter reeked of sleaze and lies and suddenly I needed a shower.

"I don't want a story about the rescue. I want an exclusive on the time you're going to spend with her during these PR events your boss and her handlers have cooked up."

I looked down into the shorter man's face. "You need to go. I'm not interested."

The guy smiled, as persistent as he was butt–fuck ugly. "I can go up to five thousand dollars if you get me a story that will put her on the front page again." He looked over his shoulder to where Kit was standing on the stage before turning back to me. "She's been such a good girl lately, we haven't had any juicy stories to report."

"And you won't get any from me."

I felt his hand dip into the pocket of my uniform and withdraw without the business card. When I fished it out and tried to hand it back to him, he backed up and shoved his hands in his own pockets.

"Mr. Butler. Don't worry. If you call me I'll be discreet. Ms. Landry is extremely touchy about her friends talking to the press."

"I said no."

"I'm a good reporter. Maybe I'll just poke around and find out what will persuade you to cooperate."

"Knock yourself out."

I was now officially over this conversation. I shoved him aside and walked towards the stage. I was within a few feet of Kit when another man decided to block my way—my boss, Captain Price. He was the only guy who was going to stop my progress right now.

"Butler."

"Captain."

He looked me over and I stood at attention, holding my breath until he gave the nod that said I'd passed inspection.

"Congratulations on your commendation."

"Thank you, sir."

"Saving Ms. Landry pulled your ass out of the fire with the Department." I looked at him to see if he was cracking a fireman joke, but his hard glare told me he wasn't. "This is your shot to erase all the bar fights and the Christmas party incident from their minds when they review your application for promotion."

Holy shit. Were they ever going to stop bringing up last year's Christmas party? It was like no one had ever had sex in a supply closet before.

"I understand, sir—"

"Let me be clear. There's lots of press here today, people with video cameras. The whole goddamn city will see this on the news as they eat dinner tonight." He nodded at someone across the room. "Don't fuck this up."

"Yes, sir."

He barely looked at me before he walked away. I was a good firefighter, but when you were trying to get promoted, your extra–firehouse activities mattered—especially when they landed you in jail and in between the wrong woman's thighs.

I shoved all that to the back of my mind and looked back to where Kit sat on the stage. I had a few moments before the ceremony started and I had a surprise for our special guest up my sleeve.

But first, I needed to properly introduce myself to Kit Landry.

THREE

Kit

"YOU DIDN'T TELL me he was hot."

I didn't even pretend to misunderstand who Bridget was talking about. Max was the hottest thing going in this room and we both knew it. Examining the hem of my dress, I shifted in the uncomfortable folding chair on the dais and rolled my eyes. I knew better than to encourage Bridget when she got on the subject of men... it never ended well. In fact, men in general never ended well for me. "I told you he was handsome."

"No, you said he was good–looking." Bridget elbowed me in the side. "Now, just so we're clear for future conversations—'good–looking' is between 'not ugly' and 'I could lick him all over'." She jerked her thumb in the direction of where Max stood with the other firefighters. "Max is clearly lickable."

I felt the rush of blood to my cheeks and neck, knowing that she'd made me go all red and splotchy. I grabbed Bridget's hand and leaned in closer to whisper, "Could you please stop pointing? I was almost a crispy critter. I didn't notice his looks all that much."

I was a big fat liar. The minute I'd walked in the door, I'd picked Max out of the crowd. He stood a good two inches taller than his friends and his broad shoulders reminded me of how safe I'd felt when he'd held me out on the fire escape. Thankfully, much of that frightening night was fuzzy, but I remembered Max. He was very hard to forget.

Bridget laughed out loud—a belly laugh that had several people looking in their direction. Shaking her head, she dabbed at her eyes dramatically. "You're a terrible liar."

I glared, knowing it wouldn't do any good. "I'm going to fire you."

"No, you won't. You love me. Besides, I'm trying to get you laid as your best friend—not your personal assistant."

"Who said anything about getting laid?"

"I did. Since you seem to have given up on that part of your life entirely, *someone* needs to worry about getting you some action." Bridget reached down to grab her PDA, which was buzzing like a bumblebee. Glancing at the screen, she groaned, "Ugh, it's Ron. I'll take care of this and you can go over and talk to Max and see if he'll help you out with your little dry spell."

"The last thing I need is a little action." Out of the corner of my eye, I spied the director of the fire department and Liam Connor, my record label president, headed over towards the stage. "I *need* to behave myself until my new contract is signed."

I had a lot of people who depended on my not fucking this up and I owed it to them. Romance—temporary or otherwise—shouldn't be on my agenda. And I had other shit to figure out. Life for me was complicated and I didn't have the energy or time to figure out how to fit someone new into the mix.

In spite of my best efforts, my eyes wandered over to where Max was standing by the stage. *Was he waiting for me?* Our eyes connected and suddenly my skin was tingly, hot, and too tight. Needing to move and break the tension, I stood up next to Bridget, rubbed my damp hands on my dress, and averted my eyes. Hell, I'd played two sold-out shows at Madison Square Garden—I could handle the hot local firefighter.

"The label is breathing down my neck to prove that I'm not going to go off the deep-end again. I've got a shit-load of my own money invested in a tour that starts in a month and a number of people who depend upon me for their paycheck." I eyeballed my best friend and drove my point home. "I don't have time for a relationship."

Bridget scoffed and gave me a slow, knowing smile. "Who said anything about a relationship? I was just talking about sex."

I stood there as Bridget sauntered away, unable to get in the last word unless I yelled or chased her down. I wasn't running in these heels. "Damn. I *hate* it when she does that."

"Does what?"

Startled, I whirled around too quickly and lost my balance, but a strong hand grabbed my arm just in time to keep me from falling over. My hands grasped the torso in front of me—a hard, muscular, male torso. I knew who it was before I looked up.

"Whoa. Steady there." Max's voice was filled with concern and I bit my lip at the sexy, deep tone. If he ever gave up firefighting, he could do phone sex. Just for me. I would pay a lot of money for that.

I was staring at him and couldn't stop. His face was finely chiseled along the cheekbones—the skin a golden olive tone. His black hair was cut short and stubble shadowed his strong jaw. I wondered how it would feel against the tender skin of my face, my breasts....

"You okay?" His brows were scrunched together in worry, his hands tightening their grip on my arms.

I was... lusting... ogling... wondering what you look like under that uniform... "Fine." Once again, the telltale hot flash crawled up my skin and I knew I was blushing. I eased his hands off my body, bit back a groan at the loss of his touch, and stepped back. I laughed and gestured towards my shoes. "I'm okay. These shoes..."

He looked down at my high–heeled sandals and back up at me—a smile tugging at his mouth. Damn, this man was so fine and I know what I'm talking about. Prince Harry, George Clooney, Johnny Depp—I've met them all—and they'd never made me feel like this.

"So, you hate when who does what?" he asked.

"That was..." *About you having sex with me.* "Um... nothing."

He shrugged his shoulders and glanced over at the director finalizing all the stuff on the podium. Turning back to me, he offered me his hand with a full, sexy smile that curled my toes. "We haven't *actually* met. I'm Max Butler."

His accent was movie–star southern, thick but not country–twangy like mine and I responded in my best "Scarlett O'Hara" impression as I took his hand, "My hero!" and giggled as a blush crept up his neck. Jesus, he needed to stop being so damn cute.

"Yeah. Something like that."

"I'm Kit." I tugged at my hand but he held it fast. My pulse was thrumming underneath his fingers and I wondered if he could feel it.

His voice was soft. "I know."

I looked around the room and noticed that we were starting to attract attention and, while I liked holding hands with the big, hot guy, this was not the focus I needed right now. The "good girl" plan required by my label didn't encourage public displays of affection—unless they were arranged by my publicist. I tugged a little harder and he dropped it, raising his own to rake it through his hair, giving it a slightly tousled effect. *Probably what he would look like when he first woke in the morning—all drowsy and rumpled.*

Damn Bridget and her suggestions. Now that I had it in my head, I couldn't stop my mind from drifting to X–rated fantasies of Max.

His voice pulled me back to the present. "...I have something for you."

I blinked several times, trying to focus on his words and not the way his jaw was covered by the beginning of the sexiest dark stubble. "I'm sorry. What?"

Max's eyes twinkled mischievously and I wondered if he knew where my thoughts had drifted.

"I have something for you. The brass wanted me to present it to you at the ceremony but I get the feeling that you wouldn't want an audience for your reunion."

I was now thoroughly confused, craning my neck to watch him as he walked behind the stage, leaned over and picked something off the floor. When he straightened, I saw what he had in his hand and my heart did a somersault, the bottom fell out of my stomach and the tears that would ruin my hour–long makeup job threatened to do their worst.

My guitar case. Jolene.

"Oh!" I slapped my shaking hand over my mouth and resisted the urge to knock over the three people in between me and Max and my baby. He sauntered over, holding her as gently as you would a baby, before placing the case on a chair.

"The case got a little wet from the sprinklers, but I checked her out and she sounds fine. No signs of warping or any damage."

I couldn't speak. What the hell could I say to even touch what I was feeling at the moment? This instrument was more than a bunch of wood and wire. It was the one link I had to my life before Nashville and the girl who existed back then.

"Oh, my God. Thank you," I managed to whisper over the tightness that had overtaken my throat. I blinked hard and fast, willing myself not to give in to the tears that this moment probably deserved. But I was a professional pretender and, while I didn't think I would mind showing my hand to the man who'd witnessed my panic attack four floors above the ground, I wouldn't do it in front of all these people. All these strangers. "This is the kindest thing..."

I leaned over and opened the case and hovered over her. I always did this, savored the moment just before I touched her for the first time. This guitar was more important to me than any lover, our connection elemental, and I respected the hell out of it. She'd gotten my ass off the street and made it possible for me to take care of the people important to me.

And with the songs I'd been writing lately, she was going to help me get back on top.

"We were told that the building and its contents were a total loss. We already filed a claim for the insurance," I said, finding my voice. I closed my fingers around her neck, cradled her body, and lifted her out of the case. The wood was cool but it would soon warm up to my body temperature, an extension of me in every way. I threw the strap over my neck and felt myself exhale down to my marrow. "I never thought I'd see her again. Jolene belonged to my grandpa."

"A Martin 1944 D–28."

I looked up at Max, not even trying to hide the surprise on my face. "You know guitars?"

"A little. My Grandpa Butler loves them and I absorbed a little over the years."

I experimented with a soft strum, testing the sound. She sounded wonderful. "You play?"

"Doesn't everybody who was raised in this town?" He was quick to add, "Not well enough to do justice to this beautiful lady."

He reached out to touch her his long fingers stroking the neck with a reverence that told me he understood how special she was. He brushed my hand and I closed my fingers over his, giving them a squeeze that didn't even come close to expressing my thanks.

Max raised his eyes from my guitar to look at me and I caught my breath at the connection that arced between us. It was like Jolene was a conduit for all the untapped, raw interest we had in each other. I knew then that my attraction wasn't one–sided. If I wanted it, all I had to do was reach out and take it. Max would meet me more than half way.

Someone bumped into me from behind and I snapped back to the present. The room was even more crowded than before and people were watching us. I closed my eyes, centering my emotions and putting on my game face. When I opened them again, Max was staring at me, confusion clouding his eyes.

He started to speak, but the sight of the director taking the podium signaled that the ceremony was about to begin. I reluctantly put Jolene away and tucked her case behind the stage. We took our seats next to each other on the dais and listened while Director Bates praised his firefighters for their bravery and dedication to the people of Nashville. I wholeheartedly agreed; their bravery had saved me from an untimely death, but I couldn't focus because right now I felt really, really alive.

Max was sitting close enough for me to feel the heat pouring off his body and it kept my senses on high alert. I shifted in my seat to ease the tension building in my belly.

Maybe Bridget was right. It *had* been too long.

Finally, we stood up so I could present Max with his commendation. Next to me, he stood at attention as the director read aloud the account of his brave actions the night he'd saved me from the fire. Max looked tense, uncomfortable; as if he disliked all of the attention. I put it in the column of one more thing I liked about him.

The director finished his recitation and turned to me, handing over the ribbon to pin on Max's chest. I reached up to do my duty, but hit a snag right away—he was too tall for me to reach comfortably without having my skirt ride up and show the whole world my assets. He looked confused by the delay until I motioned for him to lean down a little— a move that caused a ripple of laughter in the crowd and a small smile to form on Max's lips that softened his features.

Tearing my eyes away from his face, I focused on the task at hand and murmured so only he could hear, "Thank you for saving my life." My hands were shaky with emotion as I struggled to get the ribbon pinned on his chest.

"Well, I couldn't let you die in a bathroom, now could I?"

I laughed softly. "No, I guess you couldn't."

Finished with his ribbon, I rested my hands on his chest and leaned up to kiss his cheek.

Under my hands, his chest constricted with his swift intake of breath at the moment my lips touched his skin. I inhaled deeply, soaking in his scent of cedar wood, citrus, and warm male, while the blood pounded in my ears and my skin grew warmer. Pulling away, we both exhaled slowly as our eyes locked in a heated exchange of shock and desire.

There was no mistaking the look of desire in his eyes, and I'm sure it matched the one in my own. I wanted him with jaw-clenching intensity and the part of me that was all woman unfurled after being packed away for so long. I might as well have been back on that fire escape, because this felt just as dangerous. More dangerous.

Behind me, the gathered paparazzi began to call out above the murmuring of the crowd.

"Give him a real kiss, Kit!"

"Is that how you thank a hero?"

"Kiss him!"

At the sound of their voices, I glanced over my shoulder. Everyone was smiling encouragingly; the press wanted the photo, the other firefighters were cheering on their boy.

I looked back at Max for his opinion.

A smirk pulled at the edge of his lips. "I *did* save your life."

I narrowed my eyes, not really mad at the suggestion. "That's not fair."

He shrugged his shoulders the slightest bit and grinned. "Chicken?"

Oh. Hell. No.

Determined and rising to the bait, I lifted my face,

slowly closing the distance between our mouths. This would be quick, fun and flirty, and over before it began.

I had no fucking clue what I was talking about.

The first press of our mouths was like being hooked up to a live wire. We both broke contact in surprise but quickly began again, the lure of such intense pleasure already addictive.

I was the one who took it deeper, running my tongue along his, dipping inside to taste him. I couldn't help myself; it was like putting my favorite dessert in front of me and saying that I could only have a sample. Good luck trying to stop me.

Max groaned and grabbed my hips, his fingers lightly digging into my flesh—tugging me closer and turning the kiss hotter, wetter. His mouth slanted over mine and his tongue stroked past my lips, taking what he wanted and what I freely gave. My knees went weak, and I clutched the fabric of his uniform, holding him close as the kiss went on and on.

The sound of whooping and clapping startled me and snapped me back to reality. This wasn't good.

I distanced myself from Max, only far enough away to end the kiss but not far enough to lose the physical contact of his hands on me. I was breathing hard, my breasts swollen under the tight dress, my lips tender and tingly. Max was panting, his face hard and eyes hot.

Painfully aware of our audience and my management and label president glaring at me from the other end of the room, I tried to pull back further but Max shook his head, holding me in his grip.

"We shouldn't have done that," I said.

"Maybe not, but I want to do it again," he answered, his

smile intimate and naughty enough to make me shiver. "And I want to do more."

I sucked in a breath. I had thought the fire was dangerous, but I was wrong. Max was the thing I needed to worry about.

"You're no angel," I whispered.

"I'm glad you finally figured it out."

FOUR

Max

"I STILL CAN'T BELIEVE you kissed her."

I paused in my inventory of the truck equipment and shot a look over my shoulder towards Dean, who was leaning against the threshold of the open bay doors of the firehouse. It was a gorgeous early summer day and I was happy to take on a duty that let me enjoy the outdoors for a while. Turning back to my task, I replied. "Actually, *she* kissed me."

Dean scoffed. "Technically."

"No, *not* technically, asshole."

Dean laughed in my face, ignoring my shitty tone. "Well, you *did* kiss her back and I know I saw a little tongue action."

The sight of his waggling eyebrows made me laugh out loud. He wasn't wrong. I'd seen the video of the kiss over and over, and sure enough, it was clear that the kiss was way more than a TV kiss peck of the lips. In fact, some commenters on YouTube said that it should be marked as inappropriate for people under eighteen. My mother had even called and lectured me on the types of kisses that were appropriate in a public forum.

The director had flagged me down after the press conference and chewed my ass about proper conduct in uniform, but it rolled right off my back since I could still taste Kit on my lips.

I turned, crossed my arms, and leaned against the truck. "I wish everyone would stop talking about it. It was a little publicity stunt and it'll never happen again."

"Frustrated much? Wishing that Kit would take that kiss a lot further?"

"Fuck, yeah." I wasn't going to deny it. I wanted her and now that I'd gotten a sample of just how sweetly hot she was, my bad mood was directly related to the lack of opportunity to pursue it. "I haven't heard from her since she was swept away by her management team right after the press conference. I don't have her number to call her."

"You could call her manager," Dean suggested. "I'm sure he'd be happy to organize your booty call."

"Fuck off." I didn't want to do that, but it looked like the joint PR events might not be happening after all. If I wanted my shot with Kit, calling her handler might be my only option. I'd give it another day. "At least the press stopped following me around."

"Is that one reporter still calling you?"

"The guy from the Daily Scoop?"

"That the douchebag from the ceremony?"

"Yeah. He somehow got my cell phone number and he's even approached my mom at work. There's no way in hell I'm going to give him a story, but he still keeps calling." I curled my hands into fists; I'd made sure he'd gotten the message the last time he'd shown up in person. That dude could haul ass when he needed to and my six–feet–three–inches in his face was good motivation. "He threatened me the last phone call; told me that if I wasn't part of the solution then he'd make it my problem and get the scoop on me, as well."

"You? What could he possibly have on you?" Dean asked.

"Nothing. Even the last time I was hauled into the captain's office for fighting in a bar was old news. But, we both know the director wouldn't like any kind of bad publicity and it could screw up my chance at promotion." I squinted into the sun shining into the firehouse, and counted down the six weeks until I could put in my request for a team leader position. At twenty–three, I was still junior to lots of the guys who would apply, and my chances weren't great, but I needed to send a message that I wanted it. My interest would lead them to offer me lesser opportunities and that would make me more competitive the next time I applied. The politics of the job were not my strong point, but I was learning. Moving up in the ranks was determined by more than running into burning buildings. "All he wants is some dirt on her so he can get a byline, and he doesn't care who he hurts to get it."

I'd lived in Nashville my whole life and it didn't take long to notice how the press constantly hounded the local celebrities. Yeah, they'd chosen a career in the public eye and it wasn't as bad as what people talked about in Holly-wood or New York, but there had to be limits. Being a fan, I'd followed Kit's stories this past year and rooted for her to pull out of her tailspin. Her crash and burn had rivaled Britney—minus the extreme haircut—but she was clearly trying to get beyond that and all this guy wanted to do was tear her down for the price of a daily tabloid cover price.

And truth be told, I'd saved Kit's life and that created a bond of sorts between us—at least one that required some degree of loyalty. But, even if I didn't feel that connection with her, I possessed a highly developed sense of self–preservation. If I gave a story, then the possibility existed that *I* would become the story as well—at least for a short time.

No. Thank. You.

I'd keep my mouth shut, figure out a way to get in touch with Kit, and get her in my bed for at least one night. As it was, I was thankful my fifteen minutes of fame was over.

Dean's voice interrupted my train of thought. "Are you going to tell Kit about that guy?"

"No. Why should I? She's got a whole team of people keeping an eye on him, I'm sure. Soon I'll no longer be worth his interest."

Dean stepped into the bay and leaned up against the truck. Oh, shit. He had his serious face on and that meant I was getting a lecture about my lack of a committed relationship at the ripe old age of twenty–three. "The heat between you two was pretty clear to YouTube viewers worldwide. Maybe you want to think about trying to get beyond casual with Kit."

"Dean, I'm glad that you've got your happily–ever–after with Shannon, but that's not gonna happen for me. I don't want that. I'd suck at that two kids and minivan thing." I pushed off from the truck and walked over to the open bay, gazing out onto the street. "I tried that once and it blew up in my face."

"Yep. I remember." Dean pointed at his chest. "Front row seat, remember? I'm not saying you'll live happily ever after, but what's wrong with living in the moment? Just having fun and seeing where it goes with no restrictions in your head about the shelf–life? You plan the end before you've even got the condom on the first time. Maybe you just see how it goes for once." He smiled and patted me on the back as he headed towards the residential part of the station. Now he could answer my mother truthfully when she asked him to help me "find a nice girl and settle down".

I turned back to my task as I mulled over what Dean had said. Have a little fun with Kit Landry? Sure thing. Over and over, and all night long.

Anything more than casual? Not going to happen.

But, I couldn't stop thinking about that kiss. How she'd tasted, how she'd felt in my arms. Despite the difference in our size, she fit perfectly against me—like she was made to be there. We had chemistry, alright. But that was all it was or would ever be.

"Excuse me, can you tell me where I can find Shannon Jones?"

The voice came out of nowhere and I lurched up, banging the top of my head on the edge of the truck door. Biting back the "fuck me" that could get me written up, I straightened, turned, and found myself looking right into the eyes of the woman I'd just been obsessing over.

Kit was standing there in my station, an expression of surprise and then concern on her face as she glanced to where I'd clonked the living shit out of myself just seconds before. She was wearing a low–cut, little blue sundress and cowboy boots and everything else was miles of bare skin and dark curls. My brain went mushy. Maybe I'd hit my head harder than I'd thought.

Her voice was full of concern as she moved closer. "Max, are you okay? I didn't mean to sneak up behind you."

I stared at her like an idiot. In person, I was reminded again of just how gorgeous she was. She walked towards me and I couldn't move, couldn't take my eyes off of her. If you looked up "dumbstruck" in the dictionary, you'd see my goofy–ass face pasted right next to it.

I still hadn't answered when she stopped in front of me. Standing on tiptoe she touched my recent injury. "Are you sure you're okay?"

Her voice was feminine, with a whiskey–edge that tied my gut up in knots. Her hand was cool on my over–heated skin and, as she moved closer, I could smell her sweet, summery, honeysuckle scent. All I wanted to do was pull her lush curves against my body, take her mouth, and find out exactly where this crazy chemistry would take us.

I definitely had a head injury because suddenly I realized that I had her close enough to do all those things and I wasn't doing anything about it.

Get your shit together, Butler. Carpe the fucking diem.

I grabbed her by the waist and pulled her towards me, turning us so she was backed up against the door of the fire truck. She still held her packages in her hands and I missed the feel of her touch on my body, but I could work with what I had.

She stared up at me, her big, blue eyes wide with shock but mostly what I saw there was curiosity. She licked her lips and that was all the invitation I needed. I leaned into her, bypassing the prize of her mouth to press a kiss to her throat, just above the place where her pulse pounded against her skin. She was delicious all over, sweet and warm, and I wanted to drag her down to the floor and bury my cock inside her body for hours.

I looked down and realized that my hands were shaking, my breath as quick as hers—and I hadn't even kissed her yet.

"When we fuck, it's probably going to kill me." It came out as a growl, as I tipped her face up to mine and wasted no more time in taking what I wanted.

Kit didn't play games, no pretending that she didn't want this, too. She opened to me, meeting my tongue more than halfway when I dove inside. She was as hungry as I was and the kiss was anything but the usual finesse I used on women. There was no slow seduction here. It wasn't in my power to play games. I was at the mercy of whatever she would give me.

I slanted my mouth over hers, barely giving her a chance to take a breath before I went at her again like I was starving.

And I was famished. For her. It was the craziest thing I'd ever experienced, but I wasn't going to let a little insanity stop me. It never had before.

I wrapped my arms around her waist, inserting my body in between her legs. The skirt of her dress rode up high on her thighs as I pressed my hard–on against the hot cleft of her pussy. I rolled my hips against her and she dropped the bags in her hands with a thud against the concrete, weaving her fingers into my hair with a pressure that brought a little pain with the pleasure.

I didn't care. She could do whatever she wanted to my body as long as I got to do exactly what I was doing right now. As long as she let me do this and so much more.

The blast of my lieutenant's voice over the station intercom was the biggest cock block of my short life. He wasn't looking for me, but it made Kit pull back from the kiss and that was tragic. I held on tight, brushing my lips against her, light as a feather but as intense as bungee jumping.

"What are you doing here?" I asked, pressing a soft kiss against the side of her mouth.

"I was looking for the paramedic, Shannon Jones." One of her hands left the spot where they were looped around my neck to point at the floor by our feet. "I've got the T–shirts and tickets that I promised. She told me she would be around today."

"You could have sent somebody else with those things. No need to come down here yourself," I teased, taking a chance that she'd shown up in my house without her entourage because she couldn't forget the kiss either. My gamble was rewarded by a soft laugh and an embarrassed flush on her cheeks. Busted.

"I wanted to see you." She pulled back, ending our kiss and replacing her smile with a frown. "To make sure you were okay."

"I'm fine. Why wouldn't I be?"

"I know the press was following you after we..."

"After we kissed." I leaned back in and reminded her of what we were talking about. She sighed the minute our lips touched and I decided that the feel of her fingers in my hair was just about the best thing ever. I knew that standing here like this was insane in a busy firehouse, and it was only a miracle that we hadn't been found yet. Time to cut to the chase. "It *was* a little crazy. It's over. Thanks for asking, but that isn't what we should be talking about right now."

"It isn't?" She picked up on my tone and her lips curled up in smile. "Then what should we be talking about?"

"Our date."

"Oh? Do we have a date to talk about?"

"We will, once you say yes."

"I'm not supposed to be dating," she bit her lip, her eyes losing some of their glow from a few minutes earlier.

She was a grown woman, twenty–one and independent—who could tell her not to date? "The label, my management. Part of my deal was to concentrate on getting ready for the tour, writing music for the new album. Not dating."

Oh, the mile–wide loophole her team had left for me to plow through. I'd been getting around parental restrictions since I realized what fun girls could be when their mamas weren't looking and how easy it was to get them out of their panties.

"Don't call it a date—an outing. Community outreach. No press. No pressure. Just you and me hanging out."

"I don't know."

That wasn't a yes, but I could hear her excuses crumbling like an old brick wall. It was time for the big guns.

"I *did* save your life."

Kit narrowed her eyes. "What exactly is the shelf–life on you using that to your advantage?"

I sensed that the prize was almost mine and I worked hard to repress my grin. That grin always got me in trouble. "I don't know. Until I get what I want."

"And what do you want?"

"I want you."

"You're very direct."

"I don't see any point in skirting the issue, since all I want is to get under yours."

She laughed, a small hand with black and silver fingernails clapping over her mouth to stop the giggle. I didn't know if that was a good sign or not, especially when she wiggled out of my arms, removed her phone from a bag at her feet and held it out to me.

"Give me your phone. Program in your number."

I did as she asked, wondering if she was ever going to

give me that 'yes' I was looking for. When we were done, she bent back down and gathered her bags from the floor.

"Okay. One not–a–date." She walked past me towards the door to the main part of the firehouse. When she got to the door, she turned around and gave me a look that said that I was in for a wild fucking ride with this girl. "But if you want another one—you'll have to rescue me again."

"Lucky for me, I have my own fire truck."

FIVE

Kit

"I CAN'T BELIEVE you eat that stuff."

I shoved the last piece of the sugar–covered funnel cake into my mouth and licked my fingers. Max watched in slack–jawed awe as I smiled up at him. "What? You bring me to a carnival and I'm going to eat carnival food."

"Come to think of it, I'm not as concerned about *what* you're eating as in *how much* you're eating." He raised a hand and counted off on his fingers—as if I needed reminding. "A corn dog, cotton candy, ice cream, and now a funnel cake." He waved in the general direction of my body. "Where do you put it all?"

I looked down and checked out my outfit—jeans, a tank top, and flip–flops. None of it screamed "country music star" and that is exactly what I wanted; a low profile. Max had called that morning and I'd taken twenty minutes to throw on some clothes and sneak out of the house. With my hair pulled up in a ponytail, a baseball hat shoved on top of my head, and only mascara and lip gloss on my face, I was not what people would be looking for, even in Music City. I couldn't be expected to walk around like I was performing at the Grand Ole Opry all the time, could I?

"I run three miles every day, and do yoga. I don't think my figure suffers for it." I waved my hand along my body, inviting comment and ogling.

Max didn't disappoint. His eyes followed my lead, and lingered.

The impact of his gaze was as powerful as a touch and my body reacted with a slow spiral of desire. No part of me had forgotten our kiss yesterday and all of me wanted another chance to feel that good again. Max was like a drug and I was seriously considering getting another fix as soon as possible. But we needed to get some ground rules established first—I couldn't afford to proceed without making sure we were on the same page. My career might depend on it.

And I had lots of people depending on me.

He shifted closer until he brushed against me from breast to thigh. His height forced me to look upward to meet his gaze, as his hand lightly caressed my arm with a sensual touch that created a series of shivers under my skin.

He smiled down at me, his grin telling me that he knew exactly what he was doing to me. "I think you," his eyes moved back down my body and back up to my eyes in one long sweep, "look more beautiful today than you've ever looked before."

I stared at him, my mouth suddenly as dry as the desert, my brain cells scrambled. Now, I knew that Max was a sweet-talker and probably used it to get a new woman in his bed every night, but his look told me that he was looking at the girl and not the star and, damn, was that sexy.

And scary.

I could handle men looking at me as a conquest, a trophy for their arm, but I was unnerved by the way that Max treated me like something more. I knew he was a fan, but that had never been a thing between us. So, it often took a while for a guy to see me as just a regular person—if they even wanted to see me that way. Too many times I was just a meal ticket, a way to get their foot in the door to the music business or a chance to get more face time with the press by being seen with me. Many of my so–called friends and former lovers dove for cover when I detonated last year. It was a tough lesson to learn, but one I would never forget.

But Max felt different and I was still trying to decide if this was a sign to stick around or run for it. He made me feel normal and this was unfamiliar territory for me. I was both thrilled and terrified. It was why I had agreed to go out with him in the first place—other than the crazy sexual heat between us. I had a shot at having something normal for at least a little while and it made me want to lean into him, wrap my arms around him, and just be Kit. What a concept.

As if he could read my thoughts, Max's large hand tugged at my waist, pulling me closer to him. My breasts pressed against his chest, my nipples tightening in response to his touch and residual lust he'd left me with since that crazy kiss at the firehouse. I wasn't the only one feeling the effect of proximity. Max's cock was heavy where his jean–clad body pressed into mine and I would have given anything to pull that zipper down and see if he could deliver on the promise he made with his every touch.

Heavy lidded with desire, his eyes darkened and I licked my lips as he lowered his head to kiss me.

"Oooph. Sorry, buddy." I heard the apology from whoever it was that bumped into Max, jostling him and breaking us apart before I succumbed to the sexual lobotomy that happened whenever Max was near.

I didn't know what I was thinking. Anybody with a cell phone could grab a photo of us kissing and I'd have my label on my ass so fast they'd break the sound barrier. This man made me sloppy.

Max was nothing but pure, unadulterated, yummy distraction and I really couldn't afford a distraction right now. I needed to be good. I needed to rehearse my tour and write songs and give radio and TV interviews and whatever else I was told to do until they agreed to keep me on the label.

When he returned his gaze to mine, I cleared my throat and attempted to sound casual, to ignore the way my fingers itched to reach up and touch his hair. "Beautiful, huh? Makes me wonder why I spend money on all those stylists and make–up people if you think I look better now."

He shoved his hands in his pockets and flashed a sheepish grin. "Don't get me wrong, you look amazing on stage." His gaze lingered over me once again. "But I like this Kit. You look like a normal girl."

I smiled at that and sauntered over to the arcade area. I was intrigued by this turn in the conversation. "A normal girl? I'm not what you expected?"

"No." He shook his head. "Fuck, no."

"Why?"

"I guess I expected the party girl who goes to fancy Nashville parties." He glanced over at me and then around the small, local carnival. "I mean, I had no idea if you would like this sort of thing, but you've been awesome." Max chuckled. "I can't remember when I had such a great time hoping my date wouldn't throw up on me on the Tilt–a–Whirl."

I punched him in the arm and Max hammed it up by rubbing the place where I'd made impact, as if I'd really done some damage. The guy had a good foot on me in height and one hundred pounds in weight and was built like a Mack truck. If he decided to take me right then and there, all I'd be able to do is hang on for the ride.

It wasn't lost on me that I wouldn't mind taking that ride.

Laughing, we walked down the row of stalls containing various cheap stuffed animals and carnival employees hawking their game as a sure–winner. One guy with a shaved head and goatee caught Max's eye and cajoled him into winning a prize for me.

I learned something about him at that stall—Max never backed down from a challenge and he had a killer arm. When I wasn't distracting him.

Thirty minutes later, we were walking back to the firehouse and I was carrying the largest stuffed frog I'd ever seen.

"I can't believe how rigged those games are." Max frowned as he glanced over at me. "I think the only reason that guy let me win is because he thought you were pretty."

"Thank goodness! We might have been there all night if we'd waited for your aim to improve."

"Hey!" Max replied in a wounded tone. "I know what you were doing with all the touching and blowing in my ear. No fair distracting the pitcher."

Laughing, I stumbled on the sidewalk and the grip on my frog slipped. Max reached out to grab him but I resisted. "Hands off! I can carry Merle all by myself."

Max snickered. "Merle? Merle Haggard? You *aren't* naming that frog after one of the greatest country music stars of all time?"

I sniffed. I thought the name was perfect. "Merle will have a place of honor on my tour bus this summer. It's only fitting that he has a name fit for a country music frog."

He sounded unconvinced. "If you say so."

Laughing easily, we walked along in a comfortable silence and I thought about the afternoon with Max. It had been the most fun I'd had in... forever.

"Thank you."

Max looked over at me, his expression puzzled. "For what?"

"For today." I stopped next to my truck, dropped Merle onto the hood, and turned to face Max. "Thank you for giving me a break. For letting me be a 'normal' girl for the afternoon. I don't get a whole lot of normal in my life."

He shook his head. "You know there's something wrong with a girl who has the world at her feet, but can't do what she wants once in a while."

"I did what I wanted for a while and it got me in a lot of trouble. Now, I'm paying for it. I have to be a good girl now."

"I get that, but when do you stop paying?" He stepped forward and tipped my chin up with his finger and leaned down so that I could almost look him in the eye. "It sounds to me like you need to take your life back."

"That's the plan."

"So, what's stopping you?"

Me. The answer was right there but I clamped my lips together, unwilling to spill my guts in the Harris Teeter parking lot.

He moved closer to me—so close I could smell him, feel his body heat. Like a magnet, my body swayed forward slightly and I grabbed what little control I had left and backed up against my truck. Not a smart move. Max took a couple of steps forward and caged me in between his body and the truck.

Max leaned in and nuzzled my cheek, murmuring into my ear, "I'm going to end this non–date by kissing you."

I normally didn't like bossy men who crowded me with their bodies, but Max was breaking all the rules for me. I got off on it; he made me hot, wet, and itching to find a horizontal place with a door where we could get naked and sweaty.

Swallowing hard, I was breathless when I answered. "This probably isn't a good idea."

My body involuntarily arched into his and I exercised restraint I didn't know I had in order to resist reaching up to run my hands over the hard muscles covering his chest.

And then he did that bossy, sexually aggressive Max–thing and broke down one more barrier. He reached down and hooked his fingers in my belt loops, pulling my lower body close and nudging a hard thigh between my legs. Deliberately, he shifted his leg up and pressed against my core, and the pleasure was so good I moaned low and deep in my throat. He responded by rocking his cock into me again, his eyes hot and aggressive.

"Fuck. I love that sound. It makes me hard." Max touched a curl lying across my shoulder. "Even if this is the worst idea ever, I don't care."

His hand grazed my collarbone and his eyes drifted down to where my nipples poked out against the thin cotton of my tank top. The slight lift of his mouth assured me that he knew exactly what he was doing.

It pissed me off. Not in a bad way, but in the totally sexy, arousing way that led to long sweaty nights in a big bed where we worked out the power dynamic.

I let my own gaze wander up and down the length of his

body. So big, strong—I took another peek at the bulge in his jeans—and definitely interested. For the past year, I'd been out on dates with slick, phony, musicians or Brad Pitt–wannabes—all arranged by my label's publicity team. It had been a long time since I'd indulged in what it felt like to be young, healthy, and sexy. Part of my treatment had focused on reclaiming who I was and this was a part of myself that I had yet to bring back online. At my core, I was a steady–relationship kind of girl, not the fling kind of chick, but maybe Max was the guy to help with my first step back into the land of the sexually living.

It didn't have to be anything serious. That was definitely in my plans, but Max would be a very enjoyable detour.

I trailed my hands up his chest, caressing the hardness underneath his T–shirt. He shuddered as I scraped a nail over his nipple. Smiling, I wrapped my arms around his neck, caressing the smooth skin of his nape and tangling in his hair. He pushed against my hand, silently begging for more, like a big cat.

His big hands trailed down my body, grazing the sides of my breasts and momentarily cupping their fullness before drifting lower to pull my hips even closer. He leaned in, his nose tracing a path of fire across my jaw, my neck, and landing just behind my ear. "I'm going to kiss you now. Last chance to object."

Rubbing my body against his, I had nothing. My head told me that this was a really bad idea—why tempt myself with something that couldn't go anywhere? I was sure one word from me and Max would let me go.

But I wasn't going to say it and he knew it. I wanted this. Wanted him. It was time for me to rejoin the world of sexually active twenty–somethings and to enjoy myself. Just for the sake of sex. Just for the sake of feeling good.

Moving my face to the side, I found his lips with mine and murmured, "Stop talking about it and do it already."

The kiss was not what I expected. He'd been fast and frantic before, but this joining was slow and sweet; just a gentle brushing of lips against lips. But it still burned me alive. The heat from his touch started at my mouth and caught fire as it raged through my system. My fingertips were glowing, my toes curling, and fire surged low in my belly. I pulled back a second to catch my breath and found myself looking into his eyes.

I didn't think it could get any hotter but Max knew how to play me better than any Nashville musician I'd ever worked with. He cupped my jaw with one hand to hold me in place and that little gesture flipped my switch and I spontaneously combusted, leaning up to take his mouth for my own. He tasted of mint, spicy male, and pure pleasure. His teeth nibbled on my lower lip before soothing the sting with a warm lick of his tongue. I gasped and he took full advantage, invading my mouth with a slow, teasing thrust.

I *really* needed to write a song about this.

Linking both arms around his neck, I drowned in the kiss, pressing my body into his hands as they roamed my back, over my hips, and down my thighs. Groaning against my skin, Max covered my neck with hot, open–mouthed kisses and the skin exposed by my skimpy tank top. I felt him tug on the fabric with his teeth.

"I want to pull this down and suck on your tits until you come for me."

"Yes." I wanted that, too.

I grabbed his head between my hands and forced his

lips back to my own and it was my turn to control the mesh of tongue, lips, and teeth.

Max let me have my way for ten seconds before he grabbed my ass and lifted me off my feet. The movement prompted me to wrap my legs around him, bringing my aching pussy into direct contact with the hard length of his cock. Best. Position. Ever.

"Hey, Max! Whoa! Sorry, man!"

The voice rudely ripped through my sexual haze. Panting and flushed, I stared up at Max, his bewildered expression surely mirroring my own. Both of our gazes drifted over in the direction of the voice of the intruder.

Dean, embarrassed, waved his fingers at us while Shannon peeked over his shoulder.

Damn and double damn.

And then it hit me. Anyone—fans, the press—could have seen me wrapped around Max in the middle of this parking lot.

I looked down and realized I was *still* wrapped around Max.

Bad. Bad. Very bad.

Scrambling, I struggled out of Max's arms and hit the pavement, quickly adjusting my clothes. This whole thing was crazy, and I needed to grab my frog and get the hell out of here, before Max worked his voodoo on me again and I actually fucked him in the parking lot of the Harris Teeter.

I just needed some space. I needed to let Max know what this was and wasn't. Set some ground rules.

"I should go."

I turned and grabbed Merle, moving towards the door of my truck. My hands shook and I was cursing the blasted door lock when I heard Dean over my shoulder. "Nice frog."

Resting my forehead on the window glass, I took a few steadying breaths before I turned to face him. He was smiling and I flashed him a grateful look for breaking the ice. "Thanks. His name is Merle."

Dean nodded. "The Hag. Good choice."

I looked at Max and gave him an "I told you so look", that he brushed off with a wave of his hand and roll of his eyes.

Dean cleared his throat. "Sorry about the interruption. We came looking for you two because we need a favor. Shannon, the love of my life, has gotten us involved with a bowling league." His facial expression was classic whipped male and I had to giggle when Shannon punched him in the shoulder. "Anyway, we're short two people tonight and need you to fill in."

Shannon took over, her bouncy delivery making me smile. "No pressure, but we'll have to forfeit if we don't get two more bowlers." She clasped her hands in a pleading manner. "Please?"

"You don't want me," I said. "I can't bowl."

"Don't worry. We just need the bodies."

I looked over at Max. This was totally his call. Hanging out one-on-one was cool, but maybe he didn't want me around his friends.

Max crossed his arms over his chest, his face expressive but hard for me to decipher. He watched me for a few seconds, trying to gauge my reaction, too, I guess. Finally, he gave a quick nod.

"I'm in if you are. You said you didn't get a lot of normal in your life." His lip lifted in a smirk. "There's nothing more normal than bowling."

Yep, I'd said that and I'd meant it. Lately, I was always living cautiously, following the plan with no deviations. I didn't have to be in the studio tonight; no rehearsal, no appearances until early tomorrow morning. Why the hell not?

I closed and locked the door of my truck and turned back to the waiting group. "Okay. I'm in."

Pleased, Dean smiled and nodded. Shannon clapped her hands; talking a mile a minute as her boyfriend led her away.

"You really okay with this?" Max asked.

Was I? Did I want to spend more time with him? Get a chance later to talk about what was and wasn't brewing between us?

"Yep. I'm cool with this."

Max grabbed my hand in his, weaving our fingers. "Good. We'll have fun."

"Yeah, yeah, yeah. But, tell me this." I matched his grin as we followed the others across the parking lot. "Why does normal have to involve rented shoes?"

SIX

Max

"HOLY SHIT. SHE REALLY IS TERRIBLE."

I stood with Dean on the side of the bowling lanes assigned to the league and watched Kit bowl the first ball on her last frame. We both tensed as the ball careened down the lane and finally landed in the gutter—again. I shook my head, as Kit turned to Shannon and lifted her hands in defeat. Shannon stood up and embraced her as they both laughed at something Kit said.

I checked out her scorecard. Straight gutter balls. "Well, she *did* warn us."

"I know, but it usually isn't true." Dean's face was contorted with laughter and disbelief as he raked a hand over his face. "People just say that kind of stuff to be modest."

"She should have let us put up the bumper guards." I watched her as she grabbed the ball for her second roll and lined up on the lane. I leaned forward slightly as she walked forward, swung her arm out, and sent the ball down the lane. She was still bent over at the waist, anxiously watching the ball progress towards the pins and I couldn't help but enjoy the view. Her ass was fine and I vividly remembered what it felt like in my hands when I'd kissed her earlier today.

I could still taste her on my lips and smell her perfume on my clothes. Straightening, I discreetly adjusted my jeans over the permanent hard–on that appeared whenever she was around. What I'd intended to be a light, sexy kiss had blown up into something so hot that I was amazed my lips weren't scorched.

"Sorry about interrupting your make–out session in the parking lot earlier," Dean said.

"No worries; it isn't like I won't get another one."

"Yeah? You going out with her again?"

"It wasn't a date." I'd told Dean all about Kit's reservations to call it an actual date. "I wonder how long her label and manager are going to keep her on such a short leash."

"If you believe the papers, she cost them a shit ton of money. They're just protecting their investment."

"I guess."

"So is this it or are you going to have another non–date?"

"I want to. She's very cool." Truth be told, she was one of the most fun girls I'd ever spent time with and we hadn't even made it to a bed yet. And I wanted to take it that far with her. Over and over again, for at least one entire night. "I think she's into me."

Kit glanced over her shoulder at me with a big smile before returning her attention to Shannon and the fans who had just realized who Kit was.

Eyeing the exchange, Dean commented. "If the look on

her face is any evidence as to how she feels, she's into you in a big way."

I continued to watch her as she laughed and joked with the rest of the bowling team. In the midst of a group full of strangers, she exuded warmth and friendliness—and she was so damn hot.

Yeah, I'd fantasized about her, but the reality was so much better. And the crazy part? If the kiss was any indication, then Dean might be right, and she also felt this wild chemistry between us.

We were going to fuck each other. For one night? For more? I had no idea, but it was something we needed to iron out. I always made sure the women knew where I stood and Kit was no different just because she was a celebrity. As soon as we got that straight, I'd consider it a green light.

I didn't know if she was looking for a picket fence, but I wasn't offering one.

Forget the whole movie–of–the–week bullshit about a regular guy and a celebrity; they had the cold reality of the situation to deal with. I'd brushed up against the life of the rich and famous in this town since I was a kid and had ended up way the worse for wear. Frankly, I didn't know how she dealt with all the lies and bullshit in the music industry, but I did know that my future plans did not involve being in any tabloid.

Kit was smack–dab in the middle of the very public fishbowl in which she had chosen to live her life, and anyone who wanted to be with her had to take that on. Always watching what you did, what you said, what you wore—it was exhausting to think about it. And now she was faced with having to play the part of the good little girl for the court of public opinion.

A good girl. The words reminded me of the Daily Scoop

reporter. The guy still called every day and I continued to refuse his offer. It must fucking suck to have assholes like that following you around all the time, buying your secrets from people who went cheap.

After today, I had some secrets to share—at least some insight into her world and what she was really like. For some reason she trusted me, at least enough to let down her guard a little bit. If I was a dick, it would be so easy to use that trust and get her to reveal so much more. And if I got her to give into this attraction, and didn't mind sharing the details? I could be at least five grand richer for the price of an afternoon at the local carnival, a condom, and a cell phone video camera.

"So, what are you gonna do now?" Dean's voice cut into my thoughts, dragging me back to the present.

"I'm going to have the talk with her and then see where it goes."

"Don't."

"Dean, don't start."

"Max, I know I'm starting to sound like a broken record, but why do you set rules that kill any chance of you having more? You don't have to marry her." He leaned in like he had a secret to share. "There's this thing called *dating* and some people think it's a fun way to spend your evenings and weekends. You do it until you want to make it permanent because you love each other or you break up and change your statuses on Facebook. Why don't you just try it and see where it goes?"

"It's not my thing. You know that."

"All I know is that every woman isn't Sarah. You've got to let go of the past."

"I'm not the one who keeps bringing her up." I reined in my temper. He was my best friend and he thought he was doing the right thing, but it was getting old. The disaster with Sarah went down four years ago and I'd learned my lesson and moved on. "Just fucking drop it."

"Hey Max!" Shannon skipped over to us, slinging her arm around Dean's neck. It was hard to maintain the tense atmosphere when she was around. "Kit says she'll be ready to go in a few minutes." Her face beamed with excitement. "I can't believe I got to bowl with Kit Landry! I have to call my mom!" She was practically levitating with excitement as she skipped away, dragging Dean in her wake.

I decided to sit down and observe Kit while she wrapped up the last autographs. She gave each person focused attention, asking questions about them and their families. Her entire vibe was warm and approachable and she seduced them all with her authenticity. It was no wonder she had so many loyal fans.

This afternoon with Kit had rocked my world and I didn't want it to end today. Not yet. But, I wondered if she would be up for what I had to offer.

No strings. A little fun between consenting adults.

It was all I could offer. Ever.

There was only one way to find out.

Fifteen minutes later, the last fan walked away, excitedly looking at his photo with Kit now saved on his cell phone. She wandered over to me, smiling apologetically. "Sorry about that. Occupational hazard."

I stood up, letting her lead the way out of the bowling alley and towards my truck. "No worries. I liked watching you work." I gestured towards a few fans still in the lot. "They love you."

She climbed up into the cab and I rounded the truck and was seated before she answered with a heavy tone. "They love the image. They don't know me."

I was surprised at first by the answer, but there was truth in it. Hell, until the past few days, I'd been one of those people and even now I didn't pretend to know her well at all. "If they got to know you, they would find lots to love."

"I wonder." She leaned against the window and sighed. "Getting to know someone means looking beyond the image and taking the good with the bad—including the ugly secrets."

I couldn't disagree with her. "I guess you're right, but that's true even if you aren't famous. How often does anyone really let others see the deepest, darkest parts of their life?" I thought of all the reporters—and one in particular—who circled her like vultures. I turned to face her in the darkened truck cab. "We *all* have secrets."

She sighed and laughed softly. "Ignore me. I'm just tired."

I tried to see her in the gloom of the truck; something in her voice sounded off to me, like she was carrying something heavy. I didn't have the right to pry and I guessed that she wouldn't tell me even if I asked. Why should she?

"Well, I've gotten to know you a little and I like what I see."

I watched Kit, noting how she nervously bit her bottom lip—a move I found entirely adorable. And sexy. She was about to bolt, and I knew this might be my one chance.

Needing to touch her again, I moved closer, pressing my body against her and nudging her back against the seat of the truck. I rested my arms on either side of her tiny frame as she tipped her head back to look into my eyes. Her hands drifted up to rest on my chest, her fingers alternately clenching my T-shirt and petting my chest.

My body jolted with the electric shock from where we

connected and, just like that, I was *right there*. Hard as rock and dying for her. In the silent cocoon of my truck, I leaned in close, touching our foreheads together, listening to each other breathe as the seconds ticked by.

Tracing lazy circles along the soft skin of her breast exposed at the top edge of her tank top, I murmured, "I want to fuck you and I think you want me to."

"I do." She laughed softly when I paused. "What? You expected me to play it another way? I don't do games, Max."

"You shocked me a little," I admitted.

"My work life is full of games. Half–truths and strategy. I don't want that in my bed."

Jesus. She was me. Without a penis. Thank God.

"What do you want in your bed?" I leaned in to bury my face in her hair, the warmth of her skin against my cheek and her sweet scent surrounding me.

"You. For three weeks," she murmured, arching her neck when I began pressing a series of soft kisses on her skin. She was melting under me, her body heating up with the fire we had growing between us. "I don't have time for a relationship. I'm three weeks away from the most important tour of my life and I shouldn't be thinking of anything except work."

"But..." I lifted my head to look at her, needing her to say the words to seal the deal.

"I want you and I plan on having you. A lot."

"Any way you want me. Any time. I live to serve."

"Good."

I leaned forward and brushed a kiss across her lips. When her lips opened slightly, I slipped my tongue inside and leisurely explored her mouth. It was like I had the key to unlock her. She opened up under me, her legs spreading to accommodate me as much as possible in the front seat of my truck. I could take her here. Peel off her jeans and panties and slide in where she was hot, wet, and tight. It would be a fast and hard fuck that would take the edge off and then we could head back to my place.

I broke off the kiss to lay out my plan of action when my phone went off.

Fuck me.

It was the ringtone for the department and I knew I had to answer it. My chances for getting lucky tonight were about as good as winning the actual lottery.

I picked it up and accepted the call. "Yeah?"

Dispatch told me exactly what I didn't want to hear with a hot willing woman in my truck. My plans for Kit Landry were going to have to wait. I hung up and moved back behind the wheel.

I looked over at her and wished I hadn't. A tousled Kit, lips wet from our kisses, her tits on display under that tiny tank top was not a vision I wanted to trade for sweaty guys, smelly fire gear, smoke and flames. "I'm not on duty, but I'm secondary and they need all hands who are fit for duty to report."

"That's cool. You've got to go." She leaned over and kissed me, her hand trailing down my chest to settle on my cock. She stroked me lightly, making my eyes cross with the pleasure of it. I felt like fucking Superman when I managed to keep my hands on the wheel and off her. "We've got three weeks. I'm not going anywhere."

And at that moment, I wondered if I'd gotten in over my head with Kit Landry.

SEVEN

Kit

"HE OFFERED TO DO WHAT?"

I settled back into the chair and glanced around the open, utilitarian warehouse space the label had provided for rehearsals of my upcoming tour. I took a sip of my coffee as Bridget worked through her emotions. I wasn't surprised. My band, my friends and companions for the past five years, stuck by me through the ups and the downs of my crazy career and they worried about me—especially after the train wreck my life had been just a year ago. But Bridget had sat right by me through the whole thing, never once breaking eye contact or dumping me.

I'd been cruel to her at times—coming down from the alcohol and pills hadn't brought out the best in me. She'd taken it like a champ, called me out like a true friend, and forgiven me when I asked for it. She is my sister, my secret keeper, my most trusted companion and she wasn't on board the Max train. Not even a little bit.

Bridget was now looking at me with expectation, so I took a deep breath and plunged right in. "I went over to the fire station to take the photos, T-shirts, and tickets and then he asked me out. We had a good time and then... one thing led to another."

"Okay, I got it. He's the reason you disappeared the other night." She took a big gulp of her coffee and pointed at me across the table. "Get to the point where he offered the sex."

"Keep your voice down!" I glanced around the rehearsal space, noting with relief that none of my band mates seemed to have overheard this particular conversation. "He didn't offer the sex until I asked for it."

"Oh, that makes me feel *so* much better."

"Bridget, it wasn't like that." I thought about how to ease her mind and explain my reasons for this. "He makes me feel something I haven't felt in a long time. With Max, I feel like 'Kit the woman' and not like..."

"'Kit the merchandise'. 'Kit the paycheck'."

"Exactly." I pulled my hair off my face and into a scrunchie on top of my head.

"He sleeps with a lot of women," she mumbled, suddenly engrossed in the design of her Starbucks cup.

I gave her the hairy eyeball. "Did you check up on him?"

"Ron had your security team do the usual checks. He's a good firefighter on the job, but he's run into some trouble in his personal life."

"Like what?" I instantly regretted asking. This felt invasive. Unfair. Max and I weren't about details. And if I was looking for any semblance of a normal thing with him, I shouldn't act like a paranoid celebrity.

"He's got a hot temper. Won't back down from a fight but he doesn't seem to go looking for them." She paused and I knew the next fact was a whammy. "And he slept with the Fire Department Chief's niece..."

"Was she legal? Married?"

"...in the maintenance closet at the department Christmas party."

"Oh." It wasn't funny but I couldn't help the chuckle that spilled out. "Not a career–enhancing moment."

From the look on her face, it was clear that Bridget didn't find this as funny as I did. What did I care about who he'd slept with before me? His past wasn't any more my business than mine was his. Although, to find out about mine all he had to do was Google me or follow the hashtag #dumbassdecisionsaboutmen on Twitter.

"What the hell, Bridget? You told me to do this."

"Honey, I know I told you to jump his bones, but I didn't think you'd actually do it. You *never* do what I tell you to do. You want something more in your life than tour buses and hotel rooms and I *totally* get that, but this guy—he could just be using you. He could sell his story to the tabloids and ruin all your hard work. The label *would not* be happy with another scandal."

I thought about my life. I'd given up a lot in the pursuit of my career and taking care of my responsibilities. Then I'd fucked the whole thing up when I'd missed concerts and album deadlines because Jake had broken my heart. I understood it now. I knew where the feeling of no control came from, why I'd spent a year watching myself do all the things I did from a distance in my head. In fact, everyone had been briefed by my doctor on why I'd lost it—but emotional breakdowns weren't an acceptable excuse in the music business. Unless they increased your digital download sales.

The label was giving me one last chance to prove that I was still a good investment, and I couldn't afford to blow it. Some of the label management was looking for any excuse to drop my contract and they were all watching me like a hawk. Even at my young age, I wasn't the newest thing to hit this town and I could feel the hot breath of all the new arrivals on the back of my neck.

My head was telling me to stay away from Max—but the way he made me feel was addictive. With him, I felt like I could be myself because that was who he really wanted and this wasn't going to last beyond this brief period in time.

"I'm in a good place. I'm taking care of myself and following the diet and exercise plan put together by the nutritionist. We've built in lots of down time on the tour..."

I looked around to see if anyone else was close by. Bridget was one of the few people who knew why I'd really gone into rehab and that secret would be a gold mine for any reporter who got their hands on it. The label and my management team had told us that market tests showed that "alcoholism trended better than crazy".

Their words. Not mine.

So, I'd come out as a drunk—which wasn't a total lie because I'd had a drinking problem. But my reaction had been extreme because I was also hypomanic—bipolar disorder's manageable, but lesser known, little sister. I understood why it was necessary to pick the more marketable of my personal defects, but it didn't mean that I was thrilled with adding yet another secret skeleton to the pile in my closet.

I was tired of the lies. I was tired of an image that was put on me five years ago. I was ready and strong enough to make the change. If the fans followed—that was great. If they didn't, I would change my course as necessary.

"I've got my illness under control. I respect it and I'm on program."

"I know you are," Bridget said and I didn't miss the worry in her tone. I had scared the shit out of her for a long time and she was still waiting for the other stiletto to drop.

My mother had suffered terribly from bipolar disorder. Actually, we'd all suffered—living with someone suffering from that illness and going untreated was a living hell. And it was hereditary. It had been somewhat inevitable that I was going to have to deal with some emotional issues, but I'd been as shocked as anyone to find out that my mood swings, alcoholic binging, and the disruptive behavior were due to my hypomania. I was learning to live with it, forging ahead, and that meant enjoying every aspect of my life.

"I love what I do and you know how important it is for me to provide for the people I love. But, I've pushed aside having anything for myself for a long time. Not since Jake have I..." I faltered. I wasn't a good enough liar to say that it still didn't get to me. He'd stomped on my heart big time and, even though it had scarred over, it never quite pumped the same again. "Max is here and I want this now."

"We hit the road in three weeks."

"Yeah, we do; and when we go, this fling will end."

"What about finding someone to have a real relationship with?"

"I want that. And I will have it, but we both know now is not the time."

"Look, Kit." Bridget lowered her voice to prevent anyone overhearing. "Your illness isn't the only thing you need to keep under wraps. Are you sure this is the right time to bring someone new into your life? Someone you need to trust not to play 'kiss and tell'?"

She was so right; I had no argument. I could count on one hand the number of people who knew my mother wasn't dead, but living at the Shady Grove Assisted Living home. Years of drug use and drinking due to her mental illness had fried her brain—literally. Now, she lived quite happily with private nursing care in her world of dolls, crayons, and everything a young child would enjoy. Some days she knew who I was, and other days something would trigger a mania and she would slip into the peace the sedative injection would grant her.

I was a young, poor, and hungry kid when I agreed to the lie of her death and that was my only excuse. They agreed to move her out of the state home and I signed the confidentiality agreement. Back then, I'd had no idea how much the secrets and lies would weigh on me and there wasn't a day when I didn't want to go back in time and say no. No matter who came into my life, I was lying to them from day one and that fact always stood in between. Jake had told me that I kept my heart locked up in a room with no door and that, no matter what he did, he was never going to be able to get in. It was why I had fought for him when he left. He was right.

I plopped my head down on the table in frustration. Just yesterday, a blogger had printed the news that the fire in the studio was deemed "suspicious" by the NFD. The information would have eventually been made public, but the article also disclosed the details of the meeting with the label reps and my management, including the fact that I'd been questioned about anyone in my life who would want to hurt me. It was clear that the leak was on the inside and the label was furious.

Hell, I was furious. Whoever it was better hope that someone else got to them before I did.

On some level, I knew Bridget was right. I didn't know Max and I had all this crazy shit going on. I had secrets. Big ones. Now was *not* the time to start expanding my circle of friends—but I wanted Max. And something about him told me that I could trust him.

You want to trust him.

This year of celibacy wasn't by choice. No one had tempted me enough to take the chance of having someone turn on me and spill it to the press.

Background checks really killed the mood.

My head still on the tabletop, I mumbled, "I just want to have sex. Good sex. Up–all–night–sex."

Bridget lifted my hair from where it hid my face, her eyes filled with genuine concern. "Take a breath. Slow down to your usual pace of slower–than–molasses and think about this." Her face lit up with her next idea. "Call Paul!"

No way was I calling Paul. He'd retired from being my manager and I'd bothered him enough during the Jake fiasco. Paul had left his beautiful ranch and come to me when I'd hit the bottom, checked me into rehab and made sure I was fit to face the public again. No, I couldn't bother him with this.

"We have a lot to do before the tour starts."

I jumped at the sound of Ron Harris' voice just over my shoulder and I hoped to God he hadn't heard what we were talking about. The last thing I wanted to discuss with him was sex. Looking up, I groaned at the pile of documents in his hands. Ron was an excellent manager. He organized, planned, and coordinated like the professional that he was, and I knew my recent revival was due in no small part to his hard work on my behalf.

Lately, though, we'd had quite a few differences of opinion and it had strained our relationship. Ron wanted me to take on more projects and tour longer and farther. He wanted me to record the same kind of music I'd put on my last album. I wanted a little breathing room to explore other options both in my personal and professional life. I wanted to go with the music that had poured out of me since I'd walked through the fire and survived.

Clearly, we needed to talk.

Ron plopped down the tour itinerary on the table and what looked like four million promotional photos for my signature. "We need to discuss some stuff. We have a few new requests for appearances, and the label..."

I cut him off. "Ron, I don't want to add any more appearances to the next three weeks. The band needs to spend some time with their families and I want a little time for myself."

Ron stared at me like I'd sprouted a third eye. "Are you kidding me? You can take time later when you can only get booked at Branson."

Bridget flipped through the papers Ron had placed in front of her. "Australia? New Zealand? A Christmas special? Ron, you really need to loosen up. Kit has to take care of her health, pace herself."

He stopped her with a hand in her face and Bridget looked like she wanted to bite him. I would have paid to see that.

"Look, in the three years since I've taken over Kit's management, she's tripled her income and is now one of the most recognized faces in country music. In spite of her lapses, her smaller arena shows are selling out in a matter of hours and her face is on at least one magazine cover every month. Give me another year and follow my plan, and you'll be back to headlining at the largest concert venues in the country."

"All this," Bridget gestured towards the papers on the table, "doesn't have to happen in the next three weeks. Kit wants a little space..."

He interrupted in a voice loud enough to make surrounding conversations come to a halt. "Kit doesn't know what she wants."

Enough was enough.

"Stop!" Silence descended as I took control of the situation. I focused first on Bridget. "I really appreciate you looking out for me, but let me handle this, okay?" Bridget nodded and I turned to Ron.

"I appreciate you keeping my career afloat when I was sick, but I'm back now and I call the shots. I love your ideas, your enthusiasm, but you can't make plans without asking me. You need to get a life. I don't have one and I *know* you don't because you're usually with me."

I reached out and squeezed his hand. "Ron, once we hit the road I am yours one hundred percent, but right now I need some space... time to take care of some personal matters. You got me?"

Ron stared at me for a few seconds, clearly measuring what he was going to say next. His face tensed with determination as he patted my hand and said, "Now, Kit, you're on the verge—"

"'Of something big'. I know." I interrupted the speech I'd heard many times before.

It appeared that taking back control of my life was starting now.

"Ron, I'm serious. No more stuff added to the schedule."

Ron looked at Bridget and gestured towards me in a

"you talk to her" motion. Bridget shook her head while I rose from the table and moved towards the band.

The conversation had solidified my decision. I didn't know Max and having an affair with him was a risky proposition—especially for someone in my position. But Max was a delicious opportunity I was not passing up.

EIGHT

Max

"I DON'T KNOW how you do this all the time."

Flashes were going off all around us as we stood on the sidewalk in front of the Bluebird Café. I could barely hear anything with all the reporters yelling out her name, but I knew she was right there beside me. Normally Kit was a force of nature, but in the spotlight she was a tsunami, a hurricane, and a tornado all at one time and everyone she came across was fighting for the chance to get pulled in.

It was insane and she was the eye of the storm. Calm. Serene.

She fucking owned this place.

Kit leaned into me, grabbing my arm and looking up at me with a smile on her face. "This is one of the fun parts! All you gotta do is smile and look pretty."

"Well, you've got that down."

"You're kind of pretty yourself, Mr. Butler," she teased as the flashes doubled in frequency as they recorded every move we made. "So, on a scale of one to ten... how badly are you hating this right now?"

"I'm ready to have a seizure." According to the press release, I was here as her guest—a thank–you–for–saving–my–life present. I had no choice but to deal with it but it didn't make it any less painful.

"Okay, drama queen; we're done. Come on; I hear there's food inside."

She gave one last wave towards the crowd and pulled me through the front door and into the calm of the Bluebird. I'd been here once or twice with my grandfather before, to listen to someone play and I'd always liked the small, cozy place. No flash; no sparkles—just a place to enjoy great music with nice people.

"I thought big industry parties were all held in expensive hotels," I said as she grabbed my hand and drew me through the crowd towards the bar. Everyone spoke or nodded to her and most of them gave me a curious glance and then a second when they saw us holding hands. I squeezed her fingers before asking, "Is this okay?"

We made it to the bar and she ordered a club soda and a beer before answering my questions.

"This is the number one party for a song I wrote and I got to pick the venue. I didn't want to spend the evening at some stuffy hotel." She squeezed my hand again. "The press inside was hand–picked by me and my label. This is cool."

"Can I kiss you like I want to?"

"No." Kit laughed and nudged me with her elbow. "You'll just have to control yourself for an hour or two."

"That's easier said than done when you look like that."

Kit looked more like a star tonight than anytime since I'd met her, with a short sparkly black dress, hair curly and flowing down her back, and heels that gave her another three inches. She wore makeup, but underneath she was still Kit—right down to the crimson streaks in her hair.

"Uh huh."

"Are you fishing for compliments?" I accepted my beer from the waitress and took a sip, letting the liquid cool me down from the heat that always pounded on Nashville in the summer. Even the A/C in the café was struggling to keep up with the number of bodies in here tonight. I noticed that several of the people were looking at her, clearly judging whether they could interrupt us. She was the party girl and needed to make the rounds. I was just the "plus one". I placed a hand on the small of her back and nudged her towards the crowd. "I refuse to inflate your ego any more than it already is. Go see if one of these people will tell you how gorgeous you look."

She was immediately sucked in by a crowd of people who hugged and kissed her in congratulations. Watching her was becoming one of my favorite activities and I settled back against the bar—the best seat in the house.

I'd surprised no one by calling her first. The emergency call had been a bad one and it took most of the night to clear up but before I hit my rack at the station, I'd called Kit to arrange our next non–date. We'd come to an agreement about what this was and I was anxious to make it happen. She was constantly in my thoughts and those were the kind that had me waking up hard and aching for her.

She told me to pick her up for this party and suspended in the air between us was the knowledge that when I took her home tonight, I wouldn't be leaving.

"Having a good time?"

I turned, surprised to find Ron, Kit's manager, standing beside me. He didn't like me and was really bad at hiding it. I was reserving judgment on him.

Okay, that was a lie. I thought the guy was a dick.

I sat back, waiting to see what he wanted because there was no way he was there to become BFFs.

"Kit said she needed some time before the tour starts to take care of some personal matters," he said, scanning the crowd, smiling and nodding when he made eye contact. "I'm guessing that you're the 'personal' in the 'matters'."

"I hope so." What was I doing? I wasn't playing games with this guy. If he was going to dig into things that were none of his business, then he was just going to have to deal. "I know I am. What's it to you?"

"Everything about Kit concerns me. It's my job."

"And?"

"Kit knows what she needs to do and that isn't a distraction with a slick line, a rubber, and a truck parked off in the woods somewhere."

"Meaning that I should leave her alone." I laughed. This guy had brass balls. "Why are you trying to cock block me, man?"

That got his attention. He turned to eyeball me, his gaze calculating. If this guy was trying to figure me out, he was going to be really disappointed. He didn't even know who the fuck I was.

"I'd like you to keep your dick in your pants and away from Kit, but if you can't, please keep it off the Internet. No sex tapes. No tell–all interviews."

"I think I can guarantee that I have no plans to plaster my ass on YouTube."

"If you need an incentive, I can make it worth your while."

Okay, he'd shocked me. I turned to fully face him because I needed to watch him as he pimped out Kit.

"Are you offering to pay me to sleep with her or not sleep with her?"

"That's up to you," he said.

"This is what is fucked up about this business. If you're who she's got looking out for her, then I feel sorry for her."

He scoffed, "I didn't realize you were trying to play knight in shining armor."

"Anybody who met her would do the same thing." I was done with this douchebag. Kit was getting ready to take the stage and I sure as hell would rather listen to her. "Nice talking to you, Sir–Pimps–A–Lot."

I found a seat next to Bridget in the front, just as the head of her record label took the stage. Kit made her way to the front and I openly ogled her legs. They were spectacular and I'd be lying if I said I couldn't wait to feel them wrapped around my waist later tonight. The view and the fantasy went a long way to lift the bad mood that talking to Ron had started.

Kit caught me and winked, causing several people to turn and look my way. I winked back at her and she laughed, drawing the attention of her label president. She caught his look and immediately toned it down a notch or two in the fun department.

"Don't encourage her," Bridget whispered in my ear, her smile taking the edge off the scolding. I opened my mouth to respond but never got the chance because the ceremony began.

"Ladies and Gentlemen, I'm Liam Connor, the president of One More Song Records and we are here to celebrate the latest number–one song written by our own Kit Landry." He paused while we all clapped and a couple guys in the back added wolf whistles to the mix. Kit looked embarrassed by the attention, dipping her head and hiding behind her curtain of dark curls. "No one is prouder of how far she's come since she signed with us at the tender age of seventeen." He turned to her, waiting until she looked up at him to continue. "She went from a homeless kid living on the street, to three multi–platinum albums, sold–out arena tours, and twenty number–one songs written and recorded by her or the biggest names in this business. These are just a few of the things I can list that make her a great artist. But what makes her a great person is the way she walked through the fire and came back to us, healthy, happy, and filled with the same, signature Kit Landry country music."

Kit tensed at his last few words. It was hard to see if you weren't looking, but I had my eyes trained on her and she didn't like what he was saying one little bit. The room remained quiet as he reached for a large framed print of the sheet music for the song and turned back to present it to Kit.

"Congratulations,   Kit,   on   your   latest number–one song."

The room burst into applause, and flashbulbs went off as the photo opportunity was played out on the stage. And as soon as it started it was over, and Kit was on the stage all by herself, looking out at the crowd with a smile as everyone quieted down. She was poised, everything you expected a star to be, and I remembered that she was only twenty–one. A kid, by most people's standards and she was doing what most people only dreamed about and had survived having the devil on her tail.

"I'm never good at speeches, so I'll say thank you the best way I know how."

She nodded at a couple of guys just off stage and they joined her up there, pulling up three chairs. Kit turned and lifted Jolene out of her case and joined them in the intimate circle under the spotlight.

She pulled the microphone closer to her and spoke into it, her low voice weaving a net that caught all of us. You had to stay and listen to every word she uttered; there was no way you'd have the power to walk away. *This* was how she'd sold all those records. This was why she'd get back on top.

"Songs come from inside you. I write because I have all these things—pain, joy, longing, anger—inside me and they have to get out. I've had a lot to say lately as I've been working on the new album and... well... it's different from what I've recorded before." She took a deep breath, making eye contact with people as she scanned the room as if she was looking for allies. "Nobody stays the same. I hope y'all like what I have to say."

The guitars started a slow strum, the three of them playing as one on a melody that could only be described as delicate. The notes paused on a second in time, hung in the air like smoke, and then Kit's voice added the element that I didn't know was missing until I heard it. The lyrics were written to a lover, telling him to change his mind about trying to get her back. It was a plea to leave her alone, between the lines an appeal to come back and push her over the edge and a question of whether she would survive either option.

It was sad and hopeful and raw and gritty and unlike anything I'd ever heard her sing before. It blew me away. I had no idea how she did it and I was in awe of her talent. For her not to do this would be a waste.

She was in her element. I couldn't tell where she ended and the guitar began.

Kit sang in that spotlight, her eyes closed as she laid her heart and soul on the ground for everyone to see. This song was more than a love song; it was a tale of a life hard fought and won against demons. It was Kit's testimony for anyone who looked deep enough to see it.

I ran into burning buildings and *this* was the bravest thing I'd ever seen.

She opened her eyes and the fire that blazed out was even brighter than the spotlight shining down on her. I couldn't have looked away if I'd wanted to and I realized that I didn't, even when she locked her gaze with mine and seared my soul for a few seconds before moving on to brand the next person in the room.

I glanced around, gauging other people's reactions to the song. Most were clearly enjoying it, moving their heads to the beat, tapping fingers idly on the tabletop in time with the rhythm. Everyone, except Liam Connor.

He stood to the side of the stage, mostly in the shadows, his expression dark and disapproving. Hell, the guy looked like he wanted to walk on the stage and rip the guitar out of her hands.

"What's with Liam Connor? Did someone pee in his beer?" I asked Bridget.

She glanced at him and cursed under her breath. She leaned over to me and whispered, "That's what trouble looks like."

"Why? Everyone loves the song."

She grabbed her drink and took a sip before patting my hand like I was four years old. "You'll need to ask Kit about it, but remember: the first rule of the music business is that it has nothing to do with the music."

NINE

Kit

"WHAT THE FUCK was that supposed to be?"

I didn't have to turn around to know who was behind me or to know what his face looked like. Liam Connor was always in a bad mood around me lately—I'd lost him money and that was *the* cardinal sin, in his book. I'd also deviated from the agreed–upon playlist at the last minute. Spurred on by my recovery, the great progress during tour rehearsal today, and the way Max looked at me, I was feeling good and empowered and in control for the first time in a long while and I'd decided to flex.

"It was material for the new album. Everyone's heard my other stuff and I figured I'd thank them all for their loyalty by giving them an exclusive sneak peek."

I turned to look at him and it was exactly as I expected. Face red and hard with his displeasure, he crowded me into the back staff room of the Bluebird where I'd gone to take a restroom break after my performance. He was a big guy, a former college football semi–star who'd moved into the music business after graduation. He wasn't above using his size to make a statement, but I'd seen it all before. I'd faced shit down in my head that was scarier than Liam.

"I haven't approved that song for the album."

"According to my contract, you don't get approval on content unless it violates the morals clause. I get creative control over my music."

"Yes, but I can refuse to release an album if I'm not happy with the final product."

Shit. He could. The label ultimately had the last word and it would be difficult for me to force them to release it or to get the rights to take it elsewhere. I wasn't even sure I had the cash to buy out my contract and I didn't want to go down that road unless I had to.

"Liam, did you see the audience? They were eating it up." I deliberately took out any agitation in my voice, hoping to get my way by gently shaking the sugar tree.

"This crowd is all the 'music is art' group, but they aren't a commercial audience. They aren't your demo-graphic, your fan base."

"I'm twenty–one; my fan base is growing up with me. They would love that song." I took a breath and tried to plead my case. "I'm not the girl you signed five years ago. I've changed, grown. My image needs to change, too."

"I think you need to focus on how much you owe this label and how much you cost us with your little detour from your contractual obligations before you decide to change what's been proven to make money."

Ouch. That hurt and I must have shown it on my face because he had the bad manners to look like a smug dickhead. I knew I'd lost them money, but they'd also recouped a bunch of it by releasing a "greatest hits" album while I was in rehab. But my alternative was to tell them to shove it up their bottom line and see if some other label would buy out my contract. Nothing was guaranteed with my track record. I was hoping to get back on top with this tour and a successful next album, and then I'd have more options.

"Fine, Liam. Obviously we have a lot to discuss about the new album."

"I think you need to be prepared to do some listening." He nodded at me, spun on his heel and walked back into the café to navigate the danger zone of having his mistress and his wife in the same room at the same time. I'd taken no end of happiness by adding them both to the guest list. It was petty and mean and I was not sorry.

I walked over to the staff lockers, slamming a door in frustration. I knew I had to make good on my promise to apologize for my failures, but having to kiss his ass was a whole other story. I needed to talk to my legal team about my power over this album. I wouldn't go to Ron; he sided with Liam and thought the status quo was the way to go. Once I knew where the lines were, I'd figure out which ones I wanted to cross and which ones needed to go entirely.

"Hey, you okay?"

I turned to find Max standing in the doorway, partially blocking the noise and people in the Bluebird. He took one look at me, glanced behind him at the crowd and shut the door. He stalked over to me, eyes locked on my face, and even though I wanted to look away, I couldn't. Instead I did what I did best. I hid.

"Don't do that," he said.

"Do what?"

"That thing where you shut down." He reached up to brush a curl off my face and I leaned into the touch in spite of myself. "You did it the other day when I gave you your guitar. For a couple of minutes you were real and then it was like you flipped a switch and this mask came down."

I just stared at him. I knew exactly what he was describing. I'd started doing it when I had come to Nashville on my own at sixteen. It was self–preservation to keep people at a distance and it had stuck once I'd become a celebrity.

"It's Super Kit," I mumbled, wishing I had a better way to describe it.

"Super Kit?"

"Yeah, that's what Bridget calls my alter ego. The make–up, the costumes, the band behind me—they're usually a dead give–away." I flexed my arms and struck a pose like a cartoon superhero. It was lame, but Bridget and I had done it so often when I needed a laugh that it was second nature. "Super Kit! Able to fill arenas in a single night!"

Max didn't laugh. Instead he cupped my face with his large, calloused hand and looked me right in the eyes, his own searching for something I wasn't sure if I wanted him to see or miss. He was warm and I was freezing in the A/C, and it took super human strength not to latch on to him just to steal his body heat.

And cop a feel. I could be honest with myself about wanting to grope his ass at the first available opportunity.

"I could use one of those costumes," he said.

"Sorry. It's one–of–a–kind. I made it myself."

He pulled me close and I rested my head on his chest and wrapped my arms around his waist. We couldn't stay in here forever. The rumble of the crowd was just beyond the door but I would take this moment for an opportunity for

calm before launching back into the fray. It was nice to have someone on my side. Really nice.

I inhaled deeply, indulging in the amazing combination of hot male and spicy aftershave. Yum. His body was hard beneath the cotton of his shirt and his muscles bunched and rippled when I touched him. His hand caressed the skin exposed on my shoulders and back and the sensation from the touch raced under my skin, lighting me up and starting a slow burn deep inside.

His voice rumbled in his chest, just under my cheek. "A job that requires all that armor doesn't sound like much fun."

I rolled my eyes and poked him in the side. "Says the man who wears a ton of protective gear every time he goes out on a call."

"Point taken." Max pulled back and smoothed the hair back from my face. "But that's a physical danger. Your costume sounds more like it's designed to protect your feelings."

Uncomfortable with the turn of the conversation, I pulled out of his embrace, turning to trace the name on the locker closest to me. "I love what I do." I tried to play it cool but, even to my ears, my voice sounded defensive so I paused to collect my thoughts. "Dolly Parton said that those of us in the music business have the same problems as everybody else. Money, fame—nothing changes that—we just get to do it in public." I smiled to myself, the rightness of my new music bubbling up in spite of the smack–down from Liam. "The music makes it worth it for me. It always comes back to the music."

Max's arms looped around my waist, his front pressed against my back, head resting on my shoulder. His voice rumbled in my ear and I felt it down in my bones. "But you still need the costume?"

I sighed and leaned into the warmth of his touch. "You meet people and they have expectations of you because of the image. The trick is figuring out who you can trust enough to let them see behind the costume."

"And people you know?"

Somehow he'd zeroed in on what had put me in this funk. Smart, nosy bastard.

"My label, my management—they don't want me to change anything about the costume."

"And now it doesn't fit."

I turned around then, staying within the circle of his arms, and eyeballed him, wondering how he'd gotten all of this so right. He didn't wait for me to finish.

"That song... it was amazing, but Liam Connor was the only one not thrilled about it. Then Bridget said some cryptic shit about the music not being about the music and Liam left you back here in a mood and slamming doors." I let the shock show on my face. I was impressed. His lip tilted up in a sexy grin. "I'm more than just a pretty face and big dick."

While I desperately hoped the second part was true, he'd accomplished what he'd sought to do. Make me laugh and shake off the fun–killing mood.

We stood like that for a few moments while his words settled between us. I was more comfortable with Max, almost a stranger, than I was with people who surrounded me every day. He'd been real since the first time we'd met and he treated me like a normal girl, even though my life was anything but ordinary. I liked him and I ignored the whisper that said I could do a lot more than like him if our timing was different.

Curious about him, I turned the tables. "So, your turn. Do you love what you do?"

Max backed us up until my back was pressed against the cool metal of the lockers, the sharp contrast causing me to give an involuntary shiver. He placed one hand against the lockers, tracing the line of the skinny strap on my dress with his fingers. That gave me the shivers, too—for an entirely different reason.

He broke eye contact with me, instead focusing on the movement of his hands, his face losing some of its usual playfulness.

"Yeah. After high school someone close to me died and I wanted a job that helped people."

"Because you couldn't help your friend?"

He nodded. "I considered teaching like my folks, but the thought of a job stuck in a building all day didn't appeal to me. I signed on with the NFD and I have no regrets. I'd like to get promoted, be a shift leader someday, but I still love it."

I gazed up at him, struck by his simple sincerity. Max seemed like such a *real* guy underneath all the swagger. I didn't doubt that he would deliver on everything his body and sexy mouth promised, but there was more to him. I'd met lots of people and I think I'm a good judge of when I'm being fed a load of crap. I hadn't always been adept at figuring it out and that had led to lots of heartache, broken promises, feeling used, and dating losers.

Lots of losers.

Losers who used me for rides. Losers who used me for a place to crash. Losers who used me for music connections. Losers who used me so they could sell the story to the tabloids.

I was pretty sure Max wasn't a loser. But I had to be sure.

I already knew he had a truck.

"Do you have a home, a place to sleep?"

He was amused and baffled. "Yep. And I have a mortgage to prove it."

"Do you want to be in the music business?"

"No, I can definitely say that I have *no* desire to be in the music business."

"Are you going to sleep with me and sell the story to the papers?"

I cringed at how awful the question sounded actually spoken aloud. A quick peek to check his reaction and his thunderous expression told me that I'd definitely pissed him off.

Max grabbed me and dragged me against him. His eyes were almost black as he loomed over me, trapping my body between his long, hard legs.

He claimed my mouth in a kiss that was dominating, full of anger at my question, and the pent–up sexual heat that had simmered between us since we first met. Suddenly ravenous for him, I nipped at his lips and he plunged his hands into my hair, holding me still while he reclaimed possession of my mouth.

I gasped when he pulled away and held my face in between his hands. Max's voice was rough and edgy. "I want you. I want to do things to you that might be illegal in a few states. I want you in my bed, my truck, on a blanket by my favorite lake..." He moved even closer, grinding his cock against me and making my toes curl from the combination of his hard arousal and his words. "I want to lift up this skirt, push aside your panties and fuck you hard against this wall, but I *do not* want to tell any reporter about it."

His face was hard and intense and so damn sexy that I wanted to kiss him. So I did.

I licked his bottom lip and kissed the corner of his mouth. My hands wandered; I couldn't touch enough of him and I cursed the clothes that kept me from feeling the direct warmth of his skin. Max read my body like a book and he zeroed in on my neck, pressing kisses on the sensitive skin behind my ear, at the place where my pulse pounded under my skin. His hand returned to the strap of my dress and then drifted lower to cover my breast.

I squirmed against his body, needing more of him than I could take here with a roomful of people just five feet away. I pulled back and soaked in the delicious sight of a spun–up, on–the edge–of–control Max and I knew what I needed to say.

"Take me home, Max."

MAX

"You live *here?*"

I heard Kit laugh softly from the passenger seat of my truck. The directions she'd given me didn't lead to the fancy, celebrity neighborhoods and farm–mansions that surrounded Nashville. Instead, she directed me to a part of downtown that wasn't trendy, hip—or totally safe. A few blocks off Music Row, I pulled into an alley behind a building that housed an all–night Laundromat and a used bookstore. I'd plugged in the code Kit had recited at the gate and pulled in to park in a spot right next to a solitary door.

I continued with my question. "Is it safe for you to live here?"

"Yes. It's safe." She dug in her purse for her house keys

as she exited the truck and I followed. "I have an alarm system and most people don't know I live here—the celebrity home maps have it all wrong because they list my old place. I've never had any problems, but recently we've stepped up security with cameras that are monitored 24/7." She gestured to cameras mounted all along the back of the building.

Recently? What the hell did that mean? It was absolutely none of my business, but I tugged her close to get a better look at her face. "Is there a problem *now*?"

She hesitated and I willed her to tell me the truth. The thought of someone trying to cause trouble for Kit made me want to howl as all of my protective instincts woke up. That link between us because I'd saved her life? Yeah, that was kicking in big time.

She pulled away from my grasp and walked towards the building. "My life is always a little complicated, people wanting access that I cannot allow. My people are taking care of it. They tell me there's nothing to worry about." Her tone was clear that, even though she'd answered my question—the subject was closed.

I let it go. My three weeks in her bed didn't entitle me to a full access VIP pass to the rest of Kit's life.

I followed Kit over to the ugly security door and up a set of steep stairs. So far, I was unimpressed with the digs of a country music star but when I reached the top, it opened into a loft space that stopped me in my tracks. As she flipped on lights and threw her keys on a table, my gaze flickered over the open space, taking in the tall windows, the exposed brick, the living and kitchen area, and the area that was clearly her home office—the walls were covered with gold and platinum albums.

"Surprised?"

I turned to see Kit, observing my reaction. "I like it. I'm just surprised you don't have one of those big mansions with security gates and a pool." I shrugged and smiled at her. "You know, 'Super Kit's' house."

"This place is just for me. Plain old regular Kit." She turned away from me and nervously fiddled with something on the table behind her. She'd been all sexy and brave at the Bluebird but now that we were here—in the moment just before we took the leap from strangers to lovers—she was nervous.

I watched her and marveled at how she constantly surprised me with her different sides. Kit was funny, sarcastic, sweet, and strong. But, now she was vulnerable and tender—and I wanted to walk over and hold her until she didn't look so lost. I wanted to help her with the problem with her label and management team. I was hard–wired to do it. Hell, I ran into burning buildings for a living.

I was three steps in her direction, when what I was contemplating hit me like a ton of bricks. This thing between us was *not* about becoming part of her life. This was about three weeks of fun and no strings. I couldn't afford to forget the ground rules.

Turning, I walked over to her display of awards and albums, and let my gaze wander over the signs of her success. Among the display were many photos of Kit with famous musicians, actors, and someone who looked suspiciously like the President of the United States. Fuck me.

Shaking my head, I looked around and noticed a guitar and piano surrounded by stacks of paper that, upon closer observation, were filled with lyrics and musical chords.

"Sorry about the mess." I turned around to find Kit standing behind me. "I'm a complete slob when I'm writing."

She started to pick up the papers and I squatted down to help her organize the piles. I was impressed by the volume of work. She may have been a party girl in the past, but now she was clearly working her ass off. Letting out a low whistle, I said, "You sure do have a lot of songs here. Are these about anyone I know?"

She winked at me and smiled. "I never write and tell."

"Protecting the guilty?"

"Something like that."

Placing the last of the papers in her hands, I laughed, "So, are you going to write one about me?"

"Nope." Her tone was instantly chilly and I physically felt the temperature change in the room.

Shit. I'd touched a sore subject and wasn't sure how to proceed. *That's what happens when you forget the ground rules. Just sex. No talking. Talking always gets you in trouble.* She was still silent so I decided to go with the humor angle. "You wanna think about that a minute before you just shoot me down?"

"Sorry, but I won't be writing a song about you."

Warily, I watched as she got up and took the papers over to a desk. Still looking down at her work, Kit continued, "I only write songs about men I fall in love with or who break my heart." She turned and caught me with her gaze. "We aren't going to do anything crazy like fall in love or get hurt, are we?"

Oh, hell. I'd walked into a minefield and had no clue where the danger was. Removing my tongue from the roof of my mouth, I swallowed hard and searched for the words that wouldn't get me sent home with a major case of blue balls.

"No. We aren't going to do anything crazy."

We stared at each other and I recognized what passed

between us—a silent agreement—that we would not cross over the line that was drawn in the sand. I was fine with it since I had no intention to go there again. I knew what held me back—broken promises, disappointment, loss. If half of what was printed in the magazines was true, I knew Kit had her reasons to stay away from the pitfalls of love and relationships, as well.

Now that we understood each other, it was time.

I stood up and walked over to where she stood, leaning against her desk. I watched her closely, taking the cues from her. She remained silent and still for so long that I'd almost decided the affair would end here, but then she reached out and gently brushed her thumb across my lower lip and my stomach dropped a couple of feet. I was hard, aching, and I had never wanted a woman so much in my life.

Stepping forward, I pressed the entire length of my body against hers, groaning with the enjoyment of all her sexy curves. I lifted my hand to cup her face as my desire surged to flashpoint in about thirty seconds. I moved my hand back until my fingers wove into her hair, wrapping several curls in my grip and tugging her head backwards. I bit back my own groan when she gasped, her lips parting on the sound. Starving for her taste, I took her mouth in a bruising kiss. Our tongues tangled together in a slow glide and I thought I controlled the kiss until she pressed her body against my cock and my brain short-circuited.

Releasing her mouth, I stared into her violet-blue eyes, lost to everything but the sensation of being here with her, right now.

"Now see? You *are* Super Kit." I licked my lip, tasting her on my mouth. "Because when you go all soft and hot in my arms, I'm *sure* I can fly."

She half-laughed and half-moaned when I nipped at

the soft flesh behind her ear and then licked it softly to sooth the sting.

"Kit?"

"Hmmm?"

"Let's go to bed."

TEN

Kit

"YES."

It was like the one word flipped a switch for Max and he'd decided that we'd waited long enough. I agreed completely and only let out a little squeal when he lifted me in a fireman's hold over his shoulder and carried me across my loft to the bedroom. He stopped at the edge of my bed and slowly lowered me to the floor, making sure that every inch of my body stroked along his on the way down.

"I didn't get to do that the night we met, so..." His grin was contagious and I found myself smiling back at him.

"You could do it again." I took a step forward and ran both of my hands over his chest. I had this urge to touch him, to feel his warmth and let it burn me up. "But next time, we need to be naked."

"That's how we did it at the fireman's academy."

"Really?"

"Thank God, no." Max laid his hands on the bare skin

of my shoulders, stroking down with a light touch along the length of both my arms. I closed my eyes in pleasure. This simple gesture woke up all the nerve endings under my skin, making every inch of me super sensitive, tingly. I moved against him, needing to do something to alleviate the heavy weight of lust in my belly, between my legs.

His hands briefly circled my waist, skating over my hips; the heat from his touch searing me through the fabric of my dress. I looked up at his face and saw him watching his hands progress down my body, stopping at the hem of my dress. He toyed with the fabric, pausing as if he were considering his next move.

"I want to take this dress off you, lay you down on your bed and fuck you until neither of us can move."

"Yes." I loved how direct he was with his wants and needs. It was such a turn-on to be free of the double-talk and bullshit in my life. I nodded—it was all I could manage with the excitement making my skin tight, my mouth dry.

He kept his promise, his long fingers clutching the fabric and lifting it over my head in one, long move. The air in the room was chilly against my bare skin, the only protection I had against the cool air was my bra, thong, high-heeled shoes and Max's body as he invaded my space and pulled me up against the hard length of him.

He kissed me, bypassing the slow build-up and coaxing my mouth open with the sensual swipe of his tongue along my lower lip. The man could kiss, his every move calculated to evoke the image of what he could do with his cock and by the time he lifted his head for a deep gulp of much-needed oxygen, I was wet and squeezing my thighs together against the ache.

Max walked us backwards, stopping when I felt the

brush of my comforter against the back of my legs. He leaned back, taking another lingering inventory of my body.

"Fuck, but you're gorgeous," he whispered, reaching a hand towards me but stopping short of actually touching. I bit back a whimper, shocked at how much I craved that press of his fingers against any part of me. I needed him that much.

I didn't have the usual urge to make excuses for my cup size, to cover up the freckles that peppered my breasts or to shield my slightly rounded belly from his view. Something about the way he looked at me told me that he was pleased with what the saw, wanted it under him, around him.

"Sit down." Max did touch me then, one finger placed in the space between my breasts where the crisscross of satin was highlighted with a tiny bow. He pushed me back with a gentle shove and I did as I was told, glad to be off legs that I wasn't sure would hold me up much longer.

Max peeled off his jacket, draping it over the bench at the end of the bed. Next was the shirt—pulled out of his waistband—each button undone with a slowness that made me dig my nails into the coverlet. I wanted to do this task, wanted to expose inch upon inch of his flesh to my eyes and my hands but I didn't move. I wanted to see what he would do next. Needed to let him lead me down this path, to show me just how good this could be.

The snowy white shirt joined the jacket on the bench and he stood in front of me, his skin glowing golden in the dim light of my lamps, the moon glow coming through the window. His shoulders were broad, the muscles on his body honed to a fine point, flat brown nipples in the light whorls of dark hair that covered his chest and led in a narrow trail down into his waistband.

His right bicep was covered in a tattoo—a red heart,

bisected with a sword and surrounded by long, angel's wings. It was gorgeous, perfectly highlighting the finely cut muscles of his upper arm and rippling with every flex of movement.

He didn't tease either of us, unfastening his belt and button and unzipping the fly while never looking away from my face. I was watching his progress but I knew he was zeroed in on me, no doubt cataloging my quick breathing, hard nipples, and shaking hands. Max was in control of this and I was happy to go along for the ride and just play passenger for a change.

He toed off his shoes and socks and then lowered his pants, stepping out of them and placing them in a pile with his other clothing. He stood before me for a few seconds in a pair of black boxer briefs, his erection pressing hard against the soft cotton, but soon those were gone, too, and he was naked. I sucked in a breath, the exhale stuttering out with the impact of just how fucking gorgeous he was.

His cock, hard and flushed, stood up against his belly and while I watched, he wrapped his long fingers around it and stroked it from root to tip. Max walked two steps forward and stood right in front of me, his hand still working his length in a slow deliberate glide. My mouth watered with what I knew was coming next. He'd tell me to suck him off and I couldn't wait to taste him, to feel the weight of him against my tongue.

I was not expecting him to lower himself to his knees, place his hands on my thighs and spread me open. He moved in closer, settling inside the notch of my legs and kissed me sweetly, a brushing of his lips against mine. I wove my fingers in his hair, pulling him in closer and trying to speed this up. I knew he wanted me the way I wanted him—so what was with the slow roll?

"Let me enjoy you," Max murmured, in between kisses. I felt his hands travel around my back meeting in the middle to undo my bra. He pulled away from my mouth and dragged the lingerie with him. "I've been waiting forever to suck your tits. I bet they're as sweet as they look."

He dove back in immediately, covering my neck with a trail of hot kisses that took a detour over my collarbone and ended in the valley between my breasts. His stubble rasped against the tender flesh as he pressed his face against me, his breath warm as he closed over a nipple.

His tongue was just as good on my body as it was on my mouth, and I gasped at the way he lit me up from inside. This was more than pleasure; this was ecstasy—the kind of thing that you only read about and never expect to experience. I moaned, long and loud, as he sucked on me, traveling to the other one to deliver the same mind–blowing attention.

I was so strung out on what he was doing to me that I almost didn't notice his one hand sliding low, stopping at the edge of my thong. He stroked back and forth there, one finger tracing the edge of lace with a deliberate slowness that caused my thighs to clench together. I was *this close* to coming and he hadn't even taken my underwear off.

His finger finally dipped inside—low—even lower until he parted my flesh, petting my clit with a slow stroke that set off sparklers behind my closed eyelids. I threw my head back, bracing my weight on my arms. My legs fell open—an invitation he couldn't ignore. He didn't.

Max abandoned my breast and dipped his head lower. Soft kisses against my belly tracked his progress until his hot breath, rapid and hollow, skated over my skin. He pulled down the thong, maneuvering it off while keeping my heels on and then spread my legs wider, opening me and exposing me to whatever he wanted.

"I want you to come on my mouth." He looked up at me, his eyes heavy-lidded with his own passion. I could see his cock, hard and heavy in the frame created by my legs and it made me flash hotter, higher. "Then I'm going to slide inside you and make you come again. You okay with that?"

I could only nod. I didn't have enough blood in my brain to actually respond verbally, so I let my body do the talking. I reached up and grabbed his hair and pushed him down towards my sex.

He groaned, the vibration of it combining with the first swipe of his tongue. I shorted out—there was no other word to describe the electric shock that zinged through my body. My toes curled in my heels, my hands abandoning his hair to grasp huge sections of the coverlet, my legs opening even wider in spite of the overload of sensation. I did not want to back down from this. I wanted it all.

His tongue swirled, lapped, and stroked every inch of me as I watched from above. I could not look away. Could not stop sounds coming from me as he drove me higher and higher. Max slid a finger inside me and found that magic sweet spot that was directly related to the "off" switch in my brain and I was nothing but one big nerve ending. Only feeling, only here in this moment with him.

His mouth continued to work me and his finger eased in and out of me, sliding, pressing until I was there... and then over.

I came apart, shaking and falling back onto the bed as he drew the orgasm out. The huge explosion had died down but with his attention, smaller firecracker orgasms rocked my body and matched the sparklers going off behind my closed lids.

I declared this my own personal holiday—complete with a second round of pyrotechnics as soon as possible.

"I'm going to fuck you, Kit. I can't wait." He was staring down at me, rolling a condom over his erection.

I nodded, loving the weight of him as he lowered his entire body on top of mine. It was delicious perfection, and I was immediately overtaken by the sensation of his hard, blunt length sliding into my body. I was ready for him, slick and soft, and I opened up like he was meant to be there. I arched into him, drawing him deeper until he was fully inside me.

I opened my eyes and he was staring at me, his face hard, eyes intense and he began to move. Long strokes where he almost left my body, the ache of loss sharp in my belly. And then he was there again, his cock filling me and touching every spot that built the fire inside me again.

I lifted my legs and wrapped them around his waist, bringing him closer to me, his stroke deeper and Max closed his eyes. He threw his head back, tendons tight in his throat, low grunts escaping him with every thrust.

"Fuck me, Max," I cried out as I dug my fingers into his back, dragging him even closer to me.

"You're so hot. Wet." He gazed down at me again, the words forced out between his clenched teeth. "I *knew* it would be this fucking good. I want to see you come again. I want you to come all over me, Kit."

The hard planes of his abdomen stroked against my clit with every stroke and I needed little encouragement to get there again. It was white hot, and I shattered like glass around him as he shoved his hard length into my body with a desperate edge. He leaned down and took my mouth, his tongue invading me as his hips slammed against me one last time.

I swallowed his moan as his entire body went rigid, the muscles on his back like iron under the sweaty silk of his skin.

It was amazing; over the top. He'd probably ruined me for sex with anyone else, but it was worth it. Every girl should experience a guy like Max. It should be a constitutional right.

I giggled, letting the absurdity of my thoughts wash over me and Max lifted his head to look down at me. He slid out of my body and lowered himself to the bed, one long, heavy leg pinning mine in place. He laid a hand on my belly, a show of possession that I didn't mind.

"Usually women don't laugh after sex with me. Should I be worried about my performance?" he mumbled against my neck, his breath warm.

"Um... no." I pushed back a little to look at him. "Wait. Are you fishing for a compliment?"

"Kit, every man wants you to stroke his ego after you've stroked his cock. It's crazy, but we're built like that in our DNA." His lips turned up into a sensual smile that promised a reward if I delivered. "So, c'mon. Humor me."

"I need to write a song about it."

"Really?"

"It will be a number one. Fans will riot if I don't write it, scream if I don't sing it. You'll be mobbed by women everywhere you go."

"I could deal with that," he was laughing now, his body shaking with it.

"Well, then let me get started on it right away," I said as I moved to get out of the bed. "I don't want to lose the inspiration."

He yanked me back, rolling on top to pin me to the mattress. His smile was still there but it was more feral than cute and I shivered with the promise I saw there. It was going to be a long night.

"You can write that song later." He leaned down and kissed me by the ear, whispering, "Right now you need more inspiration."

Yes, I did.

ELEVEN

Max

"OH MY GOD, THAT IS AMAZING."

I watched in fascination as Kit devoured the ice cream I spooned into her mouth. She sat cross–legged on her bed, holding the gallon of vanilla ice cream that we'd liberally doused with chocolate sauce and her spoon. And she was naked—boldly, completely, and unashamedly naked.

Ice cream and a naked Kit. I could sell this to Ben & Jerry's and make a fortune.

But that would require me to leave this room.

Not a chance.

She scooted closer and scooped up a spoonful of the ice cream to feed to me. I kept my eyes on her and groaned when her tongue darted out to touch her bottom lip, her teeth biting into the swollen plush cushion of her mouth when I closed my own over the spoon and sucked off the sweet dessert. Her hair was tousled around her shoulders, cheeks flushed in the afterglow of her orgasm, ice cream dribbling down her arm. She was natural, uninhibited, and the sexiest fucking thing I had ever seen. My cock was already hard with the idea of having her again.

Sex had always been good for me. What was there not to like? I love women—their curves, tits, ass—every single thing about them was to be enjoyed to the fullest. It was a mandate. They were God's gift to my unworthy gender and we were supposed to worship their bodies at every opportunity.

But Kit... she was something else entirely. Maybe I'd built her up in my mind after watching her for so many years, but what had happened between us wasn't because of her picture on the cover of *Rolling Stone*. That shit had nothing to do with celebrities and fans—that was all raw chemistry between a man and a woman.

"That tickles." She squirmed as my tongue snaked in between her fingers and slurped up the melting ice cream. "If you don't stop, I'll..."

"You'll do what?" I kept my tongue working on her fingers. She didn't pull away. In fact, she inched closer.

"I'll, umm..." She laughed and shook her head in confusion. "...I don't know what I'll do, but it'll probably require hospitalization."

"You don't scare me. I grew up with three sisters."

Kit managed to pull her hand away from me and settled back in the bed. She dipped the spoon and fed me another mouthful. "Three sisters? Are you the only boy?"

I shook my head. "Nope. I have a younger brother. I'm the second oldest of five."

"Five? That must have been fun, growing up with such a big family."

And then I remembered—she was an only child. That explained the longing in her voice and the idea that having to share a bathroom with three sisters was anything but a living hell.

It was my turn to use the spoon. "Yes it was a madhouse. My parents should be sainted since we all lived to adulthood and weren't sold to gypsies."

"Your parents are teachers?"

"My dad is the school superintendent in Lively—a little place just outside of Nashville where I still live. My mom is a kindergarten teacher, and my sisters, April and Elizabeth, are as well. My brother, Josh, is in law school and the baby, Ashley, is still in college at the University of Tennessee."

"Did you go to college?"

"No. Straight into the NFD after high school, but I'm taking classes towards my degree in psychology." I winked at her. "So, you can lie down on my couch and tell me all of your secrets."

She laughed and shook her head, the movement causing her bare breasts to sway, the nipples tight and pink against the paleness of her skin. I settled back against the headboard to enjoy the view and thanked God again for how utterly at ease she was with her nakedness. She was such an odd mix of the public persona and the private parts—all in all, a pretty amazing combination.

But the question remained—how much of the public Kit was the real Kit?

Now was as good a time as any to find out. "I can't remember. Did you go to college?"

She shook her head. "No. I have my GED, but I haven't had any time for college." She set down the tub of ice cream and absently plucked at the sheet twisted around her legs. The nervous gesture reminded me of how her fingers manipulated the guitar strings and I wondered if she even knew she did it. "A college degree is definitely on the list of things I want to do. I'll go when my career slows down."

"Why didn't you get to finish regular high school?"

"I quit high school at sixteen to work and support myself."

I watched as she retreated even further into herself. She wasn't backing away from me, but there was a barrier there —like she was shielding herself from whatever difficult memories my question had brought to the surface. I didn't need to know her story bad enough to kill this mood or bring her down. I opened my mouth to take it all back, but she stopped me with her response.

"My daddy died when I was fifteen and I started working to help support myself and my mama." Kit swallowed hard. "By sixteen she was..." Kit blinked rapidly, briefly focusing on a point just over my shoulder. She stopped, took a deep breath and continued with a voice that had a rough edge. "She was gone and I was on my own. So, I quit school, got my GED, and started working—waiting tables, cleaning houses, singing a little here and there, until Paul Bryant discovered me at an open mic night at the Bluebird Cafe." She looked at me, her smile strained, but there. "I didn't have a normal life or the typical American dream situation, but it worked out all right."

"Is that what you want?" I clarified when she looked baffled. "Normal. The house in the suburbs, two kids, a minivan."

"Yeah. Not today. Not tomorrow, either. I just want..." Kit paused, clearly revising her answer in her head. "Actually, I guess I just want somebody—my somebody. It's been a long time since I've had anything other than the music."

Oh shit. All kinds of alarm bells were going off in my head. Just like earlier when we'd discussed her writing a song about me, I'd stepped into a minefield. Any time a woman started talking about wanting a permanent relationship, it was 50/50 on how it would end.

"You don't want that," she said, reading my silence or my expression like a piece of sheet music. If I was a dick, I'd use this moment to my advantage. Cash in on her honesty and lie to make sure I got to fuck her again. I was many things, but I wasn't that big of a dick.

"No. I don't."

"Ever?"

"No." We stared at each other, the weight of my confession and her dreams threatening to bury this fling alive. I asked the next thing I wanted to know. "Who taught you to write music and play the guitar?"

At that question, Kit smiled and I felt the tension pooled in my gut ease off. Keeping this casual was proving harder than I'd thought it would be. I liked her. She was interesting and I wanted to know more about her. But I reminded myself about the ground rules: I wasn't here to bring her down. I was here for the good stuff—for both of us. *Keep it loose, Butler.*

"My daddy gave me my first guitar. Jolene—the one you rescued from the fire. Both he and my grandfather played and I learned by watching them. Song writing... well, that just kinda came to me. Just like performing in front of people—once I did it, I was hooked."

"So, you'd do it even if you didn't have a big contract?"

She laughed, but the light didn't quite reach her eyes. "I might get to find out the answer to that question."

I didn't like the worry that settled on her face and I remembered very clearly how upset she'd been just a few hours ago at the Bluebird. Her label was playing hard–ball. I reached out and tried to pull her close. Kit resisted, her body stiff and tense. "Lots of people would kill to get one chance in the music business. I'm getting two—so, no bitchin' allowed."

"No way. You paid your dues. You should get to call the shots."

"And I blew it. As far as everyone is concerned, I'm back at square one." She sighed. "As much as I'd love to push back and tell them to shove it, I'm not in the strongest position to make demands."

"So what? You just..." I stalled out. I really had no idea what any of this meant. "What does that mean?"

"It means that I write the songs they want me to sing and I wear what they want me to wear and I go to work." Her hands clenched into tight fists, so hard her knuckles were white. The tone in her voice was frustrated, angry, and it was clear to anyone that even though this might be the deal, she wasn't happy about it. "It doesn't matter that I'm not that girl anymore. I'm a product and the goal is to sell as much of me to as many people as possible."

I scooted closer and enveloped her in my arms. When she didn't resist the caress, I brushed a kiss across her temple. "It'll be okay."

She looked up at me with vulnerable eyes and it just about did me in.

Kit snuggled her face into my chest, and I lightly stroked my hand up and down the smooth planes of her back—the silence stretching companionably between us. *She's so small and taking on Liam Connor and his label.*

This was dangerous territory. Kit was quickly becoming more than a fantasy and I was a sucker for people who needed me. The combination was going to get me in trouble unless I remembered why I was here.

I fixed and protected on instinct, a combination of my

training and what my mom called my "white knight, Nean-derthal DNA" and Kit was pushing all my buttons. Not good, but I knew it and that would keep me straight.

Kit stirred in my arms and I loosened my hold enough to lean forward and reach for the tub of ice cream. Her fingers stroked my back and I jumped a little, the featherweight glide across my skin causing me to shiver with pleasure.

"Sorry. I didn't mean to startle you. I just wanted to..." her voice drifted off as she explored my ink. People often paused when they first saw the tattoo on my back, so I was used to her reaction.

A set of angel's wings covered the broad expanse of my back, the detail on each feather making them come alive as the muscles moved under my skin. One wing was the typical angel's wing—white with deeper shading of the lightest grey. The other was black, tipped with the darkest blood red.

"When did you get this?"

"Just after I joined the NFD."

"I know what they are, but what do they mean?"

"It's my light and dark. A reminder of the best and worst of me."

"Why?" I felt her shrink back from me and I turned and caught her wrist. "I shouldn't pry. I'm sorry."

"No. Don't apologize." I was used to explaining them. Some people got it and others got the hell away from me. I thought I knew what Kit would do but I could be wrong—it had happened before. "I have both sides inside me—the good and the bad—and I don't pretend to know which one is stronger. It depends on the day, on the moment. But I know there have been times when I hurt people... a person... and I can't ever take it back."

"So, this is your punishment?"

"No. A reminder. Both sides are equal and have their place, and I don't pretend to try to be a good man all the time. I am who I am, but I do try not to deliberately hurt anyone."

"It's your code."

I shrugged. It was as good a word as any. It had been called an excuse, a shield. "I call it real."

"Do you have any?" I was entirely focused on her when I'd stripped her down earlier, so focused that I couldn't remember if I'd seen any ink. I was torn between whether I wanted her to have one or not. Her skin was so smooth and perfect; I almost hated to think of her fucking it up with a design. But, on the other hand... ink on a woman in the right place was seventh layer of hell hot.

"On my back."

I had to see it. I scooped her up and flipped her over onto her stomach. She protested with a mild "Hey!" but relaxed when she realized what I was doing.

My fingers traced the design, a heart surrounded by barbed—wire and a honeysuckle vine, and I recognized it as the logo for all her albums, T–shirts, and other merchandising. The heart was designed to look solid, but a little battered and bruised. I guessed, after hearing her earlier story about how tough life had been for her, that the design was more than just a kick–ass logo. It was Kit, once again exposing her heart and soul to the world.

"When did you get it?" I slid my fingers a little lower on her back, glancing over the sweet swell of her ass.

"I got that in Texas about two years ago. Jake..." she stumbled over the name of her famous ex–boyfriend, the crazy asshole who'd dumped her for his ex–wife co–star. "...well, he had a fit. Hated it. But, I designed it myself and I haven't regretted it." She glanced back at me, flipping her hair over her shoulder in a sensual move that shot heat right down to the erection that had waned but had never fully gone away.

"It's beautiful."

I leaned over and kissed the tattoo, letting my lips and tongue linger over her silky skin. Kit stretched out, humming in pleasure as my fingers roamed. That sound was addictive. I could make a career out of touching her just to hear her make that sound over and over again.

"It tastes good, too. In fact..." I glanced over to the gallon of melting ice cream and back up at Kit, "...I wonder if you taste good all over."

Kit's eyes grew wide as I flipped her back over, grabbed the ice cream, and drizzled the gooey dessert all over her breasts and stomach. She sucked in a breath at the cold and tried to scoot away, but I held her in place with my body and lowered my head to enjoy my dessert. I lapped up the ice cream, giving little bites here and there to heighten her pleasure. Circling her breast slowly, I laved her nipple with my tongue, knowing how much she loved it. Her tits were sensitive and I knew that if I reached down and stroked her slit, she'd be wet for me.

Having licked her clean, I lifted my head to gaze down at her. Damn, I thought I'd visualized every possible scenario with Kit as my ultimate fantasy girl, but I was wrong. Like this—stretched out and open to me—her eyes begging me to take her, to do whatever I wanted. Fucking heaven.

I couldn't have imagined this fantasy. My imagination wasn't that good.

"Max, are you just going to keep looking or are you going to do something?"

The question made me laugh and get rock hard at the

same time. She was a unique mix of innocence and pure sex and the combination made me want to spend hours, days, even weeks exploring the limits of her sexuality.

Oh, I was going to do something alright.

"I'm going to make you come again with my mouth and my hands and then I'm going to slide my dick into you and make you come all over me." Her eyes widened, a soft "oh" escaping as she reached for me, her body inviting me to take exactly what I wanted. "So, yeah... I'm gonna do something."

Her eyes followed my movements as I parted her thighs and ran my hands over her soft skin. Shifting down so that my shoulders rested between her legs, I soaked in the sight of the thin line of hair covering her sex, the pink folds already wet with her arousal.

She writhed against me, moaning low in her throat. My dick twitched against my belly, urging me to just grab a condom and mount up. We'd both enjoy it; I could get her off that way but I wanted more. I reached beneath me and grabbed my cock at the base, willing it to settle down so I could do this right.

"Kit, what I want to do to you."

Her eyes were glued to where my hand stroked my erection. "Anything. Just do it."

"Get on your hands and knees. Ass up high."

She complied so sweetly, lowering her head to the bed as she offered herself to me. I moved in behind her, covering her back with my body. My cock nestled perfectly between her cheeks, providing just enough heat and friction to keep me on the edge. Kit pressed back against me and I closed my eyes against the almost–too–good sparks of sensation that rippled up my spine.

I was no newbie, but Kit had the ability to bring me down fast.

I pushed her long, thick hair over her shoulder, pressing kisses along the delicate bones of her spine as I made my way down her back. I paused to linger over her tattoo, tracing the heart with my tongue as she moved under me with her restless need.

"Max, please."

"I know, baby. I'm right there with you." I moved lower, kissing the soft flesh of her ass and lower until I could see the core of her. I lowered myself to my stomach, stretching out on the bed, hissing with the contact as my dick rubbed along the soft sheets. This wasn't going to last long.

I went down on her, my tongue swirling, lips suckling on the tender flesh as she clutched the sheets under her with a growl. I was dying to see her fall apart, to give me her pleasure so I worked her hard and fast—no slow build–up here. It was as if I'd never had her before, as if I hadn't just come an hour ago. Nothing would satisfy until I was inside her.

"Max," she cried out as she came hard, her body half–collapsing onto the bed, the sheets twisting even tighter in her hands.

I lingered as long as I could, drawing out the little shudders that continued to make her moan but I was lost, desperate, almost out of my fucking mind. I reached over to the pile of rubbers on the bed and opened the wrapper, sliding it on one–handed while I looped the other under her body and pressed up on her belly, urging her back on her hands and knees.

I pushed inside her slowly. She was still soft and wet for me and it was easy, the warm, tight clasp of her body almost taking my knees out from under me. I slid out and back in, watching my dick disappear inside her and overcome with the way she offered herself to me so sweetly.

"Fuck, Kit. I wish you could see this." I ran my hands along the length of her back, speeding up my strokes as she began to push back against me. She cried out softly with each thrust and I loved that sound. It was erotic and full of surprise that anything could feel this good.

I leaned over her back, moving my hips faster as my own climax began to spark in my spine, my balls. Her hair had fallen forward, exposing her neck to me and I kissed her there, inhaling her scent. She groaned, her arms shaking where they held her up.

"Max, please."

"What, baby?"

"Touch me, I need it," she begged.

"You want me to touch your breasts?" I reached under and palmed her right breast, caressing the hard nipple, loving the way she shuddered under me. "I bet I could make you come this way. Is that what you want?"

One of her arms gave way and she fell forward and I went with her, my body driving deeper into her. The tight clutch of her body almost tipped me over but I wanted her to find her pleasure first. I needed to see it one more time.

Kit began to arch up against me, her movement continuing the deeper thrusts. She was close and I was beyond ready.

I left the sweet weight of her breast and drifted lower, searching for the place where we were joined. Kit was already there, her fingers wet with her lube as mine joined hers in the caress of her clit. Knowing she was touching herself flipped my switch and I was crying out, hips pounding into her as I rode out my orgasm and hers.

We collapsed fully onto the bed, chests heaving, sticky with sweat and ice cream.

"Oh, my God," Kit laughed. "Three weeks of this will probably kill me."

I laughed with her, settling into the curve of her body. Normally I was on my feet, pulling up my jeans and heading for the door but I couldn't move. I didn't want to move.

"We never talked about sleeping over," I hedged, letting my tone carry the question.

Kit rolled over, her head resting on my chest as she tangled her legs with mine.

"If you leave right now, I'll kill you."

I guess that answered that question.

TWELVE

Kit

"I HAVEN'T MADE out in a closet since high school," Max said.

I squirmed in his arms as his soft laugh vibrated over the skin on my neck while he covered me with hot kisses. The storage closest in the back of the rehearsal space was dark, intimate, and just large enough for a party of two.

Rehearsal had been long, but productive. The band was clicking, my voice was strong, and the new material was blending seamlessly into the set list. The tour was selling out, too. I wasn't playing the largest arenas—the label wasn't taking a chance on my singing to empty seats—but the medium–sized venues were full. We were even talking about a couple of nights at Madison Square Garden if the numbers kept rising.

I'd been going over a new song, when I spied Bridget leading someone into the rehearsal space—Max. The sight of his tall, muscled frame encased in blue jeans and a red T–shirt made me mess up my lyrics as I struggled to resist jumping his bones in front of my band and the press covering the rehearsal. His mouth curved into a smile—he was laughing at me even though my screw up was entirely his fault.

I barely remembered the introductions, the television interview with the two of us, or the tour of the rehearsal hall. In all honesty, I hadn't been able to pay attention to anything but the way Max was devouring me with his eyes.

Bridget had cleared her throat and made some comment about getting back to work and for us to "go get that room, already".

So, we did.

The first available room I could find was the storage closet. Which is how I ended up on a table, with my legs wrapped around Max and him nibbling on that spot on my neck that made me nuts.

"Funny, I figured you were an 'under–the–bleachers' guy."

He tightened his arms around me and nipped at my earlobe, making me shiver. "Oh yeah, but that didn't work in the winter." I pressed a warm kiss to his collarbone, inhaling his masculine scent as he continued. "It was harder to get a girl to go into a storage closet with you. I worked on Susie Miller for three months and I never did close the deal. But when spring rolled around... well, she *loved* the bleachers."

I looked up into his smiling face and laughed out loud. "You're a dog."

Max swooped in to reclaim my lips, murmuring "woof" just before he thrust his tongue into my mouth. I wrapped my arms around his neck and my legs around his waist. His body molded into mine perfectly and I shivered at the shot of pure pleasure that raced through me.

I eased off the kiss, stroking the silky strands of hair at the nape of his neck. "Well, I have no experience in closets or under bleachers, but this was the most convenient place for this." Breathless, I leaned in and pressed my forehead against his. "I really needed this."

Talk about an understatement.

Since having sex with Max two nights ago, my mind had constantly drifted back to the way he'd aroused me with his hands, mouth, and body. I'd drifted off to sleep in his arms after the orgasm-inducing gallon of ice cream, but woke up alone in my king-size bed.

My first thought had been, "I miss him" and it scared the shit out of me. I hit the floor and the shower and didn't even think about hitting the snooze button.

"I didn't like waking up alone. I was sleepy, and sticky from all the ice cream." I narrowed my eyes, as I pulled aside my top to display my shoulder. "You even gave me a hickey!"

Max examined the spot and grinned, no apology anywhere on his face. "I'm sorry about that."

"No, you're not."

"No, I'm not." He leaned over, placing a kiss on my bruise and then moved up my neck to whisper in my ear, "But we both know that if I'd woken you, I would've been late to work."

I bit my lip, stifling a moan as his thumb brushed against my nipple through my shirt.

Max kissed my mouth lightly. "Besides, I left a note and I called you."

Oh, yes, he'd called.

And sent text messages.

The texts were funny, sweet, and so sexy that I'd walked around overheated and distracted—much to the amusement of Bridget and the band and to the annoyance of Ron. But damn, it felt so good to be flirting, making a guy crazy for me, anticipating the next time we could be together. I felt like a normal woman for the first time in a long time. And it felt really good.

Max kept kissing me. Nothing heavy or intense, just a leisurely tracing along my neck, my shoulders, his mouth traveling down to caress the tops of my breasts. It was sexy and romantic and I regretted missing high school if this is what happened during study hall.

"Did you get any work done last night?" he asked. "I wouldn't want to be accused of keeping you from your work."

I laughed. "Oh no, we wouldn't want *that*." Needing to touch him, I traced my lips along his strong jaw. "Lucas and I wrote until one a.m. It was amazing. I had *no idea* what a few orgasms could do for my creativity."

"Well, I guess I could be persuaded to continue giving them to you." His eyes twinkled with good humor. "Anything I can do to help you pull off the 'must see concert event' of the summer."

I paused, pulling back a fraction to get a look at him. I raised an eyebrow. "I see someone has been reading at the grocery store checkout."

He shrugged, the dimple on his right cheek drawing my attention for a second. The dark stubble on his jaw, the inviting fullness of his lips—they were all too distracting. "It was a long line."

The tips of his ears flushed pink and I realized he was embarrassed. It was so freaking hot, I itched to strip off his clothes and see if he'd turned red all over.

I reached out and stroked his cheek. "Didn't anyone tell you not to believe what you read in those magazines?"

"Why don't you tell me what I *can* believe?" He captured my hand and pressed a kiss to my palm and then held it against his chest. "It said your tour is called 'Beauty and the Beasts' and you're on the road with Mac Daniels and Tyler Grant. Mac drives a Harley and looks like a member of Hell's Angels and Tyler is a pretty–cowboy wannabe."

I laughed. "A pretty–cowboy wannabe?" *Tyler wouldn't like that.*

"It also said you two were lovers once."

I nodded.

Max looked down to our intertwined hands, continuing in a subdued tone, "And the rumor is that you will be," he made a couple of air–quotes, "rekindling the romance on this tour."

Wow. He *really* did read the magazines. I leaned down a little to look him in the eye. "Like I said, you can't believe everything you read in the magazines."

He watched me, his eyes searching mine before he leaned in and kissed me softly. "Good to know. I don't want to be getting in the middle of something."

I brushed my hands over his shoulders, enjoying the play of his muscles underneath his T–shirt. "If I were 'in the middle of something', I wouldn't be here with you."

Shortly after my break–up with Jake and while I was in what I now knew was a manic episode, I'd been lovers with Tyler for a short time. He was the rebound guy—a poor choice on my part—and I'd broken it off. Touring with him wasn't a problem for me, except for the fact that Tyler had never made it a secret that he was open to trying again—to me or the press—and I'd been portrayed as the callous woman who'd broken his heart.

What a load of crap. I'd pegged Tyler early and still stuck to my assessment. He knew that a relationship between us would help his career get to the next level. Country music fans loved a good love story between their stars—June and Johnny, Faith and Tim, George and Tammy —the list was legendary. He was hoping to add our names to the list.

I'd been encouraged by Ron to give it a go when I left rehab, but it was a non-starter for me. Unfortunately for Tyler, he wasn't the one who was distracting me to the extent that I flubbed lyrics I knew like the back of my hand.

I kissed Max and leaned back. "What about you? I'm not getting in the middle of something, am I?"

Max barked out a short laugh. "That would be a 'hell no'."

"That sounded pretty definite."

"A guy has to know his limitations." He shrugged. "We covered this the other night."

I watched him shut down right before my eyes. Max was pretty open, but the subtle shift in his shoulders communicated as loudly as a neon sign that he wasn't going to talk about it anymore. That was fine. We weren't about having a relationship, so he didn't owe me any explanation.

"So, how much time do you think we have in here before you have to get back to work?" he asked.

"Well, I told the band to 'take five' and that's really just a figure of speech, so... Oh!" I arched my neck as Max leaned in and nuzzled the sweet spot behind my ear, his lips soft and his breath warm. I needed to get back, but a few more minutes wouldn't hurt anybody. "So... I guess we have some time... not long though... I'll be missed."

"Then we better make the most of it."

Max cupped my face with his large hands and I lost all thoughts of rehearsal, reporters, and my job as he claimed my mouth. He kissed me over and over again and made me breathless and achy. I knew what he could do to my body and I just wanted to get back here as soon as possible.

I was so lost in the taste and feel of him, that I entirely missed the voices outside the closet door until it was too late. We broke apart, blinking at the sudden onslaught of light that flooded the dimly lit space. Ron stood in the door-way, and he didn't look happy with me. I knew the look because I'd seen it a lot lately.

It brought me crashing back to earth and reality. It was not a soft landing.

Max uttered a quick, "What the hell?" and shifted to shield me from Ron, but I knew the gig was up. Adjusting my clothes, I eased down to the floor and braced myself for the fight I knew was coming.

"Kit! What the hell are you doing in here?" I winced at the outrage and disbelief in every word. "We have a rehearsal hall full of musicians, reporters, and countless other people here on the clock and you're in here making out like some teenager. I know you're going through some sort of mid–twenties life crisis." He waved his hands in the general direction of Max. "But can you at least keep your panties on long enough to do what needs to be done?"

He wasn't wrong.

My face flushed hot with embarrassment as I imagined what this must look like to him. The evidence of my selfish and unprofessional behavior was hard to ignore—my clothes were in disarray, lips swollen. I'd taken one look at Max's sexy bod and blown off my responsibilities. This was not the game plan. Max was the after–hours playtime, not the afternoon delight.

Before I could speak, Max advanced on Ron and when he spoke it was with serious menace. "You better watch your mouth when you talk to her. I don't know who you think you are but—"

Not easily intimidated, Ron cut him off. "I'm the one who's here to keep her career afloat," he sneered. "What are you doing here? Getting your rocks off with a celebrity so you can brag to your friends? Or sell it to some tabloid?"

Max's hands clenched into fists, his jaw tight as he stepped closer to tower over Ron. "Why don't we take this outside and you can say that again right before I knock..."

Okay, that was enough. I didn't know what the hell was going on between these two but I didn't need this crap right now.

Stepping between the two of them, I pushed them apart. "Are you both out of your mind? You are *not* going to 'take this outside' and beat each other to a bloody pulp." I turned and pointed a finger at Ron. "As you pointed out, we have reporters here today and the last thing we need is to give them a front row seat to a front–page headline that will piss off the label. Am I clear?" I eyeballed them both until they nodded in agreement.

Max grabbed my arm and turned me to look at him. His voice was hard and edged with frustration, "Kit, you can't let him talk to you that way. He deserves to get his ass beaten."

"And you think you're going to be the one to do it?" Ron jeered and Max advanced on him again while growling something about "teaching him a lesson about talking to a woman like that".

I shoved Max back and rounded on him. "Max, zip it. While I appreciate your help, this is none of your business— so, back the hell off."

Ouch. I hadn't said that the right way, but it got my point across.

Max flinched, his face turning to angry stone. "Fine. You want to let him talk to you like you're dirt, you go ahead." He backed up and lifted his hands in a dismissive gesture. "I'm outta here."

Damn. My heart squeezed in my chest as I watched Max stalk off, his back and shoulders rigid with anger. I wanted to go after him, but I had to take care of things here first. As Ron had pointed out, I did have a rehearsal hall full of people waiting on me and I needed to keep my head in the game. Once again, my personal life had to wait.

But it didn't mean Ron was going to get away with acting like a total ass.

I turned to look at Ron and I didn't hold back anything I was feeling. I was going for the Wonder Woman/Xena Warrior Princess vibe but it probably looked more like "woman on the edge". Either way, it did the trick. The smug look slowly melted off his face.

"Ron, if you ever speak to me like that again, *I will fire you.* Tour or no tour, I will drop–kick your ass on to the street so fast it'll be next week before you realize what happened." He opened his mouth to sputter out some excuse and I nipped it in the bud. I clearly needed to estab- lish some boundaries. "My personal life—who I do or do not sleep with—is none of your business as long as I keep it private. Don't *ever* think you can pull that kind of crap with me again. Am I clear?"

He kept his mouth shut and just nodded his agreement. *Smart boy*.

I turned my back on him, walked out of the closet, and made my way back to the rehearsal area to finish my job.

Once that was done, I could find Max and make it right with him.

THIRTEEN

Max

"KIT'S MANAGER IS A REAL ASSHOLE."

Bridget's eyes widened as her head swiveled in my direction, and I would have laughed if any part of what just went down was even remotely funny. I looked over to where Kit had reentered the rehearsal hall with flushed cheeks and a murderous expression on her face. Ron slumped out behind her and touched her arm to try to get her attention, but Kit shot him a lethal glare and gave him her back.

Good. She was pissed off at that jerk.

And she looked so hot when she was pissed.

I had lost my mind. One minute I was angry enough at Kit to chew nails and then—poof—turned–on to the point where I wished I had a pillow to throw on my lap. God, this woman tied me in knots.

I really needed to get out of here.

I groaned and slid down onto the couch next to Bridget.

I stared at the ceiling, breathing deep and trying to get my crazy emotions under control. I'd done what I always did, jumped in and gone immediately to solving the problem by slamming my fist into someone's face. I hadn't done it this time but I'd been damn close.

Bridget tapped me on the arm, her voice anxious. "What the hell happened? I thought you and Kit were off playing 'seven minutes in heaven' in the closet."

I lowered my gaze from the ceiling and noted the concern etched in Bridget's face, despite the sarcastic humor in her question. Jesus.

"We were in the closet doing... stuff... when Ron walked in and started whaling on Kit to get back to work." I ground my teeth together, my anger still fresh when I recalled the way he'd spoken to her. "Then he insulted her and I lost my cool and threatened him."

"You did what?" Bridget stared at me with her mouth hanging open. "What did he do?"

"He got in my face and we were getting ready to take it outside..."

"You didn't hit him, did you?"

"No. Kit jumped in and told me to butt out of her business." I rose from my seat, intending to leave. I didn't pretend to understand the dynamic between Kit, her manager and the label, but I knew it was fucked up. "And that is what I'm going to do. I can't sit by and watch Kit get treated like shit by that guy. Between Ron and Liam Connor, she seems determined to be a fucking doormat."

I turned when Bridget touched my arm.

I expected her to blast me for criticizing Kit, but her tone was low and calm. "Listen, I need to explain something to you. Kit and Ron—they're in a weird place right now."

"Does that weird place allow him to insult her?" Bridget wasn't going to defend this guy, was she?

"No. It doesn't." Kit's best friend paused and creased her brow in concentration. "They've been fighting a lot lately. He's been riding her pretty hard about jumping through hoops for the label until her new contract is signed. She's focused on making it work, but she's tired. It's caused a lot of strain between them." Bridget gestured around the rehearsal hall. "Remember I told you that the music business isn't really about the music?"

I nodded.

"Kit's contract isn't just about her. It's about all of these people having work. Right now seventy–five people depend upon her in order to make a living and she already feels guilty about the way she screwed up and let them all down. At twenty–one, she's the CEO of a multi–million dollar corporation and it's been like that since she was a teenager." She squeezed my hand as she continued. "Kit's life hasn't been easy. She works to make sure that she can stand on her own and take care of her people. They're her priority—even ahead of her own happiness. So she's not going to just fire Ron when he's being a jerk. This tour is too important. She isn't going to face off with Liam when she isn't sure she can win the fight."

She stood up, giving the "one minute" sign to a young guy holding a clipboard and gesturing for her to come over before turning back to face me. "I know you think she's being a doormat, but she doesn't just have herself to consider." Her mouth formed into a crooked half–smile. "So, cut her a break, okay?"

I took a look around the rehearsal hall. There had to be fifty people working here today and more behind the scenes. How many people did it take to run a tour that lasted months? My gaze settled on Kit. She stood with her band and Tyler Grant, readying their instruments to rehearse a song and all the while Tyler kept hitting on her. A touch here, a squeeze there. A constant public pawing that was starting to piss me off. Kit looked tense, stressed, and so unlike the carefree, sexy woman I'd held in my arms a mere twenty minutes ago.

I looked at Bridget, all the anger gone now. "So, who takes care of Kit?"

"Ha!" She scoffed at my question and patted a hand on my shoulder like I was a little kid. "That's the million dollar question. Kit doesn't let anyone close enough to take care of her. Someone is going to have to make it happen."

She glanced back over her shoulder at the clipboard– guy who was now hopping up and down impatiently for her attention. Returning her gaze to me, she considered me for a long moment before leaning closer, so I was the only one who could hear. "Are you the one?"

I watched her walk away, too stunned at her question to answer. What did she want from me? To be "the one" for Kit? Hell, that wasn't what I signed up for. Even though I cared about Kit, liked her even, a long–term place in her life wasn't going to happen.

Across the room, Kit approached the microphone and launched into a duet with Tyler that I recognized as a hit from a couple of years ago. She turned into a different person once the music started.

She was the woman from the Bluebird again. The creases disappeared from her forehead, she smiled as she interacted with her band, and even Tyler trying to cop a feel didn't faze her. She was in her element, queen of all she surveyed and at peace with the world. With sudden clarity, I understood why Kit wanted these three weeks. Right now, the only place she had to let go and be herself was on the stage.

I remembered my question—who took care of Kit?

For the next three weeks, it would be me. I could do that.

I was strangely at peace with my decision. I could show her a good time and take her away from all the pressures of her job. I'd keep my nose out of her business shit since my involvement only put more stress on her and blurred the lines on what this fling was all about. *Just be the boy–toy. Keep it casual.*

I sat there for another hour, watching Kit rehearse and conduct business with her staff while I figured out a plan to show her a good time. A few quick texts and it was set. Tomorrow was my day off and I planned to make good use of our time together tonight.

She looked exhausted, and when she turned in my direction and I gave her a tentative smile, she cautiously returned. Wrapping up the job, she walked over to where I sat on the couch and joined me on the sofa.

Her hair swirled around her, creating a curtain for her to hide behind. I couldn't see her face but her voice was tired. "I didn't think you'd stay."

"Yeah, well... neither did I." I shrugged my shoulders and huffed out a short laugh. "I figured you'd call security and kick me out." I nudged her with my elbow. "Thanks for not doing that, by the way."

She slid her glance over to me and when she responded her tone was even, but firm. "Max. I appreciate your standing up for me but you... can't." I opened my mouth to justify my actions but she held up a hand and halted any excuse I had. "You're a good guy but I've got to handle this stuff on my own."

Keep it casual.

"No problem. I got out of my swim lane. It won't happen again."

She looked surprised. I guess she was expecting a debate.

"Seriously, I'll be a good boy. I promise." I smiled at her as I crossed my heart.

"I doubt that." Kit groaned and buried her face in her hands. "I'm so sorry for letting that get out of hand. I shouldn't have yelled at you." She lowered her hands and looked at me finally, regret shining in her eyes. "Forgive me?"

"No. No. I stuck my big fat nose where it didn't belong. Besides, Bridget explained to me..."

"What did she tell you?"

"Is there something she shouldn't have?"

"That's not an answer."

Kit looked seriously alarmed, so I jumped in to soothe her fears. Looking around to make sure no one was watching us, I touched her hand. "No deep, dark secrets, I promise. She just explained a few things."

I leaned closer, breathing in her scent. She leaned into me, her head resting on my shoulder and my heart clenched in my chest. Her body was warm, relaxed, and so soft pressed against me. I squeezed her hand and waited for her to look up. When she did, I took one look at her tired eyes and decided on my next move.

Standing up I dragged her with me, heading towards the doorway. "Come on. Let's get out of here."

She dug in her heels and tugged until I stopped with a sigh and looked down at her. She smiled sweetly at me, but I wasn't fooled. Especially, when I heard the steel in her voice. "Where are we going?"

"It's a surprise."

She shook her head, wrinkling her nose in protest. "I don't like surprises."

I pushed her out the door. "Somehow I knew you were going to say that."

FOURTEEN

Kit

"SO, WHERE ARE WE GOING?"

Max rolled his eyes at me for the hundredth time and shook his head. "You really don't understand the concept of 'surprise', do you?" He continued with exaggerated patience. "Let me explain this again. If I *tell* you where I'm taking you, then it *isn't* a surprise."

I stuck my tongue out at him and shot death–ray glares at his smug face. "I don't like surprises."

He snorted, but kept his eyes focused on the road. "No kidding."

I stared out the window of his truck, moodily watching the passing scenery. I *really* didn't like surprises. Surprises always ended badly. Even if the planner tried to orchestrate the perfect thing to do, it was always a toss–up as to how the surprisee would take it. I'd watched a reality TV show where a couples' anniversary party started—and ended—as they stumbled through their front door half–naked, with her hand down his pants. Not good.

For me, the memory of a time when I had no control over my life was too fresh for comfort. I'd worked so hard to gain control, to plan when things were going to happen. I wasn't good at *going with the flow*.

The past year had made me really want to hold on tight. When you can't always control your body, it adds a whole new layer of control freak to the mix.

"You don't have to gloat over there. It's not like you don't have your faults." I wanted to bite back my remark the minute it passed my lips. I'd been edgy since my fight with Ron this morning. That whole scene had been happening more and more lately and I knew that, sooner rather than later, I'd have to do something about Ron.

Max laughed at my attempt to put him on the defensive. He drawled out his response with a nonchalance that made my teeth grind together. "I'm sure I do. In fact, *I* am also a control freak." He cut me a sideways glance. "It takes one to know one."

I squirmed in my seat as he hit too close to the mark. "You guys have to stop watching so much 'Dr. Phil' at the firehouse."

He was shaking his head. "No, no. I'm serious. I get it. You have life smack you around and you try to keep it from happening again by holding on real tight. For the most part it works, but it's exhausting."

Yeah; no kidding. I watched his profile as he drove. "But, sooner or later something breaks free."

"And bites you in the ass."

Max made a turn off the road, his face clouded by the thought of whatever had taken a piece out of his hide. He'd mentioned a bad breakup. *Must have been a bad one. Is there such a thing as a good one?* I reached over and laid my hand on Max's thigh. He glanced down and laced the fingers of his free hand with mine.

He pulled off the main road onto a dirt path that snaked alongside corn and soybean fields. Cattle grazed in the far distance as the day surrendered to the pull of the night. The sky was purple and orange and shot with reddish gold. I lost track of the turns he made as we wound our way through the beautiful hills of Tennessee.

He pulled the truck into a stand of trees bordering a pond and came to a stop alongside at least two dozen other trucks and vehicles. A bonfire flickered from a clearing surrounded by portable folding chairs.

It was a party.

Not one of the industry parties I was used to attending. This one had a couple of kegs, music and a bunch of twenty–somethings enjoying the fact that they were young. This was not what I expected but my heart sped up with excitement.

Max hopped out of the truck and grabbed two chairs from the back before coming over to the passenger side and helping me out.

"You okay with this?" he asked, his arm around my waist as he pulled me close.

"Yeah. Very okay." I leaned into his touch as we navigated the sea of folding chairs, coolers, and couples dancing.

Trucks were pulled up around the perimeter and people sitting on open tailgates waved at Max as we passed by.

"Who are all these people and where are we?" I asked as he claimed our spot by the fire and set up our camp chairs.

"The usual crowd. People I went to school with, firefighters from other stations. They're all cool so you don't need to worry about them being weird about who you are."

"I'm off the clock?"

"Absolutely. No Super Kit here." He dragged me close again and pressed a kiss to my forehead. "Just be a twenty–one–year–old woman with a hot date who can't keep his hands off you."

"I like the sound of that."

"Good." He leaned in to kiss me but we were interrupted by Dean and Shannon appearing out of nowhere. They were good at that—it was *their* superpower.

"Here's a beer, Max. You obviously need to cool down," Dean handed over the bottle with a smile. "And here's a Diet Coke for you, Kit. Max told us it's your favorite."

"It is. Thanks."

"Everybody," Dean shouted out and most of the party-goers turned to listen. "This is Kit and we're all under direct orders from Max not to mention that she's a celebrity and not to ask her for an autograph. No photos and no requests for her to sing at your wedding. I'm looking at you, Tara and Glenn." A pretty girl stuck her tongue out at Dean while the guy who must be Glenn flipped him the bird. "Any violators will have their nuts crushed. Direct quote. Carry on!"

"Dean, you're a jackass." Max shoved his friend, but Dean kept laughing.

"Did you really say all that?" I asked Max.

"Yep."

"Including the nut–crushing thing?"

"Yep." He stuck his hand into the back pocket of my denim skirt and smiled. "I just wanted you to have a good time."

I stared at him. Damn, but he kept surprising me. First Jolene, and now this.

"Good surprise, Max."

"I'm sorry." He cupped his hand to his ear. "Can you repeat that? I'm not sure I caught it."

"Don't push your luck, buddy."

We all sat down, the warmth of the fire just enough to chase away the chill of the summer evening as the sun went down.

"So, how was the Bluebird thing?" Shannon asked.

"It was good," I answered. "More friends than industry people there and that's how I like it." I nudged Max with my elbow. "And our guy did fine. Didn't even break out in hives when they took his pictures."

"The miracle was getting him there at all," Shannon said. "Max is the only person in this town who goes out of his way to avoid anything about the music industry. Ever since Sarah died."

Even if I hadn't been looking at them all, I would have felt the tension descend on the three of them like a downpour. Max tensed and looked ready to beat feet back to his truck while Dean was concerned and Shannon stricken with regret. Whoever Sarah was, she was not a happy conversation starter. I was dying to ask about her but I'd told Max to stay in his box not an hour ago so I needed to give him the same courtesy and respect the boundaries of our fling.

"Well, you handled it like a pro and I'm glad you came," I said, reaching over to grab his hand and weave our fingers together. The tension in his muscles eased when he figured out I wasn't going to push the topic.

"Kit sang this amazing new song. Had the crowd eating

out of her hand," Max said with a smile in my direction. "It's going to be her next number one."

"From your mouth to Liam Connor's ears."

"Forget that asshole. He doesn't know a good song when he hears it."

"My favorite is 'Troubled Times'." Shannon shot a glance at Max, daring him to stop her from violating his rules. "If you don't mind, can you tell me about it?"

"I don't mind. I love talking music with people who love it as much as I do." I noticed that several people around us were listening so I pitched my voice a little louder and smiled to include them. "I wrote it when I first got to Nashville. I had two hundred dollars, my guitar, one pair of shoes and three pairs of jeans and T-shirts in a backpack. I was staying at a shelter trying to dodge the cops and social services because I didn't want to be in the system."

Max let go of my hand and placed it on my upper back, his strong fingers warm against my skin as he offered me his support. I accepted it, letting it be what it was.

"I was pretty low and feeling pretty sorry for myself but there was this guy at the shelter who had this dog he couldn't bring inside. One night while he was sleeping, somebody killed his dog. He found him the next morning tied up where he left him." I could still see the image of the old man hunched over the body of the animal, weeping as he held him in his lap. I'd never heard such a lonesome sound in my life. "He was heartbroken and all I could think is that I'd thought I was the only person who had trouble. Somebody else was always going to have it worse than me until it's my turn to be the one on the bottom. I decided then I wasn't going to borrow trouble."

"Live with what you have," Dean added.

"Yep. Sometimes it's good, sometimes bad."

"That must have been hard, growing up on the streets?" Shannon asked.

"I survived." I shrugged it off, refusing to go back there and let it have any of my present. "I was so busy getting by that I didn't realize I'd missed so much until years later. I never got to hang out at a party like this. No football games. I didn't even learn to drive until two years ago."

"Really?" Max was surprised. "I was driving on the farm at twelve."

"I was too young and then I rode the bus or walked when I first came to Nashville. Then when I was old enough to get my license I had people driving me everywhere." I smiled at the leap that my life had made when Paul Brandt found me at the Bluebird.

"So what else didn't you get to do?" Max asked. He waved his arm as if I could have the universe. "Your wish is my command."

I looked around the party, watching the couples sway to the music.

"I never danced at a prom or any school dance."

Max followed my gaze and turned back to look at my face. He put his beer bottle on the ground and stood, lifting me with him. "Come on. We'll fix that right now."

He walked us over to a place near the perimeter of trucks, the firelight not quite reaching as we stepped into the shadows. He wrapped me in his arms and pulled me in close, nuzzling the sweet spot behind my ear that turned my insides to mush.

"Pretend the moon is a disco ball and the trees are crepe paper streamers." He chuckled against my neck. "Dean is spiking the punch and I'm not hearing any part of the power ballad played by the DJ because I'm trying to figure out if you're going to give it up after the dance is over."

"I'd say your chances are looking good."

"Excellent."

We swayed to the music and I closed my eyes and let him lead. He was warm and strong and I was content to just be held as one song led to two and three. This was up there with one of my best moments ever.

"Thank you, Max. You're sweet to do this for me."

"Are you kidding? You never pass up a chance to hold a beautiful woman close. Dancing is the perfect excuse."

"Sure." I laughed, my cheek resting against his chest.

"Trust me. You do this right and you are 'in like Flynn' later. Women eat this up. I know what I'm talking about."

"So what other opportunity do you never pass up?" I looked up at him and caught my breath. His face was all dark angles and shadows, his eyes hot with desire and mischief. What had been a light and playful sexual tension morphed into something sharper, darker, hotter. His voice was rougher when he spoke.

"You never pass up the chance to do this. Especially with a kickass, passionate woman who knows how to survive."

Max kissed my cheeks, eyelids, and finally my mouth. A simple slide of lips that spiraled into a sensuous thrust and parry of velvet tongues against each other. I wrapped both arms around his neck and hung on for dear life because— have mercy—my knees had liquefied and I doubted they would support me if he let go.

"You also never, never, pass up the chance to take a woman down to the lake in the moonlight and fuck her." He held me close, nuzzling my hair sweetly; his tender actions contradicting the raw passion of his words. I breathed him in until I heard him speak, his voice barely a whisper, "I want to see you, Kit. Under the moon and under me."

Damn.

I wasn't going to lie to myself. My heart was *right there* —ready to fall for him if I let down my guard for one minute. Hell, I already liked him. And why wouldn't I? He was passionate, tender, funny, and endearing. Everything I wanted in a guy.

And absolutely unavailable.

We'd set clear ground rules. I'd tried this relationship stuff before and it hadn't lasted. How could it when I spent two–hundred–fifty–plus days a year on the road? Emails, phone calls, and stolen weekends only held it together for so long and then it fell apart. Not suddenly and violently, but wrenchingly, achingly, and in slow motion like on every tabloid TV show. It was a goal to change whatever I needed to in order to have a relationship but that was tabled for a little while.

Right now I had three weeks. Three surprising, sexy, fantasy–fulfilling weeks.

And now, I had a surprise of my own.

Removing myself from Max's embrace, I led him away from the crowd, past the line of trucks and deeper into the gloom of the woods. The lake shone with the moonlight and it was enough to see Max, to find a stand of tall trees that was shielded from the eyes of anyone else from the party.

I pushed him against a tree. As my eyes adjusted to the dimness, I saw him clearly, arms crossed across his broad chest, intently staring at me.

"Your plans are going to have to wait."

He lifted an eyebrow. "Is that right?"

"You might want to hold on to that tree."

I took one step, then another, until I stood right in front of him, our chests touching with each heavy breath. I dropped to my knees at his feet, never breaking eye contact so I saw his expression morph from surprise to "fuck yeah" in a few seconds.

I reached up and unfastened his belt, the top button on his fly and then grabbed the tab on his zipper. He kept his eyes locked on me, the tension in his jaw growing with each click of metal against metal until I reached the end. He'd done me the favor of going commando, so I reached inside and grabbed his cock, stroking it slowly as his knees gave slightly.

I licked across the head, moaning at the salty taste of his pre–cum. His fingers dug into the bark of the tree as he groaned. I'd told him to hang on for the ride.

"What am I going to do to you, Max?" I smiled, as I recalled his words from the night before. "I'm going to do everything."

FIFTEEN

Max

FUCK. She was going to kill me.

I did what I could as she took me in hand and then into her hot, wet mouth—lock my knees and try to stay upright.

There was just enough moonlight for me to see my cock slide in between her pretty little lips. My skin glistened in the night as she sucked me and I fisted my hands with the extreme effort not to grab her hair and take over the slow ride of torture and ecstasy she was taking me on. Moments slid into minutes as I battled with myself to keep my orgasm at bay. It was a workout and sweat dampened my skin then turned cool with the breeze off the lake. I shivered.

She stopped. Oh, Jesus. I almost whimpered at the loss of pleasure.

"Is that good? Anything you want me to change?" Her lips were already swollen and slick with her effort as she stuck out her tongue and licked that spot under the head that made my eyes cross.

It was an effort to keep my eyes open. I didn't want to miss a minute of this. I'd spent a lot of time fantasizing about Kit and I realized that my mind wasn't dirty enough for where she could take me.

She glanced at where I clutched the tree and shook her head.

"Why don't you put those hands to use?" She shook out her dark curls, her expression wicked and mesmerizing. "Grab my hair and show me how you want it. Take control, Max. I can handle it."

Holy hell.

"Are you sure?"

She answered by placing her mouth a hair's breadth from my cockhead, her expression telling me that if I wanted it, I had to take it.

"I hope you mean it."

I wove my fingers in her curls, my palms flat against the back of her head as I took a deep breath and eased myself in her mouth. She was hot, scalding, and sucked me with a tight hold on my dick. She took almost all of me as she tested just how far I could go and still make this good for her.

Kit's eyes shone as they watched me, little sounds of pleasure escaping with each thrust and vibrating around me to add another layer of sensation.

She let go of me, giving me total control of this joining and I set up a rhythm. Not slow. Not fast. Calculated to keep us both on edge, to bring us within sight of the ecstasy but unable to catch it. My body was tight with the effort to make it last, that telltale tingle of warmth in my lower back alerting me to the fact that I was about to lose control.

I was a great collector of blowjobs. I'd begun early with several girls in the hayloft on my family farm and I loved them. Sitting back and taking my pleasure, the God–like control, the carnal bliss at watching a girl work hard to get me off. I loved it. I was a guy and, like any man, I was a pig when my thoughts turned to how down and dirty it could get.

But nothing—not a goddam thing—prepared me for the sight of Kit on her knees, her mouth open for me, her tongue tasting every inch of me.

"Kit, I'm going to come."

She moaned around me and her eyes fluttered closed. I looked down and the picture before me finished me off. Kit's right hand had disappeared under her skirt as she brought herself to a body–jerking orgasm. The knowledge that she got off on this little scene pushed me beyond the edge and I fell into the chasm. My eyes slid shut, my hips thrusting forward as I tried to pull out.

Kit shook her head and gripped my hips to keep me where I was and I shot. I couldn't stop. I couldn't slow down. I could only hang on to her for dear life as she brought me down to where no woman ever had before.

Aw fuck. I was a goner. I was hooked on Kit. She was going to have to beat me off with a stick for the next three weeks now that I knew just how fucking awesome we were together. Damn, it was going to be hard to let her go when our time was up.

Beautiful. Smart. Talented. A sex kitten in and out of bed.

If I was smart, I'd keep her.

I'd never been a smart guy.

"Goddam. Look at you," I whispered, my voice rough and harsh to my ears. "You're gorgeous."

I pulled out of her mouth and yanked her to her feet.

I slid my hand through her hair to cup the back of her

neck. She shivered as my lips took a slow slide across her jaw, cheekbones, and barely brushed across her lips. It wasn't enough.

I plunged into her mouth, taking the kiss directly to that crazy point where I was ready to forget where we were, strip her down and take her on the ground. My hands shook, groin tightening when I tasted me on her tongue. I let her go.

She barely contained the protest on her lips as her eyes fluttered open and met my gaze. She swayed a little on her feet. I knew what she was feeling—my world had tilted on its axis, too.

I shoved myself back in my jeans. "My place isn't far from here. This party needs to go there now. I've got a big bed and I want you naked in it all night. My neighbors aren't close enough to hear anything and I feel like making you scream."

She grabbed my arm and tugged. "Let's go."

I smiled and followed her up the path, deciding to leave my chairs for Dean to bring to me tomorrow. I wasn't going back to the bonfire because if someone tried to start chit chatting, I'd kill them.

I overtook her, clasping her hand in mine as I planned our exit. I was so caught up in Kit and the evening ahead that I didn't notice the cop cars until they turned on the blue lights and hit the siren for a couple of cycles.

I hadn't thought anything could bring me down from my Kit–induced high but this was a buzz–kill.

People scattered, running in opposite directions as they desperately tried to avoid the four police officers. I heard truck doors slamming, engines starting as some lucky bastards made their escape.

We weren't so lucky.

They didn't cuff us but they wasted no time in assisting us into the back of the police car while the several other people they'd caught were leaning up against the second vehicle in a straight line. We sat in silence mainly because I had no fucking clue what to say. I'd had some crazy shit happen on dates but I'd never been arrested for trespassing.

The officers recognized Kit and they were just a few steps away discussing exactly what they were going to do. They'd come here expecting to round up a bunch of rowdy underage drinkers and ended up with a hodge–podge of members of the fire department and a woman whose picture was on the cover of this week's People magazine.

"Kit. I'm sorry."

"It's not your fault." Her voice was low, tense. I wasn't dumb enough to say that it was okay when this clearly was not. "I'll give Ron a call when I get a chance. He'll clear this up."

What she didn't say was obvious—getting us out of the slammer would be easy but keeping it out of the press wouldn't be. It would be impossible to keep it from my boss.

I opened my mouth and then shut it. I really had nothing here.

A truck pulled up, its high beams temporarily blinding us all. A collective protest went up from the crowd and luckily the driver killed the lights. A farmer hopped out of the cab and made his way over to the cops. He was in his mid–fifties, wearing a ball cap, T–shirt, jeans and boots and an expression that said he was fucking pissed. The cops immediately went on alert.

"Sir, you need to get back in your truck and leave."

"This is my land—"

"That's fine, sir, but you still need to go."

"I'm sick of all these kids coming here and leaving their

trash and messing with my crops," he boomed out, determined to have his say.

This wasn't anything new. For as long as kids have grown up in the country, they've partied in barns, hunting sheds, and open fields, and the property owners have hated it.

"I understand, sir." The larger officer moved over to the man, exposing us to his line of sight. The farmer peered into the vehicle, curious to see who was in the back of the car. He looked away and then returned his gaze to our faces and I knew the minute he recognized Kit. The cops knew it, too; their bodies tensed as he leaned over and shouted, the thin line gone and replaced with a huge grin.

"Is that Kit Landry?" He didn't wait for anyone to answer, taking off his hat as he waved at her. "My name's Brian Wood. I'm a huge fan. My wife is, too. We have every one of your albums."

Kit leaned forward, giving him a small wave and a smile. "Thanks so much. I really appreciate it." She turned towards me and gave me the "go along with it" look. "This is Max."

I waved, following her lead.

"You're that guy who saved her from the fire."

"Yes, sir. Nice to meet you."

Kit took over the conversation again, stepping out of the vehicle and over to Brian. "I'm really sorry about trespassing. We didn't mean to."

"Don't you worry about that; just some harmless kids." He waved off her apology and plowed on as if it was the most normal thing in the world to fan girl all over her while Nashville's men in blue stood by with people they'd arrested based on his complaint.

"She's going to be upset that she missed meeting you.

We couldn't get tickets to your concert here. The cheap seats sold out too fast."

Kit reached out and touched his arm, giving him an even bigger smile. "I'd be happy to get y'all tickets and VIP passes to that show as an apology for tonight."

"You can?" He looked at the officers, nudging them with an elbow and chuckling. "That would be so nice. Very nice."

"It's my pleasure." She gestured towards the others still lined up against the other police car. "And we can let everybody go?"

"Oh sure." He could have agreed to let aliens give him an anal probe as focused as he was on digging his phone out of his pocket. He fished it out and held it up with an even bigger grin. "Can I get a picture?"

"Absolutely." Kit took the phone from him and handed it over to the big officer who took it with a smile. I bit back a snicker at how she'd manipulated this entire situation. It was genius. Somebody should have started a slow clap in tribute.

Brian looped a burly arm over her shoulders and pulled her in tight. Kit's eyes got a little bigger with the surprise at being manhandled, but she recovered and smiled for the photograph. In between the time to set up the "just in case" second shot, she turned to me and winked. The expression on her face was pure mischief and it looked good on her. Really good.

I laughed out loud and she joined me. We were both crazy, relieved from dodging the bullet and high on being together. Nothing about this night was what I expected but I was glad I hadn't missed it. And if I believed in that emotion, I might have fallen a little bit in love in the back of that cop car.

SIXTEEN

Kit

I WASN'T LAUGHING NOW.

My hands shook and my vision went blurry as I threw the pictures onto the island in my kitchen and reached for the edge to support myself. My entire body had gone slack, my skin prickly with that feeling that usually preceded throwing up.

The tabloids were full of my little run–in with the law the night before but the coverage was all about how I'd given the property owner the VIP passes and tickets. Brian had wasted no time sending the pictures of us together to a local affiliate and the story he told was the kind of good publicity I could never buy.

But this. What I was looking at was the kind of story that sunk careers and sent you to Branson.

The Daily Scoop had provided the entire package to me and my label as "a courtesy" before they printed them all. I was welcome to provide a comment and they'd be happy to run it. I was going to find this Earle guy at the Daily Scoop and rip his balls off. It wouldn't stop the story from running but it would make me feel better. My ears were still ringing from the irate telephone call from Liam Connor and the sound of him breaking a vase in his office. I didn't know which one he'd shattered but I would find out later at my command appearance in his presence.

Fuck.

I looked down at the photos and papers on my counter and came up short with any way to make this mess any better. This was ugly. This was likely the final nail in the coffin of my career.

The pictures were dark and grainy but what was in them couldn't be denied.

Me.

On my knees.

With Max's cock in my mouth.

And as if the photos weren't bad enough, the accompanying article was ugly. It made me out to be a two–timing slut with Max and Tyler and hinted that I had started drinking again. Just what I needed right now when the label was going to such pains to maintain/fix my image. As Liam had screamed, "America's fucking Sweetheart does not suck off some guy like a twenty–dollar whore." I bit back my reply that she obviously did, but I wisely kept my mouth shut. I wasn't billed as a Pollyanna but this was really over the top and country music sponsors were largely conservative. They overlooked my multicolored hair, the tattoos, and my songs that talked about sex and drinking, but this was going to cost lucrative endorsements for me personally and for my tour.

Bridget and Ron walked over and each took their turn viewing the pictorial train wreck. Their expressions morphed from concern to absolute horror as they saw the photographs. I sat on the nearest barstool, unable to do anything but stare at the shiny silver surface of my fridge.

Bridget sat down beside me and grabbed my hand. "Kit, honey, this is gonna be okay. Your lawyers are going to stop them from printing the article and it will all blow over."

I wasn't convinced, but I appreciated her effort.

"This is bad, Bridget, and we all know it." I leaned forward, resting my cheek on the cool granite countertop. "I wouldn't be surprised if the label used my morals clause to ditch my contract."

"You've been thinking of buying it out."

"There's a whole world of difference between walking away and getting kicked out."

My door buzzer sounded and I glanced at the clock. It was Max. He'd texted to say he'd be over this morning. I wasn't the only one whose boss was going to be less than thrilled about our sex life getting front page headlines. This new development was going to get him in serious trouble.

"Ron, can you let Max in?"

He cursed, but walked to the door, looking at the video monitor before buzzing him up. When his footsteps got to the door, Ron ripped it open and walked away, but not before giving Max a dirty look. I had no clue what was going on between the two of them, but psychoanalyzing their relationship was the least of my priorities.

"Lover–boy's here."

"Kiss my ass, Ron," Max replied as he walked over to me. He didn't like what he saw because he stopped in his tracks about three steps in front of me. "What happened?"

I gestured towards the pile of career–ending shit on my countertop. "See for yourself." I needed to warn him. "It's bad."

He picked up the sheaf of papers and as he progressed I saw his complexion go from tan to shockingly pale. His hands shook, from anger or what, I don't know, but he was messed up and my heart went out to him.

We weren't just fuck–buddies. We were friends and I hated to see anyone brought down because of me.

"I'm sorry, Max."

His eyes were blazing when he looked at me. Anger... it was pure fury. "For what?"

"You would have never been a target for those vultures if I wasn't in the mix. They are after me and I dragged you into this with me."

"Yeah, I'm sure you had to do a lot of arm–twisting for him to let you give him a blowjob," Ron sneered.

I turned on him. "Ron, shut the hell up. I know what I did. I know you don't approve, but it's done."

"You would have never let this happen if it wasn't for him."

"What the hell are you talking about?"

"You used to be careful." Ron advanced on me, his face screwed up with his own frustration. "You used to know what had to be done and you'd do it. You avoided trouble like him."

"Kit is entitled to live her life—" Max joined the argument, but Ron cut him off.

"Oh, what the fuck do you know about it? You can't even keep your dick in your pants long enough to get through the department Christmas party!" He laughed when Max took a step back, his surprise written all over his face. "What? You didn't think I had you checked out? I knew you were bad news for her after the deep–throat kissing at the commendation ceremony. I told you to stay away. But what the fuck do you care? You got your rocks off and now this affair is over, so get the hell out."

"Don't act like you know what's going on between me and Kit."

"What? Is this a love match now? Are you going to live happily ever after?"

I sucked in a breath at his words as my heart did a leap. I locked eyes with Max as we both faced off over the words that still hung in the air like fog.

Jesus. Why did I wish that Max would answer him? Why did I want him to tell Ron it was different than what he'd said? I was standing on the edge of making a very big mistake when it came to this man and the involvement of my feelings. Every fiber in me screamed for me to tread carefully and I was listening.

"I don't think our status is the issue here. We need to figure out what we're going to do about this story and these pictures. Now," I said.

The silence that followed was complete as we all calmed down. Not even my appliances had the balls to make a sound while we all brainstormed a way to get out of this mess.

Bridget spoke first, her voice low and cool. The eye of the storm, as always. "You have a meeting with Liam Connor at two. I think you're going to want to meet with your attorneys and security before that one."

"I put a call into the firm and they are looking into a legal injunction to stop the Daily Scoop from printing the pictures," Ron offered, scrolling through his phone. "I have Mandy at the office checking the Internet to make sure they aren't out there already. We need to get Earle Foster to name his source."

I was still staring at Max so I saw his reaction to the

reporter's name. He jumped and then rubbed his jaw with a large, calloused hand while walking towards the big bank of windows that faced the street, a nerve twitching in his left temple.

I braced for impact. I'd had enough bad news in my life to know when it was coming.

"He approached me to get a story on you, Kit."

"What?" This was the first I'd heard of any reporter approaching Max. "Why didn't you say anything?"

"I didn't think it was important," he said as he swiveled to face me. "I would never take the money or sell your story and I figured he would go away..." he sighed. "Dean told me to tell you. He told me you'd be hurt if you found out this way." He clenched his fists at his side in frustration. "We were supposed to be about having fun and I didn't want to weigh our time down by bringing up all the crap you were trying to forget. I never thought he would find another source at the party. Never."

"So which one of your buddies sold you out?" Ron asked.

Max sighed and kept his eyes locked on mine. I wanted to reach out and touch him, as if a physical connection would help me sort this out. Did I believe him? My track record with men wasn't great. It would have been no surprise that I'd been fooled—again.

Oh, but I wanted him to be the real deal.

"I have an idea," Max said.

"Give me the name," Ron's finger hovered over the screen on his phone. "I'll send our security guy over there."

"No," Max said, turning to look at Ron. "If I'm right, then he's my problem and I'll deal with him."

"That's unacceptable," Ron barked.

"Too bad."

"Fine." I put my hands up to stop round two. I was about two seconds away from losing it and I needed to get a plan on the table before I fell apart. "Max will check and let us know what he finds out. But that doesn't answer the question of who dragged the Tyler/Max love-triangle stuff into it."

Max scoffed. "Not me. All I know about Tyler is what you've told me, which is nothing."

I turned to the others. "Okay."

I looked at Ron and he avoided my gaze and I knew... I just *knew*.

I stared at him; my teeth ached from grinding them together. "Are you telling the press I'm dating Tyler? *Cheating* on Tyler?"

"Absolutely not." Ron flushed brightly, his pulse pounding in his throat.

I watched him closely and I could read him like a book. In typical Ron fashion, he was calculating how much I knew and whether he could convince me to do what he wanted. *Son of a bitch.* My vision blurred; my ears rang as I sank to the couch.

"I didn't tell them you were seeing Tyler. But we both know that a strategic use of 'no comment' is very useful."

My eyes crossed in exasperation. "Ron. Are you insane? What are you thinking? They made me look like a nympho in that article. It almost sent Liam into a stroke."

"Kit, get your head out of your ass and back into reality." His tone was even but the edge was scathing. "Music is not enough to keep an artist on the charts anymore. You need to keep your face on the magazine covers and your name on the lips of every talk-show host. Hell, you aren't even on the A-list for Jimmy Fallon anymore. When were with Tyler, your numbers went through the roof. The fans loved it and you were at the top. A love triangle is just that much better."

I stood, needing to move. "Ron, have you looked at our numbers lately? They're growing and my interview requests are steadily increasing. I'm co–headlining the number–one concert of the summer and it's not because of who I'm sleeping with. My music is enough to keep me at the top of the charts."

He snorted in derision. "I am well aware that your success is not because of who you're sleeping with." He pointed a finger at Max. "This guy? Who is he anyway? Some nobody whose asshole buddy sold all of your bedroom secrets to the tabloids."

Max stepped forward, his voice hard with anger. "The last time you spoke to her like that, I backed off because she asked me to." His hands clenched at his sides in a white–knuckled fist. "But it won't stop me this time. Do you have any idea what you're doing to her? Don't you have any loyalty at all?"

Ron sneered. "Oh, you're one to talk about loyalty to Kit. You're going to fuck her and then move on. Get out of my face and let me do my job."

I stared at the two of them arguing and my brain hurt with the effort it took to process all the crap thrown at me in the last twenty–four hours. I knew what I had to do. Ron wasn't going to be happy and neither was Max. Fuck; I wasn't happy about it, either.

"Ron, call the publicist and issue a denial of any romantic relationship with Tyler." He sputtered to say something and I raised my hand to stop him. "Also, confirm that Max and I were seeing each other but that it's over." I heard Max mutter a low "fuck, no" but ignored him. "I'll call Tyler and warn him. This will hurt his ego and he'll be an ass on tour, but that's how it'll have to be. I'll record that duet with him as an apology."

Ron shifted on his feet, his face red with frustration and his jaw clenched with the effort to shut up and do as he was told. Finally, he gave a curt nod of agreement.

I looked at Bridget and took a deep breath. "I want a drink..."

"Kit." Bridget's voice was soft, understanding of what I was asking in her eyes.

"So, I need you to clear my calendar today after my meeting with Liam so I can go talk to Cyrus. I'll be okay." Cyrus was my sponsor and he knew everything. He was the one safe place I had when I was like this. When I was at the crossroads of good and bad decisions. I was feeling edgy, like I was craving something I couldn't name. I knew the signs of my illness and I knew when I needed help. A good talk with Cyrus and I'd get past this.

Right now, I needed air and space and to get away from their sad, scared, concerned faces looking at me. I walked out of my kitchen, turned the corner and bolted up the stairs that led to my rooftop terrace.

I emerged at the top of the stairs, sunshine warming my icy limbs and boosting my energy level a little bit. I stood at the railing, watching the people on the street below and wondered how I'd arrived at this place in my life. I was faced with so many decisions, and no path looked familiar or correct.

I needed to deal with Ron. He was somebody I didn't know anymore and I wasn't sure I wanted to. At twenty–one I was bone–tired, overwhelmed, and more scared than when I'd arrived in Nashville with no job, no money, and no home.

"Kit."

It was Max.

"Go away." I just couldn't deal with him right now. I was starting to feel a little out of control and I needed to focus, to work through my exercises that were designed to help me deal with panic attacks, my cravings for alcohol.

"No. I want you to talk to me."

"Not now. I need time to think."

I felt him walk up behind me and, even though I antici-pated his touch, it still moved me. I wanted to turn and let him hold me and lose myself in him but playtime was over.

"I swear I didn't talk to the reporter."

"I believe you."

"You do?" He turned me to face him, his face holding too much hope for me to string him along.

"It doesn't matter. I have to focus on fixing this and I can't worry about this thing between us. I just can't."

Hell, it hurt to say it but I was right. My life was too crazy, too fucked up to try to navigate whatever this was. And no matter how much I wanted to take the time to figure it out, I was out of that commodity.

"I can help you deal with this. Don't shut me out."

"I've got people to help me with this."

"People on your payroll. People with their own agen-das." He pointed back towards the stairs. "You can't trust Ron. You know that, right?"

I just stared at him. I wasn't going to argue with him about it. The possibility of parting ways with Ron had been on my "to do" list and, with the last conversation, it had moved to the top. Max took my silence as agreement and plowed on.

"Kit. Let me help you."

"No. I can't." He tried to pull me close and I pushed him away, shifting just out of his reach. It was too hard to do this when he was touching me. "Just go away. Call Ron if you need help dealing with the NFD."

"So that's it? What about our three weeks?"

"I'm sure you'll find a suitable replacement in no time."

"What if I don't want to?"

"Don't." I sighed.

"Don't what?" he asked, stepping closer and backing me up against the wall. "Don't let me help you?"

"Don't make this more than it is!" I snapped, pressing both hands against his chest to force him to give me space. My hands were shaking and I clenched them at my sides, hoping he didn't see the tremor. "We set the parameters of this and nothing included you becoming any part of my life. Because, newsflash Max—this is my life. It's complicated and messy and I don't have time or energy to..."

I lost steam when he stepped forward; cupping my face in his large, warm hands. His eyes were fierce, contradicting the gentleness of his tone.

"Stop," he said. I shook my head, raising my hands to pull his away, but my actions stalled and I ended up wrapping my fingers around his wrists, leaning into his touch. "Just stop and let me help you. You don't have to do this by yourself. Not anymore."

I wanted him. Wanted to let him stay and be my rock. But what I hoped he was offering and what he meant did not match.

"Max. Nothing has changed." I found the strength to pull his hands away and step backwards. "We knew this had a shelf–life when we started. I'm calling it early. You need to go."

"And if I don't want to end it?"

"It doesn't matter. I do."

I'd known it would hit the mark and I had excellent aim.

Max looked as wretched as I felt and *I* was the one killing this thing. Whatever we could have been was done.

"Kit."

I lifted my hands to keep him from coming any closer. "Please, Max."

He stared me down, waiting me out to see if I would cave.

"This isn't over right now. I will not accept it. I respect that you need space to deal with your shit but I'm not going anywhere."

All I could do was stare at him. I had nothing except the headache that was now spiraling behind my right eye. I must have looked like I meant business because after a few moments he nodded and turned his back on me. I watched him as he progressed across the terrace, never taking my eyes off him as he descended the stairs and disappeared.

I wanted to call him back so badly it was like a physical ache in my marrow. Every part of me hurt with the effort to stay where I was. I turned and leaned on the terrace wall and reached for my phone.

There was one more person I needed to worry about. I thumbed the screen and placed the call. The phone rang once, twice and then the voice of my mother's nurse came across the line.

"Lilah? It's Kit. No, no I'm okay." I closed my eyes and steadied my voice. If I didn't, Lilah would worry about me and I needed her to focus her emotions elsewhere. "How's she doing today? That's good. Listen; let me know if anything weird happens. No... nothing to worry about... the publicity is heating up and it could get a little crazy... I won't be there tomorrow... okay, call Josef or me if you need anything... I mean it—*anything*. I'll be there as soon as I can... Bye."

I ended the call and brushed away the tears that burned my eyes. I was so tired but I had to hang in there. A few meetings. A potential lawsuit. Liam Connor was going to be a dick and I needed to bring my A–game. We'd figure it out. I'd paid for the best lawyers and security for a reason. Same shit, different day in this business.

I wiped at my cheeks, cursing the stupid tears that were running down them and a fucking reporter named Earle Foster.

SEVENTEEN

Max

I WALKED into the firehouse looking for one person.

"Max," Dean called out as I walked past him.

I didn't even slow down. Dean's known me long enough to understand what was about to go down. He ran up behind me and our movement drew the attention of the rest of the guys on duty. I was going to have an audience and I didn't give a shit. The more people to back up how this went down, the better.

I found Bobby in the truck bay and I knew the minute he saw me. Fear has a look and he was the poster child for terror.

"How much?" I advanced on him, using my height and bulk to my advantage. He cowered and I was glad. *Be very scared, motherfucker.* "How much did he pay you for the pictures?"

"Man, c'mon." Bobby backed up two steps and I followed him. "This is how it goes. She's a celebrity and she should know better than to blow you at a party where everyone can see."

I hit him. I was aiming for his fucking ugly mouth but he dodged and I landed it on his nose. I felt the crunch and saw the blood. I'd likely broken it and I didn't care one little bit. When I was done with him, his nose would be a minor problem.

"You asshole. You broke my nose!" The pain pissed him off and gave him a backbone because he got up in my face and kept talking. "I'm your *brother*. You're coming after me because I sold some pictures of a drunk, shitty singer who's probably fucked half the town to get her record deal? Dude, you of all people know what women will do to get a contract. They've all been on their backs."

"Bobby—" Dean's voice cut in over my shoulder, his tone full of warning. "You don't want to go there."

"What? We don't talk about Sarah. Everybody knows that she fucked around on him with that producer."

"This isn't about Sarah and I asked you a question... how much?" I was like ice, stone–cold and serious about getting my answer and the SD card.

"Fuck you." Bobby spat blood on the floor and dared me to make my move with a "come on" wave of his fingers.

That was his second mistake. I jumped him and beat him with every ounce of anger in my body. I punched him until he fell down and then I pinned him to the ground for another round. He was tough and he landed some good punches on my face and stomach. I tasted blood but it didn't slow me down—I had purpose. I didn't do this for me. I was doing this for Kit and for the vulnerable look in her eyes when she said she wanted a drink and for the tears she cried when she'd thought I'd gone inside.

And I did this for the way my chest hurt when she'd pushed me out of her life and ended us.

"Butler! Stop this now!" The voice of my captain barely pierced the haze of fury, but his arm latched around my neck as he yanked me off Bobby got my attention. He manhandled me up and shoved me towards Dean with a terse "keep him on a leash" and then he leaned over to jerk Bobby to his feet.

"What the fuck is going on here?" He was looking at Bobby when he asked the question, but he turned to me for the response. "Butler? You're still in deep shit with the director and me over your trespassing. Don't think we didn't hear about it because your new friend got the charges dropped."

"Yes, sir."

"So why did I come in here and find you beating on a brother firefighter? In *my* fucking house?"

I didn't want to tell him but I had no choice. I wasn't going to add insubordination to my list of infractions. "He took pictures of me and Kit at a party and sold them to a tabloid reporter."

"And what were you doing in these pictures? Anything that would violate department rules?"

"No, sir."

I knew what his next question was going to be and to say that telling him the answer was the last thing I wanted to do was an understatement. Not just for my sake; he was the one who'd caught me fucking the director's niece at the Christmas party, so my sexcapades weren't a big mystery. I didn't want everyone to know about Kit. We'd been secluded, in a private area and Bobby had followed us. There was a good chance that no one else knew about it. And if Kit's lawyers succeeded in getting the article stopped, then I didn't need to expose her actions to all the guys standing around and watching the show.

"So what was in the pictures?" The captain's tone told me he wasn't going to ask again.

I walked closer to him, close enough so only he could hear me. "We're having sex in the pictures. She's giving me a blowjob."

To his credit he didn't even blink, only a muscle twitch by his left eye gave away any reaction.

"I see." He looked at Bobby. "Is this true?"

"Yes, sir."

"And you accepted money?" Bobby nodded and he bit back a foul curse. "How much?"

"One thousand dollars."

I saw red; my jaw clenched so hard that pain shot up my temple. He'd gone cheap when he'd thrown her under the bus. Fucking Bobby.

"Where are these pictures? Did you make copies?" Bobby mumbled "on my phone" and "no" and the captain held his hand out. "Give it to me."

Bobby handed it over and I watched as the captain pulled out the SD card and handed it to me.

"Give this to Ms. Landry. I'll call her manager and let him know that if she wants to sue Mr. Taylor, the department will fully cooperate."

"Yes, sir." I shoved the card in my pocket, knowing it was not the end of this. There was no way I was getting away with whaling on Bobby, no matter the reason. It was NFD policy.

I was right.

"Butler, you're suspended for two days without pay for fighting at the house. I'll write it up and you have five days to grieve the reprimand."

It was a light reprimand, since I could have received a week without pay but it was going in my jacket. As of right now, I could kiss the next round of promotion boards good-bye. Fuck it. I'd do it again.

"Taylor, get cleaned up and report to my office immediately. You're suspended indefinitely, pending a full review. I don't think I need to tell you that your behavior casts a pall on the department and violates every tenet of common decency." The captain's voice was like a whip and I was really glad it wasn't aimed at my ass. "And bottom line, that's a shitty thing to do to a brother. How is he or anyone else here supposed to trust you to have their back at a call?"

The message was loud and clear: Bobby might lose his job.

Look at me not giving a shit.

Everyone filed out of the bay since the show was over, and I turned to head out to my truck and head home. It had been the shittiest day and there was a six–pack and my back porch calling my name.

But I had to do one thing first.

I dug in my pocket for the SD card, holding it out to Dean. He looked confused, but took it from me, no questions asked. This was why we'd been friends our whole lives.

"I'll call Bridget, Kit's P.A., and tell her you're bringing this over."

"Why don't you deliver it?" he called after me as I walked out of the bay and into the sunshine.

"Because she doesn't want to see me anymore."

And there wasn't a damn thing I could do about it—no matter how much I wanted to.

EIGHTEEN

Max

IT WASN'T any surprise at all to find my mom waiting for me when I got home.

I pulled into my yard and parked my truck alongside her little Prius in the shady spot under the magnolias my great–grandparents planted many years ago. She was sitting on the broad front steps of the farmhouse that had been in my family since before the Civil War. It was mine now, my early inheritance from my Grandpa Butler who held the note that I paid every month. He was living it up and charming the ladies at the Augusta Senior Living Village now.

I climbed out of the truck, grabbed the beer off the passenger seat and walked over to sit next to her. She didn't waste any time making her point.

"Dean said you got suspended for two days."

"Fucking Dean." I didn't even dodge the smack she leveled against the back of my head for my language. Some families put money in a jar for every curse word; we had my mom's half–hearted attempts to give us brain damage. I pried the top off a bottle with my keychain and handed it to her and then opened my own.

"You want to talk about it?"

Did I want to? No.

Was she going to stay here until I did? Yes.

"Are you going to tell me how you ended up in a sex tape with Kit Landry?"

I made a mental note to kill Dean the next time I saw him.

I turned and faced my mother. She was looking at me with the same look she'd worn when she'd caught me half–naked on the living room couch with Tamara Riggs. She'd calmly sent Tamara home and then proceeded to pierce me with her steady gaze until I confessed everything and will-ingly listened to the "sex talk". Ten years later, she still knew how to make me talk.

"It wasn't a sex tape." I cleared my throat and took a drink from my bottle. "It was just... you know... pictures."

"Uh, huh." She sounded skeptical and reached over to adjust the collar on my shirt. "You two seemed to have hit it off."

I needed to tread carefully here. She was circling in for the kill. "Well... you know... we've become friends."

"That's great, Max." She smiled and took a sip from her own bottle.

I knew it was coming. There was no way my mom was letting me off the hook on this one. As a rule, I didn't talk with my mom about the women I slept with. My dad, either. I didn't bring them home, so there was nothing to discuss.

Her voice was deceptively soft and sweet. "Would that be what they call 'friends with benefits'?"

"Mom!"

She turned back to me and shrugged her shoulders. "Did I get it wrong? That's what Ashley told me the term is these days."

Why in hell was she talking to my little sister about this?

Pain started throbbing at my temples. I covered my eyes. "No, Mom, you got it right."

"Good." She sounded inordinately pleased with herself and then confused. "So, what does that mean exactly?"

Maybe Ashley hadn't explained *everything* to Mom.

"It means that it's... umm... casual."

"I see." Her voice was slightly disapproving.

I waited and occupied myself by watching the bees buzz around the honeysuckle on the fence. I knew this trick. My mom would sit quietly and patiently wait for her victim to cave in under the weight of the silence and spill the beans.

Oh, hell.

"Mom, we're just hanging out until she goes on her tour. Well, we were. It's no big deal." How could I explain this? And why wasn't I telling her that Kit kicked me to the curb? She'd said it was over but I wasn't ready for her to end our time together. "Kit works too hard and she's got no one to take care of her. We started just to give her a break, to have some fun, that's all."

My mom turned and nailed me with her cool, gray eyes. "Max. What are you doing?"

"I just told you."

She shook her head slowly. "You just told me you care about this girl enough to notice that she needs someone to take care of her." She stopped me when I tried to interrupt.

"It doesn't surprise me that you stepped in to try to help, but I *am* surprised you picked her."

"Mom. We're spending some time together. End of story." I needed to make this clear. "This was never going to be anything more than these three weeks. Our worlds wouldn't work together."

"Here we go again," she sighed, and set her beer bottle on the deck with a loud clunk.

"What does *that* mean?"

"Ever since Sarah died, you've divided up your life into these tiny little compartments. Work. This house. Sex." She smiled at the look of surprise on my face. "I'm your mother; I'm not deaf, dumb, or blind."

"Mom."

"Don't '*Mom*' me."

Her voice had that scary "don't mess with me or you're grounded" tone, so I shut up and let her finish.

"Sarah cheated on you and then she died and you never got the chance to come to terms with what happened. No one blames you for having lots of 'friends'." She gently smoothed back my hair from my face. "But you can't expect to live like this forever to protect your heart."

I ducked out from under her touch and away from her piercing gaze. "I don't want to talk about this."

"Big surprise. You've never been a talker—so be a listener." She chuckled lightly and patted my knee. "Some of the best things in life are the ones you don't see coming."

Smiling, my mom stood up and handed me her beer, leaned over to kiss me on the cheek and walked down the steps. She got to her car and paused, shouting across the yard, "Call your dad. He wants to know if you kicked Bobby's ass. He's always hated that guy."

I laughed, lifting my bottle as she drove away. Leave it

to my mom to come by, bust my balls, and get me thinking about shit I did not want to think about. Like Sarah, relationships, and Kit Landry.

The last few hours had been a nightmare—worse for her. The thing with Kit had been going along fine and now it was a mess. And while I'd normally be out of here with all the crap happening, I wasn't headed for the door even though she'd opened it up and told me to find my way out.

What the hell was I doing?

I knew what.

Kit was amazing. She was easy to talk to, to laugh with, and she was the hottest little firecracker I'd ever had in bed. I was only signed up for a three-week gig and I was already dreading the day when she would no longer be part of my life.

I wanted my three weeks. After that? I had no clue.

NINETEEN

Kit

YOU KNOW it's a bad day when the main evidence in a lawsuit is a picture of you giving a guy a blowjob.

I exited the judge's chambers with my full entourage behind me—Ron, Bridget, my attorney, and my bodyguard. In spite of what the public thought, my life was more late night drive–thrus than red carpets but I was glad for the perks today as we headed out the back of the Federal Courthouse and avoided any press in the front.

I settled into the backseat of the black Suburban, kicking off my heels as I sank down into the leather seat. I leaned back and closed my eyes, wishing I could take the day off but I only had time for a quick nap, rehearsal, and then a late flight to New York City for several promo appearances.

"Well, I'm glad the judge ruled in our favor," Bridget said.

"Judge Fairfax is known to be fair and sympathetic to

violation of privacy cases," my attorney, Patrick Sweeney, commented while he checked the messages on his cell phone. "The Daily Scoop has to destroy the photographs and they cannot print *that* story, but they *can* still run one about your love triangle with Max and Tyler."

"I'm not involved with Tyler," I grumbled, not even opening my eyes. I don't know why I bothered to protest; that story had taken hold and was running on every major media source. Ron was getting his wish, as my record sales and radio play were picking up. He never passed up the chance to give me an "I told you so" look.

"If they base the story on 'unnamed sources' then they can do it," Patrick explained. "I've got a paralegal at the firm who will be monitoring their stories on you. If they screw up, I'll be all over them."

I looked over at him, reaching out to give his hand a squeeze. "Thank you so much. I don't know what I would have done if they'd printed those pictures."

"Well, let's try not having public sex again and we won't have to find out," Ron muttered from the front seat of the car.

I ignored him. I'd been doing a lot of that since yesterday in my apartment when I'd discovered he was stirring up the Tyler crap in the press. Patrick shot me a look and I knew he was thinking that I needed to do something about my manager. I was glad I had him working on that, as well.

"I'll call the NFD later and tell them the ruling. As you can imagine, they were concerned about the photo getting out as well since it also involved one of their firefighters. They will use your statement and today's case in the disciplinary hearing against Bobby Taylor."

"What about Max?" I asked, looking out the window as

downtown Nashville slid by. I had another two weeks here before hitting the road and I couldn't wait. On tour, I could just focus on the shows, the music, and my career. It was my norm, my comfort zone, and I was so ready to get back there. But I couldn't even fool myself that I wouldn't miss Max. I would; very much.

"He was suspended for the fighting, not the photo, so there isn't much I can do for him unless you want to send a note and try to get it lifted from his record."

"He did beat the crap out of Bobby for you," Bridget said. "I think it's the least you can do for a guy who is such a hero."

"I can't believe he got the SD card for me." Dean had shown up and handed it over and filled in the blanks on what had happened at the firehouse. Max had done it again —saved my ass from the fire but I still couldn't call him.

If I did, then we would keep going for the next two weeks and I'd be in danger of getting in over my head. I was already into him and fourteen more days wouldn't slow that down. The other night at the Bluebird I'd sung a new song, the one about not wanting to risk getting too close because I knew I would fall. At the time, I didn't have anyone in mind but now I did. The song seemed almost like wish fulfillment.

I could fall in love with him.

I was half-way there already.

I wasn't sure if he would ever feel the same way.

Max wasn't a player. He was a straight-up guy who didn't want any type of commitment and I got that. I didn't really understand the why but I knew it involved a woman in his past. I knew that fighting against a memory was the hardest thing to do and I didn't want to lose that battle a second time.

But I owed him thanks for what he did for me and it was a debt I could not fail to pay, no matter what it might cost me.

TWENTY

Max

I WAS ACTING like a crazed middle–school girl.

While the rest of A–shift was downstairs in the TV room, I flopped down on my bunk in the firehouse and hit the speed dial on my phone. Again.

Kit was in New York making the rounds of the talk shows, but I persisted in trying to talk to her about what happened.

The love triangle story had broken and the number of reporters stalking me was ridiculous. I wondered if they really thought my response to their questions was ever going to be anything but "no comment".

I wasn't ashamed of being with Kit, but I was embarrassed for her and what the article and photos made her out to be. Most people congratulated *me* on scoring big, while some of the public treated her like a fallen woman. Luckily, her real fans stuck by her and the sales for her concerts had skyrocketed. I guess the saying was right—the only bad publicity is no publicity.

My only real problem was the reaction of the NFD— they weren't thrilled, but after a very long apology session with the director and a statement from Kit, I was off suspension, had received my back pay and the incident was wiped from my record.

But Kit wasn't so forgiving.

Since the day in her loft, she'd frozen me out of her life. She refused to take my calls or answer my emails and texts. I was one restraining order away from stalker status but I couldn't stop myself. I'd tried to give her the space she'd asked for but after four days, I was officially going out of my mind. I had to talk to her.

Kit was one of the strongest women I knew and I cringed at the thought that I was part of the stress that had brought her to her knees. Not telling her about the reporter was stupid. But letting her find out about it the way she did was worse than stupid.

I let the phone ring and I jumped with surprise when I heard a real, live voice come over the line. Kit's voice. Not a recorded message.

"Max."

It was the same, sexy voice I heard in my dreams. Not the sparkly, pre–packaged version she used in interviews, this was the totally genuine voice that latched on to something deep inside me and wouldn't let go. I refused to think about how close that something was to my heart.

I hesitated, waiting for her to tell me off and demand I lose her phone number.

"Max? Are you there?"

"I'm sorry."

"What are you sorry about?" I heard her breath catch

over the line, giving away her emotion. I wasn't the only one struggling with what this had become. "You got the SD card for me. Thank you."

"I'd do it again. I'm no Boy Scout or even anybody you'd take home to your parents, but I'm not an asshole and I'm not cruel."

"I believe you."

"But?"

"I'm not in a place to handle what's going down between us. This has gotten complicated." Kit sighed heavily, her voice edgy. "I want to trust you, but my head's telling me I don't really know you."

I cut her off. "You *do* know me." I leaned into the phone, as if I could get physically closer to her by focusing on her voice. "You know me. Just like *I know you.*"

The moments passed like an eternity until she spoke and I could breathe again. "I don't know how to cut you off right now."

"Then don't. I'm holding you to my three weeks."

"And then?"

"One day at a time." I lived in the moment all the time. Why treat this any differently?

The silence on the line stretched out but I could be patient. I knew when I was going to get my way and Kit was already considering it. She hadn't shot me down, so I was still in the game.

"One day at a time," she said.

I closed my eyes. The relief I felt at her words almost made me dizzy.

Not wanting to overstep the boundaries of our "friends with benefits" arrangement, my next question was cautious. "I heard you after I left."

"What do you mean? Heard what?"

"I don't know who Lilah is, but if you're in trouble—"

She cut me off right away, the fear in her voice when I expected anger, freaking me out.

"Max... I can't talk to you about that."

"Kit, please."

Her voice was firm. "Max. I can't. Not right now."

"Alright. Alright. Don't worry about it." I hadn't missed that she'd said "right now"—did that mean she might someday? Did I want her to? This whole situation was fucked up, totally out of my comfort zone but I couldn't find the energy to back away. I also hated to rock the boat with my next comment, but it needed to be said. "You can trust me. I hope you know that."

Surprisingly, she shifted the subject entirely. "Who couldn't you trust, Max? Who is Sarah?"

I sat up and swung my legs over the side of my bunk, my entire body rigid with tension. Now it was my turn to let the silence stretch out between us as I considered my options. I could refuse to answer her questions or I could offer her the trust I kept asking of her. "So, we're going to have this conversation?"

"Is there a reason why we shouldn't?" Kit countered softly.

"Oh, I can think of about a million." I chuckled, my throat dry. "Including the one that says this is crossing the line of the terms of our agreement."

"You said we know each other. This will help us get to know each other better."

"Uh huh." Fuck it. I could do this. Kit and I had already crossed the line; what was going on between us was so blurry, I'm not even sure I could find the chalk line.

"Sarah was a girl I loved. She broke my heart and then she died."

"Oh, Max. I'm so sorry."

I swallowed hard, fighting every instinct to shut down this conversation because thinking about it made it feel like yesterday instead of six years ago.

"We lived together and I found out she was cheating on me with her boss, a record producer. He was older, had more money, and she fell for every slick line he fed her. I was in the fire academy, making no money, and all I could offer her was little pay and a future of wondering if this was the time I never returned from my shift."

"How did you find out?"

"I saw a text from him and everything suddenly made sense—all the traveling together, the nights she was working late at the office." I swallowed hard because this is where the story got rough. There were some things you never got over and this was mine. "We got in a fight at a party and she took off in her car. She'd been drinking, so I followed her and when I caught up with her, she'd flipped it on a curve. It was too late."

"Oh, my God, Max."

"When Dean found us, I was working on her even though I knew." I coughed, my throat tight. No matter what Sarah had done, no matter how much she'd hurt me, she didn't deserve to take her last breath on the side of the road. "That's my story."

"You still love her." It sounded more like a statement than a question to my ears but I heard what she was asking.

"No. But I did." I was in for a penny; might as well give the pound of flesh, too. "I really did and then I was really hurt. I never want to feel that way again. I just don't think the high is worth the low."

As the words passed my lips, I realized that I wasn't so sure anymore. Just two weeks ago I would have guaranteed my answer, but with this woman in my life my limitations felt more like shackles instead of safety nets.

"Enough about me. If I keep this up then I'll have to turn in my man–card."

She laughed and just the sound loosened the tightness that I'd been carrying around since she'd kicked me out of her apartment.

"So, Kit. What's your story?"

"Don't you read People magazine?"

Her laugh was awkward and I recognized it for what it was—a lame attempt to avoid the spotlight. She wasn't getting off that easily.

"Didn't you tell me not to believe anything I read in a magazine?" When she hesitated, I leaned into the phone and whispered, "Baby."

"Yeah?"

"Just tell me."

"I loved Jake Cooper and he loved me. I know he did no matter how it turned out. For a year, we were able to keep it together. I cut back on my touring and he turned down a movie but eventually our careers demanded more of our time. He wanted me to scale back my ambition, but I couldn't make the leap. I was afraid."

"Afraid? Of what?"

"Career suicide. Lost opportunity. Missed chances to make money and secure the future for me and the ones who depended on me. It was only a few years ago that I was a homeless teen living on the streets. Jake grew up in the suburbs in a gated community and he had no way to understand where I was coming from."

I knew what came next. Unless you were living under a rock, the whole world knew.

"Things were bad between us and then he went to

Japan to work on a movie and I stayed in the U.S. His ex–wife was his co–star and they started sleeping together again."

"What an asshole."

"Yep. But, that wasn't the reason I left him."

"I think it was reason enough."

She hummed in agreement. "I ended it because I wasn't the woman who was going to make him happy. The things he wanted us to do to be together—it wasn't wrong. That's what normal people do and I figured that if I couldn't or wouldn't do it for him then I needed to let him go." Kit attempted a non–committal tone as if the decision hadn't been a difficult one to make, but the pain in her voice gave it away. "We loved each other—I loved him—but it wasn't enough."

I remembered the headlines that followed Kit the year after the break–up. There were the missed concerts, the delay of her album because she was a no–show at the recording studio, and the reports of drinking and rehab.

Kit guessed my train of thought. "Everything printed about me was true. The drinking. The men. I missed work because I was drunk or hung over or in some random guy's room. I haven't had a drink in a year. Haven't wanted one until recently." Her voice was weary. "I've been hitting extra meetings, talking to my sponsor as I work through it all."

Okay. So we were both fucked up when it came to relationships and that was never destined to end well. I should get out now while the getting was good but I knew I wouldn't.

I'd thought I was a fan before I met her but "Kit the Singer" was only a fraction of what the awesome "Kit the Woman" was. Jake Cooper had been a clueless douchebag and I was running for the second place title because I intended to walk away when this was all over. Or would I stay? I had a lot of thinking to do in the next two weeks.

Voices came over the line and I could hear Kit murmuring to someone in the background. When she came back on the line, her voice had switched into business mode. "I have to go."

"Hey, don't worry about it. You go do what you have to do and I'll see you when you get back to Nashville. Okay?" My fingers itched to touch her and I would have given anything to kiss her at that moment, but that was going to have to wait.

She agreed and ended the call and I flopped back on my bunk and stared at the bed above me. The crisscross of wire that supported the mattress on the upper bunk perfectly matched my emotions.

My head was telling me not to get involved any deeper with Kit but I knew it was too late. I *was* involved. I wasn't calling it a love match, but friendship was definitely in the mix and that made all the lines a little blurry.

And for the first time since Sarah, I didn't mind.

But it did scare the shit out of me.

TWENTY ONE

Kit

"IS THAT A NEW SONG?"

Surprised by his question, I strummed my guitar and looked over to where Max was lying on the picnic blanket. We hadn't talked much since our telephone call. I'd left New York for a short press junket in the Northwest and bad weather in Nashville had pulled Max into a double–shift at the station that ended early this morning. I'd expected him to grab some sleep and then call me later, but he'd called before eight and asked if I wanted to go fishing and have a picnic.

I'd thrown together a cooler full of food and drinks, and grabbed my guitar just in time to meet him downstairs in his truck. We'd driven in silence to private Butler land far out of Nashville.

So far we'd eaten, with Max inhaling the fried chicken, but his fishing pole was still in the truck. He'd collapsed on the blanket and I watched him.

Max didn't look good. Haggard and exhausted, he had dark shadows under his eyes and his usual, easy conversation was nonexistent.

I knew what was wrong and I let him have his peace. The TV news and the newspaper were full of what Max had dealt with on his long shift. With tourist season in full swing, the bad weather had caused several major accidents with several fatalities. One accident resulted in the deaths of three people, one being a child, and Max's station had responded to the call.

So, I didn't press him to talk. I had no idea what to say that would soothe his hurt. He needed time to process everything that had happened and I was content to sit by and work on the song I couldn't get out of my head.

I still owed him an answer to his question. "Yep. A new one. But, the words aren't coming to me." I struggled to articulate what I was feeling since I couldn't get it on paper. "It's not a love song, it's not a sad song, it's..."

"It's bittersweet."

I closed my eyes and looked up into the sky as I continued to strum. The sun shone a warm red behind my eyelids. He was right. It was bittersweet and needed the perfect lyric. But that would be for another day. I needed to concentrate to the get words down and I couldn't do that, knowing what Max was dealing with.

I opened my eyes and looked at Max. His eyes were closed, his chest rising and falling in a rhythm that usually led to a nap. Damn, but he was beautiful. With the sun glinting off his ebony hair and his tan skin gleaming, he looked like a dark angel. I laughed at that word choice—he'd always been my angel.

"I like this place." I soaked in the crystal clear lake, the grassy lawn leading down to the pier and the beautiful, old shade trees. It was secluded, quiet, and perfect for getting away from what troubled you. "Is this a favorite?"

"One of them. I come here to relax. To get away." His voice was gravelly and he cleared his throat before continuing. "Thanks for coming. I've never brought a woman here before."

My stomach did a triple somersault. What did that mean about how he felt about me? Something between us had shifted, changed. It was still too early to tell but I felt like we were on the edge of moving into new territory for us; something that would take longer than three weeks to figure out.

I'd missed him in New York and he'd preoccupied my thoughts more often than I liked. The week between the awful day in my loft and when I'd finally taken his call had been terrible. It was crazy how much I missed him and how much that fact didn't bother me. But, what I wanted in my personal life was the total opposite of what Max wanted in a relationship. Realistically, this was all it could ever be and I had to accept it.

I placed my guitar in its case next to the blanket and stretched out next to Max. He reached out with one arm and dragged me closer, our knees touching, eyes locked on each other. I reached out and stroked his face. He closed his eyes, leaning into my touch.

"Do you want to talk about it?" I asked.

He kept his eyes closed. "No."

I kept up the stroking, running my fingers through the soft strands of his hair, a whisper–light trace across the stubble on his jaw, down his muscled bicep. He wasn't asleep.

"Are you ever scared?"

He opened his eyes, dark lashes and the darkish circles on his skin making the amber stand out.

"Fuck, yeah; every time."

"Then why do you do it?"

He shifted up on one elbow, looking down at me, the sun behind him making his tanned skin deepen to a bronzed gold. He didn't give me his usual Max smile. His eyes were somber, the lines around his mouth and eyes tight with tension.

"Are you ever scared? To do what you do?" he asked.

"It's not the same."

"Answer the question." He toyed with the top button on my sundress, slipping it through the hole.

"Yes. I get scared."

"So why do you do it?" Another button slipped through the hole, the rough callouses of his fingers awakening the nerve endings under my skin

"Because no one else can do what I do. Nobody else can sing my songs."

"So ask me again." He leaned forward, kissing the skin he was exposing, a lick of his tongue, a nip of his teeth.

I arched into his touch, squirming underneath him as my belly grew warm and my nipples hard. I could barely think about the question with him all over me.

"So why do you do it?" I asked as he put his finger in his mouth and then lowered the wet digit to circle my nipple, blowing on it gently.

"I do it because nobody else can. It's my song, in a way."

He lifted up and stared down at me, desire mixing with something else in his eyes. Sadness. Regret. Grief. I bit back the tears in my eyes. He didn't need that from me.

I cupped his jaw, stroking over his lower lip. "Was it bad today?"

He closed his eyes, his jaw tight. "Yes."

"Can you talk about it?"

"I—" He swallowed hard, fingers gripping the blanket. I wanted to take the question back. He'd come here to forget and I'd invited his nightmare. "There was a kid. We couldn't get them out."

I gasped, understanding the horror immediately. The TV screen had been filled with the car fire.

"What do you need?" I would give him anything but I didn't know where to start. He needed to give me an idea and I would let my heart show me the rest of the way.

"I need you." He lay on his back, on the blanket, his eyes fixed on me. "I was back at the house, putting away the gear, getting cleaned up and all I could think about was you. Do you know why?"

I shook my head.

"Because when I look at you, everything else fades. It just disappears and I can breathe again." He reached up, his fingers toying with a curl, wrapping it around his finger. "I need you to make it all disappear. You're the only thing I want to see."

I leaned over, lowering my lips to his mouth. I pressed my lips to his, the sweetest glide filled with every ounce of my feeling. I pulled back, watching him until his eyes opened in a lazy, sensual motion.

"Just look at me."

Max stared at me as I sat up completely, shrugging off the sundress and letting the sunshine warm my skin all over. I let my fingers dance across my skin, my breasts, in between my thighs. I was teasing myself, enticing Max with the movement. Drawing him into my spell.

"Just look at me," I repeated as I slipped off my bra, one strap at a time, letting the weight of the cups pull it down.

The breeze off the lake was cool against my fevered flesh, tightening my nipples into hard peaks. I needed his touch, the wet slick of his tongue on my body, but this was about Max.

Max's eyes were hot and needy as he watched my progress, his hand rubbing against the erection filling the front of his shorts. I snaked a hand around my back and undid the clasp, throwing my bra to the side. I hooked two fingers into my underwear and slid them off my body until I kneeled in front of Max in nothing but my skin.

I was wide open. Pouring everything I had, everything I felt, into this moment with him. He looked me over, his gaze scorching me as he drank me in.

"Just look at me."

I leaned forward from my kneeling position and undid the button on his shorts, pushing them down and off his body. He was hard, large and hot as I closed my hand around him, squeezing and stroking until he writhed under my touch. He never broke eye contact with me and I was wet just from the sounds he made. Rough. Needy. Raw.

"Fuck. More." He groaned, writhing under each stroke of his cock. His fingers clenched the blanket at his sides, twisting the fabric. He was gorgeous, skin smooth and damp with sweat. "Please, Kit. More. I need you."

I ached to touch myself, to ease the deep need building between my thighs, but I held off. This was about Max. This was all for Max.

I straddled his waist, reaching for the condom I'd stowed in the basket. I placed it on him quickly, positioning my slick center over him.

"Just look at me."

I slid down his length, gasping with the fullness of him.

He was so hard, so thick. I stroked my hands over his chest, enjoying his masculinity.

He reached up and cupped my face, caressing my cheeks with his thumbs. "You're so beautiful."

I blinked back the tears. I was not safe with this man. I wanted to protect him, to soothe him, to laugh with him, to be with him. He'd worked his way inside my heart and I'd done nothing to stop him. It was as if my heart knew what my head would not admit.

He was it for me. He could be—was—my everything.

I traced the contours of his face, his cheekbones, his eyelids, his lips, and then back up to lightly caress the dark shadows underneath his eyes. "You look so tired. You should be at home sleeping."

His sooty black eyelashes fluttered open, the desire swirling in his eyes causing my breath to catch in my throat. Max reached up, grabbed my hand, and pressed a kiss onto the palm.

"I need you, Kit." His gaze caught my own in a stare of unapologetic need and desire. "You're all I need."

"Max."

"Always need you."

He pulled me down and kissed me, his tongue thrusting inside my mouth with a brutal, possessive hunger. I claimed him back, elated to know that I was not alone in this feeling. I needed him to know that he wasn't alone, either.

I released his mouth and sat up, beginning that slow rise and fall that would bring him release, maybe bring him comfort. I was so wet, my body clasped him on each stroke and I felt the loss of him when he pulled out and the hunger building each time he thrust back in.

I want you.

I need you.

I love you.

I used my body to tell him all the things that I would not say. All the things I knew he did not want to hear. But I shouted them in my head as we rode the wave together. When I came it was sudden, wrenching a long, deep moan from me that I shouted into the open air. Max groaned, his fingers digging painfully into my hips as he shoved me down as he thrust upwards, going deep inside me. I felt him come, swelling inside as he found the oblivion he needed.

I collapsed against him, our bodies slick against each other and warm with the sunshine and our exertion. Max held me and I held him, our bodies shivering with the after-shock. We held each other until the sweat cooled on our bodies and our heartbeats slowed down in tandem. We held each other as we both fell asleep—Max finding his peace and me finding my home.

TWENTY TWO

Max

"SO, what are you trying to do? Feel good or forget?"

I looked up from the bourbon in my hand and into the face of my best friend. He leaned heavily on the bar and shook his head at me like he already knew the answer to his question. "Dean, don't start. I'm not in the mood."

Dean signaled to the bartender to bring him a beer. When he turned back to me, his voice was brimming with sarcasm. "Yeah, I needed you to tell me that. *Thank God*, I came over to get that newsflash."

I took a drink from my glass. "What do you want?"

"I want to know what has you heading straight for the hard stuff." He nodded towards the glass in my hand.

I knocked back another swig of the whiskey before looking at him. "I'm fine."

"Go sell that shit somewhere else. Are you still thinking about the shift? You took off pretty fast after the debrief."

I sighed and slammed my glass down on the bar, spilling

some of it on the counter. *Dean's just worried about you. No need to bite his head off.* I tried again with less asshole in my tone. "No. I'm okay about the shift. I just..." I struggled with how to describe what was eating me up. "I'm just..."

Giving up, I grabbed my second drink and glanced over his shoulder across the room. My gaze automatically found Kit, beautiful and animated, as she posed for pictures and signed autographs for some of the crowd at Stoney's, a local bar and grill owned by a retired fire-fighter, Mike Stoneman. Always gracious, Kit happily complied with her fans' requests. As usual, she was making every person feel as if they were the only person in the room.

Dean interrupted my thoughts. "So, where did you go? I tried your phone for hours."

I took another drink, grimaced at the bitter taste, and savored the burn. A couple more of these and I wouldn't give a shit about the shift or anything else. "I went to the lake." I anticipated his next question and muttered, "With Kit."

Dean's arm paused in mid-air as he lifted his beer to his mouth. His eyes shifted to me as his mouth dropped open in shock. "You never take women to the lake."

"I know."

"Not even Sarah."

"*I know.*"

Dean placed his beer on the bar and rubbed his hand over his face. "Is that a good thing?"

"I don't know." And I didn't. I stared at the mirror over the bar, watching Kit's reflection as I remembered the events of the morning. "I don't know. I got off the shift and she's the first person I thought to call." I glanced at Dean with a shrug. "I needed to see her."

Dean stared at me like I'd just spoken in pig latin. "Well, that's good. Right?"

"I don't know." Damn, I sounded like a broken record. "I just needed to be with her."

I'd known in my gut that she was exactly what I needed. And she was perfect. She'd known when I'd needed to sit and brood and when I'd needed to laugh. Then, she'd offered herself to me, so sweetly and openly, and I was unable to do anything but bury myself inside her body and make love to her with a ferocity that shocked me.

Make love to her.

Not just sex.

Oh hell. I'm in trouble. I squeezed my eyes shut at the memory of the way I felt the minute I'd entered her soft, warm body. I'd worried I was going to be too rough, that I would hurt her. And I was right. I *was* going to hurt her.

"I'm falling for her," I said.

"Oh."

"Yeah. Oh." I opened my eyes to see Dean gearing up to launch into a "this is great" speech and I cut him off. "It won't work. I can't do it."

"Bullshit. That's just Sarah talking."

My frustration bubbled to the surface and I growled. "No. That's the truth. I'll fuck this up eventually. I don't know how to do this."

Dean's face flushed with anger. "Bullshit. You'll figure it out like the rest of us assholes."

I refused to debate this with him. I knew me. I knew my limitations and I would fuck this up and when I did, Kit would dump my ass and I would be in the hurt locker. It would be ten times worse than Sarah and I just couldn't do it.

I already needed her too much.

Dean nudged my shoulder as Kit headed over to us with her cheeks flushed and eyes bright. Her cheerfulness faltered when she glanced in my direction. God only knows what she saw in my face because I felt like I was raw and ripped open.

"You want a drink?" Dean asked.

"Just a Diet Coke, please."

Kit glanced towards me, her eyes lingering for a moment on my bourbon. I did not make eye contact with either of them, instead watching the activity in the mirror over the bar.

Dean ordered her drink and pointed towards the crowd in the bar. "I can't believe you got Stoney to smile. I didn't think he actually *had* teeth."

Dean nudged me again, and I tried to join in on the conversation, but I couldn't stop thinking about what I knew I had to do. Minutes crawled by and I seethed until I couldn't stand it any longer.

I put my glass down and touched Kit's arm to interrupt her conversation with Dean. "We need to go."

My voice was more gruff than I'd intended and she pulled away from my touch with a confused and hurt expression on her face. I sucked in a breath and gave myself a do–over. "Don't you have an early photo shoot tomorrow? We should go."

Nodding, she shot me a questioning look before turning to Dean and making her excuses to leave. On autopilot, I took her arm and headed out of the bar and across the parking lot towards my truck.

Kit stopped and turned and faced off with me. I couldn't look at her.

"Max. Are you okay?"

Just do it Max. End it. I looked at the neon sign on the

bar and avoided her eyes as I hedged. "I'm just tired. I need to go."

The bustle of traffic and the distant sound of a siren filled the silence.

"Do you want to go to my place?"

I shook my head, my eyes still glued on the garish neon. "No. I don't think so. I just need to go home."

"Okay… you just want to call me tomorrow?"

I turned to face her and she faltered. What she saw in my face caused her features to cloud over with a wariness I hated to see. I hated that I was the one to put it there.

I fought the urge to hit something as I ended the best two weeks of my life. "No. I don't think I should call you anymore. This needs to end now."

She stepped back and raised an arm up over her stomach, as if reacting to a physical blow.

Determined to get it over with, I plowed ahead. "You were right. We both knew this was going to be a short-term thing. I just think we should end it now. It would be better."

Her eyes searched my face as her mouth struggled to form words. She cleared her throat, her voice raw. "Did I do something wrong?"

"No. It's not you. It's me."

Fuck, that was a terrible thing to say. I was an asshole.

She might have been hurt two seconds before but now she was pissed. "I can't believe you used that line on me. You're dumping me with one of the worst excuses ever." Kit walked up and poked me in the chest. "If you want to end this, then just tell me why it's over. Don't hide behind some lame-ass line you think is going to spare my tender feelings."

Unable to maintain eye contact, I looked over to a group of people exiting the bar and struggled to say something that would soften the blow. But I didn't trust myself to speak and not take it all back. I turned and Kit was no longer standing beside me. She was walking towards the sidewalk and talking to someone on her cell.

What the hell?

"Yeah I need a cab at Stoney's... that's the one... I'll be waiting." She clicked the phone shut and continued walking on the sidewalk towards the front of the bar.

I sprinted to catch up to her. "I'll drive you home."

"We're done, Max. I called a cab and it'll be here soon. Just leave me alone."

I stood there on the sidewalk as she waited for her cab.

You can't just let it end this way. Time to be a grown–up and be honest about why this was such a colossal mistake.

Desperate, I blurted out the truth. "I can't do this. I like you."

Kit's face registered surprise for the briefest moment and then she was pissed again. "You *like* me? You sound like a middle–school boy."

She was right. I tried to figure out a way to explain why I had to get out before it was too late to salvage my heart.

"The other night, Shannon got to pick the movie at the station and she chose the chick flick where that British guy hooked up with the movie star. You know the one I'm talking about?"

Kit nodded. "I know the one but what does that have to do with us?"

"I'm getting to it." I took a step closer. "At the end, she comes to him and lays it all out there. Tells him she loves him, the whole nine yards, but he turns her down. He explains that he's just a regular guy and when she dumps him he'll have to deal with seeing her face on TV, in maga-zines—everywhere—and he wouldn't be able to handle it."

"And?"

"That guy? He's me. I wanted to be with my fantasy-girl and then walk away with no regrets just like I always do, but I didn't expect to care about you. I didn't expect to need you." I tentatively reached out, capturing her hand. "And I do need you. So fucking much. This is more than a fling to me and I have to get out while I can. Because *when* it ends, *when* I fuck it up, I'll be the one having to live in this town with your face and music everywhere."

I stroked my thumb gently over her palm, memorizing the way her tiny hand fit inside my own, the softness of her skin. She was the most beautiful thing I'd ever seen. Funny, open, giving and way out of my league. I had to get out now before I couldn't walk away.

She looked at me and I hated the sadness etched onto her face.

"In that scene, she also reminded him that all this stuff was just nonsense—not real—she was just a regular girl," she said.

She stepped forward and placed her hand on my chest and I leaned into the warmth of her touch.

"I'm just me, Max. All the famous stuff, it isn't me. I thought you knew that."

"If you'd stayed the fantasy, I could handle it. But you didn't. That's why I need to walk away now."

It was the truth, but I wished like hell I could take it back. Kit looked at me for a long time, like she was trying to see if there was any argument to make and I knew the second she knew it was useless. She nodded slightly and it was done.

I stepped closer, pulling her into my arms and holding her close as I memorized her soft curves. I buried my face in her hair and inhaled her unique scent. Even though it couldn't last, I didn't regret being with her. She pulled back and gazed at me.

"It was this morning, wasn't it?"

I just stared at her, unsure about how to answer her question.

"That was real—what happened between us. It was real," she said.

"Yes, it was."

"You don't want real."

"I—" Oh fuck. "I don't need real."

"That's bullshit. Everybody needs real." Kit reached up and touched my cheek and I leaned into it. I couldn't help myself. "We just tell ourselves we don't want it because we're scared."

That hit too close. Too close. "I don't need it."

"Sure you don't." She dropped her hand and I missed her warmth. "We could be good together. You're going to regret this, you know?"

"I already do." And that was the most honest fucking thing I'd ever said in my life. "I just can't go where this is headed. What you want is not what I want. That hasn't changed."

As her cab pulled up, she shook off my touch and I braced for the final goodbye. It was for the best. I had a chance to land on my feet if I got out now.

Everything was in slow motion as the cabbie rolled down the window and asked if Kit was his fare. She said something to the guy but I couldn't hear it over the roaring in my ears. When she turned back to me, she had a fake smile pasted on her face and her eyes were bright with moisture. Standing on her tiptoes, she softly kissed me, and then climbed into the cab.

I watched the cab turn the corner towards Kit's loft and drive away.

And then she was gone.

I knew it was the right thing.

It was the grown–up thing.

Being a grown up sucked.

TWENTY THREE

Kit

"KIT!"

"Tyler!"

"Look over here!"

I pasted a smile on my face and struck a pose for the cameras on the red carpet constructed by the label in their large, opulently appointed lobby. The event, a party to cele-brate the kick–off of my tour, was loud, crowded, and seemed to go on for hours. My feet hurt in the ludicrously high heels my stylist had picked out for me, and my jaw ached from the constant smiling for the photographers.

And my heart hurt.

The dull ache had started three days earlier in the parking lot outside of Stoney's Bar, when Max kicked me to the curb. *No, that was harsh. He didn't kick me to the curb— he broke up with me. And he didn't even do that because we weren't together.*

"Kit, darlin'."

A couple of times I'd almost called him, but my finger stalled over the "call" button and I'd closed the phone without dialing. His position was clear and I needed to respect it and move on. I couldn't have him. I'd known it from the beginning. Now I needed to get on with my tour and life; without Max.

"Kit, darlin'. Are you ok?"

Tyler's voice jerked me back to the present, back to the glare of the lights and the click of the photographers' cameras. Dazed and disoriented, I leaned into Tyler's side as he steadied me. Tyler gazed at me with affection and desire and I pressed closer, selfishly seeking comfort where I could find it. Tyler smiled in reaction and his gaze shifted down to my mouth while his grip on my waist tightened. Alarm bells rang faintly in my head as he leaned closer, brushing his lips against mine in a soft kiss.

I sighed, all the tension in my body easing away as I returned Tyler's kiss. He was familiar, safe, and it was so easy to just lean in to him and forget all of my angst about the tour, Ron, and Max.

Max.

Oh no. This is wrong.

Ignoring the flashes going off like the Fourth of July, I pushed away from Tyler and stumbled back in the direction of my dressing area. Reporters were yelling at me but I waved them off and ran as fast as I could in those ridiculous shoes. I needed a few minutes to remember who the fuck I was and who I wasn't. I wasn't a woman who kissed one man while I thought of someone else.

Tyler was close on my heels, so I sped up, made eye contact with my security, and nodded my head in Tyler's direction. My mountain of muscle quirked an eyebrow at me and nodded just before he closed in and blocked the door that I quickly opened and closed behind me.

Once inside, I let loose a strangled scream, ripped the ridiculous shoes off and hurled them across the room. The sudden peace and quiet in the room sucked out the last ounce of my adrenaline and I took the few steps to my dressing table and sank down on a chair before my legs gave out. Stricken, I stared at my reflection. I was proud of my ability to slip into my alter ego and handle any situation life threw at me. I *never* lost it in front of the press. Never let the mask slip.

"Super Kit" was invincible.

I sighed, grabbed a makeup brush and started touching up my face. I was disgusted at myself—I'd used Tyler. I was a jerk and, in a colossally dumb move, did it in front of a ton of photographers. My hand stilled in applying the makeup as I gave myself the ass–chewing I needed. "Get your head in the game. You have too much riding on this tour to get sidetracked by emotional bullshit."

A knock on the door halted my lecture–for–one. "Not now, Tyler. Give me a minute!"

"It's not Tyler." Bridget's voice was muffled through the door. "Can I come in?"

I went over to the door, opening it just enough to let Bridget and my attorney, Patrick, into the room. Surprised, I reached out and gave him a big hug.

"Patrick, what are you doing here? Don't you have a new baby at home?"

His eyes twinkled at the mention of his newborn son. "I'm on my way there right now, but I wanted to drop off the papers you had me draw up." He handed an envelope to me, his smile dimming with the change of subject. "Are you sure you want to give Ron such a generous severance package?"

I sat down on the couch and drew the papers out of the envelope. "He was the key to my success and I can't forget that fact. Even if—" I faltered as I looked over the papers and then up at my two friends. I was confused.

"What's this?" I pointed at the top three papers.

Bridget and Patrick exchanged a look and suddenly I knew what was going on here. "Ron has been the one feeding information to the press about your activities with Max, your supposed relationship with Tyler. He's also made questionable deals for you where he got kick-backs. Big bribes. Lucrative bribes. My team found evidence that goes back almost to the beginning of your professional relationship." He gestured to the pile. "He has not done his duty to you and I think you should fire him for cause and refuse to give him a severance package."

"Can I do that?"

"According to his contract, he forfeits his severance if he violates the terms and conditions of his contract."

"And you can prove that he did?"

Patrick nodded. "*And* that he was planning to continue with your next album. I have an inside person at the label who states that Ron had meetings with Liam Connor and promised he would kill the new songs, your new sound. He was going to get a bigger cut directly from Liam on your new contract, as well."

"Really?" I sat back on the sofa and part of me wasn't surprised at all. Things between us had been rocky at best— hostile on a good day lately—but I couldn't believe he would actively stab me in the back. But I had to be realistic about where I was in my career at this moment. "I can't fire him now. I'm about to go on tour."

"Kit, I called Paul Brandt," Bridget joined in. "He said he's on the next plane and he'll stay until we find a replacement for Ron."

Paul would be able to hit the ground running. And he would come to me if I needed him—and I needed him now. I didn't want to drag him into this but I didn't see any choice.

I stared down at the papers lying on the table, wondering what else could go wrong. I needed to focus and make a decision now.

"Do it. Fire Ron with no severance."

"He'll probably sue."

"Great. Just what I need—another scandal." But I was past worrying about that. I needed to act and deal with the fallout, whatever that might be. "Do it anyway and get Paul here. We don't have much time."

I'd made my decision and the rapid knock on my door and "five minutes Ms. Landry" indicated that my duties at the party wouldn't wait for this latest development. Rising up from the couch, I mentally prepared to deal with the crowd waiting outside my door. A squeeze from Bridget, and a "hang in there" from Patrick was all I had time for before I opened the door and entered the party full of press, label management, and Tyler. Kissing him now seemed so minor in comparison to everything else that was falling apart in my life.

Josef, my head of security, stuck close to me as we moved through the crowd, heading towards the area set up for the speeches and the press Q & A. I shook off the drama of the last few moments, put on my "Super Kit" persona, smiled, and waved hello to those who called out good wishes. Someone came up behind me, too close, and I figured it was Tyler. I turned to ask him to walk over to the podium with me.

It wasn't Tyler.

I stepped back from the microphone shoved way too far into my personal space. "I'm sorry, but the press conference will start in a few minutes. Okay?"

The reporter, one I didn't know, pressed forward. "Why'd you lie, Kit?"

Confused, I looked over my shoulder, making sure Josef was watching the exchange. I gave a nod in the reporter's direction and began to walk away. He kept after me, still shoving that damn microphone in my face. The scene was starting to draw attention and conversation muted as we passed by.

Josef stepped in behind me, his deep voice asking the reporter to back off. I didn't turn around. I knew better. If I turned around it was like feeding a feral cat. You do it once and they never fucking go away. Years of dealing with aggressive paparazzi had taught me to keep the smile on, the chin up, and keep on walking. However, the next question shouted at me was enough to make me break all my rules.

"Kit, why'd you lie about your mother?"

Ice settled in my veins as the words sunk in. I turned, my lips stiff. "What?"

The room, now so quiet you could hear a pin drop, heard every word he said in reply. "I asked why you lied about your mother being dead when you've had her locked away in a private sanitarium for the past five years?"

The floor heaved. I could actually feel the blood draining from my body. Ron. Max. My stupid kiss with Tyler. The stress of the tour. All of it came crashing down on me as my vision turned red and my hands shook with anger.

I came out swinging like Sugar Ray Leonard or Mike Tyson. I caught him by surprise and the first punch caught him in the face. Pain shot through my hand but I didn't care. He groaned, dropped the microphone, and went down on one knee as he clutched his bleeding nose.

I went for him again, grabbing his shirt as I yelled at him. "What do you know about my mother?"

The reporter sneered as Josef grabbed him from behind and hauled him to his feet. He kept talking. "I'm talking about the fact that she's a pathetic mess, a trashed out junkie, and a whore." He spit blood onto the floor near my feet right before my security team dragged him away. "I was going to give you a chance to give me an exclusive, but you had to go and act like a crazy bitch. Now, you can deal with it."

I went for him again but Josef's two strong arms around my waist restrained me. I fought him but it was futile. I'd hired Josef for his brains and his bulk and he was using both right now.

"I'm fine. Fine. Let me go," I said.

He did as I asked and I pushed my way through a crowd that, in the wake of my fury, parted like the Red Sea.

This was bad.

I needed to check on my mom, and then I needed to figure out the plan for damage control because the label was going to flip out. This could be disastrous for my career, but I'd be damned if I was going down without a fight.

MAX

"Good morning, Mary Sunshine."

I blinked at the light pouring through the windows of

the firehouse kitchen and tried to figure out who the fuck was talking to me. I stumbled the last few steps, rubbing my eyes and stretching my arms. Dean was seated at the bar, so I nodded to him and went straight to the coffeemaker, poured a cup, and gulped down the first hot swallow. It burned, but the jolt of heat was exactly what I'd needed. I leaned against the counter and noticed Dean staring at me.

"What?" I was annoyed, and I made no attempt to disguise that fact.

"Nothing. I'm just surprised to see you here this morning."

"I *am* on shift with you."

Dean took a sip before he continued with poorly-disguised sarcasm. "You had a hot date last night. I figured you'd be sleeping over at Alison's place."

Oh shit. "Look, Dean, if you have something to say..."

"All I'm saying is that you usually spend the night with Alison when you guys hook up. I figured last night was no different."

Dean paused and took another leisurely sip of coffee while I waited for the other shoe to drop. When it came, his disapproval made me wince.

"I guess I was wrong about you after all. You rebounded pretty damn quick. I mean, you broke it off with Kit three days ago and then you show up last night with Alison." Dean fixed me with a level stare that made me squirm. "I was wrong about you not being mercenary enough to handle this whole affair thing. You're a pro."

"I didn't sleep with Alison."

"Look man, it's none of my business. You can sleep with whoever you..."

I cut him off. "You're right. It's none of your fucking business, but since you decided to stick your nose in anyway, shut up and listen to me." The silence between us crackled and I took the time to steady my temper. "I didn't sleep with Alison. Nothing happened. When it came down to it, I couldn't."

Dean sighed and rubbed his hands over his face. When he looked at me he had that sad and concerned look that he did so well. I preferred pissed.

"What happened?"

I didn't even know where to start. I wasn't even sure what happened last night, only that it ended with Alison pissed and my sleeping alone at the firehouse. Damned if I knew what to say. The women usually waited until after I fucked them to get mad at me.

Dean solved my dilemma by asking what he wanted to know. "Did you go to Alison's after you left Stoney's?"

"Yeah. She wanted me to stay over and I thought I was into it. But, I just couldn't. Nothing felt right with her, and I ended up making a really lame excuse and left. I didn't want to drive all the way out to my house, so I came here."

I sat down on the barstool next to Dean. Alison had been really hurt when I bailed on her and that was the last thing I'd wanted to do. But I did it anyway. "I knew the minute I kissed her that it was a no–go." I decided to say what had been rolling though my head on a constant loop for three days. "I can't stop thinking about Kit."

Talk about an understatement.

I'd thought about her every second since she'd left in the cab. I'd reached for the phone to call her so many times that I'd locked it in the glove compartment of my truck to take away the temptation. I dreamed about her and woke up so hard I wanted to crawl out of my skin. I thought about her when I was on calls—something not only dangerous to myself but also to my fellow firefighters.

When Sarah died, work was the only respite from the constant gnawing in my gut. The vision of her lying half in and half out of the car and the last terrible words we spoke to each other showed up in my dreams. But this time, even work wasn't helping. And as I'd predicted, I couldn't even listen to the goddamn radio without her songs coming on and in this city, good luck trying to find a non–country station. I was fucked because there was no getting away from it.

"Call her. Admit you screwed up," Dean said.

"I can't."

"Then figure out how to get over her."

"I can't."

And I don't want to.

Suddenly, it was clear. No matter how this had started, I needed her in my life. She was everything I wanted and by some fluke of the universe, she wanted me. The morning at the lake, the way she'd known what I needed, known how to soothe the hurt from my shift, had scared the crap out of me. I might run into burning buildings but she was the brave one that day. She'd made herself vulnerable and open to this thing growing between us. I'd seen it in her eyes, heard it in the way she'd said my name, and saw it in her hurt expression when I'd stood in a dirty parking lot and threw it away.

I jumped when Shannon poked her head around the corner. "Max! You've got to turn on the TV. Kit's in trouble. She got in a fight or something."

Not waiting for her to finish, I grabbed the remote for the kitchen TV. I punched a button and the local country music channel blazed to life with a picture of Kit kissing Tyler. I jerked back. *No fucking way.*

Shannon touched my arm and murmured, "Ignore that. It's nothing."

When Kit pulled away from Tyler, with a horrified look on her face, I let out the breath I'd been holding. In the next second, I lost all ability to speak as Kit launched herself at a reporter and clocked him with a right jab to his jaw. The man fell to his knees, but instead of backing off, he snarled something at Kit which caused her to hit the guy repeatedly until Josef pulled her off and took her away from public view.

What the hell?

"She's got a nice right hook," Dean said. I ignored him.

The TV program reverted to two reporters speaking animatedly, while a mug shot of a woman—a woman who looked like an older, tired version of Kit—was displayed on the screen. I turned up the volume, and focused on the screen and the perky, female anchor.

"*...breaking news regarding country music star, Kit Landry. Last night at a label press party, Kit was approached by a reporter who disclosed that her mother has been institutionalized for the past five years. This news comes as a shock to the star's fans as it was commonly reported that her mother passed away several years before she came to Nashville. The usually cool and collected singer was removed by security after she physically attacked the reporter.*"

A male anchor picked up the story while a photo of Kit flashed onto the screen. "*That's right, Tammy. The story, which appeared in this morning's edition of the Daily Scoop, states that Elizabeth Landry was repeatedly arrested for drug possession, drug dealing, and prostitution while Kit was growing up. According to the article, she finally suffered an overdose which left her mentally disabled one year after Kit's father died in an accident. It also reports that Kit took over her care and moved her to a private sanitarium just after her first record deal was* signed. *The real question is why Kit lied about her mother for all this time."*

Tammy nodded vigorously as she responded, *"Well, Jim, the singer is holding a press conference at her label head-quarters in about an hour and her team says she'll answer everyone's questions. Her publicist also announced that her manager, Ron Trent, has been fired and her previous manager, Paul Brandt, is coming out of retirement to take over until a permanent replacement can be found. All of this is right on the heels of Kit's return after a stint in rehab after a year of erratic emotional behavior leading many to ask if the singer suffers from the same illness as her mother. Stay tuned. We'll carry the entire press conference live in an hour."*

I turned off the TV and rubbed my hand over my face. My mind reeled with all the information. Kit had been carrying around some serious secrets the past few years. Secrets she couldn't share with me since I'd given her no reason to think I'd stick around. That was going to change.

I pushed through the crowd of people coming into the kitchen and headed towards the door and my truck. Just as I turned the doorknob, a hand closed around my arm, pulling me back. It was Dean.

"You going where I think you're going?"

"Yeah. I'm going to see Kit. I don't know how I'm going to get to her, but I've got to try." And then I remembered—I was on duty today. "Shit. You'll tell the captain and get someone to cover for me?"

"You know I will." Dean reached around, opened the door, and pushed me out the door. "Go get her, man. And don't take no for an answer. She needs you and you need her."

I nodded and, in spite of the angst twisting in my gut, I

sprinted across the parking lot, jumped in my truck, and pulled out. I wasn't entirely sure Kit would see me. Reaching for my phone, I pulled up Bridget's number and hit the "send" button. If Kit had her phone off or wouldn't take the call, Bridget was my best bet.

She picked up on the third ring and did nothing to hide her surprise. "Max?"

I pulled out onto the road and headed towards downtown Nashville. "Yeah, Bridget; it's me."

She didn't hesitate to let me know where I stood. "Look Max, this isn't a good time right now. I need to get back to Kit and you're *the last* person I want to talk to right now."

I cut her off before she got wound up and hung up on me. "I'll cut to the chase then. I'm coming to the press conference and I need you to get me in. I need to see Kit."

Bridget laughed into the phone and I could picture her shaking her head in disbelief.

"Max, you broke it off with her because you couldn't handle whatever was happening between the two of you. Now the shit has really hit the fan. Why would I let you within ten feet of her?"

"You're right. I was a chicken–shit and bailed on her. I'm not gonna argue—"

"Thanks for your honesty. I'm hanging up now."

In a panic, I blurted out the first thing that came to my mind. "No, don't hang up! I'm the one. That's why you have to let me in. I'm the one!"

"The one *what*?"

The words rushed out of me so easily, I knew it was the truth. "Remember, when I asked you who took care of Kit and you told me nobody took care of her? Then you asked me if I was the one who would do it and I couldn't answer you?" When she didn't say anything I plowed on. "Well,

I'm the one. I'm the one to take care of her. And you've got to get me in there so I can prove it to her. Please. Help me."

The silence stretched across the line for what seemed like hours. *Come on, Bridget; you know I'm right. Just help me out.* I turned on to the block that held the office of her music label and faltered at all of the news personnel and fans milling around the street. I found a spot and pulled the truck over, my hands remaining in a death grip on the steering wheel.

Bridget sighed. "Come around the back and I'll get you in." Just before she ended the call, her voice took on a warning tone. "But Max, if you hurt her again, I'll kill you."

I jumped out of the truck and sprinted across the street towards the woman who made me break all of my own rules. My heart pounded with adrenaline, the rush similar to what I experienced when I entered a burning building. There was no fire here but I knew my life was at stake—and God help me—this was scarier.

TWENTY FOUR

Kit

IT WAS times like this that I really missed my daddy.

I looked around the waiting room set up adjacent to the place where I would hold a press conference in less than an hour. It bustled with people from my staff and the record label—all focused on fixing the train wreck formerly known as my career. Liam Connor shot nasty looks at me from across the room and I had to dig deep into the grown–up part of me to resist flipping him the bird. *Calm down. All you have to do is bare your soul to a roomful of strangers. Piece of cake.*

I hadn't slept in twenty–four hours. I was running on fumes, ibuprofen, and a Red Bull Bridget had shoved into my hands about two hours ago. Breakfast of champions. Even though this was stressful, I was more than a little relieved that my secret was out and I didn't have to carry it around anymore. Ron had done me a favor when he'd spilled the beans about my mother, but I still hated his guts.

I still didn't understand why he hadn't told everything about me but I wasn't going to wait for that other shoe to drop.

I'd talked to Lilah an hour ago and my mother was in her room with extra meds to keep her from getting upset. While security kept the reporters out of the Shady Grove Assisted Living Facility, the additional noise and bustle agitated my mom and the other patients.

I'd taken care of one responsibility—on to the next couple hundred obligations.

I looked around and couldn't find one person I wasn't responsible for in this room. Even Bridget was both a friend and an employee, and I was terrified of letting them down. I'd already jeopardized everything by trusting Ron.

"It wasn't your fault."

I jumped as a big hand settled on my shoulder. Turning around, I looked up into the clear, blue eyes of Paul Brandt —the man who had been my father figure, my boss, the biggest pain in my ass, and my biggest supporter. God, I loved him. I was humbled that he, with no questions asked, had left Texas to help me.

He tapped me on the nose in that way he did to cheer me up. "It wasn't your fault. You trusted him and he betrayed you. Nobody blames you and you shouldn't blame yourself."

I broke eye contact, the shame leaving a bitter taste in my mouth. "Paul, I should have known."

He cursed under his breath before grabbing my elbow and leading me away from prying ears. His eyes laser-locked on my face until I was forced to look him in the eye.

"Kitten, you listen to me and take it as the gospel truth. This was not *your* fault. You had a viper in your camp and didn't even know it. You've always taken responsibility for everyone around you, but you can't control the bad choices that other people make." He towered over me, and leaned in close and gentled his tone. "I love you and you're the bravest kid I know. You took care of your grandparents, your dad and, then, you took care of your mother whenever she strolled back into town to get clean." Pain flashed in his eyes as he recounted the sad details of my life as if I didn't already know them. "You've spent your life taking care of other people and let your own needs fall by the wayside."

I was irrationally defensive and angry at his words. "Paul, I worked hard to make things better for the ones I love. I'm not going to apologize for doing what was right."

"Honey, it ain't right if it makes you take responsibility for something that you didn't see coming. Kitten, I've watched you give and give and not take anything for yourself." Paul counted his points off on his fingers. "You don't go on vacation. You haven't tried any of the new projects that have been offered to you because they don't fit your current image. Hell, you gave up Jake because you thought that he deserved to be happy more than you do."

I opened my mouth to argue with him, but he was right. I'd been afraid to want things for myself when, one day, they'd be gone. I lived on the fringes of my own life. But I didn't know if I had the strength to do it differently in the future. Max had been the biggest risk I'd taken in a long time and look how that had turned out.

Hugging Paul tightly, I mumbled against his chest. "Have you been watching Oprah again?"

"Dr. Phil." When I raised an eyebrow at him he protested, "What? The man's a genius."

Laughing, I released him and turned towards the mirror mounted on the wall behind me to fix my makeup which was probably messed up from all the emotional crap going down today. "I promise I'll think about what you said." I pulled out my makeup. I could still feel him watching me and knew my answer didn't satisfy him.

"Think about it? Kitten, you need to get a life. A life that includes a man who loves you and is looking out for you." He paused. "Bridget said there was someone who she thought might be that guy."

I froze mid–swipe. "Bridget talks too much."

Paul laughed. "Maybe so. But you don't tell me squat, so I'm glad she does." He sidled up next to me and leaned back against the table, his arms crossed casually in front of his chest. He wasn't fooling me.

"So, he wasn't the guy?"

I dug into my bag looking for my mascara and maybe avoiding looking at him. "Didn't Bridget fill you in?"

"I'd rather hear it from you."

I gave up and put down the tube of makeup. "He wasn't interested in a relationship. Not a bad decision, considering my rock–n–roll lifestyle. He ran for the hills. Smart man."

"Yeah, but you didn't want him to be so smart. Did ya?"

I ignored the question. I'd dodged the same questions from Bridget for two days after Max had broken things off. Max wanted out and getting back together with him wasn't up to me. For once, none of my celebrity perks could get me what I wanted, because celebrity was exactly what he *didn't* want.

Paul rubbed the back of his neck and chuckled softly as I resumed applying my makeup.

"So, this guy... was he a blonde or brunette?"

"Brunette. Why do you want to know?"

"Just curious." He shrugged and stroked a hand along his jaw. "Bridget said he was a firefighter, so he must have been a big guy. About 6'3"? Broad shoulders and biceps as big as my thigh?"

I dropped the lipstick tube in my hand and leveled a look at Paul. "How could you know that?"

With a slow grin he jutted his chin in a direction over my shoulder. "Because I think he just walked through the door."

Spinning around, my eyes scanned the crowd until I zoned in on the tall figure walking towards me with Bridget.

Max.

His face was blank, but his eyes were the same—golden topaz and filled with simmering heat that caused my heart to go all squishy. Sweet Lord, I'd missed him.

Too much.

I backed up against the table and crossed my arms in front of my chest as he came to a stop right in front of me. My body instinctively leaned towards him and I clenched my hands into fists to keep from touching him. *He's just here because of his hero complex.*

Looking at his handsome face, my emotions bounced from anger, to hurt, to hope, and to relief at just seeing him one more time. And that made me mad all over again.

I swallowed hard and turned loose the first words that came to mind. "What the hell are you doing here?"

TWENTY FIVE

Max

I HAD EXPECTED her to hit me.

I drank in everything about Kit. I was close enough to smell her perfume and feel the heat of her body. She was rigid with hostility, so I resisted the urge to drag her into my arms and bury my face in her glossy curls. I let my eyes linger on her face, her beautiful face, her graceful neck, and the creamy swell of her breasts in the V–neck of the dress she wore. Finally, my gaze drifted back up to her eyes and when one eyebrow quirked up in a silent inquiry, I remembered that she was still waiting for me to answer her question.

"I came to see if you're all right. You've had a rough couple of days and I thought you could use a friend."

Tears pooled in her eyes for the briefest second just before she blinked them away. Once she'd harnessed her control, Kit met my eyes with the friendly but distant expression I recognized from countless interviews.

"Super Kit" was in the house.

Only her voice, a little shaky, gave away any inner turmoil.

"Thanks, but I have lots of friends as you can see." She waved a hand around the room at the clusters of people surrounding her. "I'm good. No need for you to worry."

She wasn't going to make this easy on me and I didn't blame her. I took a half step closer, gathering enough of my balls to reach out and run a finger along her arm. She inhaled sharply at the contact but didn't move away. The big guy standing next to her moved a little closer—not a direct threat, just making sure I knew he was there.

"I'm glad you're good." I sounded lame and stupid and I cursed my sudden attack of nerves. Our future depended on this moment and I was scared shitless—not of saying too much, but of not saying enough of the right thing.

I decided to go for broke. "I screwed up. I never should've ended things with you, and now that I've got my head out of my ass I'd like another chance."

No taking it back now. This was agony. While I stood there, her expression changed from surprise, to confusion, and then my least favorite—stubborn resistance.

Shaking her head, Kit backed away from my touch as if she were trying to become a part of the table behind her.

"Look, I don't know what the shelf–life is on feeling obligated to a person once you've saved their life, but we're even. You don't have to worry about me. I pay a lot of people to do that."

When I inched closer, she bit her lip and groaned in frustration. "Max, you need to go. I heard what you said loud and clear. This was just a fling and it's over."

Anger at her words, her denial, made me impatient as I stepped even closer, bracketing her body with my larger frame and blocking out everything else. This needed to be about us and only us for at least the next few minutes.

"This was always more than a fling between us and you know it. What we had—" I corrected myself. "What we *have* is something real and I'm done running."

Kit's gasp mingled with those of Bridget and the large man, but my eyes never left her face. I didn't care what the others did as long as they didn't get between me and this woman.

Kit was scared, her breathing shallow and frantic and she swallowed convulsively. I could see her mind churning out excuses but she leaned towards my body in an unspoken expression of need, her body betraying her deepest desire. She wanted me, too.

The moment was broken when a man approached and signaled to Kit with the "five-minute" sign.

I was out of time.

I brought the conversation back to where it belonged—on the fact that I wasn't going anywhere.

"Kit." She turned her attention back to me and I leaned in close so she couldn't look anywhere else. "I'm not asking for you to make a choice right now, but I *am* going to stay here and help you through this and then I'm going to prove to you that we belong together."

I grabbed her hand and waited as the long moments stretched between us. If I had to get down on my knees and beg, I was prepared to do it.

"You can stay." Kit's voice was quiet and shaky as she withdrew her hand. "Let's see if you feel the same way after the press conference." She nodded at me and turned to follow Bridget out of the room.

I smiled like a goofball and didn't even try to pretend it

wasn't for her. I was done hiding how I felt about this woman.

She slipped back into "Super Kit" mode right before my eyes. Shoulders back and focused control on all of her facial expressions. Now that I knew the real Kit, this persona was understandable, but very unsatisfying. I wanted the girl who laughed at my stupid jokes, seduced me at a bonfire, and soothed me on a picnic blanket.

A big hand landed on my shoulder.

"Paul Brandt. I was Kit's manager and I'm filling in since she kicked the weasel to the curb."

I laughed at Paul's reference to Ron. I couldn't have agreed more.

"Max Butler. Kit's..." I struggled with the right words to describe my relationship with Kit.

"I heard what you said, son. I think I have a pretty good idea of what you are to Kit." He looked me up and down with an assessing glance and then motioned for me to follow him. "That took balls. I wasn't inclined to like you, but that impressed me."

I shrugged off the compliment. "I run into burning buildings for a living."

"Uh huh, and I bet that's easier than what you just did."

Walking briskly in the same direction Kit had taken, Paul pushed through a door and suddenly I could hear the rumble of the crowd gathered at the press conference. I spied Kit talking to Liam Connor just behind the side curtains on the stage. He was waving his arms around, clearly agitated. Kit, on the other hand, was focused and ready for the battle.

Paul was watching the scene as well. "That's our girl. Tough as nails when she has to be. The label pinheads are mad at her. They want her to read a prepared statement, but she insists on going off–script and speaking from the heart." His laugh rumbled deep in his chest. "It's the right call. She connects with her fans like nobody's business."

I nodded but I couldn't tear my eyes away from Kit. "Yes, she does. She doesn't give them every part of herself, but what she does let them see is genuine."

But, nobody knew what a big secret she had carried around. I shifted uncomfortably with the knowledge that she hadn't shared it with me.

Paul seemed to read my thoughts. "She didn't trust anybody with the secret of her mama, son. I was with her two years before she let me know about it. She's so used to being the boss that she doesn't know how to lean on other people."

I wearily rubbed the back of my neck. "I get that, I really do. But, I don't understand how she does it."

Paul huffed. "Kit had to grow up fast with very little stability in her life. Believe it or not, this craziness is where she's the most comfortable because she created it and controls it. It's become her safe zone and she is terrified to do anything that'll rock the boat." He leaned over, lowering his voice as people gathered around them. "You seem real determined to stick around so here's a little advice: she thinks being happy—having something for herself—is selfish because it distracts her from her responsibilities. If you want her, you're gonna have to convince her that she can have it all."

I was interrupted from responding as Liam walked to the podium and kicked off the press conference. Every eye in the room was on Kit and I was no exception. I examined her—looking for signs of stress, nervousness, fear—as I willed her to know that I was there.

As if she sensed my focus, Kit turned her head just

enough to meet my gaze and my heart stuttered to a stop in my chest. I lifted a hand to wave at her and she did the same to me. A small gesture between us but it was enough for her to know that I was here. If I had my way, we'd have lots of time to talk, to say all the things that needed to be said.

Maybe she didn't think she deserved it all but I wasn't going to stop until I'd changed her mind.

TWENTY SIX

Kit

MAX WAS HERE.

Twenty minutes ago, I couldn't imagine anything making this ordeal bearable, but now Max was here and I felt peaceful, almost calm. The fact that my entire outlook was changed by his merely walking through the door should've scared the hell out of me but the moment my fist connected with the nose of that reporter, something inside me had broken free. Other than the absolute conviction that I would not let this moment destroy my career, the rest of my life was up for grabs.

I was shocked, and thrilled, at the way Max maneuvered his way in here and insisted on staying. I had considered fighting him for a moment, but who was I fooling? It was exactly what I'd been hoping, aching for. I just hoped that when he heard what else I was going to reveal at this press conference, that he would want to stay.

Liam finally stopped yapping and signaled to me that it

was show time. I scanned the crowd, noting many familiar faces, most of them wearing expressions of concern and encouragement.

I took a deep breath and began. "Thank ya'll for coming here today. I'm sorry for all of the trouble this has caused and hopefully I can make it right. My mother, Elizabeth Landry, is not dead as I have previously let everyone believe. She is alive and has been in a private nursing home since I signed with my label. Her current condition is the result of a drug overdose six years ago during which she suffered severe brain damage. She functions at the level of a three- or four-year-old child and has seizures when placed in stressful situations."

I gripped the podium, not even looking at my notes. I knew what I wanted to say. "I would like to tell you that I lied about her being dead solely because it was in her best interest, but that would be untrue. Yes, I wanted her to be safe and in a healthy place, but I lied because I was embarrassed." Tears gathered in my eyes so I dipped my head and wiped them away before pressing forward. "My mother is bipolar. Her mental illness was undiagnosed and untreated for a very long time and even after we knew, she refused to stay on her medication. To make the situation worse she became an alcoholic, an addict, and she sold her body for drugs. She'd leave for a while and then show up strung-out and broke. The pattern was always the same: she would clean up, make promises to stay straight, and then go back on the street. It was bad enough when my father was alive but when he passed, her care fell on my shoulders. As you can imagine, it was a heavy burden for a fifteen-year-old girl."

It was so quiet in the room I could hear the air rushing

in the vents. For someone who was used to crowds of singing fans, this was a little unnerving.

"My life was consumed with dodging the foster care people and surviving as best I could. Early on, a reporter assumed she was dead and I let the lie continue. I was embarrassed. I was tired of having to explain that my mother was a junkie. It was more convenient to let everyone believe she was dead."

I paused and looked around, meeting every eye squarely. I was done with the shame. This was way off script and Liam Connor was going to have a fit. He'd have to get over it. I wasn't going to have any more secrets hanging over my head.

"If you know anything about bipolar disorder then you know it is hereditary and after my episode a year ago, I started treatment with a psychiatrist and was diagnosed as suffering from hypomania. It is a form of bipolar disorder that causes those of us with the illness to have manic or depressive episodes. When I had an episode after my break–up with Jake, I started drinking heavily, forgetting my obligations—you all reported on it so I will spare us all the gory details." I paused to take a breath when the crowd laughed quietly. "I do not require medication and I am treating my illness with diet and exercise with the help of my physician. Of course, I am under constant medical care to treat my mental illness and my alcoholism. I am truly sorr..."

I heard a loud scuffle behind me and I turned around. The voices got louder; the activity just off the stage became chaotic and people jostled to see the cause of the disruption. The press started mumbling, most of them rising from their seats to get a better look. I had no idea what was going on until the source of the noise was rushing towards me.

"You bitch!" Ron, disheveled and drunk off his ass, lurched onto the stage and headed straight for me. "You stupid bitch! You can't fire me!"

Stunned by his appearance and his venom, I stumbled backwards and tried to dodge his fists. Ron grabbed my arm and ripped the sleeve of my jacket before I could get away from him. Stumbling, I fell down and my head hit the table. I was conscious but so disoriented that it was impossible to differentiate between the stars in my eyes and the flashes from the cameras.

Ron followed me down, yelling at me with breath rank with alcohol and I curled up in a ball to avoid his blows. I was getting desperate when Ron's weight was suddenly lifted off me. Struggling to catch my breath, I grabbed a chair and stood up just in time to see Max hit Ron squarely in the stomach.

Ron staggered back two steps, shook it off and lunged towards Max—spewing filth and hate about me. Flailing wildly, his fist connected with the side of Max's mouth, drawing blood. Max wiped at the blood, glanced at his hand, and with a smirk hauled his fist back and nailed Ron right upside the head. Ron went down like a tree and, just like that, the circus was over.

My ears were ringing from hitting the table. I was swept up by Max as Josef and the hotel security staff descended upon the fallen form of Ron. Max murmured in my ear, "I've got you" and the chaos of the press shouting and cameras flashing faded into the background as he carried me off the stage and towards the back of the building.

I hung onto Max, as Paul and Bridget led us through back offices and down the stairs to the back entrance of the building.

"Are you okay? Can you stand?" Max peered down into my face, his hand reaching up to smooth back my crazy hair.

I nodded, holding on tightly as he lowered me to the ground; his arm looped around my waist, holding me firmly at his side.

Liam Connor appeared at my side, his face flushed but his suit impeccable. Apparently he'd avoided the drama.

"Kit, you weren't supposed to talk about *your* mental illness," he said.

"Nice security detail dickhead," Max said, putting his body in between us. "I'm getting her out of here."

"We need to talk," Liam insisted but Max cut him off with a shove to the chest.

"Not now."

"Don't put your hands on me," Liam growled.

"Fucking leave her alone."

Paul stepped up and inserted himself between them, his voice the only calm in the middle of all this crazy. "We aren't going to do this now. You hear me?"

I watched as the two men faced off, Paul's bulk beating Liam by about forty pounds and three inches.

"Fine. I want her in my office tomorrow." Liam gave up more easily than I thought he would but he couldn't resist giving Max a dark look as he turned to go. He was not happy and I wasn't looking forward to our chat.

Bridget fished her keys out of her pocket and handed them to Max. "You take my car and get her out of here. She can't go home, and the usual places will be mobbed. You have somewhere in mind?"

"Yeah," Max grabbed the keys. "I'll take her home with me. It'll take them a while to figure it out and she'll be safe there."

"Kitten, you okay with this plan? You feel safe going with Mr. Butler, here?" Paul asked.

I don't want to be anywhere else. I tightened my grip on Max. "Yes."

Paul nodded and swatted Max on the shoulder. "All right then. You get going and we'll take care of this mess."

Max loosened his hold and looked down at me, his gaze concerned and tense and filled with something else I was afraid to name. He hauled me up in his arms and planted a swift, hard kiss on my mouth. "You ready?"

"Yes." I looked up at him, biting my lower lip before making my request. "Can I get you to take me somewhere else first?"

TWENTY SEVEN

Max

THE SIGN at the entrance read "Shady Grove Assisted Living Facilty" wasn't what I expected at all. In my head, I envisioned something out of One Flew Over the Cuckoo's Nest complete with Jack Nicholson yelling at us as we walked the hall to her mother's room with scary medical equipment lining the hallways.

This place was more like a resort. Security gates at the beginning of the compound opened when I asked Kit for the code—the only thing she'd spoken since we'd left except for answering "no" when I asked if she needed Shannon to come by and look her over. I was uncomfortable with the silence, my gut tight and muscles taut with everything that had already gone down today and what I knew was coming.

I had no idea what to expect. No idea what kind of shape Mrs. Landry would be in. And I was scared. This was important, these moments would determine if I got the chance to be with Kit or whether we were over. This was a test and I'd never had the chance to study.

I followed the way Kit pointed with a shaking hand and that pretty much wrecked my soul. My White Knight syndrome was in overdrive when it came to this woman and I was amped up enough to fight whatever dragon showed its face. I would slay anyone and anything to wipe that tremor from her muscle memory.

We passed a large building with a sign that told me it was the social hall surrounded with tennis courts and a pool. This was not a nursing home—I remembered from the search for Grandpa Butler that this place consisted of separate villas purchased by the resident where they could have live–in help to assist them with day–to–day living. I also remembered that it was as expensive as fuck.

"This is it. Number 22," Kit said and pointed me towards the two–car garage. Whoever was inside knew we were coming because one of the doors went up and I pulled in.

"Wait." Kit laid a hand on my harm when I reached for the door handle. "Wait until the door is completely down."

"Is that how you avoided being seen?" I asked.

She nodded. "Nobody saw me coming or going. It was crazy enough to work."

"What about visitors?"

"My mom doesn't get any visitors other than her doctor." She looked over at me in the gloom, her fingers tensing under my own. "You'll see."

The door to the house opened and a woman in her mid–fifties with dark blonde hair and glasses stepped into the opening, motioning us inside. I jumped out and hurried over to Kit, helping her out of the car and noticing her try and hide the wince when she moved. She wouldn't let me call Shannon but I'd check her over later.

"Katie," the woman called out when she pulled Kit into a total body hug. Kit wrapped her own arms around her neck and they stood there for a few moments. From the shaking of her shoulders, I could tell Kit was crying and I could do nothing but stand by in impotent rage and hope I got the chance to beat the living shit out of Ron. It would be worth the loss of my career to see that guy bloody.

"Hey. Hey." The older woman pulled out of the embrace, looking down at Kit with eyes and cheeks damp. "Why don't you introduce me to this guy? You've never brought a bodyguard before. Is it that bad?"

Kit chuckled and shook her head, wiping her fingers under her eyes before turning to me. "Max this is Lilah Pierce, my mom's nurse. This is Max. He's..."

"I'm her boyfriend," I answered, focusing on Lilah so I missed the reaction on Kit's face. I didn't need to see it, I'm sure it matched the answering hammering of my heart in my chest. I couldn't believe how easily the word had slipped out and I didn't know why I said it. Boyfriend status was something that was granted, not taken, and we had not talked about it. But I took the slide of Kit's hand into my own as silent agreement to this step in whatever direction we were headed.

"She's having a good day. We had lunch a little while ago and she'll have a nap in about an hour." Lilah cut a glance to me. "I think she'll be okay with a new face today. You might want to read to her."

I followed both down a hallway into an open kitchen and sitting area to a covered, bricked patio. The area was partially shaded from the sun and protected from anyone's view by a high privacy fence. There was a seating area and on one of the two sofas sat Elizabeth Landry, Kit's mother.

She looked older than she was, hair mostly gray and pulled back in a ponytail. Thin with slumped posture, her skin was rough and looked like she'd spent way too many hours in the sun without sunscreen. When she looked up and saw Kit, the smile was warm and a little shy.

Kit let go of my hand and walked over to her mom and sat down but she didn't reach out to hug her right away. She sat still, hands on her lap while she spoke softly to the woman who had given birth to her twenty–one years ago.

"Elizabeth doesn't always like to be touched," Lilah explained beside me. "It might take a few moments for her to warm up to Katie being here."

"Is it because of the stroke?"

"Yes. Her reaction to touch, noise, food, all varies according to the day. I could give a long medical explanation but the bottom line is that her brain was fried by the abuse it took and now it just doesn't work right. We aren't sure how she will react and sometimes it can be violent so we normally don't initiate it." Lilah motioned for me to sit down at the table with her, both of us pulling up chairs. We watched Kit and her mom, the older woman now resting a hand on her daughter's knee listening as Kit read the child's book in her hand.

"Why do you call her Katie?" I asked the first thing that came to mind, needing to understand this whole situation better.

"That's what her mother calls her. Her given name is Katherine," Lilah said. "Kit is her stage name."

I wondered what else I didn't know about the woman I'd fallen for. Judging from her announcement at the press conference it was quite a lot.

I sat there watching them for half an hour, Kit reading a book my three-year-old niece knew by heart while her mom giggled and laughed and chanted back her favorite parts. Kit would end the book and Elizabeth would beg for her to read it "one more time" which Kit would do right away.

It was sweet and heartbreaking. Here Kit was, once again taking care of one more person in her life. Once again the question popped into my mind: Who took care of Kit?

It would be me. I was the one who could do it.

Lilah rose from her chair and walked over to them. "It's time for you to lie down, Elizabeth."

They both looked up at her, the disappointment of having their time ended as clear as the blue Tennessee summer sky. They both stood to say their goodbyes.

"Bye Mama. I'll see you next week."

"You read to me again?" Elizabeth asked, her concern genuine and earnest. "You read to me?"

"Yes, Mama. I'll read to you."

They both stood there and even from where I sat, I could see Kit's entire body leaning forward, willing her mother to embrace her. Pleading with her to allow a touch. I held my breath, sending up my own prayers that Kit would get the touch she so clearly craved.

It wasn't happening today. Elizabeth turned to Lilah and smiled, shuffling off into the house with her nurse close behind her. Kit watched them go, her arms wrapped around her body as if to chase away a chill.

I walked up behind her and laid a hand on her shoulder. She spun around and launched herself at me, the sobs wracking her body. I stood firm and strong, a wall built for her to rail against, to push against as she fought to exorcise these demons.

I rubbed her back, kissing her hair and the skin over her temple as she calmed down.

"I'm sorry for falling apart like that," she mumbled against my chest. "I'm sorry."

"After the day you've had you deserve to let it all out. I'm here. Do what you need to."

"I won't..." She stuttered over her words. Clearing her throat and beginning again. "The way she is... I won't be like that. It's not her illness, it was the stroke from the overdose. I'm sick but... but that isn't..."

Jesus. She was worried about that?

"Kit, I couldn't care less if that was how you would end up. I want you. We'd figure it out together."

She didn't answer and I could feel the tension in her body as she thought about it, analyzed whether it was realistic for the long term. I could withstand the scrutiny. I could prove I wasn't going anywhere if I had to.

We stood still for a while as I held her, neither of us speaking. There wasn't much to be said. This situation sucked all the way around and there wasn't a damn thing I could do about it—except give her an escape.

It was time to take Kit home with me.

TWENTY EIGHT

Max

"KIT, IT'S ALL CLEAR."

I glanced over to where she was crouched on the floor-board of the car. Eight years on the job at NFD had come in handy. I knew the city like the back of my hand and the crisscross of little known backstreets and shortcuts had enabled me to get her away from the press. A glance into the rearview mirror confirmed that no one was behind us as we entered the Lively city limits.

Kit maneuvered into the seat and groaned as she stretched her limbs. She rubbed her head and winced in pain.

I'll kill that guy if he hurt her.

"Are you sure you're okay? Do you want a doctor?"

Kit winced again as her fingers touched a tender spot. "No. I'm fine."

"My cousin, Robert, is a doctor and he lives nearby. I can call him."

"No, I'm okay. Just a little sore." As I turned off the road and on to a private lane marked "Butler Farm", Kit leaned forward to peer out the front window. "Is this *your* farm?"

"Partially. I bought the land with my cousins Robert and Amy two years ago from my Grandpa Butler." I pointed towards a lane that led to a modern house. "Robert built that for himself and Amy's husband farms her part." I turned the car down a long, tree–lined driveway that led into a clearing where a large white farmhouse stood surrounded by roses. I pulled to a stop at the steps that led to the wide, wrap-around porch before turning to Kit with a grin. "I bought the house and 10 acres. Stay where you are and I'll help you out."

I jumped out of the car and rushed around to meet her. She ignored my order and emerged, disheveled, but steady on her feet, with her shoes in her hands and her torn jacket thrown over her arm. Kit stopped abruptly and looked at the house and the yard with wide eyes.

"Max. It's beautiful! I expect the Waltons to come out any minute!"

I chuckled as I led her up the steps to the front door. "I wish. I could use John Boy's help with the heavy lifting." At her perplexed expression I guided her through the door, explaining, "I'm renovating."

I watched her face as she entered and viewed the interior of my house for the first time. I kept the architectural details intact, but removed some walls and put in large banks of windows to let in the sunlight. From the front door, were the original maple floors as they led through the open family room and kitchen anchored by a large stone fireplace.

I led her into the kitchen before I asked, "Do you like it?"

Her smile gave away her answer. "This is gorgeous. It's amazing."

I didn't try to hide my pride as I showed off my home. "I do what I can as I get the money and I bribe the guys at the firehouse with beer and burgers to help me out. I'm done with renovating the back rooms. I enclosed the back porch with glass to make it a three-season room but I still need to work on the living room, study, and dining room." I motioned towards a large staircase. "It has five bedrooms upstairs—four now—I took a small one and made it into a master bath and walk-in closet."

I was babbling. I shut up and brought her hand up to my chest. "I should've brought you here sooner."

I understood why I hadn't. Bringing Kit here meant I couldn't ignore my feelings for her. Now, with Kit standing in my home, I could see a future with her in this house. In my life.

I saw all of the emotions swirling in Kit's eyes—fear, vulnerability, desire and an emotion I hoped I wasn't misreading. *Stay with me. Make this place a home.* The house was silent except for the sound of the grandfather clock ticking in the hall and our heavy breathing. I reached out and grasped her waist, pulling her close. She melted against me as I cupped her face and leaned in to sample the sweetness of her mouth.

I don't know how I ever thought I could give this up.

I brushed my lips softly against hers, barely a promise of a kiss before I pulled back. My hesitation was met by a whimper from Kit as her hands laced through my hair and pulled me back to her mouth. My first real taste of her was electric. The slide of velvet tongues flamed my passion and I angled my mouth over hers possessively—the pressure on my cut lip making me wince.

Kit pulled back, her lips wet from my assault but her eyes full of concern. "You're hurt." Her thumb brushed over my injury gently and that touch made me feel like a million dollars. "You're bleeding. Let me clean that up."

I tightened my hold on her as she tried to pull away. "I'm fine."

She cupped my face between her palms, her voice low. "Let me take care of you."

I nodded and led her to the family room. Sitting her down on the couch, I retrieved the first aid kit from the kitchen and returned to sit down beside her. I soaked Kit in as she busied herself with pulling out the necessary items with her small, slender fingers. She refused to meet my gaze, her face a mask of concentration as she swabbed and cleaned my lip with careful motions. Content just to have her near, I took the time to gaze at the face I'd missed so much. Even tired from the events of the past few days, she was still the most gorgeous girl I'd ever seen.

"I think you'll live." Her eyes traveled over my face and down my body looking for signs of another injury. She "tskd" when she spied my knuckles, scraped raw and a little bloody from hitting Ron. She smiled as she cleaned the abrasions. "It must have felt good to finally hit the weasel."

I laughed. "Yeah, it did. He was asking for it." My tone sobered as I continued. "I'm sorry I wasn't able to stop him before he hurt you. I'm sorry I let you down. That *I* hurt you."

Kit dipped her head, hiding her face from my inspection while she silently busied herself with applying the ointment. Her motions stilled as she sighed and brought my hand up to rest against her wet cheek.

I cupped her chin and tipped her face up until I could see the tears. "Kit. Baby, don't cry. You're killing me."

Her violet eyes were darkened with confusion and pain and I held onto her hand, anxious to keep the physical connection.

"Max. This is so... I... I just need to know what you want."

What did I want? That was easy.

Her.

"What do I want? I want to stop missing you. I want to stop looking for bits of paper with lyrics on them showing up in my pockets. I want to stop thinking of that stupid frog when I hear a Merle Haggard song. I want to hear your songs on the radio and know they're about me." I leaned in closer, my hands gripped her shoulders, lips only a breath away from hers, and our eyes locked. "I want you in my bed. In this house. In my life. Underneath me. Around me. I want my name on your lips as you come apart all over me."

My hands clenched with need as I pressed a brief kiss against her mouth before saying the thing I never thought I would ever say again.

"I want you to tell me that you love me because I love you and I honestly don't know how to live without you."

TWENTY NINE

Kit

HE LOVED ME.

Max loved me and wanted me. I was breathless and I took a deep breath to calm my erratically beating heart as I inched closer and pressed my mouth against his.

"I love you, Max."

He slid his arms around me and pulled me close, groaning in his chest as he swept inside my mouth with his tongue. *More. All of you.* I wove my fingers into his hair anchoring him in place for my greedy mouth. It had been too long. We scrambled against each other—desperate to feel skin against skin, soft curves against hard angles.

I was hungry for him, reaching under his shirt, rucking it up to lift it from his body. I needed to see him, to feel him. I trembled and Max hissed into my hair at the first touch of my palms against the sleek, heated skin of his abdomen and around to the muscled expanse of his back.

"Baby, you always make me feel so good." Max breathed

the words against my cheek before he savagely reclaimed my mouth. "Let me make you feel good. You know how much I love to see you come."

His words made me shudder as his calloused hands covered my breasts, rubbing my nipples until they hardened underneath the silk of my dress. With one hand, he tunneled under my hair and unfastened the halter top, letting it fall down to expose me to the burn of his gaze and the rough caress of his hands.

"Make me come. Please." I wanted nothing more than to lose myself in him, in how he could make me feel. Max could make all of the crap of the last twenty–four hours go away and I needed the oblivion. I needed him.

I moaned and arched upwards as he took a nipple in his mouth, sucking and nibbling on it until it was hard and sensitized to the point of pleasure/pain.

It was almost too much. I was slick between my legs, clenching them together in search of what he offered, what I knew he could deliver. I tugged him up my body but he refused to let me control this lovemaking.

"Kit. I need to fuck you. I need to know you're mine."

"I'm yours."

"Yes. You are."

His look was feral, his movements rough as he lifted me up, unzipping my dress and pushing it down and off my body. I shivered as he stripped off my thong, and blazed a trail down my body with his lips and teeth—nipping and laving my skin, stopping only to push me back on to the couch and expose my nakedness to his gaze.

I was possessed. Taken. Like every touch and every look branded me as his.

For as long as I remembered, I'd wanted to belong to someone and now I did.

He watched me as he pushed between my thighs and tongued my wet core, making love to me with his mouth. His pace was unrelenting as he pushed me higher and higher, as if he needed to seal our words with this physical act. My body went boneless as he pushed inside me with two fingers, pumping sleekly and deeply. Without warning, my body bowed off the couch and I pushed up against his mouth as my climax washed over me like a wave of fire.

He was burning me alive, branding me and I'd never craved anything more.

"Fuck, you taste good. Like honey."

Max rose up, unfastened his jeans and shoved them down his legs, his cock hard and stiff against his stomach, a delicious drop of pre–cum on its tip. Before I could tell him how much I wanted him, Max leaned over me, capturing my mouth in a kiss that tasted of my arousal as his cock brushed against my slick, sensitive sex. Mindlessly filled with the need to have him inside me, I struggled up against him, urging his body to fill me, stretch me.

Breaking off the kiss, he ran his tongue up my jaw and let it circle the outer shell of my ear before dipping down to nip at my earlobe. He pulled back and I protested, silencing my complaint when I saw that he was pausing only to put on a condom.

I gasped as he entered me with one thrust, kissing me roughly and holding my hips in a bruising grip. I didn't want him to be gentle and he wasn't. I needed this connection to erase the last few days of being apart.

He pounded into me, hard and deep, and I met him thrust for thrust, our cries mingling along with the sweat on our straining bodies. Max grasped my thighs and lifted me higher against his body, angling me in a way that allowed him to rub against my clit with every push and pull. I tightened my grip on his biceps, his eyes locking with me just as my climax hit and pulled him over the edge with me.

He collapsed on top of me, panting harshly while his lips tenderly skimmed my forehead, cheeks, lips, and finally settled against my neck. His weight was a comfort, a solid reminder that I wasn't alone. I was loved.

He shifted to the side and pulled a blanket over us as we settled into the couch. Max caressed my face with gentle hands, urging my lips up to accept his gentle kiss. He broke it off and whispered against my cheek. "I love you."

"I love you, too." I snuggled into his embrace, rubbing my face against his neck and inhaling the unique scent of Max, sweat, and our lovemaking that lingered on his skin. In spite of this perfect moment, doubts were crowding into my mind and I clung to him, wishing we could stay in this moment forever. How would we really make this work?

Max sensed my struggle and pulled back to look into my face. "What's going on?"

"Are you sure?" I traced his jawline, loving the scratchy feel of his beard against my fingertips. I shivered as I remembered how it had felt against the skin of my thighs and breasts. "Our life will never be normal. Even if I cut back, this will never be a regular kind of life together."

Max shifted and leaned up on one elbow. "I know that. But, I can't live without you. I tried and it didn't work." He kissed the tip of my nose and smiled. "Besides, I'm beginning to think that normal is overrated. We'll figure it out. We'll make our own normal."

"That sounds so good. I want that." Brushing aside my doubts, I snuggled into his embrace as he shifted back on the couch. I was happy. Max loved me and it *would* be different this time.

Like he said, we would find our own normal—together.

THIRTY

Max

I WOKE SLOWLY from the most amazing dream.

It was always the same; Kit in my bed, dark curls spilling over my sheets, as I worshipped every inch of her deliciously fuckable body.

This morning was even better, because the pictures in my head were in Technicolor and my sheets even smelled like her. Groaning, I rolled over, pulling my pillow against my face, inhaling the delicious scent of Kit—a combination of summer, honeysuckle, and pure sex.

Lying there, the smell of fresh coffee and the sound of her sweet singing wafted over me and made me smile.

It wasn't a dream.

I shifted under the sheets as memories of last night drifted across my mind. I was hard, aching as I stroked up and down slowly, drawing out the pleasure. When I woke up with Kit on the couch I'd picked her up and carried her up the stairs to my bedroom, placing her gently on my bed.

In the twilight, Kit had climbed on top of me—driving me crazy with her soft hands. Her mouth had been hungry, sweet, and I'd let her lead the way. All of her doubts from earlier seemed to disappear as she took control of my body. Drawn in by the spell she cast over me, I made no effort to hide just how desperately I wanted her. She teased me with her lips and hands, and it had taken all my strength to resist taking over as she grasped my cock in her small hand and led me into her body.

That time was slow and sweet. No words were spoken. She'd fallen apart in my arms and I'd held her close as my climax surged through my body, leaving me sated and spent. Unwilling to break our connection, I'd stayed inside her as we drifted back to sleep.

We needed to talk. To figure out how this was going to work between us. She had doubts and so did I but I wanted to figure them out together. For the first time in forever, the thought of committing to someone didn't scare me. I wanted it and I was going to have it.

I got up, determined to go down to the kitchen and drag Kit back to bed. Breakfast could wait. I dragged on a pair of jeans, and left them unbuttoned, padded barefoot down the stairs, and skidded to a stop when I got a good look at the scene in my kitchen.

I leaned against the doorway and watched her make my house into a home.

Kit was standing at the stovetop, my shirt reaching to the middle of her thighs and her hair tousled from the night in my bed. She sang softly to herself as she bustled around, preparing pancakes and eggs.

"You look good in my shirt."

Kit looked over her shoulder, eyes wide with surprise but warm with love. I pushed away from the wall and walked over to her, wrapping my arms around her waist and pressing my front against her back. She melted against me and sighed as I pressed a soft kiss to her neck.

"Good morning."

She sighed again as my mouth traveled up to the sensitive spot behind her ear. Her voice was breathless and I smiled at her reaction to me. "Good morning to you." Kit gestured at the stove. "I was making you breakfast."

I nibbled back down her neck as I snaked a hand under the edge of my shirt to caress her silky thigh. "I was hoping to have breakfast in bed."

She moaned as my fingers brushed against her wet folds and higher to caress the smooth skin of her belly. She wriggled against me, rubbing her ass against my erection. Holy shit that felt good.

"I made you pancakes...Oh!"

I was done playing unless I was doing it in my bed. I lifted her over my shoulder, snagged the bottle of syrup off the counter and turned to head back to the bedroom. Kit squirmed in my hold and squealed as I smacked her ass. "Hold still. You're gonna love it, baby. I'm gonna lick every inch of—"

The sight of someone standing in my foyer brought me to an abrupt halt.

"Mom!"

Holy shit. My dad was also standing at the front door, a grin twitching at the edges of his mouth.

Kit was absolutely still, but I could feel her groan of embarrassment buried against my shoulder. I slowly lowered her to the ground, and once her feet hit the wood floor, she turned and faced my parents, fussing with her hair and tugging the oversized shirt further down her legs.

It was kind of cute. We'd laugh about this someday but

from the feel of her elbow jamming into my side, I didn't think it would be anytime soon.

My dad cleared his throat, breaking the embarrassed silence as he strode towards the kitchen. "Coffee smells good. Think I'll get a cup."

"How did they get in?" Kit whispered.

"They have a key."

Kit took off up the stairs with a mumbled "going to put some clothes on" and I followed my dad into the kitchen. The passing of cups, milk, and sugar busied our hands as we studiously avoided the fact my parents had clearly interrupted an intimate moment.

Taking a sip of the hot brew, I asked, "What are you guys doing here so early?"

Kit made her reappearance, wearing a pair of my sweatpants, and I handed her a cup, pulling her close beside me.

"We tried to call but no one answered." My mother reached out and grasped Kit's hand in compassion. "We saw what happened to you, dear. It was terrible." She turned to me, her eyes filled with pride. "And we saw what you did to protect her."

"Proud of you, son." My dad patted my shoulder and then shifted to lean against the counter. "When we couldn't get you on the phone, we figured you two were squirreled away here. There's a bunch of reporters camped out at the top of the lane. Robert blocked the road, so they can't get down here unless they crawl through the woods." He flashed an apologetic glance towards Kit. "We probably gave away your location, though. I think the ones who were camped out at our house followed us here. I'm sorry."

Kit smiled back. "Don't apologize, Mr. Butler. Welcome to my world." She sighed, and put her coffee down on the counter. "I should apologize for disrupting your life."

"It's John. And you didn't do anything you need to apologize for. This will all blow over and we'll be back to normal before you know it."

"Damn! That coffee smells good! Is there more?"

I turned to see Dean, followed closely by Bridget, saunter into my kitchen and head straight for the coffeepot.

"The door was open so we just came on in." Smiling at the Butlers, he introduced Bridget before he continued, "The station, Kit's loft, are all a mob scene. Bridget called me once my shift was over and she followed me in your truck."

"The label needs you back pronto. The buzz has all been in your favor, but with the tour kicking off in three days, they are howling to get you back in town for promo work. Paul's working out the details but we need you. Sorry," Bridget said.

I watched Kit closely; her expression was tense. I gathered her close to my side and pressed a kiss to her hair as she asked, "What about Ron?"

Weird looks passed between the four visitors and my stomach clenched in response. "What's going on guys?"

Dean was the one to answer. "Ron's still in custody. Both you and Kit need to go and give statements so they can press charges. That's the good part." He rubbed the back of his neck and hesitated. "The bad part is that he's saying you assaulted, threatened, and harassed him, Max. He's hired a lawyer who keeps talking to the press and stirring it all up."

I shrugged. "So what? He can't prove it."

Dean continued. "The department has placed you on administrative suspension without pay until this gets cleared up. The director's pissed and wants to talk to you today. You *know* how he hates bad press."

"I protected her. What the fuck did they expect me to do? Let that asshole hurt her?"

"It's not just the fight." Dean held a hand up to stop me from interrupting. "You left the shift to go to Kit. I tried to cover, but they know. You were AWOL."

Shocked, I released Kit and walked over to the large fireplace that dominated the family room. Leaning on the mantle, I breathed in deeply, controlling my temper and collecting my thoughts. This was manageable. I would talk to the chief and the police and get back to work.

"What?" Kit asked from behind me. "You left work to come to me?"

I turned and faced the bank of upset and concerned faces in front of me. "Of course I did. You needed me. I'd do it again if I had to."

"Could you lose your job?" Her expression told me that she already knew the answer and it was not going to go over well.

"Yes."

"And you would do it again?"

"Yes."

"What about your promotion?"

I scoffed. "Not going to happen now."

Kit stared at me, her expression unreadable. I didn't know her well enough to understand every nuance and right now I cursed that fact. She closed her eyes briefly, cutting herself off from me completely. I made a move towards her and her eyes flew open and she bolted, heading out of the kitchen. She was clearly upset.

Following her, I caught up with her in my room just in time to see her pulling on her clothes. "Kit, baby? What are you doing?"

"I'm going. I've got to fix this mess."

"Okay. Just hang on a second and I'll get dressed and go with you."

She stopped, her eyes only briefly meeting mine before darting away. She clutched her shoes to her chest and scurried past me and into the hallway. "No. I'm going alone."

I grabbed her arm and spun her around to face me just before she reached the stairs. "Kit. I'm going with you. Remember last night? We do this together from now on."

Tears pooled in her eyes as she shook her head, her voice a broken whisper. "No. This won't work."

Shock rolled through me and loosened my grip on her, allowing her to slip down the stairs. I barely registered the others as they piled out of the kitchen just in time to witness my life falling apart.

My voice was loud and harsh as I shouted at her retreating back. "What do you mean, *this won't work?* We've barely gotten started and you're giving up?" I raced down the stairs two at a time and caught her at the bottom. "What about the fact that we love each other?"

"Max, we both know that isn't enough. Our lives are too different and mine has already ruined yours. Your parents have reporters camped on their lawn and you're practically a prisoner in your own house. Not to mention the fact that you might lose your job!" She wiped at her wet cheeks with the back of her hand. "My life is in chaos and I go on tour in a few days and I'll be gone for months. Trust me. We've been living in a bubble—a wonderful bubble where the press left us alone and we didn't have to deal with reality. But trust me, those days are over and the reality of my life will tear us apart." Her breath hiccupped in her chest. "I don't want you to end up hating me because I can't be what you need."

"What are you talking about?" I saw the fear, heard it in

her voice. I was scared, too, but I was more afraid of losing her and never taking the chance. I reached out, pulling her close to me. "Kit, don't do this. My job will be fine. Your job will be fine. We'll work out the rest. Together." I leaned in close to press my forehead against hers as I pleaded, "I love you so much. Just hang on to me baby. We'll be all right, I promise."

She rested against me and a little of the tension loosened in my chest. Her hand wove through my hair as she pulled me into a kiss that was full of tenderness and something else I couldn't name. With a whimper, Kit released my mouth and stepped far enough away that I could see the expression on her face. Suddenly, I knew what else had been in that kiss.

It was goodbye.

I was pissed. Anger shot through me. "So, you're gonna do this? You're afraid and you're going to run? What is this? Fucking payback for what I did?" I gestured wildly at the front door. "All this craziness? That's nothing. But you're too afraid to take the chance and even though I suck at any kind of relationship, I know I can't do it by myself." Running my hands through my hair, my voice caught as pain squeezed my heart. Jesus, this was worse than Sarah. Knowing Kit was out there and I couldn't have her might kill me. "You and me, together? It would be hard, but I know we'd be worth it. It could shatter into a million fucking pieces and it would still be worth it."

I stared at her, daring her to take the leap with me. If this had any chance of working, we both had to be committed one hundred percent.

"Max." Her voice was barely above a whisper but it was like she was shouting at me. That one word told me everything I needed to know. She was already gone.

I turned away from her, heading up the stairs to wash her smell off my body and burn the sheets.

THIRTY ONE

Max

MY EYES WERE gritty from too little sleep.

Three weeks had passed since Kit walked out of my house and my life. The last time I'd seen her was the day after she'd shot us all to hell. I'd arrived at the police station to give my statement just as she was leaving and our eyes had met for the briefest moment before I turned away. I couldn't stand the sight of her when I couldn't have her. She looked beautiful as always, but in that second, I saw the pain and hurt that shadowed her eyes but, for once, my hero complex didn't take over. She'd made her decision and she could live with it.

Just like I would.

My suspension from work only lasted two days. In the end, Kit had called the director—explaining how I had protected her from Ron—and I'd been reinstated immediately. I was grateful. The job was the only thing that kept me from losing my mind. At work, I could pretend to ignore the pitying looks from my family and friends.

Just like the one Dean was giving me right now.

I shifted on my seat inside the fire truck as it raced down the street to the third call of the night.

"Dean, cut it out."

Dean didn't even pretend to misunderstand. "You look like shit. When's the last time you slept?"

I adjusted my helmet to block my face. "Last night."

"Uh huh." Dean continued to examine me. "I didn't ask 'when was the last time you tossed and turned and paced the night away'."

I stared down at my boots, saying nothing. I wasn't going to spill my guts and dwell on something I couldn't change.

"Max."

"Don't." I met his eyes across the truck and gritted my teeth. "She's gone. Let's just do the job."

The back doors opened and I jumped down to the ground, surveying the scene. I got my orders and made my way into the three–story apartment building, checking rooms, carrying victims out to safety—focusing on the job. Time passed quickly, and soon I was on the second floor, conducting one last sweep before calling the "all clear."

Inside, the fire was dying down but it was still loud. I heard an ominous crack but couldn't tell where it was coming from. A tingling awareness spread across the back of my neck. It was time to get out.

Instinct propelled me towards the exit just as the ceiling heaved above me. Two steps from my goal, debris rained down on my head and shoulders. I reached for my communication device but it was too late.

A large object landed across my back and I slammed to the floor under its weight. I couldn't breathe. I scrabbled to move away the heavy debris. I tried not to panic but it was hard, with what felt like an elephant sitting on my back. It was getting hotter, the noise louder, as the fire sparked back to life overhead.

I clawed at the rubble and dislodged my helmet and it rolled to the side. Succumbing to the pain, I saw the picture of Kit tucked into the inside band just before everything went black.

THIRTY TWO

Kit

THE APPLAUSE WAS DEAFENING.

I waved to the audience and left the stage of the Grand Ole Opry, heading towards my dressing room to prepare for the interview segment and then my final performance of the night. I was bone–tired. Getting here had required a red–eye flight from Florida, so I pushed open the door and headed straight for the fridge and my new best friend—Mr. Red Bull. Bridget was on the telephone, so I kicked off my shoes and plopped down on the couch.

The first set was behind me and I breathed a sigh of relief. I longed to get out of Nashville, back on the road, and away from all the memories of Max. On the road, I still hurt, but it was easier to focus on the music and the fans without seeing him on every corner. I welcomed the grind of the road. Most nights I fell into my bunk in a dreamless stupor but I still dreaded the morning when my brain clicked into gear and the pain came rushing back.

I'd blown it this time. My fear had forced me to make a rash, stupid decision that hurt Max deeply. The crazy part was that I didn't even know why I'd done it anymore. My doctor said it was a panic attack brought on by all the crap that had happened and that my sense of desolation and fear was a normal part of it.

All I knew was that I'd been overcome with the overwhelming feeling that staying with Max would hurt him.

His face outside the police station had been cold, hard, and devoid of any emotion towards me, except indifference. He probably hated me and I didn't blame him. I hated the cowardice I'd let control me, but it was too late to change it. My chance with Max was over and I had no one to blame but myself.

I popped one eye open when Bridget signed off her call, ready to ask about the details of our flight, when a phone rang—the "Stand By Your Man" ringtone signaling that it was mine.

Bridget scooped it up off the dressing table and flipped it open with a cheerful greeting. Her smile slipped as she listened briefly, murmured for the person to hang on, and held the phone out to me. Her voice was grim.

"It's Dean. It's about Max."

My hand stilled in mid–air. It was bad news. I knew it. Maybe the worst news. With icy fingers, I took the phone from Bridget and brought it up to my ear.

"This is Kit."

"I thought you might want to know." Dean's usually jovial voice was tense and anxious. "Max is hurt. We're on shift and he was in a building when it collapsed."

I found it hard to speak around the band that was constricting around my heart. "Is… is he okay?"

Dean paused as people shouted around him. I could

hear him cup the phone closer to his mouth. "I don't know the extent of his injuries. We got him out of the building and he's on the bus headed to NashGen. He was unconscious. Hold on a second." Dean answered a series of rapid questions and came back to the phone. "Look, I gotta go. I'll see you at the hospital."

I sat there, unable to move, as the dial tone sounded in my ear. Only two thoughts swirled in my mind: one, I had to get to Max, and two, that if I got the chance, I would make him love me again.

I jumped off the couch, my focus on getting to Max.

Bridget was right behind me, scooping up purses and keys.

"I'm going with you."

I hit the backstage hallway and broke into a run. People moved out of my way while casting puzzled looks in my direction. Paul came jogging up and stopped my momentum with a hand on my shoulder.

"Kit, where are you going? We have a show in," he looked at his watch, "ten minutes."

I leaned on his arm, scared shitless and close to losing the battle to keep it together. "Max is hurt. He could be—" I bit my lip, unable to voice my greatest fear. "I have to go to him."

"You know, if you walk out of the Opry, the label will tank your new contract." His voice was firm; matter-of-fact. No judgment there.

"I don't care." *I would give up my whole career for Max to be alright.* I'd figure out the career part once I knew he was okay.

Nodding, Paul kissed my forehead quickly and pushed me towards the door. "Good girl. I'll fix it here. Go!"

Bridget and I bolted out of the artists' entrance of the

Opry and headed straight for her car. I was silent as we careened through traffic, praying for Max to be alright. Could you be okay if a building fell on you? Would they let me see him? The fifteen–minute ride was torture and I barely let the car come to a stop outside the ER before I jumped out and bolted for the entrance.

The waiting area smelled like antiseptic and burnt coffee and was filled with firefighting personnel, EMTs, and policemen. Ignoring the pointing fingers of those who recognized me, I scanned the crowd for Dean. Giving up, I approached a nurse to ask about Max, when I heard my name shouted above the noise. Turning, Dean waved me over.

He grasped my arm and led me to a room filled with firemen. "He's still unconscious and they moved him upstairs."

"Can I see him?"

Dean pushed me through the door. "We'll see. I'll take you up."

We emerged from the elevator on the third floor and immediately stepped into a waiting room full of people. Several nodded to Dean, and I ignored the whispers that erupted in my wake. It seemed like an eternity until I turned a corner and entered a hospital room where John and Olivia Butler sat, next to a hospital bed.

I blinked, my eyes adjusting to the low light in the room and the hushed hospital sounds of machines whirring and soft–soled shoes squeaking on tile floors.

My heart fell to my feet. I forgot how to breathe.

Max sat on the edge of the bed, shirtless with a pair of scrub pants. His face and body were covered with scrapes and cuts. It was the bandage on his head, tinted red with blood just over his left temple that made me weak.

I wanted to run to him and make sure he was all right but his hostile demeanor stopped me. His amber eyes grew dark when he saw me, suspicion and hurt tightening his jaw.

"What are you doing here?" he asked, not an ounce of welcome in his tone. I'd made a mistake. I was too late.

"Dean called me," I stumbled over my tongue, suddenly realizing how far out on the ledge I was with no safety net. "I wanted to see that you were okay."

"I look better than I feel," he answered, his tone flat and emotionless.

"Oh."

"You've done your duty. You can go."

"Max!" His mother scolded him from her perch by the bed. I blushed with embarrassment. I had no right to be here.

I moved to leave but a hand on my arm stopped me.

"Are you a friend of my grandson?"

I turned. A much older man, who possessed Max's strong jaw and large build, was watching me closely. Startled, I looked around. Their faces were worried, frantic. I had no right to be here.

"I'm sorry." I offered an apology towards Olivia Butler. "I should go. I'm intruding."

I turned to go, but gentle pressure on my arm stopped my leaving. Max's grandpa held me back, his face kind and full of understanding.

"Young lady, the important thing to remember is that you came." His curious gaze examined me and I remembered that I still wore my costume from the Opry. "I can presume from your lovely outfit that you were at quite a fancy shindig and left in quite a hurry."

"I was at the Opry. I have a show tonight."

"I see." His eyes were gentle as he squeezed my hand in encouragement. "You don't walk out of the Opry for just anyone. My grandson must be very important to you."

"Grandpa," Max said in warning from across the room.

I blinked back the tears gathering in my eyes, my voice barely above a whisper. "Very important." I swallowed back the fear and told the absolute truth, making eye contact with Max as I spoke. "He means everything to me. I love him." I started to back out of the room. "But I was scared and I have no right to be here. Not now. I'm sorry."

I really did turn to go this time. I wasn't welcome. Too late to salvage what we'd had. I'd get on my tour bus and back on the road. Sooner or later, I'd forget him. In the meantime, I'd get a shitload of good song material.

I was two steps out of the door when I heard his voice.

"Wait."

I froze, not really sure if I'd heard him or imagined it like I had in so many dreams the last few weeks.

"Kit. I can't get off this bed without falling down. Get back in here." His mom whispered something that sounded like "you're being rude" and he added, "Please."

I eased back into the room, staring at him from the spot just inside the door. Max just stared at me and I had no idea whether he wanted me to stay in place or go to him. The air in the room crackled with everything between us, the uncertainty and longing I saw in his gaze.

"Can you give us a minute?" Max asked his parents and Grandpa and they all hustled to beat feet out the door.

A soft chuckle escaped the lips of Grandpa Butler as he walked past me. He stopped and whispered his two cents. "Trust me, darlin'; I've seen him mope around these last few weeks. That hurt will be forgotten once Max hears you tell him you love him. Tell the boy what he's been dyin' to hear."

"Grandpa," Max barked and the older man scurried through the door with a big wink.

I liked him. Very much.

Max and I stared at each other, the seconds measuring like hours in my twisted gut. I had no idea where to start.

"You left the Opry," Max stated but every word was drenched in a question.

"Yes."

"That's not going to make Liam happy."

"No, it won't," I agreed. "But I wasn't thinking about making him happy when I left."

"What were you thinking?"

"I was thinking that you might be gone and I'd never get to ask you."

"Ask me what?" His gaze was hot and leveled at my own. I couldn't look away. I wanted him to see just how real this all was. To believe me.

"Ask you to take me back. To say I'm sorry for giving into my panic and fear and hurting you." He didn't respond but he didn't look away, so I walked towards him, my voice cracking with all the emotion just trying to break out of me. "I wanted to ask you to love me again like in that movie star film. To tell you that I'm just a girl who screwed up and wants your love even if I don't deserve it. For today. For forever."

I was standing in front of him now. So close my body brushed up against his knees. He smelled like smoke and antiseptic and Max and I just wanted to latch onto him and inhale.

"What about your job?" he asked, his voice so low I had to lean in to catch it. The movement brought me within kissing distance of him and I fought the urge to lay one on him and seal all my words that way.

"I don't know. I might not have a label. I may start my own. I don't know." I shook my head. "I know I'm stronger with you. I'm better with you."

"And if your career is over?"

"Then, it's over. I'll figure something out. I can play anywhere. I've got options."

"Uh oh. 'Super Kit' is in the house."

I shook my head. "I don't need her when I've got you."

"Stupid jackasses. They don't know what they've got."

I laughed. "Is that right?"

"Yes." He reached out and grabbed my hands, lifting them up and around his neck as he opened his legs. I slid in there, tightening my hold on him and hanging on for dear life. I know my heart was pounding like a drumbeat in one of my songs but I didn't care. Max didn't either. "I am not a stupid jackass. I know what I've got."

"And what is that?"

"I've got you."

"Yes, you've got me."

He tugged me down and our lips met in a soft sweet kiss. His voice was low but I heard every precious word.

"Don't leave me again," he pleaded. "You'll always be enough for me. The only one for me. I love *you*, Kit."

I wrapped my arms around him and held on tightly, as our mouths gently caressed each other.

I broke off the kiss as the room spontaneously erupted in applause, hoots, and catcalls. I looked over my shoulder to see the doorway filled with his family and friends offering smiles, teary eyes, and congratulations.

"Now about the whole 'Super Kit' thing." His gravelly

voice brought my attention back to his handsome face. "I kind of like the idea of you in a cape—and nothing else."

"On one condition."

He cocked an eyebrow at me. "Anything."

I leaned in closer, my lips only a breath away from his. "You need to change the locks on your front door."

"Deal."

EPILOGUE

Three months later

THE SIGN READ, "Lively, Tennessee. The place folks love to call home."

I squirmed in my seat in the back of the chauffer-driven car, excited by the marker that told me that I was five miles from the place I had wanted to be all summer— home. I had a number-one single, "Angel", on the charts and a new album due out in the Fall. I was on top of the world.

I'd decided not to renew my contract with Liam Connor and was exploring starting my own label while entertaining offers from a couple of big name recording companies. I had time to decide and was in no hurry. My life was full and my own.

The tour had been unbelievably successful with every show sold out and extra dates added and filled to capacity, as well. I'd loved every minute on stage with the fans, and the band was closer than ever. With Ron gone from the scene, the fun and camaraderie had returned in full force.

It felt like it was when I first started—before I let business become more important than the music. Before I'd let image be more important than the truth.

It had been an amazing summer.

But, each passing day I'd counted down the time to when I could return to Tennessee and to the man who held my heart. Max. I had missed him terribly. I'd flown home frequently and he'd come to see me when he got time away from the station. He'd even spent his week–long vacation on the road with me, witnessing the craziness of my life on the road first–hand. To my relief and delight, Max fit in like he was born for the road. The band loved him, the crew loved him, and the fans loved him.

Especially the female fans.

I giggled as I remembered the first time he'd attended a "meet and greet" and been bombarded with requests for photos from my female fans. At first he'd been surprised and then embarrassed as the ladies had shoved pieces of paper with their phone numbers into his hands. Once the fans had posted those pics on the Internet, it started a pattern that would continue the rest of the tour—requests for Max, photos with Max, and a pile of homemade gifts for Max.

While Max was a good sport about suddenly being thrust into the spotlight, I was careful to keep the intimate details of our relationship between the two of us and I shielded him from exposure as much as I possibly could. But, even when he wasn't with me, he was photographed by the press, as he lived and worked in Nashville. I'd worried silently that it bothered him more than he let on. When I apologized for the press intruding on a private lunch with his parents, he kissed me softly and told me to never apologize again; it was a small price to pay to be with me.

I'd shown him many times that night just how much his support meant to me.

So, when, three weeks after the night at the hospital he'd asked me to move into the farmhouse with him, I'd agreed with one stipulation—that he'd let me install the security gates currently blocking the car at the top of the driveway.

I used my remote control to open them and gathered my things together as the car drove the last mile to the house I now called home. My heart pounded like the drum solo on "Angel" at my first glimpse of the large, white house surrounded by the old–growth oaks and dogwoods planted by Max's grandparents. I blinked back tears as I thought of the love that had been made and would be made in this house.

This is home.

I'd wanted this for so long that I had the urge to pinch myself and get three independent confirmations that this wasn't a dream. If it was, then I was never going to wake up—ever.

The car pulled to a stop at the base of the wrap–around porch, and I hopped out without waiting for the driver to open the door. I'd told Max not to meet me at the airport and I was now anxious to have the reunion I didn't want witnessed by cameras and curious fans.

I scanned the yard as I thanked the driver and signed the invoice for the bill. I heard hammering coming from just beyond the rose garden and I headed around the house to find Max. The garden was in full–bloom, the flowers coaxed to life by Grandpa Butler, and the scent was strong and sweet where it mingled with the smell of fresh cut grass.

My breathing literally skipped when my eyes landed on

the best thing I'd seen in two weeks—Max in khaki cargo shorts and a tight, white T–shirt that caressed his muscles.

Will I ever see him and not want him?

He was hammering a shutter next to one of the windows on the front of my new rehearsal space and recording studio, located in the sweet little cottage that had been Grandmother Butler's private retreat. Tears came to my eyes as I remembered the day that Max had walked me down the back path to this little house and handed me the keys, explaining that he wanted to renovate it into a space where I could work from home. He'd brushed away my tears as he teased, "As long as I can visit and try my damnedest to distract you from your work."

And then he'd pulled me into the cottage and demonstrated just how distracting he could be.

Heat pooled in my belly at the memory, and I must have made a sound because Max looked up, his amber eyes widened in surprise and then crinkling up at the edges when he smiled. One minute I was riveted to the spot and the next I was crushed against his chest with his mouth devouring mine in a desperate tangle of lips and tongues. God, he was an addiction for me and I didn't plan on ever kicking this one.

Max lifted me off my feet and I wrapped my legs around his waist as he turned and walked the few steps necessary to press my back against the side of the cottage. I briefly worried about his injury but he'd assured me that he had a doctor's note that said he was fully recovered and I needed to stop worrying about him. The note really said that—an inside joke between Max and his doctor and a way to stop my constant "fussing over him"—his words, not mine.

With my weight supported by the wall, his hands were

free to roam my body, teasing under the edge of my T–shirt until his hands moved over my stomach and my ribs to cover my breasts, plucking my nipples through the lace of my bra. I sighed and rolled my head back as Max took advantage of my invitation and pressed hot, wet kisses along the exposed skin of my neck.

Max lifted his head and looked down at me, his eyes blazing with desire, heat, and love. He was so unbelievably gorgeous that he still took my breath away. His mouth widened in his trademark "just for me" sexy smile and his voice was rough with emotion. "Hey."

I smiled back. I'm sure I looked like a goof but I didn't care. This was my man and I loved him more than I ever thought I'd be able to love anyone. "Hey."

His hand reached up to caress my cheek, my eyes closed as I leaned into his warmth. He was my rock, my touch-stone, and I could feel my soul filling back up just being in his orbit.

"You're early. I meant to meet you up at the house and give you a proper welcome."

"I think this is pretty perfect." I pulled myself from his embrace and tugged him towards the house. "C'mon, I know how we can make this welcome even better."

To my surprise, Max pulled me back with a shake of his head and a mischievous grin on his face.

"No way. I want you to see your new studio before we go up to the house." He pulled me behind him as he climbed the front steps, turning to face me when we reached the top. "Everything is installed and ready to go. It just needs your personal touch."

Max opened the door, motioning for me to walk inside. I could smell the scents of drywall, paint, and carpet, and as my excitement bubbled to the top I slipped past him and took the first real look at my new recording studio. My eyes scanned the front room which served as the writing/lounge area and was outfitted with two comfy sofas covered in red corduroy, tables in honeyed maple, and an upright piano in the corner. A custom—made entertainment center held a flat screen and Max's gaming systems. Light streamed in through the large windows, making the warm yellow paint gleam like burnished gold. It was warm, inviting—and mine.

I walked towards the back rooms which housed a kitchenette, bathroom with a shower, and my studio. It wasn't as large as the ones in Nashville, but I could record demos here, write songs, and rehearse with the band instead of heading into town. Skipping back into the front room, I saw Max standing there with his hands opened in a gesture of inquiry.

"So, what do you think?"

I crossed the room and jumped into his arms, pressing kisses all over his face as he staggered under the onslaught. "I love it!" I peppered more kisses on his lips as he laughed out loud. "Thank you! Thank you! I love you!"

"This is the right way to say thank you." He curled his hand around the back of my neck and pulled me in for a slow, wet kiss that quickly turned the mood from festive to seductive as he claimed my mouth in a blatant show of possession. I whimpered and Max broke the kiss, gazing down at me with a heavy-lidded stare that told me we would be headed to a bed very soon. Fine by me. It had been too long. "You're very welcome," he nodded towards the long wall behind him, "but you haven't seen the best part yet."

I followed the direction of his gesture and had to blink. The wall was covered by a hand made guitar rack mounted on the wall. It was also made of maple, stained a golden color and carved with the most delicate design of honey-suckle and barbed-wire. Just like on my tattoo and album logos. It was beautiful and made with so much love that it shone.

"Oh, Max." I covered my mouth with a shaking hand. Never in my life had someone done something like this for me. I pulled away from his embrace and walked slowly towards the rack. My hands shook even more as I ran my fingers over the wood. It was smooth as glass, cool to the touch, and the design was intricate but beautifully simple.

Max came up behind me, his voice soft in my ear. "Grandpa Butler helped me with the carving and the stain-ing. It holds five guitars," his hand motioned to the middle section of the rack, "with a place of honor for Jolene."

I leaned forward to observe the carving below Jolene's slot more closely. The wood frame was formed into a curved point that held a more detailed carving of the full logo of the heart, vines, and wire. Something extra was carved into the heart and I leaned in closer to read what turned out to be three initials. K.L.B.

Oh. My. God.

My breath stuttered in my chest and my legs wobbled as I slowly turned around, scarcely believing the scene before me—Max on one knee with a velvet ring box in his hand and looking at me with so much love that I wasn't sure that this tiny cabin could hold it all. It wouldn't have surprised me if the windows blew out, the door flying open under the pressure of the emotion. Suddenly afraid that my legs would give out, I grabbed the back of the sofa. This was not the time to face-plant on the floor.

"Kit." He swallowed hard, his voice gravely and rough with his nervousness. "I wish I had your gift with words. I know this is fast and we're young but I've never been so sure of anything in my life." Max reached up with his empty hand and caressed my cheek, brushing away my tears. "I love our crazy life and I love watching you do all of these amazing things with your career. I want to be the one you come home to, the one you need when it gets too tough—the one you write mushy love songs about."

I choked back tears as I half–laughed, half–sobbed at his words. The tears were flowing like someone had opened the faucet and I knew that my makeup was a mess but I didn't care. All I knew was that the most amazing man in the world was asking me to spend forever with him. To make the home I'd dreamed about.

Max opened the box, removed the ring, and slid it onto my finger. The metal quickly warmed to my body temperature and it fit perfectly—like it had always belonged there.

"Marry me, Kit Landry. I love you. I swear that every fucking day of your life you will never doubt that you are the most important person in the world to me."

I didn't even bother to wipe away the tears as I fell to my knees and tackled him. We both fell backward onto the carpet but I could see him clearly when I straddled his body. His grin was wicked, too cocky for a guy who hadn't gotten my answer yet but I think he knew what was coming. "Yes, I'll marry you! I love you."

"Come here. It's been too long."

Max pulled me down to him, capturing my lips in a kiss that quickly turned from tender to needy in the span of a few seconds. It had been too long. These days, any time spent apart from him felt like it was too long.

Max tugged at the hem of my shirt, pulling away from our lip–lock only for the time necessary to lift it off my body. In less than five seconds he had my bra off, his strong calloused hands rubbing against my sensitive skin, teasing my nipples into hard points while my whole body flooded with white–hot arousal.

It never took long for him to get me there and I was on the edge, fueled by too many nights with only my hands to ease the ache. I leaned over him offering my nipple, audibly stuttering when his hot mouth closed over me. He worked me up with his mouth and tongue—the gentle pulls, the licks and kisses that got me wet and needy. Desperate for him.

"Fuck, yeah, baby," Max growled against my skin as my orgasm hit me like a bolt of lightning.

My mind went blank as my body filled with the pleasure that rolled over me in waves. In spite of it, I was still so hungry for Max that my hands shifted over his body—unable to settle in one spot for very long. With a ragged breath I opened my eyes and looked down at him, begging, "Max, please. I need you."

He lifted his head to gaze into my eyes, a muscle clenched in his jaw with his own effort to remain in control.

"Off. Off," I said impatiently while my fingers got busy unbuttoning and unzipping his shorts. He lifted his hips up and I shoved down the material far enough to give me unobstructed access to him. He was going commando and I immediately grasped his cock in my hand, stroking the long hard length, soaking in every movement of his body, every groan that escaped past his clenched teeth.

I loved every minute with Max but this moment—when I had him completely undone by his need—was a head–rush for me. But it never lasted long.

When Max took over, I was the one adrift, only anchored to this world by him and the way he made me feel like the whole universe centered on the two of us.

He groaned, running his hands over my skirt and

making quick work of getting it off me, along with my thong. Finally I was naked and he had full access to where I wanted him most. He lifted his hips so the tip of his erection prodded the entrance of my hot, slippery core. Closing his eyes tightly, he pushed inside me with one thrust. He was big and hard and it had been a long few weeks but even through the ache it felt so damn good that I never wanted it to stop.

His eyes opened and I don't know what killed me most —the fiery passion or the tenderness. His fingers dug into my hips and I could feel his legs shaking with the effort to prolong this moment for a little while longer. "Kit. I love you so much. No one else for me. Ever."

I leaned down, brushing a soft kiss against his lips. "Show me. Prove it."

With a low moan, he rocked his body against mine— sliding in and out of my body—as his mouth claimed every one of my gasps, every single sigh.

I arched my body, riding him to meet his every thrust, pulling him deeper and clinging to him as he pulled out of me.

Max broke the kiss, panting with desire as he lifted his head and licked my nipple, sending sparks of pleasure to my clit. He drew the hard peak into his mouth and suckled deeply before releasing it to do the same thing to its twin. My head swam with the sensations created by him filling me, stretching me as my second climax built low in my belly.

"Come for me, Kit." Max's voice was rough, his breathing hard and labored, stuttering with each deep thrust. "I need to feel you again. Want it. Will always need you."

His words sent me over the edge. Flying. Tumbling. I

cried out as my body seized him, drawing him deeper and forcing him to join me in the freefall.

For several long minutes, we laid together on the floor, listening to the sounds out in the garden as they filtered through the open door. The scents of summer roses and sunshine mixed with those of our lovemaking as we drifted along in our private paradise. He nuzzled my cheek, that spot on my neck I loved so much. He shifted us, placing me on my back while he leaned up on his elbow to watch me. I lifted my left hand and played with the ring on my forever finger.

It was classically styled with a large stone in a platinum setting and it was perfect. Not gaudy or showy, just right. "Max, I love it. It's so beautiful."

"I'm glad you like it." He grinned a slow, lazy smile. "I'm glad you said yes."

"What would you have done if I'd said no?"

"Like *that* would ever happen." He dodged my pinch and laughed. "I would have kept asking you. Wearing you down with sex until you had no other choice but to say yes."

"Manipulative bastard," I grumbled.

"And you're going to be Mrs. Manipulative Bastard."

I grinned up at him, liking how that sounded just fine. I dropped a quick kiss on his lips. "Thank you."

Max cupped his hand behind my neck and drew me close for a lingering kiss before resting his forehead against mine. Smiling softly to himself, he shook his head. "For what?"

Aw man, how could he not know? I reached up with both hands and made sure he heard every word. "Thank you for believing in us when I didn't."

His eyes sparkled with mischief and his smile was big enough to light up the world. I loved knowing that all that joy was because of me, of us. "Baby, don't you get it?" He wound a curl around his finger and gave it a gentle tug. "Loving you is the easiest thing I've ever done. I love being the little man at home."

I laughed at that. Life with Max would never be dull. I kissed him and then leaned back, my mind churning a million miles a minute. *The little man at home...*

"Uh, oh."

Max's voice brought me back to the present.

Busted.

His voice was laced with humor as he touched his finger to my nose. "I *know* that look. You just thought of a song didn't you?" I nodded and he pushed me up, stripped off his T–shirt and pulled it over my head.

He pointed towards the cabinet next to the piano. "That's stocked with your favorite pens and paper."

I looked over towards the cabinet but hesitated. "Are you sure? I just got home..."

Max laughed and leaned back on the sofa, his hands behind his head. He made a delectable picture—all muscles, silky dark hair on his chest, and miles of tanned sexy skin. "I'm going to lie here and recover, so you've got fifteen minutes to write down what's in your head."

I shivered at his sexy tone. "And then?"

"And then, I'm going to take you up to the house and get to work on distracting you from your job." He paused and flashed a wolfish grin. "At least for the next sixty years or so."

All thoughts of work suddenly left my mind as I pictured just how many ways Max could distract me from my work. *Oh, yum.* I backed towards the door of the cottage, pausing at the doorway.

"How long did you say you needed to recover?"

Max lifted an eyebrow and leaned up on one arm. "What did you have in mind?"

I reached down and grabbed the hem of the T–shirt. "I was wondering if you wanted to work on 'Operation Distract Kit.' You know... get started on that sixty years or so." I lifted the T–shirt up and off my body and shivered at the feral gleam that shadowed his features. "If you're recovered enough, that is."

Max growled low in his chest and leaned towards me. "Why don't you come over here and let me show you just how recovered I am?"

I laughed and turned towards the door, stepping out on the porch. "Why don't you catch me?"

Racing across the lawn towards the house where I would live and love with Max, I threw back my head and laughed.

I needed to write a song about this.

Tomorrow.

A NOTE FROM ROBIN

Dear Reader—

Thanks so much for reading my book. I really hope you enjoyed Max and Kit's story. If you did, please tell your friends and drop me a line at robin@robincovington romance.com. I'd love to hear from you. And for the latest info on my books, sign up for my newsletter.

And if you are so inclined, please leave a review on Amazon, Barnes & Noble, iBooks, or Goodreads.

I love to explore the theme of fooling around and falling in love in my books and I adore a hero who falls hard. When I'm not writing sexy, sizzling romance, I collect tasty man candy pics, indulge in a little comic book geek love, and obsess over Dean Winchester. Don't send chocolate... send eye–candy!

There are so many great books out there and I'm grateful that you spent your money and time to read my book.

Xx,

Robin

Social Media Links:

Website: www.robincovingtonromance.com
Facebook Profile: http://on.fb.me/YSW9n3
Facebook Page: http://on.fb.me/1fCyWuQ
Twitter: @RobinCovington
Pinterest: http://bit.ly/1c1Tm5u
Newsletter sign up: http://eepurl.com/qjFcz

ACKNOWLEDGMENTS

When I was growing up in a small Virginia town, I was surrounded by stories. My family (bootleggers and preachers) could spin a tale that would have you laughing and crying in turn. For that heritage, I am so grateful and I hope that I am living up to the very high bar they set for me.

On this journey, I get to walk with the most amazing people and they hold me up, drag me along, or kick my butt when I need it.

Kimberly Kincaid and Avery Flynn—I don't know what I'd do without you.

Debra Hill Hodge, Tina Payne, and Karin Evans – for helping me with the beta read. You guys sizzle!

To my Sizzlemongers – I love you guys!!!

Sara Humphreys, Laura Kaye, Gina L. Maxwell, & Tracy Brogan—Thank you for inspiring me, making me laugh, and showing me how to do this.

Washington Romance Writers, Maryland Romance Writers, Contemporary Romance Writers, the Indie Club, and the Self–Publish loop writers—So much talent shared so generously. Thank you.

To the Main Man, Little Man, and Lulu—I love you all so much. Thank you for supporting me and helping me reach my dream.

SALVATION

BY

ROBIN COVINGTON

Letting Go Never Felt So Good

Burning Up the Sheets, LLC

23139 Laurel Way

Hollywood, MD 20636

Visit my website at www.robincovingtonromance.com.

Edited by Nicole Bailey at Proof Before You Publish, Inc.

Cover design by Sweet & Spicy Designs.

Formatting by Anessa Books

Manufactured in the United States of America

First Edition May 2015

 Created with Vellum

SALVATION (NASHVILLE NIGHTS, #2)

Carlisle Queen & Mateo Butler

Letting go never felt so good.

Carlisle Queen is dying and no one knows it.

Burying the pain of losing her friends and her professional swimming career in a terrorist attack, America's former sweetheart dulls her pain with drugs, pills and parties. The bomb left her with more than nightmares; shrapnel is lodged in her back and inching closer to her spinal cord. When the doctors tell her paralysis is inevitable, she decides to take her own life rather than face a lifetime in a wheelchair.

Mateo Butler isn't anyone's hero.

Reeling from the death of his little sister and his own cowardice, he spends his nights partying and his days ignoring the medical school acceptance letters and his parents' concerned phone calls. Just a couple of months from graduation, he's facing a future filled with shame and regret. The last thing he needs is to meet the woman who compels him to be a better man.

Can they save each other?

When Carlisle and Mateo meet, the chemistry between them is combustible. They play, party and hide their true selves until one night turns their lust into something more... something real. As secrets are revealed and walls collapse, what they were and what they might become doesn't matter as much as who they are together. When the choice comes down to life or death, can love be their salvation?

For Nancy Weeks.
Thank your for your help, your open heart, and your
friendship.

CARLISLE

I taste blood.

Smoke and acrid dust swirl around me and I cough and heave and struggle to orient myself. I reach out trying to find him, searching for Aaron. He was just here.

The blood is warm on my tongue, on my chin and it dribbles out each time I try to scream. I reach out, desperate. The pain in my body like a thousand sharp knives piercing my skin, digging in deeper than I could have thought was possible. I push through it, dragging my body across the paved walkway a few inches until I find him. Aaron.

I'd know him anywhere. My lover. My best friend. The strength of his body, the long lines of his swimmer's frame. My fingers touch him, sliding off the wet and warm liquid on his skin. The smoke clears and I scream.

I wrench up in bed, my throat raw from the screams I know I tried to make in my sleep. My body is covered in sweat, hurting from the pain of muscles tensed in terror and the very real pain I've endured for the past eighteen months.

I would love for this to just be a nightmare. A figment of

my overactive imagination, the product of eating too much spicy food or reading Stephen King novels before bed. Something I could change or explain away. That would be fucking sweet.

I throw off the covers, a shiver jolting through my body when the air-conditioned air hits my damp skin. I know better than to linger in bed when this happens or to let this dream roll around in my head for too long. I make a tentative attempt to stand and the pain shooting through my back and down my right leg reminds me with teeth-gritting clarity that the bombing wasn't a dream. I have the metallic shards embedded deep in my body to prove it—morbid souvenirs from a time that should have been the best day of my life.

I lower myself back to the bed, maneuvering through the exercises I learned in physical therapy to combat the morning pain that often followed in the wake of my nightmares. My body would go into full clench in my sleep and I'd stay like that for hours, sometimes waking with a sore jaw from having ground my teeth together for so long.

Two quick knocks on my door and my roommate sticks her head through the opening. Her long fall of jet-black hair is tied up in a loose ponytail and her porcelain skin makes Olivia Yee look like a Korean doll. She is tiny too, her barely five-feet frame looks Lilliputian when she stands next to my five-feet eight-inch length.

"Was it a bad one?" Livvy asks in the voice that takes everyone by surprise when they first hear it.

Truth be told, it was the voice that compelled me to interview her as a potential roommate in the first place. I didn't need someone to help me pay the rent; my endorsement money and the insurance payout after the bombing in the athlete's village guaranteed that I never had to work again but I didn't want to roll around in this place and listen to myself think. Months spent in my private room in a rehab facility had provided enough "me time" to make me sick of the voices in my head.

With her low, husky voice, I was expecting the real-time version of Jessica Rabbit to show up the day of the interview but I was in for a surprise when a woman strolled in dressed more like Amy on *The Big Bang Theory*. She informed me of five things within the first five minutes: 1) that she was a lesbian but I wasn't her type as she "really wasn't into gingers"; 2) she had a serious girlfriend who lived in New York City; 3) she didn't really follow sports but the medals were awesome; 4) she was very sorry I had been blown up; and 5) that she was a phone sex operator to make money to pay for school.

I immediately regretted that she wasn't into gingers and the fact that I loved the peen because I fell in love with her on the spot.

"I'm sorry. Did I disturb your time with Ron?" I ask about one of her regulars while slowly easing up into a sitting position. Livvy doesn't offer to help me, she knows I'll ask if I need it. I do take the bottle of water she hands to me as she sits down on the bed. "Was I loud?"

"Nope. Ron finished early and I heard something when I walked by."

I glance at the clock. Ten forty-five at night. I'm not going back to sleep anytime soon. I'd been so exhausted earlier that I'd crashed shortly after wolfing down takeout Chinese in front of the TV but now I'm fully awake and will be for hours. Lucky for me, between the city of Nashville and living next to Nashville University, I can always find something to do.

"You want to go out?" I scoot over to the side of the bed

and quickly add when she opens her mouth to make up some reason why she can't go out, "You have one more final in two days. Go out with me tonight." I pout. "You're leaving me soon to get regular booty in NYC. Go out with me now."

She shakes her head and raises her arms to the heavens as if asking for help. "Oh, the guilt trip is strong in this one!"

I ease up onto my feet and test out the level of cooperation my legs will give me tonight.

"What's your number tonight?" Livvy asks, watching me closely from her perch on the bed. "You've had a pretty good week, yeah?"

I nod and make my way around the end of my bed, pulling off my t-shirt and shorts as I go. Nudity doesn't bother either one of us. I've spent too much time in locker rooms with other swimmers to worry about somebody seeing what God gave me and Livvy doesn't have a modest bone in her body.

Truth be told, she's actually the only person besides the various doctors and my mother who has seen me completely naked since the bombing. My lower back is a mess of keloids from the injury and the many surgeries and I don't like people looking at them. It's one of the reasons why I stick to fast-hookups with guys and no sleepovers, my body gives away too many secrets. Invites too many unwanted questions.

"I'm at a six tonight." Zero is pain-free and I don't even remember what that feels like anymore. I walk into my bathroom and turn on the shower. "The episodes are increasing in frequency just like the doctor said they would."

The times when my mobility is limited is increasing, just as the doctors have all told me. I've seen them all, from every hospital in the U.S. and a few overseas and they all sing the final chorus in unison: the shrapnel will eventually cause paraplegia or kill me. They are all very sorry but there's nothing they can do for me.

There's one guy, a Dr. Bertrand from a hospital back east, who might be able to conduct an operation that can remove all the shrapnel from my body. I'd still have increasing mobility issues but the Grim Reaper would have to take a rain check. But the great Dr. B has looked at my records and turned me down for the surgery.

I step under the spray and Livvy comes in and sits down on the lid of the toilet to talk. We do this all the time and soon we won't be able to and the melancholy rains over my body with the water.

"I'm going to miss this when you move to NYC," I say, loud enough for her to hear me over the spray. "But I know Sarah is excited to finally have you with her."

"Two years apart was longer than we thought," she agrees, her tone chock full of the pain caused by living apart from your love. "I'm glad we made it. It was touch and go there for a while."

Sarah had moved to New York for her dream job in TV and Livvy still had two more years of school to finish and a scholarship she couldn't abandon. It had been tough on them and they'd had one six-week break-up that had been hard to watch.

"So, you didn't answer me," she changes the subject. "Are the episodes worse?"

I pause, using the shield of the shower curtain to gather my thoughts. I know what she's asking me and I don't want to get into it tonight. It will kill my buzz before I even have one. I shut off the shower and pull back the fabric to grab a towel. I don't look at her.

"They are more frequent and it takes me longer to

recover. The last one impacted my entire right leg and I couldn't walk for about an hour."

"Oh shit."

"Yep," I agree with her and move over to the mirror and wipe the condensation off with my towel. The face is still the same, the long hair a dark auburn because of the water weighing it down but I'm not the same. It's the eyes, the eyes give me away every time.

The medicine cabinet door squeaks a little when I swing it open to survey the contents inside. Deodorant, Neosporin, band aids, a tube of some eye cream I never use, sit alongside the double row of prescription pain killers, anti-inflammatories, and muscle relaxants. I use the toiletry items and shut the door, using the towel to get the excess water out of my hair.

"So, where do you want to go tonight?" Livvy's voice is behind me as I walk into my closet to find something to wear.

It's balls hot in Tennessee even when the sun goes down so I grab a white cotton sundress and pull it over my head. I wince a little bit at the pain that throbs in my right thigh because of the movement but I shake it off. My tits are small enough that I don't need a bra and I gave up underwear, unless I'm wearing formalwear or jeans, three years ago. Grabbing a pair of cowboy boots, I head back to the bathroom and find her gone. I swipe on my eyeliner, mascara and lip gloss and it's as good as it's gonna get tonight.

I head down the hall to Livvy's room and find her pulling up a pair of cutoff jean shorts. She has a t-shirt on that I gave her for Christmas which reads "Screw your 'lab safety'. I want superpowers". She'd rather kiss a man than put on makeup, so it looks like we're ready to go.

"I don't want to go to a club. Let's hit a party," I say as

we both head into the living room of the apartment. We're three blocks off campus and it's the weekend between the two finals weeks. There's no need to go into Nashville proper if we want to party and I know where I want to go. "Let's go to Mateo and Zane's house."

Livvy stops rummaging through her small bag and looks up at me, the delight and surprise on her face emphasizing her doll-like resemblance.

"So, you're finally going to go to one of their parties? They've only invited you every time this entire year."

"Mateo never invited me, it's always Zane," I answer, transferring ID, lip gloss, breath mints, condoms, cash, and keys to my small party purse. I find what I'm really looking for in the side pocket, tucked into a semi-hidden space. I pull out the small manila envelope and peel back the flap, peering inside at the dozen small capsules nestled inside. I shake one out on my palm and pop it in my mouth, using a bottle of water to wash it down.

"What'd you take?" Livvy asks as she closes up her purse. She doesn't judge and she never nags but she does insist on knowing what I put in my system since she's my wingman. She also made me promise not to take anything stronger than smoking a joint without being with her. Since we're always together, that's not usually an issue.

"Molly." I don't drink alcohol, a holdover from my competitive training days and it's a bitch to have a hangover when I'm dealing with my other aches and pains. Harder drugs let me forget the pain for a while and I rarely have too much of an aftereffect.

She nods, not judging me, and waits while I put the last of my items in my party bag. Livvy doesn't always approve of how I live my life and she definitely isn't on board with my future plans but she supports me and stands by to make sure I don't go too far. I think it was all those years of pushing every limit life threw at me—body, mind, competitors—but I'm wired to take it to the edge every single time. If it scares Livvy, she deserves an Oscar because I've never even seen a flicker of alarm in her brown eyes.

"So, any reason why you're throwing the 'boy wonders' a bone now?"

I don't know why she's playing coy. She knows why I've avoided going to Mateo Butler and Zane Wyatt's house all year. Hell, I've known it since the first time Mateo walked into my freshman Spanish class and announced he was the TA. Normally a girl who goes for long, lanky blondes, his six-feet two-inch, two hundred-pound, dark-haired package of lickable man would have knocked me on my ass if I hadn't already been sitting down. And then he locked his baby blues on mine and gave me his dimpled "I'm-going-to-fuck-you" smile and I knew I had to steer very clear of Mr. Butler.

T-R-O-U-B-L-E

From the jump, Mateo and I were the definition of chemistry. We'd circled each other for the entire year, through two semesters of Spanish and study groups. Because he intrigued me more than any other guy, I'd done my recon and watched him in class, around campus, and at the many clubs where Zane performed. At first glance, Mateo only took two things seriously: his beer, and his pussy.

But I watched him pretty closely and when he thought he wasn't on stage to perform for anybody, he was intense and pretty serious for a guy who didn't give a shit. I knew a faker when I saw one, I looked at one in the mirror every day.

I just shrug and answer, "Mateo Butler is nothing but trouble."

"Well, yeah, but that's usually the first required item on your list to give a guy the time of day."

"Oh no," I shake my head, slipping on my favorite pair of cowboys boots. Worn black leather with red flame accents on them, a gift from Aaron and the evidence of his love of my hair. "Mateo is the worst kind of trouble because under all that partying and screwing around is the worst kind of deception."

"I'm dying to hear this," Livvy says, not even trying to hide the sarcasm in her voice.

"Underneath all of it..." I pause for emphasis and while I'm camping it up, I couldn't be more serious, "...he's really a *nice* guy."

"Mother fucker," she says, her smile telling me that she gets me completely. "So, what are you going to do with this potential-boyfriend-material in manwhore's clothing?"

"I'm going to see if he's up for a little fun. No strings."

"And if he's not?"

I grab my purse and pull it across my body as I head to the door. "He's up for it."

"She's here."

I look up from my place on the couch in my room where I'm drinking a beer and considering the idea of letting Amy Tyne unzip my pants and blow me like she's been offering all night. I like Amy well enough and she gives great head even though she could watch the teeth more often, but I'm not into her tonight. We started out two years ago as casual fuck buddies at my fraternity house. If I wasn't hooking up with someone else and she wasn't with somebody, we'd meet up and exchange orgasms for an hour or three. She'd come and leave and not call. It was awesome.

About six months ago we hooked up in an alley outside a downtown club and ever since then she's been texting, calling, showing up at my house "just to hang out". Tonight she invited me to a graduation brunch with her family and every single alarm I have went off in my head.

"Who's here?" I ask, pushing Amy off my lap and placing my empty beer bottle on my beat up coffee table. I stand, hoping he means who I think he means.

"Ariel." Zane waggles his eyebrows and uses the nickname we have for the woman who has been on my radar since she stepped into freshman Spanish. He's the one who started calling her Ariel and I have to admit the stupid joke makes sense. She has red hair, emerald green eyes and was a world-class swimmer until a bunch of assholes with a bomb decided to blow the athlete's village to kingdom come. "She's here with her roommate."

"It only took her all year," I say, moving past my best friend to go find the object of my lust and late night fantasies and see if she is ready to act some of them out with me.

"What about me?" Amy says from my couch, her words slurring a bit with the beer she's been drinking all night. "What about brunch?"

"I don't like brunch. Sorry." I walk out, closing the door behind me.

"You love brunch," Zane says as we head down the stairs to the party on the first floor.

"Yeah, but I hate parents."

"Only because they all love you."

It's true. I think it's the manners my folks drilled into me since I was a kid that makes all the mama's picture me as the perfect guy for their daughter. Not me. I'm not the guy you should rely on to be there through the "for better or for worse" part of anything.

Our house is always full of people but tonight is nuts because everyone is celebrating the end of the school year. Another week of exams, then graduation and college life will be over and I'll have to join the ranks of those who pretend to be adults while figuring their shit out. I might be in medical school. I might not. I'm enrolled but I just can't visualize walking into the building and actually doing it. That was the plan before my sister died but now... it doesn't feel like my thing anymore. The whole thing stresses me out so I push it out of the way and scan the crowd for Carlisle Queen.

She's easy to spot. Tall, long-legged but it's her hair that grabs my attention. Not just red, it's at least four shades of auburn and shot through with gold. I want to grab it, wrap it around my fingers. A couple of times a curl brushed against my arm in study group and my dick got hard like I was some kid in high school. I'm not ashamed to admit it; this girl does it for me. Period.

"Whoa buddy. Aren't you even going to try and play it cool?" Zane asks, right on my heels.

I follow her progress through the house, hanging back when she stops in the kitchen, waiting as her best friend grabs a red solo cup and gets in line for the keg. She makes no move to get one for herself and I'm not surprised. Carlisle doesn't drink and the rumor is that she prefers recreational drugs when she parties. I think she's come to class stoned a couple of times but I can't prove it.

"I don't think the Ice Queen likes head games," I say using the nickname she earned from the student body within the first few weeks of fall semester after she quickly shut down all invitations from the sororities and refused every date offer she received. I've watched it all from a distance and learned from their mistakes. Just like the one my buddy Pete and his roommate Seth are making right now.

"Hey. You're Carlisle Queen, right?" Pete asks continuing with the introductions after she nods. "This is Seth."

"Hi," she says, making the briefest eye contact before she scans the room. In anticipation of our eyes meeting, my skin prickles with the low burn of awareness that always happens when I'm within five feet of her.

When her gaze slides to mine the surge of adrenaline burns off every bit of the beer buzz I am feeling. When a slight smile tilts up her full lips I get the signal she's sending loud and clear: she's here for me and the game we've been playing is finally on. My dick is hard as a spike but the knowledge of how this night is going to end calms me and I lean against the door frame to watch what happens.

"This is Olivia," Carlisle introduces her roommate to the guys when the other woman appears at her side with her beer.

The guys nod at the newcomer but Pete is all about Carlisle and he steps into her personal space. She looks like she might retreat but instead she extends her hand out and lightly pushes him back the step he just took and one more for good measure. I laugh and nod when Zane murmurs "taking him out like a boss" in my ear.

"We were thinking of going back to our place and partying some more. You want to go?" Pete asks, his words slurring a little. He was one of the first to arrive tonight and he's hammered back at least a beer every half-hour. I'll probably find him passed out in my bathtub in the morning. "We hear you like to party."

He means that he's heard she likes to party and fuck. Carlisle has a good time. Never with college guys. Locals and musicians only.

"You're friend can come too," Seth says, nodding towards Olivia. "The bed's big enough for four."

I give him guts for just throwing that out there but if Carlisle looked any less interested, she'd be catatonic.

"Sorry. I don't like penis," Olivia answers, taking a long sip from her beer while throwing an "are you kidding me" look at Carlisle.

Carlisle chuckles and shakes her head. "No thanks guys. I've already got my fun lined up for the night."

She flicks a glance in my direction and I know she's talking about me. My whole body relaxes and tenses up with desire all the same time. I move forward to rescue her from the "B-team" when Pete steps in it with his two big feet.

"Can I see your medals? Are they at your place?"

"Oh no," Zane mumbles beside me and we both shake or heads.

It's commonly known that Carlisle doesn't like talking about the games, her medals, or anything about that part of her life. She wants to put all that behind her and I don't blame her. Everything she accomplished is overshadowed by what happened in the end. She just wants to forget.

And the look she's giving Seth right now says that I need to intervene before she gets his blood all over my kitchen floor.

I step forward and insert myself in between them. I look down at her but I speak directly to him.

"Hey Seth, move on buddy."

"Mateo man, stop cock blocking me."

I smile at Carlisle and she smiles back, the flash of her emerald eyes wicked and I know tonight is going to be fun. As soon as I get rid of Seth.

"Seth, she's here to see me so you need to go and stop cock blocking *me*."

He mutters some random curses but leaves anyway. He grabs another beer that he doesn't need before he and his flunkie walk off in a huff.

"If you were at all intrigued by the threesome, I think I can accommodate you," I lean down and murmur in her ear.

"Maybe another night." She reaches up and grabs the

lapel of my shirt and drags me closer, whispering fiercely in my ear. "I think you'll be more than enough tonight, yes?"

"Fuck yeah I will." I reach down and wrap my arm around her waist, keeping her close to me. She is warm, smells like gardenias, and her breast is heavy against my side. I have no interest in delaying this one minute longer. "Come with me."

I take her out onto the deck. There are fewer people here and I find a quiet corner where I can touch her and talk to her without interruption.

"You want anything to drink?"

"Nope." She places her water bottle on the railing. "That's not my preferred buzz."

"I've heard that."

"You've been checking up on me."

"I hear things." I smile and lean down until our forehead touch heads and I can feel her breath on my face. She steps into me and I place my hands on her hips. We fit together perfectly and I can't help but imagine how good it will be when all these clothes are out of the way. "I thought you wouldn't be here tonight because *you* have a Spanish exam on Monday."

I want to kiss the corner of her mouth where her lips form a tease of a smile. "I'm going to ace the written exam." Her smile droops a little. "The verbal portion... it might get ugly."

That is an understatement. I have never heard anyone butcher the Spanish language like Carlisle Queen. Yes, I'm biased because I grew up in a bilingual household but she is terrible. I once thought you'd have to work hard to pronounce things as badly as she does. Not Carlisle. For her, it comes naturally.

I open up a little space in between us but I keep my

hands on her hips, even letting the right one dip to cup the sexy, round swell of her ass.

"I think you need to practice. Use me." When one auburn eyebrow lifts I smile at her dirty mind. "That's for later. Show me what you've got."

"*Me gustaría pedir del menu*," she says and I strain a muscle hiding my wince.

"Okay, so you want to order from a menu." I nod and when her eyes light up with hope, I shake it in the negative. "That was awful. Try again." I demonstrate the proper way to say it and then urge her to try again. "Don't pick some random sentence. Just talk to me. Tell me what you want me to know."

She considers me for a moment and then the wicked gleam is back and she steps even closer to me. "*Creo que eres caliente*".

She thinks I'm hot. Good to know.

"Better," I murmur. "Try another."

"*Quiero saber cómo te gusto.*"

She wants to know how I taste.

I groan as she leans in close, her lips hovering over mine a demonstration of what she wants. I want it too. I chase her mouth but she partially turns her face to the side while keeping her eyes locked on mine. Her hands are on my chest and I know she can feel the pounding in my chest at her next practice line.

"*Te quiero a ti dentro de mí.*"

Fuck. She wants me inside her.

"That's what I want too. To be inside you, to feel your long legs wrapped around my waist." I trace her lips with my tongue, capturing her own moan on the tip and savoring her surrender. "Come with me. I want to touch you and I'm not doing it with an audience."

I enter the door we just passed through and lead her down the back hallway, heading for the stairs and my bedroom. I make it halfway down the deserted hallway and I can't wait another minute. I push her against the wall, raising one arm to bracket us in. She tips her head to look up at me and I get lost for a moment in her eyes. Usually the color of emerald, they are nearly black with her arousal. Her gaze flickers down to my mouth and I grin.

"*Voy a besarte ahora,*" I whisper, the only warning of what I'm about to do. She understands me, her breath catching just before I angle my head and take her mouth.

The kiss is hard, bruising, devouring. Months of pent-up desire and want vented in the press of mouths, the lashing of wet tongues, the clink of teeth. She moans under me and clutches the fabric of my t-shirt, pulling me closer as I dive in deeper, dominating her with my craving invasion.

She pulls back to breath, her breasts rising and falling against my chest as she struggles to catch her breath. Her lips are already a deep rose and I want nothing more than to see them wrapped around my cock.

"*Quiero más.* She wants more and she just takes it.

I groan as one of her hands travels up my body and around my neck to pull me down to her. Her lips slant over mine and I slide my tongue into her wet heat. This time it is slower, softer but the gradual build of possession flips my switch and I slide my hands over her ass and angle her pelvis forward, grinding my erection against her sex.

It is intoxicating. The curves of her body inviting me to explore with my hands. I trace the sides of her torso, ending only when I can cup her breasts in my palms, thumbs rubbing the hard nipples pressing against the thin cotton of her dress.

Carlisle breaks off the kiss, throwing her head back to

bare her neck to me and I press my lips to her throat. I drop my right hand back to her ass, under her dress where I find bare flesh and nothing else.

"Fuck Carlisle," I slip my hand a little lower, into the hot cleft of her body. "You're pussy is so wet for me." I groan when she opens her legs wider and presses her ass back on my roving hand. "I want in there so bad."

"Where's your room?" She pants against my mouth, her tongue slipping in for a quick taste before retreating to let me answer.

"Upstairs."

"Too fucking far." She breaks off the kiss and looks over my shoulder, her eyes zeroing in on the empty laundry behind us. "In there."

She doesn't have to ask me twice and I spin us both, covering the three steps necessary to reach in the room and shut the door behind us. I shove her back against it and fumble for the lock in the dark, finally succeeding in sliding it home.

I find her mouth in the dark and lift her up my body, encouraging her to wrap her legs around my waist. She whimpers and I shudder in response to the carnal sound as I begin a slow thrust against her exposed sex. I lose myself in the kiss, her taste, the grind of our bodies together. When she wedges her hand between us and strokes my cock through my jeans, I lower her to the ground and release her from the kiss.

Eyes adjusted to the dark I can see her eyes, glassy with her desire and they way she never loses eye contact when her hands undo the button and ease the zipper down. Her fingers wrap around my aching cock and I shudder with the exquisite pleasure/pain of her touch.

"Fuck Carlisle. You get me so hard."

"You're so big," she murmurs, her voice a deeper, huskier version of her usual tone. I like the way she says my name. "Mateo, I want this in my mouth. Can I?"

"Oh my God, yes. Please."

I stare as my dream girl drops to her knees in front of me and drags my jeans down to the middle of my thighs. She leans forward and licks a long, wet line from the root to the crown and across the slit.

I fumble beside me for the light switch and I flip it up. The light bulbs are cheap so the light is watery and shadowy but it does the job. I can see everything.

"I want to watch you suck me off," I say, inhaling sharply when she leans back in and takes my erection deep into her mouth. Lips clamped tight around my flesh she bobs her head up and down, the rhythm slow but leading to that slow burn in my balls, in my belly. Her fingers dig into my ass cheeks, the light tug encouraging me to thrust into her wet heat. I raise my hands, my fingers sliding into the silky, red-gold strands as I watched her take all of me.

Fuck, you're beautiful," I gasp, overcome by lust when her eyes meet mine from across the distance of my body. I know this image will be branded on my brain until the day I die. "So fucking gorgeous."

The burn in my belly intensifies and I realize I don't want to come this way. I pull out of her mouth and lift her to her feet, kissing her and moaning at the taste of me in her mouth.

"I need to be inside you. I need to know if you feel as good as the dreams that leave me hard and aching. I want to see if you're as good as the fantasies I have running through my head as I come all over myself."

She leans up and kisses me hard and fierce, pulling back

to hand over a condom and a promise. "I'm better. I guarantee it."

Carlisle

I THOUGHT we'd be this hot together and I wasn't wrong.

I'm a shivering, aroused mess and watching Mateo roll on the condom is just about the sexiest thing I've ever seen. He's long and thick and I can still taste him on my tongue.

"I want you so much," Mateo huffs out on a breath before he takes my lips again in a kiss. His fingers, rough against the skin of my thighs lift my skirt as he backs me up until I am leaning against the washing machine. He strokes upward, his touch causing goosebumps all over my skin. There is no hesitation as he finds my folds and caresses my flesh. I arch into his hand, encouraging the digit he eases inside me on a slow pump. "You're soaking wet for me. I love that."

He leans over me, his mouth devouring the skin where my neck meets my shoulder. Soft nips and harder bites leaves me writhing on the hand still buried between my legs. It is so good and I can feel the blaze and tingle of a fantastic orgasm building with every thrust of the two fingers he's using to fuck me. He is hitting all the best spots, the slow guide he's using is designed to torture me if his grin is any indication.

"Teo, keep doing that. Please," I beg. I want what he's dying to give me and I'm not ashamed to ask for it.

His kisses travel lower on my body, his free hand pulling aside the top of my dress and exposing my swollen breasts to his attention. His lips closed around my right nipple and I come, hard and long, surprising us both. He groans but keeps tugging on it with his teeth extending the waves of pleasure through several amazing aftershocks.

"Look at me Carlisle," he demands, his voice sexy with his want. I lift my eyes to his and I'm lost in the dark navy they have transformed into with what I've done to him. "That was gorgeous. You are amazing when you come and I could watch you all night long."

He lifts me top of the washer and steps in between my legs, his erection pressed against the place where I want him the most. He leans forward and kisses me, soft and tender as he enters my body in one slow push. We exhale together, our breaths meshing with the slide of our tongues against each other. I loop my hands around his neck, weaving my fingers in his hair as I pull him deeper inside me.

The stretch at his invasion reminds me of why I love sex. The pleasure, the slow burn building into a molten heat that runs throughout my entire body. Fucking heaven on earth.

"Make me come again, Teo. Please."

He groans and his thrusts become harder, more forceful. I'm making lots of noise, unable to contain the moans and pants he drives out of me with every thrust of his hips. I can't help it. He is *that* good. It's a good thing that the party is so loud.

"Fuck Carlisle, you're so fucking tight." He loses his grip on me and overcorrects, jamming me against the washing machine, causing it to slide backwards and hit the wall with a loud thud. We both laugh as he keeps thrusting, enjoying the hell out of each other as he starts to come. "Oh my God."

His hands grab my ass cheeks and lift me higher against him, the angle now the perfect position for his rock hard body to rub against my clit and I'm so primed that I join him in the freefall. His mouth on my nipple, the hard suckling sends delicious aftershock shivers throughout my body and I arch into it, my hands twisting in his hair to keep him there as long as possible.

His thrusts slow down, evolving into shallow dips and swivel of his hips against mine. I grind back, enjoying the pleasure still sparking with each rub against my clit. I slide my hands down to his ass and squeeze, relishing the way the muscles become concave with every forward push.

"Sweet holy hell," I breathe out, my heart racing in my chest like a freight train. "I don't know if it's you or the Molly but I am tingling all over. Damn."

He releases my nipple, lifts his head, and grins down at me. "It's me, of course."

"Absolutely," I nod and pull him to me to for a long slow kiss of tongues and teeth and more laughter. "I don't think I've ever come while laughing before."

"Imagine what we can do if we make it to a bed," he murmurs in my ear. "Your place or mine?" When I don't answer right away he pulls back to look at my face. "What?"

This is where it gets awkward.

"Usually I'm a one and done girl."

His hand strokes lightly across my collarbone and dips down to circle and gently squeeze my nipple. I gasp and he takes another kiss. "No exceptions? I think I'm worth an exception." He adds a sexy, teasing growl to his plea. "I haven't a chance to taste your pussy. You can't go until I show you my mad oral skills. You won't regret it."

I slump against him with desire and try to hide my smile and hang on to my principles while he touches me. I want to stay, want to invite him back to my bed but I have my rules for a reason. For his protection more than mine.

I shove back and shake my head, adjusting my top to cover my breasts and give me some breathing space to make the hard call.

"I don't stay over. I don't do beds. I don't date," I shrug at his raised eyebrow, smiling to ease the sting. "Those are my rules."

Mateo watches as I ease out of his arms, adjusting my dress. I'm having trouble meeting his gaze, afraid that he'll see the desire to make an exception on my face. This is why I waited until he was almost gone; I knew I'd want to break my rules for Mateo. I have a crush. There is no point in denying it. But it is also the main reason I need to leave.

"Well, when you put it that way, you're almost challenging me to get you to break them," He says, leaning against the washer with his arms crossed over his broad chest.

His dark hair is mussed, his jeans pulled up but unfastened so I can still see the top of his cock and the dark curls at its base. My mouth actually waters and I hesitate, regretting that I'd waited all year to sample his goodies and now I was just walking away.

I lean down and grab the purse that fell to the ground when we burst into the room.

"Sorry, I'm very firm on 'no beds, no sleepovers, no dates' rule.

"I should warn you that I am a very creative guy when I want to be." He grins even wider and I realize that I might have bitten off more than I can chew with him. "I'm also very creative."

"*Darle su mejor tiro mateo*," I say, daring him to give it his best effort.

And then I leave, wondering what I've gotten myself into with Mateo Butler.

THREE
CARLISLE

Going to see Dr. Shrieve once a month is a compromise with my parents.

I left Texas and came to Nashville to go to college because I couldn't stay with April and John Queen one minute longer without committing a crime that would have gotten me the death penalty in the Lone Star state. They are good people, the best parents, but they were smothering me.

I can only imagine how terrifying it must have been for them to see me hurt in the bombing. I remember times in the hospital when I woke in the middle of the night to find my mother crying in the chair next to my bed.

So I cannot blame them for being protective.

But after the initial shock, the agony of the surgeries and physical therapy, they refused to make the turn and see me as a grown woman. They hovered, they worried, they were on my ass like a tailgater on the freeway and I couldn't take it anymore.

I applied to and enrolled in Nashville University

against their protest but agreed to continue to see a therapist to deal with my PTSD and other issues.

It was an easy compromise to get away and live my life on my own terms.

Dr. Shrieve is in her mid-thirties, married with no children but two very spoiled Chesapeake Bay Retrievers. She is plain-speaking and encourages me to be the same. I like her. If she wasn't my doctor, we'd be friends.

"So, are you dating?" she asks, looking down at her notebook with a slight smile tugging at her lips. She asks me this every time. The answer is always the same.

"I don't date. You know this," I answer as I snag another Twizzler from the pack on the table. "I did it with the TA in my Spanish class. In his laundry room. It was awesome."

She raises her eyebrows, smiling as she looks at me over the edge of the notebook. "I thought you weren't going to do that."

"I wasn't but it's the end of the school year and he's graduating."

"So, he's another emotionally and logistically unavailable man you allow yourself to be with in an environment that you control from initiation to completion."

"Wow. Are you charging by the big word today?" I shift on the couch, adjusting my position until the low throb in my back reduces from "give me a Percocet" to "give me a stiff shot of whiskey". "We've talked about this. I love sex. I want to have an active sex life but I don't want to get involved with anyone. I can't."

"I just think you might be passing on the opportunity to have a real connection with someone. True intimacy is not found in the alley behind a bar or in a guy's laundry room. Don't you want that kind of connection?"

"I've had that, Doc. I had it and I watched him die right

in front of me with his blood and brains all over my hands." I swallow hard, the memories I rarely indulge in making it difficult to speak. "I'm not doing that again."

"You're not even allowing yourself the chance to do it again." She's stubborn this one. Determined for me to get that happily-ever-after she lives in the suburbs. "You've mentioned this TA so many times over the past year. I just wonder if there is something there to pursue."

I take a bite of the candy and consider Mateo. He's hot, intense, a smartass. If I was the old Carlisle, he'd be a guy I'd want in my bed, on dates, taking home to meet April and John. The new Carlisle needs to keep it all physical and as far away from entanglement as possible. I have nothing else to offer. "It's not a good idea. It's not fair to do that to somebody."

"So, you're still planning on taking your own life." It isn't really a question. I worried at first that she'd tell my parents or try to get me locked up but she explained that there's a difference between suicidal ideation due to mental illness and planned suicide. She's not on board with assisted suicide for herself but her east-coast-educated-yuppie upbringing won't allow her to trample on my right to choose.

We've been over and over this countless times and I throw my hands up in the air in a "really" gesture.

"Look, I wouldn't be much of a shrink if I didn't ask you about it at least every other session." She reaches over and steals a candy from my bag. "I know you're not crazy and you're not depressed. But there aren't many young women your age who plan to end their life."

"The doctors all say that I have a forty percent chance of the shrapnel doing it for me. If that is how I go, my pill stash will go to waste. I'll leave it to you in my will if you want."

"You're avoiding my point about the other sixty percent."

"I don't want to be in a wheelchair for the rest of my life." I start out looking her in the eye and then I can't anymore. She tries to hide it but I can see the pity in her gaze. It's the same look I get from every reporter, every doctor, every person I've met since the bombing. "I just don't want to live that way."

"Lots of people live with disabilities."

"And they are much better people than I am." I can't control the anger in my voice. I am really tired of explaining this again.

"I'm not saying you're a bad person. I just feel like I should continue to make sure you're aware of the options for you. Paralysis is not the end of your life. You can even participate in competitive athletics again. The Paralympics—"

I stand, biting back the wince in my right leg as I gather up my things. "I've told you at least eight million fucking times. All of that... swimming... it's behind me. You say I'm not crazy and it's because I left my past in the past and I made peace about my future. I live in the here and now more than most people, milking enjoyment out of every fucking minute."

"I didn't mean to make you angry," she says, putting her pen and notebook down on the table in front of her. "You're so young and you've got your whole life ahead of you."

"And you need to accept the fact that my 'whole life' is just going to be a lot shorter than expected." I look at her and hope she'll hear me. "I have and I'm okay with it. Really."

She stares me down and I can see the wheels in her head spinning in every possible direction. I know she doesn't really understand. How could she? Nobody can unless they've lived it and I sincerely hope that no one ever has to go through what I did. Never again.

But those assholes took more than my health, more than my career and passion, more than the man I loved. They took my control, took away my ability to form my own future. They took away my hope that each day can get better... because mine has never gotten better. It's lke I'm stuck in that moment when I knew Aaron was gone and I was left behind to bear the pain of our loss all by myself.

The timer goes off on her phone, signaling the end of our session and I let out a sigh of relief. I bend over to get my purse off the floor and I gasp at the sharp pain in my leg. I test out the sensation, tapping my foot on the floor and measuring my level of control. It hurts but I don't feel the tingle of numbness in my leg that signals another episode of limited mobility.

"You okay?" Dr. Shrieve asks, reaching out a hand that she quickly pulls back. She knows I'll ask for help if I need it.

"Nothing a little smoke break with MaryJane won't cure," I joke, biting back a laugh when her eyebrows shoot up at the mention of my recreational drug habit. She's lectured me about it before, many times, and I can't resist the chance to yank her chain.

"You didn't smoke before you came here? I'm honored." The level of sarcasm dripping from every word is epic.

"What? How helpful would it be for me to come to my therapy session high as a kite?" I tease, both of us recalling the time I showed up loaded on a dose of Molly. The good doctor was not amused and sent me home in a cab and a bill for the full session.

"I'll see you in a month," she says and points at the door. She tries to remain stern but I see her smile as I open the door that leads directly into the hallway of the office building and bypasses the waiting area of her office. It'd a privacy thing. Nobody wants to parade their crazy in front of a bunch of strangers.

I walk to the elevator and press the button for lobby, leaning on the wall a little bit as my back twinges. Once I get to campus, I'll find Livvy, go home and light up my little stash OG Kush marijuana I bought from a contact in California. It was helpful with the pain and the anxiety I experienced when my legs stopped working, however temporary.

I love this city and a few minutes later I am enjoying the ride as the bus takes me through downtown Nashville, stopping often to discharge or accept new passengers. I peer out of the window, soaking up the sights as we pass Music Row. Numerous musicians walk down the sidewalk, guitar cases slung over their shoulders. I wonder if they have melodies and words swirling around in their heads as they make their way home or to work or the next gig. Can they turn it off or does it keep them up at night until they get it all down on paper? I am a music junkie and those kinds of questions fascinate me. It was one of the reasons I chose to move to Nashville.

Swimming was like that for me. As I got closer to competition, I would plan the race in my head, committing the strategy and the strengths and weaknesses of my opponents in the database in my brain. I would practice the strokes in and out of the pool, committing the movement to muscle memory. The constant soundtrack in *my* head was the sound of the water rushing past my ears and my elevated, ecstatic heartbeat.

I miss that music. I miss the cool water on my skin, the weightless power of my body in it, the strength I exerted as I carved my path through it. I never really heard the crowds yelling or my coach screaming. Just the damn water music, my theme song.

It's why I've never been in a pool since the attack. I haven't heard the music since that day. The moment when the bomb went off it turned my paradise into a nightmare.

The bus rumbles to a stop on campus near the science building where Livvy is taking her final exam and I exit, steadying myself against the doorframe when my right foot hits the sidewalk and I lose balance.

"You okay, miss?" the driver asks, the beads on the end of her cornrow braids clinking together as she gets up to lend me a hand. Her touch is light, tentative and I give her a smile as I push away and stand on my own.

"I'm fine. A touch of vertigo," I answer as she returns to her seat. "Thanks."

I walk as far as I can, each step increasing the lack of sensation and control over my leg. My heart is hammering in my chest, sweat forming on my back and under my arms as I fight off the panic attack I can feel building in my gut. I don't know what's worse, the actual loss of mobility or the fear that this might be the time it doesn't come back.

I make it to the common area outside of Livvy's building and grab onto the back of a bench, lurching around it until I'm in position to sit down. I'm winded and my hands are shaking as I rub over my leg, cursing the pins and needles crawling over my skin. I flex my right leg, relieved to see that it obeys my command and lifts a few inches off the ground. The pain when I do this is sharp but I don't care about it.

It's the lack of feeling, pain or otherwise, that I fear. The pain is a old friend.

I pull my phone out of my purse and check the time. Another hour until Livvy is done and there is no way I can pull her out of a final. I'll sit here and wait, grateful that the weather is fine and the sun is warm on my shoulders. I shift on the hard bench, adjusting my position to ease the pain in my back, gasping when it jabs me deep. I almost double over with it, my hand in a white knuckle grip on the arm of the bench.

"Carlisle?"

A large body blocks the sun and I shiver with the loss of warmth and the aftershock as the wave of pain subsides. I gulp in air, slowing down my pants as I fight to gain control of the pain like they taught me in pain management class. I open my eyes, noting the sticky wetness of tears on my lashes, and find Mateo looking down at me.

His expression immediately morphs into concern and he drops to one knee beside me. He reaches out and touches my hand and I grab it, holding on as if he can keep the ground under my feet.

"What do you need?" he asks and I almost cry at the relief I feel knowing he is here.

"My leg." I motion to the traitorous limb and wince as another wave of pain hits me. "It hurts. I need to get home but I can't walk."

"Do you need an ambulance?"

"No."

He stares at me for a few seconds before squeezing my hand. "Can you wait here while I get my car? I'll take you home."

"I can wait."

"I'll be right back." He leans in and brushes a soft kiss against my forehead before he goes and I whimper at the loss of the comfort his presence brought me for those few seconds. I sit on the bench, practicing my yoga breathing and cursing the fact I usually skipped yoga in favor of watching *Saved by the Bell* episodes with Livvy. Fuck you Zack Morris.

A blue car pulls up to the curb and Mateo hops out, slamming his door and then running over to me.

"How do you want to do this? I can carry you but I don't want to hurt you." I look up at him, horrified by the suggestion and it must be so apparent that he chuckles a little. "Okay, I won't carry you." He kneels down by me once again. "You're tall so you might be able to link your arm around my neck and I can support you that way. It will look like I'm copping a feel but I think my reputation can take the hit."

Even through the pain, he makes me smile and I nod at his suggestion. "Let's try that."

Mateo grabs my right arm and loops it over his shoulders, his left arm tight around my waist and we slowly rise to a standing position. With him supporting me, I don't have to put any pressure on my right leg and the pain subsides a little.

"Is this okay?"

"Yeah, thank you."

"I would say my pleasure but it will be all yours in a few seconds." We make slow progress across the quad and he nods towards his car. "That's a fully restored 1964 Chevy Impala with a convertible top and I feel like I should warn you that you might have the urge to fall in love with me once you ride in her."

I laugh, rolling my eyes at his ridiculous banter. "I think I can resist."

"I wouldn't rush to judgment." He leans over and opens the passenger door, hooking my legs behind the knees and lowering me into the seat with the grace of a groom carrying his bride over the threshold. I flail a little at being man-handled but he looks at me and shrugs. "It sits low to the ground and I figured it would put too much strain on your leg to get in the regular way."

He shuts my door before I can reply and sprints around to his side and slides behind the wheel. I buckle my seatbelt as he starts up the engine and I can't help the "ohhh" that escapes my mouth when the huge engine purrs and vibrates the entire car like one of those massage chairs at the mall. The leather is supple and hugs every part of me and the chrome shines so much I can see my reflection in it.

"I love this car," I say as he pulls out into traffic. His driving is so smooth and the car rides like a boat, not one jolt causes me extra pain.

He glances over at me and grins. "I told you."

"I said I was in love with the car, not you."

"It's only a matter of time." He grins and pulls the car over and to a stop. I look out the window and realize we are at my apartment. I look back at him and he grins. "The ride was free but the distraction from the pain will cost you."

I snicker as he gets out of the car and heads over to my side. I undo my seatbelt and open my door but he stops me before I can get out.

"Are you up to it?"

"I'm not sure."

"Then that is a no. You want to do it the same as before but in reverse?" he asks, kneeling down to get to the right level. "Let's try it."

I loop my arms around his neck and he puts an arm under both of my knees and gently wedges the other behind my back. He lifts and a lightning strike of pain runs down my leg and I gasp. He stops immediately, his lips against the skin of my temple as he murmurs soothing noises and apologies.

"Jesus. I'm sorry." He adjusts his position around me, his dark head bent and his nose gliding softly against my jaw. I remember he did the same thing after we had sex. A sweet touch after all the sizzling heat. I want to burrow deeper into his embrace, lean on his strength for a little while longer.

Which means I need to get away from him as soon as possible. I have no business starting anything with this nice guy in party boy clothing. If I keep this up, I might want to keep him.

"I think I'm good," I say and when he looks at me, I nod to give him the go-ahead. "I'm on the second floor. There's an elevator."

"You got it." He lifts me slowly, watching my face closely to gauge my pain level. Once he is fully upright he kicks the door shut with his foot and starts the short trip to my place. There's no one around so the elevator comes quickly and with just a few moments of wincing pain, we are at my door and he's unlocking it and carrying me inside.

"Where do you want to be? Couch?"

"Yep." I wave at the longer chaise end of our sectional. "Over there. I can put my feet up."

He lowers me to the couch and we both sigh with relief. I lie back on the cushions and close my eyes. Thank God I'm home.

"Mateo, can you get my meds?" I ask, popping one eye

open to find him looking down at me with a worried expression on his face. "What?"

"Are you sure you don't want to go to the doctor?"

"No. I'm used to this now. It's a result of my injury and all the surgeries. I'll be fine in a little while."

He stares at me for a minute, probably deciding whether he believes me or not. Decision made he claps his hands together. "Okay where are your meds?"

"First room on the right. Right hand side table, top drawer."

He heads off in the direction of my bedroom and I hear the slide of the drawer as it opens. A pause and then the question I know is coming.

"Carlisle, there's only a few baggies of pot in here."

"There's one with a couple of rolled joints. That's the one I need."

I hear the drawer slide shut and his footsteps as he returns to me, my bag of joints in his hand.

"You don't have a prescription you can take?" he asks, handing over the bag when I waggle my fingers at him.

"I do but they knock me out. I don't want to sleep, I just want the pain to go away." I fish a lighter out of the purse lying beside me and light up, patiently coaxing the smoke that will make the bad man go away. I get it going and inhale deeply, holding it in until I have to breathe. I offer it to Mateo. "You want some?"

"Not my thing but thanks." He pauses, looking around my living room and I expect his next comment to be "nice place" or something like that but it isn't. "You get high a lot, yeah?"

"I wouldn't say a lot but probably more than the average. The pot helps me with the pain and the other... " I shrug. "... I just like it."

I take another drag and wait him out. He's got something he wants to ask and I'd bet my favorite pair of Chuck's that it's going to be about my medals.

"Is the pain bad?"

I am wrong. Color me surprised. Pleasantly.

"I have a low throb or aches all the time. The scar tissue from the surgeries are the worst but the nerve pain is the one that fucking brings me to my knees."

"That sucks."

"It really does." I settle back against the cushions and close my eyes, starting to feel the effects of the drug on my system. "I do not recommend getting blown up."

"I'll keep that in mind." Laughing, he walks over to me and presses another one of those damn soft kisses to my forehead. I keep my eyes shut and I am all about the other senses.

He smells awesome, a combination of cologne and something delicious, and I lean into it. I remember every kiss, every touch, every thrust of that night and with the MaryJane relaxing me, my body is responding in all the best ways to his proximity. He pulls away and I almost whimper at the loss of sensation but it's for the best. I can't get involved with anyone, it's my number one rule.

"Well, I've got to go out to my cousin's house and help him with some drywall. You gonna be okay?" he asks.

I open my eyes, blinking up at him in the bright sunlight spilling into the room. I'm starting to feel good with the pain subsiding to low throb. "I'm good. Thanks so much for helping me out."

"You're welcome." He hesitates and then reaches down and grabs my phone off the couch beside me. He thumbs it on and starts typing.

I laugh and reach for my phone; he zigs when I zag and I can't get it. "What are you doing?"

"I'm programming my number in your phone. Call me if you need anything. I'm your backup wingman when Livvy isn't around." He hands my phone back to me with a sexy grin and wink of those fucking gorgeous baby blues.

If I could get my hands on him right now, I'd bite and lick him all over. So, it's probably a good thing that I can't off this couch.

"Hey, thanks. Again."

He starts backing up to the door. "Call me. We can grab something to eat."

I shake my head, unable to stop smiling. I blame it entirely on the pot. "That sounds too much like a date."

"Labels. You are so hung up on labels." He smiles and steps through the door. "Call me."

"I won't."

But I'm starting to wish I could.

FOUR

MATEO

"Hey Mateo, did you get a contact high or something?" Max asks.

I jolt out of my thoughts to find my cousin and Zane staring at me from across the bedroom where we are hanging and taping drywall. This old farmhouse belonged to my grandparents before my grandma died and Max bought it from him. He lives here with his fiancée, Kit Landry, a bona fide country music star who fights for the top spots with Taylor and Miranda. They are planning to have their wedding in this house, so I've been recruited to help out. He pays in beer and pizza and front row seats at her shows, so it's a pretty even trade.

But today I'm not pulling my weight. I am cold busted. I drifted off, completely immersed in the constant replay of what happened today with Carlisle.

"Sorry, I just keep thinking about today." I place the taping knife in the mud pan and place it on the makeshift table holding the bulk of our materials and wipe my hands on my jeans. I grab a Gatorade from the cooler and toss one to each them. I told them about what happened the minute I arrived. "She's just... "

I don't know how to describe Carlisle Queen. The woman was on the Wheaties box so we all think we know her. And she was the center of the coverage that followed the bombing. She wasn't the only athlete who survived the bombing but her story was always the lead. A few hours after she stepped off the podium with her twelfth gold medal, she was in a hospital in Germany fighting for her life and grieving the loss of her friends and lover.

Aaron Daniels and Carlisle were America's sweethearts. Two kids who'd trained together for years at the same facility in Baltimore, they'd fallen in love in the public eye and everyone ate it up. I wasn't the only guy who thought Aaron was the luckiest fucker in the world. And now I had a small idea of just lucky he'd been and I wanted more than just one taste.

I sigh. "She's got me by the fucking balls, Max."

"The sex was *that* good?" He asks, lowering his bulky frame down to the floor. He's a big guy, we grow them big in the Butler family and his size helps with his job as a fire-fighter. We grew up together and he knows me as well as Zane does. "I know how much sex you've had, so I'm throwing the bullshit flag."

"He's blinded by the glitter of 'new pussy'," Zane adds from his perch on top of a big container or paint. "Blown out of normal proportions by the fact that he's had a crush on her since the nanosecond she walked into his class. It's kinda cute."

I flip them both the bird because nothing expresses my reaction to their comments any better than that. The fact that they aren't entirely wrong keeps me from hauling them outside into the yard and kicking their asses.

"Yes, the sex *was* that good but she's fun. Smart. She keeps me at arm's length, even when I'm helping her. There's this wall up. You can see through it and you can even touch her but it keeps you from getting too close." I have no idea if that makes any sense to them but it does to me.

"So, it's the thrill of the chase," Zane comments, nodding his head in understanding. "I get why she keeps reeling you in. It's not like you to go back for seconds so soon, but I get that."

I shake my head. "It's not just that. I can't put my finger on it."

"It sounds to me like she's got some pretty serious physical concerns going on. You've always had a bit of hero complex, Mateo. Maybe your bat signal senses a damsel in distress?" Max asks.

My first instinct is to deny it but he's right. I've always been the guy who is there when you need help. The guy with the truck to move your shit out of ex's apartment. The guy who will bail you out of jail. The guy who will show up when you call.

I like being that guy. It's hard-wired into my DNA. But when it counted, I failed. Really fucked it all up and let my sister, Mari, and my family down and suddenly I'm not really sure who I am anymore. It doesn't take Dr. Phil to figure out that that I've been dialing it in since then.

Carlisle has her own rules and so do I. They aren't that different: avoid anything where someone can start to depend on you. But Carlisle intrigues me enough to want to dip into the shallow end of that pool again.

"We all know I'm not the guy to rely on," I say.

"Jesus Mateo. Mari would kick your ass if she knew you

were' still beating yourself up about it," Max says, his expression equal parts anger and frustration.

"She'd remove his balls if she saw how he's ignoring the medical school stuff that is piling up at our house," Zane adds. I glare at him for outing my procrastination to Max because we both know that when my mom pumps him for info, Max will have to spill. Nobody crosses my mother or lies to her when she asks a question. Carmela Montez Butler takes no shit from anyone, ever.

"Look, that dream of medical school was one I had with Mari. She's gone and I just don't know if it was ever mine."

That is the truth. I don't remember who thought of opening a practice together, helping people one-on-one but I'm not sure it was me. And now... I don't know what the fuck I want or if I have what it takes to do a good job.

"Uh huh. It has *nothing* to do with the fact that you're punishing yourself. Paying some stupid penance." Max doesn't even try to hide his disbelief. "Just get your shit together and go. The only thing Mari wouldn't forgive you throwing away this opportunity."

I'm done with the conversation. My goal is to put off thinking about any of this shit until the day classes begin in a few weeks. If I find myself standing in front of dead guy in Gross Anatomy, then I'll know what I'm going to do.

"Zane are you still playing at that music festival thing in a couple of days?"

If they are surprised by abrupt change in conversation, the only indication is the look that passes between them that I ignore.

"Yeah, why? You coming?"

"Can you get me a spot on the sound stage? Something out of the crowd?"

His face scrunches up into a "what the fuck" face.

"Yeah. I can work it out." And then the light bulb goes on and he brushes his long hair out of his face and grins. "You want to treat Carlisle to a little VIP treatment."

I snort and roll my eyes. "She had dinner at the White House, I'm thinking that meeting you backstage is not going to be the highlight of her life." I pull my phone out of pocket. "After today, I'm not sure she can handle standing in huge crowds for all that time."

He nods. "You get her to go and I'll make sure she is well-protected from the 'little people'."

I am able to flip him and hit her number on my phone at the same time. It's a gift.

"You got her number?" Max asks. "I thought she shot you down."

"I took it off the TA list for our class."

"Nice abuse of authority. I like it," Zane says. Of course he does. If there is a rule within five miles, he's breaking it.

The phone rings and I walk out on the balcony just off the bedroom. She picks up on the third ring, laughing with whoever is with her in the background.

"Hello," her voice gets more distant for a second and I envision her checking the caller ID. "Oh wingman. What are you doing? I thought we covered this calling thing this morning."

I smile. Just her voice gets me going and I have to shift to adjust my shorts getting tighter. I need to tread carefully with this woman.

"I was wondering if you want to go see Zane perform the day after tomorrow. Your exam will be done, you will have failed your verbal portion because of your shitty accent and you will need something to distract your from your defeat."

"You suck and you need to stop jinxing me," she laughs.

"You didn't answer my question." I like that I have to chase her a little bit. It's nice for a change.

She sighs. "I told you I don't date."

"And I wasn't asking. The tickets are free and I have an extra. I'm not picking you up, you can meet me there." I pretend to think about her other rules and drag the moment out a bit longer. I can hear her breathing on the other end of the phone; it's a little elevated and I would bet my car that her heart is pounding just like mine. We just do this to each other. "There will be no bed, no sleepover but if you're up for it, I will fuck you."

The sharp inhale from Carlisle ends on a gasp and I know I've got her. It might be the last time we hook up, this thing between us has to burn out sometime, but we'll go out with a bang.

"I don't know how I'm supposed to pass that up," she says, breaking the silence that stretched out a little too long for my comfort. "What time should I meet you?"

"Eight o-clock?"

"Fine. I'll be the one with the cowboy boots and the very low expectations."

I huff out a laugh and hope I can wait to see her. This girl fucking kills me.

"Well, then the only way I can go is up."

"*Marco?*"

I send the text and look at my phone, waiting for a reply. I'm at the show, held on an outdoor stage in a huge field and there are about twelve gazillion people here. It's dusk, almost dark and I can't tell one writhing, dancing body from another. I am never going to find Mateo in this crowd without a little help.

My phone buzzes in my hand and I look at the screen, so grateful it is backlit and I can see it.

"*Polo*" pops up in the familiar blue text box and I don't have to wait for the direction I need. "*To the left of the sound booth. Back of the audience.*"

I lift my head and scan the area, finding the large sound booth elevated on a small stage and flanked by large light stands. It is on the edge of the crowd of screaming fans listening to a local band play their hearts out. I press forward, circumventing the tight cluster of people and weaving my way around the edges. I feel good tonight, my back is strong but I don't want to get crushed by people having a good time.

"*Marco?*" pops up on my screen and I stop to return the text. "*Polo. Near the t-shirt booth.*"

"*Coming to you. Don't move.*"

I do as I'm told and wait by the stand, watching as people fork over their money for stuff with the music festival logo on the front and a list of all the performers on the back. One guy working behind the counter gives me a curious look but is quickly distracted by the line of people in front of him.

I'm about to send another text when two hands cover my eyes and a rough voice against my ear says, "Marco."

I laugh and turn to face Mateo before answering, "Polo."

He looks down at me, his blue eyes scanning my face and down my body in one hot glance. I look right back and what I see makes my body pulse with the memory of how good it was between us and how much I want to do it again. He's so hot, dressed simply in jeans with a black t-shirt, a ball cap turned backwards on his head. He hasn't shaved today and a dark shadow of hair that I want to reach out and touch covers his jaw.

His eyes spark with the recognition of what I'm thinking, his grin is wide as he leans back in for a quick kiss on my lips and another murmur against my ear. "I've got a spot for us on the sound stage out of the way of the crowd. Zane hooked us up."

I grab his arm, needing to get something out of the way. "Hey."

"Yeah?"

"Thanks again for the other day. It's... " I look around the crowd and consider my words as they stick to the roof of my mouth. "I don't like asking for help." I stumble again. "You were great."

He waves me off. "I get it. What you have to deal with, it sucks. I'm just glad I was there to help out."

"Me too." And I am. "Thanks again."

"Anytime. I'm your wingman, remember?"

His grin is contagious and I nod and take the hand he extends out to me, melting against him when he tugs me close. Mateo parts the crowd, shielding me with his body as we make our way to the sound stage. Once we get there, the security guard at the bottom of the steps nods to Mateo and opens the gate for us to walk up. He leads me to a spot just behind the large table covered with sound equipment where we can lean against the railing and watch the show.

Mateo positions us so that I can rest my weight on the metal rail and moves up behind me, close but not touching as he rests his arms on the railing next to mine. In this position he is all around me, his heat and his scent completely covering me. I like it. I like the sensation that his body has captured mine, that he has no qualm in indulging in the maleness of asserting his dominance and possession in this crowd of people. Anyone who looks at us will know that we've fucked and that we will be doing it again... very soon.

I like it more than I want to but I won't let that deter me from enjoying tonight.

"Is this okay?" he asks, his breath warm on the skin on my neck and I shiver with the goose bumps it raises on my body. He notices my reaction and his groan is low and deep in my ear, moving his hands to link with mine as he leans forward enough to press his chest to my back, his groin into my ass. "Is *this* okay?"

I nod, letting my head fall back to cradle against him and I watch the show. I am not in any hurry to rush to where I know this will end. This is exciting, sexy. I'd forgotten all about this part of the seduction. My time with Aaron seemed so long ago and since him... well, you didn't get much seduction with quick one-offs against a wall or bent over a couch.

I turn my head, brushing my lips along his jaw to ask, "When does Zane go on?"

"After this band."

"Good. I love his stuff. I think I've been to most of his local shows in the last six months."

"Stalker," he teases and pulls away to grab his phone out of his pocket. He thumbs it on and pulls up the camera app. "Let's send him a picture. He was excited when he heard you were coming."

I lean in closer to make sure we get both of our faces in the shot and after a couple of pics that I hope never see the light of day, we get a good one and Mateo leans back against me, circling me in his arms as he types out a quick text and sends the photo.

"So, what did you do today now that classes are officially over?" he asks, brushing his mouth against my ear.

"I helped Livvy pack and mail boxes to New York."

"Ouch. That's going to be rough when she moves, yeah? You guys are really close."

I nod. "Today kind of sucked for both of us. She's excited to finally be with Sarah and I'm happy for her, but I'm going to miss her. She's the first real friend I've had since everything happened."

He's quiet for a few moments and I wonder if he's going to ask me questions about the bombing, about Aaron. Most people do but I realize that he's not drumming up the courage to ask, he's waiting to see if I'm ready to share. I'm not but I'm grateful for his patience.

"I worked out with my trainer. We did weights today and I'm going to feel it in my arms and legs tomorrow," I say.

"That's good. Back injuries require lots of strength training, core work and overall body. Do you swim as part of your routine? The low-impact would be great for you."

"I don't swim anymore." I manage to keep the edge of panic and anger out of my tone but my words still come out like a whip and I feel him tense up at my reaction.

"Ever?"

"No." And I clamp my lips together, unwilling to say more and trying to control the tremor that starts whenever I talk about it.

His phone vibrates in his hand and we both look down. Zane has responded and Mateo quickly presses the screen, both of us relieved to move on from the awkwardness that was creeping into our night.

Zane's sent a selfie, the stage with the current performers in the background of the picture. "*Ariel! Glad you could make it even if you have to hang out with that loser. I'll come find you after the show and rescue you.*"

"He calls me Ariel?" I ask.

Mateo glances at me, his expression a little bit confused. "Yeah. You know the whole red hair and mermaid thing. The swimming... " I keep my expression flat and his words drift off when I don't respond. He's worried about my taking offense. I let the silence drag out a little bit longer before I let him off the hook and smile. His obvious relief makes me laugh out loud.

"Newsflash braintrust, you two aren't the first to think that up." I gesture towards the phone. "Hand it over."

I type onto the screen. "*If we fuck, you'll write a song about me. It will go viral. I will have to listen to it for the rest of my life. No thanks. Ariel.*"

I hand the phone back to Mateo, noticing for the first time the dark expression on his face. Not anger. Something deeper. Carnal. Something that gets me wet and makes my body flash hot all over.

"I rescind my offer of a threesome. You know this, right?" Mateo pulls me in tight against him, his breath hot against my cheek. "There's no fucking way I can share you with anybody. There would be bloodshed. Prison for me." He punctuates the next few words with a series of small nips against the skin of my neck. "Very. Bad. Idea."

"Well, then you better make my sacrifice worth it." I snake my hand backwards between us, touching as much of his hard abdomen and even harder crotch as I can from my awkward angle.

"You already know I'm worth it. I bet you're already wet for me. Dying for it." He keeps one arm looped around my waist ensuring that I stay where he wants me while the other wanders, skimming over my bare thighs and then inching up under the hem of my denim skirt to trace the bottom curve of an ass cheek. He groans against my ear. "Fuck, I love the fact that you hate underwear."

I lick my lips. "I don't like anything to get in between me and what I want."

He laughs, the sound dark and sensual and the perfect thing to crank me up one notch higher.

"Well, you can't have what you want right now." The tips of his fingers trace the curve of my ass and I hold my breath as he makes a shallow dip into the wet, slick place between my legs. My body sags but he holds me in place in the right spot for him to make me crazy with that dirty mouth. "If you're a good girl and enjoy Zane's set, later tonight I'll bury my cock in your pussy as deep as you want, for as long as you want, as often as you want. Sound good?"

All I can do is nod and try to get my breathing under control as Mateo removes his fingers from my skirt and wraps both arms around my waist. His phone buzzes in his pocket and I feel it against my hip.

"That's probably Zane. You want to look at it?" I ask.

"Nope. He's getting enough airtime tonight. I want you all to myself."

I'm totally good with that and we remain in that position until Zane is announced and we let go of each other long enough to yell and scream and clap as he comes onstage. The crowd goes absolutely nuts and he reels them in with his sexy banter and the start of his first song. Once again, I'm bowled over with just how good he really is.

"He's awesome," I say to Mateo as we sway together to the music. "Really good. Does he have a record deal yet?"

He shakes his head. "He gets lots of work as a songwriter but he's taking his time picking the label. I think he's waiting until after he goes on tour to pick the one he wants."

"Tour?"

"He's going on tour with Kit Landry as one of her opening acts. His manager thinks he'll get a bigger deal once he's made a splash in major cities."

"How the hell did he get a gig with Kit Landry?" I turn to face him and Mateo stares down at me as if he's trying to decide if I'm joking with him or not. "What? What did I miss?"

"I guess I just figured you knew," he says and grins. "My cousin Max is engaged to Kit. Zane is one of her primary songwriters and we practically live at their house. They feed us and we provide slave labor for all the renovations my cousin insists on doing himself."

"Really? I'm a huge Kit Landry fan."

"Well, I happen to know she's a huge Carlisle Queen fan. I'll introduce you."

I nod as he pulls me into his arms and I loop my arms around his neck. We dance like that for a while as Zane rolls through his set behind us and before I know it, he's done and the next local band is being ushered on stage.

"Let's go."

Mateo takes my hand and leads me down the stairs, nodding at the security guard as we pass by. He places me in front of him, using his larger bulk to part the crowd as we make our way towards the parking area. His hands, heavy on my hips are grounding and sexy at the same time. The slide of our bodies together as we walk in tandem is like blowing air on the smoldering embers of lust we'd lit earlier tonight. It won't take much to get me going. I've been thinking of this since the last time we were together.

"Are we supposed to go catch Zane backstage?" I ask, tilting my head and giving him access as Mateo places soft kisses on my neck. The night is cooling off, not enough to make me cold but the combination of the breeze and his attention is making me shiver, super aware of every inch of my exposed skin.

"No. He'll have plenty of company for the night. Brunette. Blonde." He murmurs against the skin on my shoulder, his teeth tugging gently on the thin strap of my tank top. "I'm partial to redheads at the moment."

"For the moment?"

"Well, I have a very short attention span. Early diagnosis of sexual ADD."

"That sounds serious," I tease, skimming his forearms with my nails and loving the rise of goose bumps on his skin. "What's the cure?"

"I need to get somewhere and focus on my task. Give it my undivided attention for hours."

Getting somewhere and letting him focus on me sounds really, really good. It feels even better when he spins me around, the cool metal of a truck cab against my back and hot, hard male on my front.

He takes my mouth, simple possession with soft lips and velvet tongue as he coaxes a moan from deep in my throat. I weave my fingers through his hair, pulling him back to me every time he tries to pull away. He tastes of the beer he had during the show, red hot gum, and spicy, half-latino lover.

I travel my hands along the wide expanse of his shoulders, tracing the ripple of defined muscle in his back until I can cup his ass cheeks. Pulling him forward with one rough tug, I grind my pelvis against his hard length and curse the two layers of denim cock blocking me.

I have three brain cells that are not occupied with how I feel right now and it's enough for me to coordinate reaching between our bodies with shaky, sweaty fingers and unfastening the snap and easing the zipper down just far enough for me to feel the heat of him through the fabric of his boxer briefs.

"*Tu Me Vuelves Loca,*" he groans against my lips, dipping back in to taste me one more time, his tongue probing in sync with the rhythm of his hips thrusting into my palm. "We need to find somewhere I can get you horizontal."

He doesn't wait for my agreement, although I am completely on board with that plan, and pulls me between the cars parked in orderly rows in a large field. I think this is a farm or something when it isn't hosting a music festival and there are no lights except for the ones aimed at the festival. It gets darker and darker as we move farther from the crowd.

He stops next to his car and pulls me to him for another deep kiss, tongues and teeth and moans from us both. He breaks the kiss long enough to place his hands at my waist and lift me over the door and toss me into the backseat. He's left off the drop top and two seconds later he climbs over the side and joins me in the deep backseat.

"I don't think I can drive right now. You've got me too jacked up," he says. My eyes are adjusted to the darkness and I can see him sprawled against the seat, hair mussed from my hands, lips swollen. The sensitive skin on my neck, my chin and cheeks is tingling from his stubble, and I'm excited by the idea that I might have his marks on me tomorrow. "I feel like I've been hard for hours."

I glance down at his crotch and can see the outline of his erection through the soft denim, the patch of dark hair above the line of his boxer briefs visible in the "v" of his open fly. I move to straddle him, not lowering myself all the way down, leaving enough room for me to insert my hand under the fabric and stroke his cock. His head thuds back against the seat and he lets out a soft "fuck".

"That's what I want." I lean over, pressing my lips against his so he can feel and hear my words over the music coming from the stage. "I want you to fuck me. Now."

Mateo moves then, his fingers suddenly speared through my hair, forcing me to look at him. He looks as crazed as I feel. This thing between us is bringing out every primal and reckless instinct inside me. Inside both of us.

"People are everywhere. They could see us," he says, his voice ragged with his own need and the effort to verbalize with my fingers wrapped around his penis. "I don't give a shit but I'm an exhibitionist asshole. Are *you* sure?"

"I want it. If you won't do it then I'll find somebody who will."

I think I see an actual flash of blue fire in his eyes at my words. I wouldn't go find someone else when my body is screaming that it only wants him but I remember what he said earlier about not sharing me with anybody as his fingers stroked me. I want *that* possessive, growly guy all over me, inside me, and I will not settle for anything less.

"*Es usted un coño?*" I say, issuing my final challenge.

SIX

MATEO

I can't believe she just asked if I was a pussy.

In the worst accent ever heard.

I know what she's doing. She's pushing my buttons, controlling this scene as much as she can. Classic Carlisle. My control-freak fuck buddy whose lust runs hotter than the red in her hair. Normally, I don't like games. I don't like the push and pull of a mind fuck when I just want to screw a willing body.

But Carlisle's games? Hot. Intriguing. And they make me laugh.

My lips curl up at the corner at the taunt and I bite back a groan at the way her pupils dilate when she realizes she's going to get exactly what she wants and more. I tighten my fingers in her hair, drag her face down to mine and part her lips with a brutal kiss. Her grip on my cock tightens and I buck up into her grasp, aching to feel her touch on my skin.

Carlisle gives back as good as she gets. The nails of her other hand dig into my shoulder and I wince at the spark of pain. It only makes me harder. I let go of her hair, break away from her mouth and drag her tank top straps down to expose her breasts to me. She isn't wearing a bra and I waste no time cupping them both in my palms, dragging my thumbs across the tips.

Her head falls back and she starts with those noises that drove me fucking crazy the last time. Ragged sighs and moans as I stroke her flesh, teasing her pink nipples into hard, tight points. And then she starts with the talking and I wonder if I'm going to come in my pants like I did the first time I ever went down on Erin Delaney in this very car, on this very seat.

"Teo, suck on me. Put them in your mouth."

I want to. Jesus, do I want to do exactly as she commands but I cannot resist teasing her for a little while. I lean forward, making sure my lips skim the curve of her breast, leaving a trail of hot, moist breath as I make my way to her neck. I lick the long column of ivory flesh, nibbling the skin over her pulse point and loving the way she jumps at the contact. I take my time, dragging it out until she grabs my hair in her hands and yanks my head back to force me to look at her.

"Teo. I asked you to suck on my tits. Do it or I will kill you."

I laugh, enjoying the way her eyes narrow even more.

"Go ahead. Get mad," I tease. "It'll only make it hotter."

She growls and pushes my head down to her breasts and I give her what she wants because I'm dying to see her fall apart like she did the other night. Licking, teasing, sucking the hard nubs of flesh into my mouth. I trail my hand down to the space between our bodies and pull up the hem of her short, denim skirt. The scent of her arousal mingles with the summer scent of sunshine baked into earth, fresh-cut grass, and sunscreen to form the most delicious perfume.

My mouth waters and my dick leaks as I slide along the

moisture slicking her thighs. She is so wet that my touch glides over her folds as I caress her flesh. She grinds her body down onto my hand, seeking that pressure in the best place possible but I won't let her have it, groaning low in my throat when she whimpers above me. I finally glance a fingertip over her clit and she shudders, her weight collapsing onto me as her legs start to shake.

"Teo, I'm going to come."

I instantly release her nipple from my mouth and remove my hand from her skirt. I lift my hands to frame her face, my voice low and harsh against her ear.

"Don't you dare come right now. I want to drink it up. It's mine and that's how I want it."

"Fuck you," she growls and then her voice goes softer. "Then take it. Please," she pleads, her nails digging into the muscle of my forearms.

I shift out from under her body, leaving her to face the back of the car, knees resting on the seat, ass up in the air and the top half of her body draped over the back end of the car. Behind her, way off in the distance is the stage, the lightshow making her form look like illuminated abstract art.

I almost choke on my desire as it rises up in my chest and tightens every muscle in my body. I am primed, ready to go. But I want her to go first.

"You look so fucking gorgeous. Everything about you says I can do whatever I want to you and you'll take it."

"Anything you want," she says, her hands clenching and unclenching, gliding over the smooth-as-glass paint job. She demonstrates her submission by spreading her legs wider, her skirt rising to expose the sweet curve of her ass.

I lean down behind her, using my hands to spread her wider, finding her wet folds with my tongue. The first swipe makes her jump but the second has her pushing back against my face. I am beyond teasing at this point. I'm afraid to stroke my own dick because I'm *that close* to coming.

I angle my head and find her clit with my tongue, pressing against it in a rhythm she mimics with her hips. I eat at her, savoring her taste, drinking her arousal as she begins to shiver around me. Her legs shake, her ass muscles clenching under my palm as I caress her silken skin. She's gasping above me, her words lost in the beat of the music as I bring her closer and closer. I don't need to hear them anyway, the way her body goes completely still is what I've been aching for as she comes apart all over my mouth. I continue the pressure, taking her as far as I can, keeping her suspended in her own pleasure until she pulls away, her body collapsing in a boneless heap over the seat.

I rise from my position, pressing kisses along her spine as I drape myself over her body, only stopping when I cover her completely.

"Eres tan bella," I whisper against the damp skin of her neck, the curls tumbling over her back. I kiss her cheek, trailing down until I can claim her mouth in a soft kiss full of softer sighs and wet tongues. "So beautiful."

"Quiero que me folles," she says, her green eyes flashing with the heat of our unfinished passion.

She wants me to fuck her. No... she's begging me to fuck her.

Her terrible pronunciation does nothing to lessen the impact of her words on my cock. I'm hard, painfully hard, and I want nothing more than to give her what she's asked for.

"I will fuck you." I lean back and pull the condom out of my pocket before shoving my jeans and boxer briefs down to my thighs. The night air is cool against my hot skin but I don't care. Carlisle is running hot enough to burn me alive and I want to be consumed by her tight heat. I rip open the packet and slide it down over my length, leaning forward to slide into her body, her slick lube making it an easy glide forward. She gasps and then lets out a long, satisfied sigh that wraps around my balls. I have to fight the urge to pull out and slam back in. "I will fuck you hard and fast and deep. Are you ready?"

She nods and I pull out almost all the way and then shove my way back in. Carlisle pitches forward with the force of my thrust, throwing out her arms as she spreads herself out on the back of the car again. Her position is open, submissive and I take all she is offering, my hips snapping forward as I move in and out of her wet, willing body.

"Teo. Yes. Yes," she chants over and over, and I fall into a rhythm that brings me closer and closer to my own release. The fire in my lower belly, the ache in my balls tells me that I'm not going to last as long as I want to. That I am not going to be able to resist the tight drag of her sex along my cock, that she will take from me what I am very willing to give to her.

I lean forward, draping my body over her back once again as my thrusts become more and more shallow. I bite the spot where her neck meets her shoulder and she cries out, her hand reaching back and her fingers digging painfully into my hip.

"I need to come," she pants, her words slurred she's so drunk on our lust. "I need... "

"I know what you need," I growl as I wedge my hand between her body and the seat and rub her clit in tandem with my strokes and the heaving jerks of her body under me. "Carlisle, come. I want you to squeeze me tight in your hot little pussy. Come on."

My words and the rutting of my body against hers, pushes her over the edge and I go over with her, my orgasm making me shudder with the white-hot pleasure of it. I hear the music off in the distance but my ears are ringing, blood pulsing through me so fast I can't keep up, even with deep, gulping inhales of the sweet night air. I hold on to her, burying my face in the sweet gardenia scent of her hair, relishing the cool silk of it against my overheated skin.

"Fuck me," she says on a breath that starts out as a sigh and ends on a laugh. "Fuck me."

"Happy to but I need a minute. I'm twenty-two, not Superman."

I lift up and off her body, slowly pressing kisses on any patch of exposed skin I can find. Her skin is like silk against my lips, her taste salty and sweet.

"I could eat you up." I take a quick bite of her ass and tell her just how amazing she is. "You. Are. So. Fucking. Delicious."

We lower ourselves to the seat, a tangle of laughter and limbs. When was the last time I laughed with a lover? Never. Sure, we had a good time. Enjoyed the moment and each other. I didn't stay around or keep them around long enough to laugh together.

But I'm not in any hurry to go anywhere right now. I dispose of the condom, right my clothes and settle lengthwise across the seat, pulling her down alongside of me. The music from the festival continues, providing a perfect backdrop to our silence.

"We need to do that in a bed sometime," I say, tracing a finger up and down her arm. "I'd like to actually see you completely naked."

Carlisle stiffens slightly and I wonder what I've stepped in this time.

"I'm not girlfriend or sleepover material," she answers, her voice soft but firm.

"And I'm not asking you to move in. I'd just like to fuck you, roll over and pretend to sleep while you pick your clothes off the floor and sneak out." I press a kiss against her hair and navigate the land mine field I've clearly landed in. "You can even have a walk of shame."

"You're kind of an asshole."

"I really am but I'd still like to hang out with you again."

"Don't you have medical school or some other time-consuming activity coming up?" She looks up at me, her expression indecipherable but concerned.

"That's the plan." If she's not girlfriend material, I'm not sharing material and that includes my shit about school, my sister, or any of it.

Carlisle remains silent in my arms, the music from the stage drifting over us with the breeze. I get her, I think. She's not cold or stuck-up. A part of her is closed off except when I have my cock buried in her body. The couple of times we've been together, I've seen who she probably was before her body and her life was blown apart and then paraded through the media in the last eighteen months. When something like that happens to you, it is a rare person who can move forward without leaving the old you behind.

"Look, my wingman status remains even if we never fuck again. I'm screwed up and so are you but when I'm fucking you I forget about it for a while. I like sex with you and I like hanging out with you. Nothing more than that." I put a finger under her chin and tip her face up to look at me. Her green eyes are open but clouded with her hesitation. "I don't like to chase women, especially ones who have no desire to be caught. You have my number. You call me when you want to have some fun together. You control it all. Sound good?"

She watches me, her gaze assessing until she rolls her eyes and shakes her head. "Oh hell. You might be a nice guy after all."

I laugh, a little confused. "I try not to be a dick as a general rule but my 'Y' chromosome gets in the way once in a while."

Carlisle laughs, lying back down on my chest. "For the record, I'm not screwed up. I'm okay."

"Really? Okay?" I don't try to hide my skepticism.

"Yep." She nods against my chest before placing a kiss on my collarbone. "And by okay I mean that I'm seriously fucked in the head but I'm sick of talking about it."

Oh hell, this one is just about perfect. I look up at the stars and wonder what I'm doing with this girl.

SEVEN

CARLISLE

Aaron is in the Student Commons.

Not *actually* Aaron. I'm not having a drug-induced hallucination but my vision blurs a little at the edges and my heart jumps like it's trying to propel itself off the diving block when the race gun goes off. I look around the room and I can't get away from it. His face is on every inadequate-penis-size-compensating flat screen TV in the center displaying either his official summer games photo or live footage of him doing what he did so well.

I try to stand but I can't. It isn't the injury but the surge of nerve-searing pain that shoots from my heart and liquefies every bone in my body. He is beautiful...alive. I stop breathing with the unconscious hope that he will appear, walk right off the screen and into my arms. How many times have I made that silent plea? The wish whispered in the dark to a vast universe that doesn't care about my desire.

I am paralyzed, soaking in his face, his smile. The beard I thought I would hate and then loved. I watch as his long, toned body leaps off the block and slices through the surface of the water. His smiling face as he stands in the center of the awards ceremony, tears of pride running down his cheeks as he salutes our nation's flag. And then the pictures of us together; laughing, kissing, cheering each other on at events start rolling across the screen and the bile rises up from my stomach and I have to breathe again in order to push it back down

The media called us the perfect couple and they didn't know the half of it. Neither of us was easy to live with but we *got* each other the way that only happens if you're lucky. And fuck but we loved each other. Bone-deep and overpowering. I didn't know how lucky we were until he was gone.

And then the footage changes to the carnage, the wreckage of the athlete's village. I close my eyes and dig blindly in my bag for my phone. I didn't need to see the images when I was awake, it would spoil it for when they showed up again in my dreams. My phone is vibrating when I pull it out and I don't even open my eyes to check the caller ID.

"Hello?"

"Is this Carlisle Queen?"

I don't recognize the man's voice and when I glance at the caller ID, I realize that I don't know the number either. I look back up at the TV screen and notice the headline banner at the bottom and suddenly I understand the coverage. The final U.N. report on the bombing has been released and drags up all the memories of the time when that crazy terrorist group tried to send the whole lot of us to hell. I bet my mother's beloved labradoodle that the guy on the other end of my phone is a reporter.

"Ms. Queen? My name is James Moore from the San Francisco Gazette. I was wondering if I could get you reaction to the report—"

I've never been so angry to be right.

I turn off the phone, stand on shaky legs and weave my way in between the tables scattered throughout the room. People are starting to look, their gazes moving like ping pong balls between me and the TV screen and I just keep moving. I'm used to people staring and nobody ignores gawkers better than I do.

My phone rings again and I look at the screen. Another unknown caller. I decline the call, turn off my phone and exit the building heading across the quad. I don't want to wait for the bus and my apartment is only a few blocks away so I start walking. The sunshine is warm on my head and my bare shoulders but my teeth are chattering in spite of the sweat I can feel running down my back and prickling under my arms.

All I can see is Aaron's face. Not the ones where is he is alive and happy but the ones that live in my head. The ones the media will never have because they weren't there. They didn't see what I saw. They didn't taste the blood.

I speed up my steps, wanting to get home before the panic attack I can feel coming on hits me like the bus I narrowly avoid stepping in front of at the corner. I can see my apartment from this location and I scan the area for any news trucks, relieved when I don't see any setting up. They'll be here soon enough, never passing up the chance to ask bullshit questions about the worst day of my life.

I hit the front steps of my building, wishing I could run up them but I get to the front door soon enough. I pull the door behind me to make sure it locks and then I'm pressing the button for the elevator two, four, or seven times. I know it won't make it come any faster but its either that or screaming. I refuse to lose it in the lobby of my building.

I enter the elevator and count off the seconds it takes to get to my floor and then rush down the hallway and unlock my door. I slam the door behind me and toss my purse on the floor, leaning over at the waist with my hands braced on my knees. I struggle to catch my breath, dry heaving as stars flash on the periphery of my vision.

"Oh my God, Carlisle are you okay?" Livvy rushes over to me, her face appearing in in my line of sight as she kneels on the ground in front of me. She raises her hands to cup my face, holding me so that I have to make eye contact. "Breathe. Just breathe with me."

I'm having a panic attack. I've had them before and Livvy has had to coach me through them from time to time. Poor girl, once again I wonder what she did to get stuck with the crazy roommate.

"Carlisle, what happened?" She asks, her face getting some of its color back.

I suck in the air, mimicking her inhale and exhale until I feel my own body regulating itself. I slide down the wall, landing in a heap beside the door. I'm a sweaty, sticky mess but I pull myself together enough to get her up to speed.

"I saw Aaron." I shake my head, knowing I need to start over from the alarmed look she's giving me. ""On TV. They released the final report about the bombing. I've had two reporters call me already."

She jumps up and goes to the window, pulling aside the blinds to look outside. Another perk of living with me, the chance that reporters will camp outside your door.

"I don't see any trucks yet," she says, and turns back to me. "I'll tell my parents that we'll meet at the hotel and not here."

Oh shit. I totally forgot that this is graduation weekend. Perfect.

"I'm so sorry Livvy—"

A sharp knock on the door, followed by a "Carlisle, it's Mateo. Are you in there?"

My stomach does this flip-flop thing at the sound of his voice and I am relieved that he is here. Happy.

I cut a look at Livvy and reach up, turning the door handle and sliding it open. Teo filling up the doorway takes over my view, his face full of concern. He walks inside, shuts the door behind him and drops down to one knee in front of me.

"Jesus, are you okay?" He grabs my hand and frowns. "You're shaking and freezing. What the hell is going on?"

I stare at him, wondering why he is here. I attempt to struggle to my feet and he reaches out and lifts me, holding me against him until I'm steady on my feet. I want to sink into him, steal his warmth and just stay there for about three days. I don't now when it happened but Teo has become something in my life. What I don't really know. Friend. Supporter. Something more.

I don't want him to be anything to me. I don't want to feel the relief that coursed through me when I heard his voice through the door a few moments ago. I'm raw from the photos of Aaron, the wound of my loss is open tonight, too exposed. The fact that Mateo would be any part of healing me is terrifying.

I push him away.

"Carlisle, wait. You're shaking like a leaf and I've never seen you so pale." He looks at Livvy before reaching out for me again. I push him away. "Will you sit down before you face plant on the floor?"

"I'm fine," I insist. I'm stubborn, I know. "I just need a few moments to get myself together.

I walk to the kitchen and pour myself a glass of water, spilling some down the front of my shirt. My hand is shaking so badly that I loose my grip on the glass and it crashes to the counter, shattering and spilling its contents all over the place. I jump back at the same time Mateo and Livvy surge forward to help but I wave them away.

I don't want their help. I don't want them near me.

Livvy grabs a towel and throws it down to stem the tide of the water dripping down on the floor while Mateo pulls me close. His hands cup my face and he does that forehead touching thing that makes me get wobbly in the knees and in the vicinity of my heart and I reach the end of my rope. I want his touch too much. I want his comfort.

I squirm out of his grasp and slide past him, pushing off his hands when he tries to pull me back to him.

"Carlisle, wait... " he says, following me into my room.

"Why are you here Mateo?" I shove my bedroom door open and go to my bathroom. I pull back the mirrored door and pick up the bottle of drugs Dr. Shrieve gave me to take when I have a bad attack. "I open the bottle and shake two onto my palm, dry swallowing them before leaning over to slurp water from the running tap. When I stand upright, Mateo is giving me a weird look in the mirror. "What?"

"I think you take a lots of drugs."

I raise an eyebrow at him as my temper flares. "Do you? I don't remember asking you." I push by him and go out to my room, turning when he grabs my arm. I yank my arm out his grasp. "Get off me!"

"Getting high isn't the answer all the time. I know you had a terrible thing happen to you but popping pills isn't dealing with it."

I get up in his face, holding nothing back. He gets everything he deserves and I decide to pile on all the shit I'm want to vent to the bombers, the reporters, the doctors. My list is long and my tone is ugly.

"I never asked your opinion about how you think I should deal with being attacked and having the man I love die right in front of me along with some of the best friends I've ever had. I didn't ask for you to comment on the drugs I take or the way I deal with my problems. You are nothing but a fantastic lay and if you think there is anything more than that, you are delusional."

His lips curl up into a sneer and he gives it back as good as I gave it. "You can't function without popping something. Hell, I don't think we've actually fucked without you being high on something. I don't need to be anything to you and I don't expect to be but someone has got to tell you that you are playing a game that you can't possibly win." He points at his chest, his knuckles white he's so tense. "I don't want to turn on the news one day and hear that you overdosed on a bunch of pills and you're gone. Call me nosy or an asshole or whatever but you need to get your shit together and this isn't it."

His words hit a little too close to the mark. His words hurt and I don't need anymore pain right now. I'm done. I just want him gone from my apartment, my life.

"Mateo, you can't fix me. I'm not your goddam Boy Scout project and I just want to you to go. Delete my number. Don't call me. Just go."

He stares at me for what seems like and hour, his jaw tight and blue eyes blazing. He opens his mouth to say one more thing and Livvy interrupts, her tone soft in the midst of all this anger.

"Just go, Mateo. Please."

He transfers his gaze to her and something in her expression deflates him. He nods, never looking at me as he brushes past and leaves my room.

I stand there until I hear him close the front door and

then I turn, ready to vent to Livvy about what a judgmental asshole he is. She's standing in the doorway, the look on her face something I can't place. Diappointment? Anger? Hesitation?

"What?" You can't think he was right to say all that shit to me?"

"I think he meant well because he's a nice guy and cares about you but I don't think it was his place." I breathe out a sigh of relief and open my mouth to start the Mateo roast but she keeps talking. "But, I don't think what he said was wrong." She holds up a hand when I rush to argue. "I'm leaving you here and it scares the shit out of me that your normal reaction to any kind of situation is to get high. You had a panic attack and you didn't even try any of the exercises Dr. Shrieve taught you."

"You never said anything before," I say and I am unable to keep the betrayal out of my voice.

"I just did." She steps forward and pulls me into a hug, her body shaking with her emotion. "I know what your plans are and I'll support you with whatever you plan to do in the end. But I love you and I want you to stick around. I'm with Mateo, I don't want to turn on the news anytime soon and I find that I can't call my best friend anymore."

I'm stunned. Speechless, which is a rare situation for me, and with the pills I just took, I'm not reacting as quickly as I want and she's pulling away before I can stop her.

For the second time in less than ten minutes, a person walks out of my room without looking back.

CARLISLE

The usual crowd is at Mateo and Zane's house.

It isn't a full blown party but there always seems to be a crowd hanging out on the back deck or in the living room playing music or watching a game. This time I find Zane sitting on the patio outside, drinking a beer and strumming guitars with three other guys while a half dozen girls watch them and try to be the one who gets to go home with the musician. I recognize some of them from class but none of their smiles are friendly. I'm the perceived competition and I am the enemy until I am eliminated. Dating these days isn't that different from professional sports.

"Hey Ariel," Zane nods at me as I approach, his smirk knowing and his words coated with "I-knew-this-would-happen" gloating. "You here to patch things up with our boy?"

I'm not getting into my business in front of all these strangers but I nod. "Is he here?"

"In his room," he says and opens his mouth as if he had more to say but then shut it, jerking his chin in the direction of the house.

I walk inside the house and up the stairs, bypassing the people playing Playstation on the couch for Mateo's room. For once in a very long time, I don't regret the fact that my taking them two-at-a-time-days are over. I've got some apologizing to do and like anyone with a healthy ego, it's not a skill set I like using very often. But I was wrong and I need to own up to it.

I knock on his door and wait for the inevitable "fuck off" and I'm not disappointed. His voice is rough, harsh and unwelcoming. Well, this girl is not scared by the Big Bad Wolf routine. It takes more than a grumpy man to send me running...metaphorically, of course.

I turn the doorknob and it slides open and I stick my head in. Mateo is lying on his bed surrounded by a large manila envelope and papers, a beer in one hand and the other tucked behind his head. He's wearing a pair of old camo print shorts and nothing else and I can't help the way my eyes take off on their own journey and travel over the broad width of his chest and the sculpted perfection of his abs. His skin is dark from the early summer sun but I can see the place where his tan line ends peeking out from the open "v" of his unbuttoned shorts.

The dark happy trail entices me to follow its lead and I'm rewarded by the sight of his long expanse of skin broken only by the dusting of dark hair on his pecs and the silken swirl in his armpits. Stubble on his face just elevates his classification from hot to molten and I have to grip the doorknob a little harder to resist the urge to jump his bones.

Instead, I decided to dazzle him with my incredible conversation skills.

"Hey," I say and I have serious doubts about how this is going to end if I can't do any better than that.

He twists his head to the side and gives me the once over before turning back to his original position. "Hey."

"Can I come in?

"If my telling you to fuck off didn't stop you, I don't know if anything else will work," he grumbles before taking a sip of his beer.

I take that as the only invitation I'm going to get and move fully inside the room, closing the door behind me with a click. The noises from the rest of the house die down to a low rumble and the almost silence in his room is intimidating when I realize that this entire exercise is going to require me to fill it with words. Real words. Not the bullshit you spout at parties or the small talk you make Aunt Irma at Christmas. Real. Fucking. Words.

"Are you going to stand there and ogle me or are you here for a reason?" he asks, his voice muffled by the forearm he now has draped across his face so he can block me out. Nice try. I am completely unembarrassed by the fact that I *was* ogling him not five seconds ago. I bet money he ogles himself too when he looks in a mirror.

I take the four steps it takes to reach his bed, kick off my sandals and climb in next to him. I settle in beside him, lying on my back, so I can look him in the eye if he ever decides to stop hiding.

"You're on my bed."

"I am."

He sighs. "Why are you on my bed?"

"I'm fulfilling one of your deepest fantasies."

That gets his attention and he lowers his arm, his blue eyes narrowed and full of questions. He doesn't look as mad as he was yesterday and I breathe out my own relief.

"I'm admitting I was wrong. I'm sorry," I say.

"You think *that's* my deepest fantasy?" he asks.

"I thought it was every man's fantasy to have a woman admit she was wrong," I say, venturing out with a light smile when he huffs out a tiny laugh and relaxes a little bit. "I'm really sorry. I'm not saying I agree with everything you said but I shouldn't have gone off on you like that. You saw me at my worst, I hope."

He contemplates me for a few seconds, his brain obviously churning with the decision of whether to forgive me or not. I add something hoping to tip him into the "yes" column.

"I'm drug-free today. I had to dodge a few reporters outside my building to come here and I did it buzz-free."

"Really?" He shifts his head on the bed to align better with my line of sight, his eyes searching, examining my face. I try to meet him head-on, to let him see whatever it is he's looking for. Down deep I'm hoping he sees me and it's enough. "Thank you." He pauses before continuing. "You are a lot of fucking trouble Carlisle Queen."

His words make me sad, more than a twinge of regret making me squirm. I settle back against the bed and look at the ceiling. I can feel his gaze still on me, like a touch on my cheek and I can almost hear the questions rolling around in his head. He deserves them, he's helped me out more than anyone lately and I'm ready to share if only to show him that I'm worth all the trouble.

"I was conscious immediately after the bomb went off." I begin in a voice that hurts it is so full of gravel. "I don't remember it going off or throwing me through the air but I remember lying there with pain so bad I threw up." I swallow and feel his fingers lace with my own as he lends me his strength. I soak it in. I need it. "I was walking with Aaron and other athletes, we were going to have dinner. Afterwards, I couldn't find Aaron at first, the smoke was thick and my eyes watered from the chemicals. I was in a lot of pain but I started crawling to find him."

I blink as the ceiling goes blurry and I realize I'm crying, not heavy tears but a steady stream of liquid regret and pain and loss flowing out of me. I don't bother to try and brush them away.

"I found him and I tried to see if he was okay. He wasn't. When I got up close... half his face was missing. His brain... " I suck in a deep breath and force the image out of my head. I couldn't help it if it showed up in my dreams but I didn't have to force it on myself when I was awake. "I draped my body over his and waited to join him. I didn't want him to be alone. The reports from the paramedics and the police said they found me that way. Barely alive myself but protecting him from any other harm."

"You guys took care of each other a lot I guess," he says, tracing a pattern on the back on my palm. It soothes me, grounds me, and I allow myself to accept the comfort. "Two kids so young in such a competitive situation."

"We did. Or at least Aaron tried." I sneak a glance at Mateo, the burn of embarrassment heating my cheeks. "As you know, I'm not good with letting people help me."

"Understatement of the century."

I sigh and squeeze his hand. "I'm working on it."

"Apology accepted. Don't beat yourself up too much about it."

Mateo places his beer on the side table and moves back to me, gathering me in his arms and holding me close as I let the last of the tears flow. His chest is warm and solid and that precious thud of his heartbeat under his skin comforts me. He sifts his fingers through the length of my hair, playing with the strands as he lets me collect myself.

"You are very strong to survive that, Carlisle. I know you don't feel like it all of the time but you are."

I laugh against the wall of muscle beneath me, soaking in his scent and wrapping my arms around him. "I take the drugs to get the shit out of my head that comes rushing back when it all gets to ne too much. If I could erase those images, I wouldn't take anything stronger than the prescriptions I have for pain. Being high turns the movie in my head off for a little while. I'm not sure how strong *that* is."

"I think it's goddam strong," he murmurs and presses a kiss to the top of my head. "I never met Aaron but I think he would agree with me."

I smile at that. These two men couldn't look more different but there is a common core that they share.

"Aaron was strong but it was a quiet power. He wasn't flashy or a trash talker but he gave one-hundred percent everyday and took care of other people. It was a gift and people flocked to it. They trusted him." I peek up at Mateo and catch his gaze to watch his reaction to my words. "You two have that in common."

He rolls his eyes and looks up at the ceiling, shaking his head. "Don't put me on that pedestal. I'll fall off. I promise."

"I doubt that but I'm not trying to put you up that high. It's not your style, at all."

"You think so?"

I shake my head. "You don't strike me as a glory hound guy."

We lie their quiet for a few moments, the sounds of the party below drifting up to us. People are laughing and I can hear Zane and his guitar on the deck.

"You're probably right. Zane's the one who has to have the spotlight to survive. Not that it's a bad thing, just listen to him."

"He seems to have his future all planned out. Fame. Fortune," I say.

"A growing collection of women's underwear thrown at him on stage," Mateo says and I when I look at him to see if he's telling the truth, he nods. "Yeah. He gets panties, thongs, room keys. The worst was a set of dentures with the woman's phone number on them written in Sharpie."

"I think I want to barf."

"It was really gross but Zane said it was good to know that his demographic is cross generational."

"That's one way to look at it."

"He's a half-full kind of guy."

"Mateo, you can't act like you don't have anything special planned. You'll be off at medical school soon." I smack head with the back of my hand, remembering belatedly what happened yesterday. I lean up and kiss him on the cheek. "Happy graduation. I'm embarrassed to say that I don't have a present."

He hugs me close and kisses the end of my nose. "Thanks but this is present enough for me."

"Nice try but I'm getting you a gift. Maybe a stethoscope or a lab coat. Don't you need those things to be a doctor?"

He tenses beside me and I wonder what I've said wrong. I look up him at him but he's staring at the ceiling, his jaw tight and stiff.

"Did I say something wrong?" The silence stretches for a while longer and I decide he's not going to answer me. I've obviously stepped into something major for him. "I'm sorry if I did."

"You didn't say anything wrong, I just don't have any answer for you. I'm not sure I'm even going to medical school. That was a dream I had with my sister Mari and now I don't know if it was ever my dream or if I want it without her."

I think I know the answer but I have to ask. "What happened to Mari?"

"She died. Eighteen months ago," he answers. Six months after I lost Aaron. Rough times all around. "It was a brain tumor. Inoperable. It took her six months from the day she was diagnosed."

He sucks in a wet breath and I keep my eyes down, wanting to give him some privacy to deal with his grief. I understand the need to cry in private.

"I am so sorry. You two were obviously very close."

"We were only eleven months apart and she was my first friend. My best friend. I loved her more than anyone in the world. She was a force of nature." He chuckles and I feel his lips against my temple. "I'm not sure how well you two would have gotten along. Two strong women who are used to getting their way."

"She sounds like she was my kind of girl." I say and I mean it. I've never had any patience for a wilting wall-flower. Give me a chick with some thorns any day.

"We were supposed to open a practice together and work with patients one-on-one. The Butler family practice."

"And now you don't know if you want to do it by yourself?"

"Yep." He gestures down to the papers lying beside him on the bed. "This is the paperwork from the school, text-book lists, supplies. I need to make a decision."

"Not that you're asking but I think you should try it out and see if the white lab coat fits before bowing out. You might not actually know until you try it." I think back to my time as a new athlete and the decisions I had to make on the sport I wanted to pursue. "I thought I wanted to be a high diver instead of a swimmer when I began competing."

"What?"

"Yep." I lean up on my elbow and look down on him, smiling at his surprise. "I went to a few coaches to see if I had any talent for it and they all said no after it became clear that I couldn't do anything more than belly flop."

"So what happened?"

The last coach in Baltimore watched me swim laps one morning. I was on a neighborhood swim team and I was practicing. He said my breaststroke was the best he'd ever seen and that I was like a bullet in the water. I moved from Texas to Baltimore a few months later and the rest was history."

"And twelve medals later... " He pauses and I know what he's going to ask. They all want to know. "Where do you keep your medals?"

"Would you believe that I keep them in my underwear drawer?"

"Is that true?"

I just smile.

NINE

MATEO

I wake up in fucking heaven.

Carlisle is curled up against me as the little spoon and my dick is rock hard and nestled into the cleft of her ass. Her hair, silky and scented like gardenias is pillowed against my face, surrounding me with a smell I will always associate with Carlisle. I lean up a little bit on my elbow to look down on her and watch her sleep.

I've never seen her so still, so beautiful. Her pale skin has this pinkish glow from the warmth created by our bodies tucked here together in our private cave. I should let her sleep but I can't, I am dying to taste her first thing in the morning, to feel her surrender before she has the chance to put on her armor. I need the real Carlisle and after our talk yesterday, I might have a chance of having her in the early morning light.

My right hand is resting on her hip and I raise it up, lifting her hair away from her neck and giving me access to the smooth column of warm flesh. I start slow, soft. Barely there kisses that she'll feel in her dreams, wonder if they are real, and wake to find her good dreams are just as powerful as her nightmares.

She tastes good, like salt and crème, a sexy woman flavor that gets me even harder. I drift my hand down farther, skating over the curve of her breast underneath her tank top, teasing her nipple through the fabric, It peaks and I groan a little, my mouth watering to get a taste, to feel it roll against my tongue.

I lean over her and ease one strap of her top down over a creamy shoulder and indulge. Reaching out with my tongue, I lick the pebbled flesh watching her fingers curl involuntarily into the sheets below us. The fabric twists between her digits, punctuating the moan that escapes her as I suck her entire nipple into my hot, wet mouth. Suddenly her fingers are digging into my scalp, pressing my face down and encouraging me to continue what I'm doing.

I need no further invitation to nudge her over and off her side until her back is flat against the bed. I stretch out beside her and lean over to suck her other nipple through the flimsy fabric of her top. Carlisle arches up into my touch, begging me with her body and the sounds of want and need pouring out of her to keep going.

I stop and look up to find her gazing down at me, her emerald green eyes dark with her passion, her bottom lip red and swollen from her biting it. I move up, licking along the seam of her lips until she releases her lip from its captivity and I can draw it into mine. I am dying to delve deeper so I abandon her lip to slip my tongue in deep, sweeping alongside her own as it tangles with mine. Her arms are wrapped around my back, pulling me closer as we eat suckle, caress, and explore in the early morning light.

I break off the kiss and look down at her, unable to

contain my smile. "I can't believe I finally got you in my bed."

She laughs softly, her fingers stroking the skin at the nape of my next, teasing me with her touch.

"Well, don't waste it. You never know when you'll get me back here."

Her words sober me instantly and dive in for a kiss more bruising and demanding than I intended it to be. I want to claim her, want her to agree that I'm not the only one careening towards a point of no return. Who the fuck am I kidding? We've already passed that point long ago.

I release her mouth and pull back enough to make eye contact. "There is something between us. It's strong and it's not going to go away because we go back to a bunch of rules we made up when we had nothing to lose."

Her eyes go wide and I silently dare her to contradict what I've said, to deny what is pulsing between us like a livewire.

"This could get complicated," she whispers. "It could get messy."

"Like anything between us could be anything else. But I want it. I want you in my bed and in my life."

She doesn't answer and I can see push and pull of what she wants to do and what she thinks she should do waging a war inside her. This is not something either of us signed up for but here we are, right in the middle of it and it feels huge.

"I don't know Mateo, there's so much more you should know... "

"I know that I want you, that I crave being with you in and out of bed and I want to explore it and see where it goes. I'm not asking for you to commit right now but I want you to think about it. Can you do that?"

She nods and I renew our kiss, letting her set the pressure with the way she clutches my head and guides it against her mouth. When she presses down, I obey her silent demand to trail kisses over her jaw, her neck, across her collarbone until I am back at her breasts. I tease with my tongue, little nips of my teeth on one before transferring my attention to the other grinding my hard dick against her thigh as her body writhes and her moans gets louder.

"Carlisle I fucking love it when you lose it. Love how you scream it out, telling me just how good I make you feel."

"Teo, touch me. Come on. Do it," she demands but I'm not ready to give her what she wants yet.

I reach down with my right hand and begin a light caress of the skin of her thighs. She's so hot for me that she reaches down and shimmies her skirt up a bit higher, giving me a glimpse of her auburn landing strip. Carlisle opens her legs wider, her own fingers joining mine on their upward journey, urging them on.

"You want me to touch your pussy Carlisle?"

"Yes."

"Then ask me nicely."

She huffs out a sound somewhere between a laugh and growl and her eyes snap to mine as she joins our fingers together. "Touch my pussy Teo. Please."

I allow her to drag my hand up and I find her damp, slick and warm. I take her hand and press it against her hot button. "You touch your clit baby and show me how you get yourself off while I finger fuck you."

Carlisle does not break eye contact with me as she does as she's told. I let my gaze drop because I'm dying to see what this looks like. My fingers are darker, blunter as two of them work their way in and out of her body. The sucking pull of her sex on every retreat, as if she doesn't want me to leave.

But the sight of her own, longer delicate fingers rubbing herself in slow circles is enough to get me off if I don't keep control of myself. Her hips shift as she gets closer and I couldn't look away if my life depended on it.

"I'm going to come Teo."

I speed up my thrusts and lean over, nudging her hand to the side as I add my tongue to the mix of sensations. I want to taste her as she comes and it only takes a few tender swipes against her clit and she is shaking under me, her body clutching my fingers in a tight, wet, hot grip.

She tugs on my hair and pulls me up and my mouth is taken in a kiss. She dives in, her tongue going in deep. She wants to taste her on my lips and I let her plunder, enjoying the way she takes what she wants and that what she wants is me.

We break apart, chests heaving with our effort to catch out breath. "I want to fuck you, Carlisle."

"Yes, she nods at the same time her hands start to unfasten the button of on my shorts and ease down the zipper. I'm commando so the next thing I feel is her hand stroking me from root to tip. I shudder when her thumb swipes across the head of my cock and I reach down to still her touch, afraid I might come if she keeps that up.

I lock eyes with her and voice what I've been dreaming about. "I want you naked and underneath me. I have to see you."

Carlisle

I FREEZE AT HIS WORDS. I can't help it.

I have not been entirely naked for a lover since Aaron and the fear that Mateo will be turned off by what he sees flickers across my mind. Normally, I would hedge and find a way to avoid it but this morning, in his bed, with what is pulsing between us, I have to be honest.

"You might not like it." I gesture towards my back. "It's ugly. The surgeons did their best... "

"Let me see," he says, quietly, understanding coating the three words and soothing my fears a little.

I sit up and let him undress me. First my tank top and then my mini-skirt and then I watch hungrily as he gets rid of his shorts. His penis is hard, jutting up against his belly, the tip red and wet. I lick my lips and feel my body clench with wanting him inside me.

"Roll over baby. On your stomach," he whispers and I remember that he will see all of me. I do as he says, there is no turning back now and I lower myself to lie flat against the mattress, open to his scrutiny.

The silence in the room stretches long but I can hear him breathing behind me, his gasp when he sees the mass of scars covering my lower back. I hold my breath.

I expect his touch but what I don't expect is his mouth, pressing soft kisses along every ridge, every keloid, every dip and indent marring my skin. He is straddling my legs, his penis dragging across the skin of my thighs, still hard and urgent and undiminished by the ugliness before his eyes.

Mateo spends long moments examining me, caressing my skin, tracing the evidence of a stranger's hatred with his loving touch and I melt into it. My body relaxes with each passing second and I blink back the prick of tears in my eyes. He moves away for a moment and I hear a drawer open, the ripping of a foil packet and then he is back against me, trailing kisses up my spine until he is draped over me, his breath hot on my cheek.

"Is this okay? " he asks, and when I nod, I feel his cock pressing against my opening. I open my legs sider and we both sigh as he slides inside, full and deep. He stops once he's in, leaning over to capture my mouth in a sweet, deep kiss. *"Tesoro,* you are beautiful. I swear it."

Tesoro. Treasure. Oh fuck, he looks at my broken body and knows what a head case I am and he still thinks I'm a treasure? Holy hell. I can't hear anymore. I'll want to hear more.

"Teo, move, please." I move hips under him, encouraging him. "I need you."

"You don't think you're beautiful, Carlisle?" You think I wouldn't crave doing this if I saw your scars?" He punctuates his word by starting a slow glide in and out of my body. I whimper, the combination of his words and his body, making me crazy and my chest hurt with the way my heart is pounding. "Everything about you is beautiful, gorgeous. I wanted you the first time I saw you and nothing can change that."

I shut my eyes and try to steel my heart against his words. The invasion of my body and the seduction of his words spook me. It's too much and I need him to fuck me and I try to speed things up with my movements but he is having none of it.

"Relax Carlisle, I'm going to give you a slow, deep fuck and you'll believe me by the time I'm done," he murmurs against my ear as he does exactly what he promises. I'm so wet, so turned on that all I can do is writhe under him, welcoming him deeper inside my mind with each thrust of his hips.

Mateo never stops kissing me. My lips, my cheeks, my

neck. Always reminding me that he is the one inside, around me. There is no way I can hide in my head and make believe that this is a nameless, faceless fuck. He grounds me to this room and to the time and place and I give in completely when his hands slide up my arms and he covers my hands, linking our fingers together.

"With me, *Tesoro*. Come with me. Come all over me."

I do. It is soft and sweet but erupts electric tingles all over my skin as I fall apart. Mateo is all over me and I have his scent, his sweat, his imprint on me and it is a safe place where I can just revel in my pleasure and his pleasure as he follows me over.

He starts to move off me but I stop him, wanting to keep this closeness, this moment for as long as I possibly can. It is the only way I can explain my agreement to what he suggests next.

"Come home with me today. My parents are having a party and I want you to go with me."

"I feel like I need to warn you about my mother in advance," I say, looking over at Carlisle in the passenger seat of my car.

I turn on the road in Lively, a little town just outside of Nashville, that leads to the house where I grew up and headed to a BBQ I was dreading until Carlisle said yes. I fully expected her to go home, get cleaned up, change her mind, and cancel on me. So no one was more shocked than me when she appeared in her living room looking like an angel in a long sundress with her hair spilling around her shoulders and a sweet kiss for me.

"I'm actually pretty good with new people. Parents usually like me," she answers. I can't see her eyes behind the sunglasses but her big smile is mocking me.

She has no idea.

We get to the top of the long driveway that leads to the house and I see the small American flags stuck into the ground on each side and I sigh.

"My mom is a naturalized citizen from Cuba. My grandparents escaped and got to Tennessee by way of Florida." I shake my head as the flags get bigger as we get closer to the house. "She is the biggest patriot since George Washington and an even bigger supporter of our teams in the winter and summer games. She screamed when I told her you were coming."

If I hadn't told her I knew I would be the one on the grill, served up later with the baked beans and potato salad. But warning her gave my mom time to prepare for her special guest. I have a pretty good idea of what is going to greet us when we get to the house.

"That is sweet. I can't wait to meet her."

"Sweet is not the word I would use to describe her." As the house comes into view I groan and then laugh at what I see. "I love her but my mom is...intense."

The large, two-story white farmhouse sits in the shelter of tall trees, rose bushes, dogwood, flowering cherry and the flowerbeds my mom has planted over the years. In the few hours since I called, my mom has placed every piece of red, white and blue decorations she has on our house and anything else that can't run away. Bunting, streamers, and flags are everywhere and stretched across the porch is a handmade banner that says "Welcome Carlisle Queen. American champion".

I park at the end of the row of cars and the silence is complete when I turn off the engine. I turn to look at Carlisle and gauge her reaction. Her face is blank and her sunglasses still cover her eyes so it is impossible to know what she is thinking. I watch as she opens the door and steps out of the car, turning in a complete circle to soak it all in.

I start to ask her what she thinks when my mother appears at the side of the house and she makes a beeline for Carlisle who barely has time to remove her sunglasses and brace herself for the arms that pull her into a hug.

"Carlisle! I am so happy to have you in my home. Welcome! Welcome! This is an honor," my mother says in heavily accented English as she continues to squeeze my date like an overly affectionate anaconda. I take a step forward to get Carlisle some breathing room when I see her arms reach up to encircle my mother.

They loosen their hold but do not let go of each other and I stand by and watch as they speak softly to each other, auburn head and darker curls bent together. My mom switches to a mix of Spanish and English as she weaves her words together into a blanket of love and welcome for the newcomer. I can't catch all of it but snatches of their conversation float over to me on the summer wind; words of pride for her accomplishment and sorrow over her loss and, finally, blessings on her future.

This is my mom's superpower, to love everyone with a heart as big as the blue sky open above us. When I was kid I was embarrassed by how my mom was constantly touching people, telling them how special they were, and making sure they were loved. It's why every lonely and neglected friend we had growing up flocked to our house. Carmela Montez Butler never learned to put a filter on her heart.

And I like that she's opened her heart to the woman who is becoming important to me.

My dad strolls up to the scene and pats my shoulder with his big paw of a hand.

"Should we rescue your friend?" he asks.

"I think she's doing fine," I say and turn to look around the yard again. "You got the stuff up quick. I only called a couple of hours ago."

"Kit sent Max over to help so I think you probably owe him more slave labor."

I roll my eyes. "What else is new."

My mom lets go of Carlisle and when they both look at us, their eyelashes are damp.

"Jesus, mom. Did you have to make her cry?" I ask, dodging my mother's swat towards my head.

"Mateo! Do you kiss your *mami* with that mouth?"

"I do and she loves it." I lean over to give her the tainted kiss and glare down at her. "You could have gone easy on her, mom."

"You cannot love in half measures, Mateo. You will know soon enough." She dismisses me with

"It's fine, Teo. It was a good cry." Carlisle gives my mom another squeeze and then turns her smile to my dad. "I'm Carlisle Queen."

"Mike Butler. Welcome to our home," he says, giving her the same shoulder pat he just gave me and then points to the backyard. "I bet you could use a cold drink after meeting my wife...or a nap."

"You can both kiss my *culo*," she grumbles but takes the hand my dad is holding out to her and follows him towards where the music is playing and the guests are gathered.

"Mom, cursing at me in Spanish is still cursing," I taunt her as I grab Carlisle's hand and follow them. "You doing okay?"

She nods, her smile genuine so I relax. "It was fine. She's pretty awesome really."

"She really is." We round the corner of the house and Carlisle stops me, her gentle "oh" making me smile. "This is where I grew up."

The view in the back is as spectacular as the front. Huge greenspace leading to the man-made lake, barns and outbuildings constructed to match the house and the rolling hills of farmland. I lift my free hand and point to a spot across the lake.

"Straight over there is the farm where my grandparents lived and now belongs to Max and Kit. I have several other cousins who bought other pieces and have built houses on it as well."

"So, as far as I can see, it's Butler land." I nod and she asks, "Do you plan to live here too?

"Not anytime soon but when I do I'll either build on the east side of the lake..." I point out a piece of land to our right. "...or I will live here in this house."

I watch her face as she soaks it all in, pleased that she clearly likes what she sees here. My nervousness about bringing her here is long gone.

"I'm glad you came with me today. Thank you." I lift the hand I am holding to my lips and press a kiss to her knuckles. "I like seeing you here. A lot."

"I like being here. Thanks for inviting me."She leans over and kisses me, soft and sweet and appropriately PG-rated for any age of guest at the party.

I lean back in for another until a voice behind me interrupts us.

"Hey, there are kids around here you know."

ELEVEN

CARLISLE

Mateo curses against my lips and pulls out of the kiss.

I push down my disappointment and peer around him to see who interrupted my chance for a little bit of sugar. Whoever he is, he resembles Mateo enough for me to presume that this one of the many Butler cousins. He's bulkier but they share the same dark hair and warm smile. I like him immediately.

"Carlisle Queen this is my cousin, Max Butler. Task master and all-around pain in my ass."

I roll my eyes, smiling back as he shakes my hand. "You're the one with the drywall problem." I say.

"My only problem is the assholes who don't know how to put up drywall properly," Max shoots back with a light shove to Mateo's shoulder.

"Holy crap, can't you two act like grown men for two seconds and not embarrass us in front of the special guest?" A tiny woman with red streaks in her dark hair steps between then and they both come to heel pretty quickly. I don't even try to bite back the laugh that bubbles up.

"Aren't you going on tour soon? Mateo asks, draping his

arm around her shoulders, trying to intimidate her with his size. She pinches him in the side and he jumps away, rubbing the spot where she made contact. He uses his free hand to gesture between us, making the introductions. "Carlisle Queen this is Kit Landry. Kit Landry this is Carlisle Queen. She has gold medals and you have gold records. Discuss amongst yourselves."

"She has platinum records Mateo," I correct him as I smile at Kit. "I have them all."

"And I am a huge fan of yours as well," Kit says and steps forward to give me a hug. When we step back she cocks her head to the side and looks me up and down. "You're taller than I expected."

"And you're shorter," I answer.

"It's the heels I wear on stage. Everyone says that."

"Everything looks smaller in a competition size pool."

"Ask her where she puts her gold medals," Mateo prompts as the four of us head to a table in the shade. He pulls my chair out for me, his hand lingering on my shoulder as he continues to speak. I love his touch and it would be very easy to get used to it. "She told me she keeps them in her underwear drawer but I don't believe her."

Kit and I lock eyes as she sits down beside me and I wonder if she will guess correctly.

"The real ones are in a safe and the framed replicas are in her closet," she says and I raise my hand to high-five with her. When our palms smack together we both laugh and I decided that I like Kit Landry a whole hell of a lot.

"Wait? Is she right?" Max asks and then looks down at his fiancée. "How did you know that?"

She shrugs and then winks at me. "The real medals are pure silver with gold plating so you aren't going to keep them in a student apartment."

"So far so good," I encourage her to continue.

"And the replicas are in your closet because it feels too braggy to put them in your living room and you don't have an office yet."

"Perfect score," I grin at her and look at Mateo. "Did you really think I kept them in my underwear drawer?"

"People keep all kinds of random stuff in their underwear drawer," he protests.

"Come on genius, let's go get a round of drinks," Max says and moves off in the direction of a group of coolers.

"I'll grab you a water," Mateo says just before he steals a quick kiss and walks away.

"So, how long have you guys been together?" Kit asks as we settle in to get to know each other better. I hesitate just a little too long and she jumps in. "I didn't mean to put you on the spot. It's just that he doesn't bring dates to family stuff."

"I'm kind of surprised that I'm here actually," I say and wonder how much is oversharing in this situation. "This wasn't supposed to be a thing."

"And now it *is* a thing?"

I think back to our time in bed this morning when Mateo talked about beginnings and what we could be. It's a thing.

"It's gotten complicated really fast."

"Well, that sounds like every great love affair," she teases.

A little girl interrupts with a handful of folded brochures she's placing on each table. I smile at her and pick one up, reading the information on the front for Grace and Peace Hospice Center.

"What is this?" I ask, turning it over and noting it's a facility located in Lively.

"Today is a thank you event for the staff at this hospice center." She pauses and asks, "Did Mateo tell you about Mari?" When I nod she continues. "Carmela volunteers there now but they like to throw a party for the wonderful people who helped Mari and so many other people."

Remembering the kind words she whispered to me just earlier, I am not surprised that Carmela gives her time to a group like this.

"When I was in the hospital and rehab for so many months, there was a group who assisted the families, brought care packages by, and helped with small tasks. My mom said they were a constant source of support." I say, looking over the brochure and reading the testimonials from so many families. "Hospice must have been a comfort. It must have been terrible for them to have her go so quickly."

"She might have had a little more time but she refused any more treatment after her first round of chemo. She was so sick and she didn't want to live what little time she had that way. Mateo was furious with her and they had a huge falling out and never reconciled."

I remember the way Mateo talked about his sister and I cannot imagine him not making it right. "That doesn't sound like the Mateo I know."

"We were all blown away but he just couldn't imagine giving up and not fighting it. He thought she was quitting without fighting and he was furious. When Mari explored assisted suicide options, he just lost it. Max had to drag him out of bars and picked him up in jail once. It was a mess."

"Did she..." I swallow hard to loosen my frozen vocal cords. My grip on the brochure so tight I can feel the paper rip. "Did she go through with it?"

"Her autopsy said that she died from the tumor but I think she did it. Mari was ready and she wanted to go out on her own terms," Kit says, her voice fading as the buzzing in my ears begins to drown out the sounds of the party around us.

Unease spreads over me and gives me a chill even in the heat of the afternoon. Anger is rising fast, aimed at myself and my selfishness in indulging in anything with Mateo. A man whose sister's story is so similar to my own and clearly broke his heart. I had my rules. I broke them. And now I have to make sure that I'm the only one who pays the price.

If I ever meet the guy (or gal) who invented Caller ID, I will kiss them on the mouth.

I glance down at my phone where it buzzes against the couch cushions. Mateo. He's been calling pretty much non-stop since I insisted that he bring me home last night and didn't invite him to stay over. It would have made perfect sense to grab his hand, drag him to bed and let him fuck me until I didn't remember just how screwed up this situation really was. But I just couldn't.

I'd wondered where this connection had come from, why we kept gravitating towards each other and I had my answer now. We are both messed up in the head and everyone knows that opposites attract except when the two people are fucked up. Put two head cases in the same room and they will snap together faster than a virgin's legs on the first date. That had Mateo and me written all over it.

But I'm glad I found out about his sister when I did because that was a recipe for a disaster that would rival the Titanic, Pompeii and Justin Bieber all rolled up together. Our stories aren't identical but the conclusion would be the same: Mateo would end up hurt. I'm not ready to put a name to whatever pulses between us but it's enough of something to make me think twice about continuing it any further. It would be a shitty move and while many would say my plans to check out on my own terms is the ultimate in shitty, I'm not going to drag him any deeper into this when I already suspect that I'm in over my head.

A week of avoiding his calls and he'll have another woman in his bed and Gross Anatomy on his mind and I will be forgotten.

The phone alerts me that I have a voicemail and I pick it up, thumbing over the screen to pull up the app. My finger hovers over it and I'd be a liar if I said I wasn't tempted to hear what he has to say. I wouldn't call him back but it would be nice to hear his voice. To see if he is pissed off enough with me for the hint of a Hispanic accent to coat every irritated syllable.

My thighs clench together at the memory of his voice and I moan and it catches in the back of my throat. I swallow hard and try counting to ten to get my heart rate back to a normal level.

I swipe to the left on the screen and press the red "delete" icon when it appears and watch as it removes my temptation. If I'm thinking about listening to his message and *hoping* he has that sexy, southern Spanish drawl thing going on... well... just no.

Mateo Butler is fun and sexy, loves his mother and fixes cars with his dad. He is a guy who helps his grandpa cheat at cornhole and loves his sister so much that her photo displayed on a banner puts tears in his eyes that he doesn't even try to brush away. And then in the ultimate "fuck you" from the universe he's the lover who makes me wet with a heated look and shatters me into a million pieces with his body. He has access to a part of me that's only been touched by one other person; a part I truly thought I'd buried with Aaron.

I'd been wrong.

I consider going to New York to visit Olivia for a week or so. Long enough for things to cool off between us. Long enough for me to forget how it feels to have his weight on top of me, the slide of his rough palm along my body, over my arms, his fingers sliding perfectly into alignment with my own. I knew that staying overnight was a risk. My Achilles Heel was morning sex and when you add to the equation the fact that Mateo is such a great guy, it all adds up to the cost of a plane ticket to JFK.

Am I running? Fuck yeah, I'm running. Because the only direction my inner compass is pointing me towards at this moment is wherever Mateo Butler was. And I just can't go there. Not anymore.

I open a new tab on my laptop and begin my search for flights. I can leave as early as tomorrow morning if I stick to non-stop in first class. Perfect. I reach for my phone to call Olivia and make sure I can crash at her place. It barely gets to the second ring when she picks up.

"HRH! What's up?"

I smile at her voice, happy to hear the joy across the line. She's loving New York, loving her new job, and head-over-heels for Sarah.

"You sound happy so I guess this means you're not coming back to me."

"Sorry babe, you've got all the right equipment but my heart belongs to another."

I laugh, settling back against the couch, suddenly so glad that I called her. I miss her. She's my best friend and I send up a silent thank you to the heavens that she answered my ad for a roommate all those months ago. She was strange, hard to impress, and even harder to love. We were a perfect match.

"If I didn't love you so much, I'd write bad things about you on the bathroom wall."

"That's not really a threat since they'd all be true."

"I'll tell them you like dick," I tease.

"Oh, that's low even for you," she chuckles on her end of the phone and I can hear the sounds of the city in the background. "I'm late for work so I gotta cut this foreplay short princess. What's up?"

"Can I come hang out with you and Sarah for a little while? A few days? A week, tops." They are still in the honeymoon phase of finally living together again after two long years apart and I don't want to cramp their style for too long.

"Sure. Stay as long as you want." She does something on her end that makes her voice fade a little but I hear her question. "When will you be here?"

"I was thinking of flying out tomorrow morning."

She stops. I can't see it but I know she has by the swift inhale that travels over the line.

"Carlisle, are you okay?"

I kick myself for putting the fear in her voice. If she's using my real name, I know she's freaking out. "I'm fine. I'm still going to set off every metal detector I get near at the airport but I'm fine."

"No. You're not."

I sigh and throw her as much of the bone as I want to send over the line. "It's nothing physical. I need to see my best friend, eat pounds of frozen cookie dough, and watch an Avengers marathon."

She sighs. "Fuck. It's Mateo Butler isn't it?" And then

all traces of nice leaves her voice and the chill in her tone makes me shiver. "Did he hurt you?"

"No. No, it's not that."

"But this is about him. I'm right. Yes?" When I don't answer she demands, "What's going on?"

"He's a *nice guy*, Livvie."

Her pause is filled with horns honking and the bustle created by millions of people crammed on an island and I count off the seconds until she responds, her voice low and a little shocked.

"Well, that fucking sucks."

"Yeah. It does." I take a deep breath and try to inject something other than the panic I am feeling in my response. "So, can I come stay with you guys?"

"Stay as long as you want. Just get here already."

"Tommorow. I'll text you my flight details."

We say our goodbyes and I end the call, settling back against the couch to think about what I need to do in order to be gone a week or maybe two. With no classes, I can zip down to Texas and see my parents. The last time I talked to my mom she'd laid on the guilt pretty thick and I need to go see them or they will come here.

My phone buzzes again and I look at the Caller ID, smiling at the name flashing on the screen. Speak of the devil.

"Hey mom. That's weird, I was just thinking—" I stop when I hear her clearly crying on the other end of the line and my stomach churns with icy hot fear. "What's wrong? Is it Andrew?"

With my older brother serving in the Marines overseas, I hate that my mind always goes to the worst case scenario but I know first-hand just how very breakable we all are.

"No," she manages to say through the sniffles. "Andrew and Dad. Everybody's fine."

I let up on the death grip I have on my phone and stand up, heading to the kitchen to grab a soda from the fridge. I yank the door open and snag one of the glass bottles that hold my favorite local root beer. I pop off the cap with the opener and take my first sip while I wait for my mom to pull herself together. She's not a crier. April Queen is the one who kicked my ass when I didn't want to get up and go train, who protected me from all the crazy that happens when your kid is a world-class athlete at thirteen, and the one who held our family together when I was hurt, so I know that whatever this is...it's something worth crying about.

"Mom. You're freaking me out."

"I'm sorry Carlisle but it's the most incredible news." Her voice is muffled and I realize that she's talking to my dad. The phone makes a weird clicking sound and the abundance of background noise tells me that I'm on speakerphone. "We got the most amazing call today from Dr. Bertrand's office."

Dr. Bertrand? Who the hell is he... or she? I've seen a million doctors on every freakin' continent since I was hurt and I gave up keeping track a long time ago.

"Mom, I have no idea who that is."

"He's the doctor who can do the surgery you need to remove all of the shrapnel."

That stops me. I know exactly who she's talking about now. This Bertrand guy is the doctor of all doctors who can do this intricate type of spinal surgery to take all of the metal out of my body. If he does this, then the chance of this killing me disappears but there is a high likelihood that I will emerge from the surgery with some level of limited mobility. I could end up using only crutches after months of physical therapy but there is a higher chance I will be a paraplegic. Wheelchair bound for the rest of my life. I feel queasy and I out the soda down on the counter.

I barely register that I am asking follow-up questions. "He said he wouldn't do it. What changed his mind?"

"He looked at your latest x-rays and MRI's and thinks you're a perfect candidate. He's prepared to do it as early as next week. Isn't that wonderful news?"

"I don't know."

"What do you mean you don't know? This is the chance for you to live a long, happy life," my mom responds, her voice flattened by her confusion. "You aren't thinking of not having the surgery are you because that would be crazy. Selfish."

"I don't want to live my life as a paraplegic. I don't think I can." I sigh. "I've told you this before. That is not what I want."

"I don't understand," my dad says, his deep voice booming over the phone. "Are you saying you would rather die than be in a wheelchair?"

"I would, yes."

My parents go silent on the other end of the phone and I wonder if we got disconnected until I hear my dad's voice, low and soothing and the unmistakable sound of my mom crying.

"Mom, don't cry," I plead, knowing it will not work.

"I prayed for this... " Her voice breaks but she pulls herself together enough to scold me. "I prayed for this miracle and you're telling me you don't want it?"

"Not if it is going to condemn me to a life I do not want to live." I struggle to gather my thoughts will all the things pinging in my brain like a pinball machine. I don't want to hurt them but I don't know how I can do that and still tell them the truth. "I've lost enough already. I should get to choose how this all ends."

The voice that rings out in my ear is the one that made coaches weep and cower in the corner. April Queen was the fiercest mom in competitive sports. Nobody even looked at me sideways without her defending me, my training time, my opportunity. I saw the biggest, baddest coaches and sports professionals duck around the corner to hide when they knew they'd wandered into the crosshairs of my mom.

Dr. Bertrand held out longer than the rest and the last "no" he delivered to us sounded pretty final to me. Apparently, my mother didn't take no for an answer.

And she isn't going to take it now either.

I hear my mother take the call off speaker and pick it up. Her voice is firm, immovable. "I'm flying out in two days to help you get ready for the surgery. He wants to do this next week and you will have it. This is not up for discussion Carlisle. I will not stand by and let you kill yourself by failing to act."

She hangs up before I can tell her that I am planning to act quite decisively if it comes down to it. She wouldn't hear me anyway. My mom has made it her life to track down any and every doctor in the universe who could help me. I'm beyond grateful. I'm still walking around because she kept pushing and persuading and harassing every medical professional to look at my case and do something.

And it will take a face-to-face argument to change her mind now.

I sit on one of my barstools and let it sink in. I've been living with a death sentence hanging over my head for so long I don't really know how to feel. I gave up hoping for a reprieve so long ago that my plans to go out on my own terms was an old friend. Comfortable and predictable.

But this change, this chance, is scary and unknown and out of my control. If I have the surgery, I will have a long lifetime of shit to think about and plan and do. A life that can include so many things I'd pushed off my menu because I was never going to get the chance to order.

Now I have an all-you-can-eat-buffet spread out in front of me and instead of falling on the table and gobbling it all up I've lost my appetite. I'm numb because of something burning in my chest that feels a lot like hope and a yearning for one person.

And it scares the shit out of me because the first person I thought of when my mom broke the news was Mateo. If I have the surgery, I could have more time with him. We could be something beyond friendly fuck buddies.

I can stick around... for him.

This is too much for my brain to process. Full blown panic leaves the taste of acid in my mouth and I know I cannot stay here right now. I slide off the stool and stumble for my purse but simply dump the contents on the counter when the tremor in my hands prevents my fingers from working properly. I spy what I'm looking for and manage to get the Molly out of the envelope, washing it down with what is left of my root beer.

I toss my wallet, my keys and my phone back into the bag and head for the door. Tonight I want to be with a crowd of strangers and not think for a while.

Luckily, I know just the place to go.

My phone rings and I pick it up on the third or fourth ring.

I look at the display. Zane. He's got a show tonight at Toot's, a big semi-dive place in town that caters to a rougher crowd who like good music, hard liquor and a really good time. It also has frequents nights where a brawl breaks out and the cops have to come out and sort through the drunks and assholes. I really hope tonight isn't one of those nights because I don't want to make a trip to the police station tonight.

"What the fuck, Zane?" I growl into the phone. "I don't have any money for bail."

"Mateo listen up, all I've got is a few minutes in between sets." He's shouting a little over the noise in the background but I hear him loud and clear. "Your girl is here and she's pretty fucked up."

I want to remind him that she's not my girl. Being my girl would require her to pick up my phone calls or answer my texts. Carlisle Queen has been radio silent since I dropped her off at her house and she didn't invite me up.

But Zane sounds spooked and suddenly the Facebook status of our relationship is all background noise.

"I'm on my way."

I dress and jump in my car, breaking several moving violations to get to Toot's as quickly as possible. I pull my car into the gravel lot and park with a move that would make Bo and Luke Duke proud and I run to the building.

I get to the door and pay the cover charge and begin the process of elbowing my way through a pretty big crowd of drunk people. The bar smells of booze, sweat, too much perfume, and the desperation of people who realize it's about an hour from last call.

It isn't easy to push through and I get more than one nasty look but I'm on a mission to find Carlisle before she does something dumb. Or something dumber than coming to Toot's by herself.

I make my way to the stage and Zane is front and center, belting out a cover of a popular song and wailing on his guitar. I move forward and get as close as I can to the stage with the Zane groupies all lined up on the edge and trying to get his attention with their "pick me, pick me" boob displays. I start to wave to get his attention but he's got an eye out for me and he points towards the left side of the room, never breaking stride on the lyrics or the chords.

I twist around and I see her, the red hair is like a beacon even in the dark haze of the room. I also have her location hard-wired into my body like it's GPS. She's dancing on the floor by herself, which is good, but she's got an audience of three or four huge guys who could easily get work as extras on "Sons of Anarchy". Fuck me.

I shove my way through the crowds pretty quickly, only allowing myself to breathe when I have my hands on her.

"Carlisle!" I shout over the music while I do a quick

once-over of her body. She looks fine but she's not dressed for a night out. Jeans and t-shirt with her red and white chucks are not pick-me-up-and-take-me-home clothes and I let go of the pit in the bottom of my stomach. "Carlisle, we've got to go."

"Mateo!" Her smile is bright, her pupils blown and she is swaying in time with music from another bar because it doesn't even remotely match the beat of Zane's song. She's hopped up on something and I'm guessing it's her favorite party friend, Molly. Jesus.

"Babe, we've got to get you out of here." She nods happily and I send up a prayer that her drug of choice makes her very agreeable because I don't have time to deal with her and the three big biker guys who have moved in our direction. They look like a group of dogs who are seriously pissed that I just took away their favorite chew toy.

"Hey," the big guy in the middle shouts at me. "We were here first."

Fuck me. I'm going to kick her ass when she sobers up tomorrow. I swear to God.

I'm not crazy enough to take on three guys at once. I might do stupid stuff but I don't have a death wish. What I *do have* is years of experience on what can turn a guy off as fast as he got turned on in the first place. I use the first thing that comes to mind.

"She's underage!" I yell and then I put a cherry on that banana-bullshit-split. "Her dad's a cop and he'll kill me if he knows she was here."

I guess their prison experience wasn't something they want to repeat because they back off pretty quickly and I start moving Carlisle out of this place before the last call stampede begins. Even with her being so compliant, it's difficult to maneuver her through the crowd and when I see her wince in pain when she's jostled by a group of happy drunks, I do what I have to do.

"Hang on to my neck," I shout in her ear and I bend down and pick her up in my arms.

I look like Richard Gere in "An Officer and a Gentleman" when he takes Debra Winger away from her crappy factory job and I feel ridiculous. But it parts the crowds before us and I walk us out the front door of Toot's and get her in my car without incident. I slide behind the wheel and send a quick thank you text to Zane and tell him that I'll be at Carlisle's place.

I glance over at the passenger seat and she's out cold, snoring softly as if this is something that happens to her every day. I worry that this is a state she is in every day but since the last time I brought it up I got my ass handed to me, I'll keep it to myself.

The crowd is starting to grow in the parking lot and I don't want to be here when all the drunks try to leave at one time. I start the car and drive back to her apartment, glancing over at her often to make sure she's okay.

Traffic is light and it takes no time to get to her place and when I can't wake her up I have to execute the same move I did in the club to get her inside. It would be way easier to place her in a fireman's hold but with her back injury, I worry that I will hurt her. So I navigate the steps and the old elevator and finally get to her door.

I dig her keys out of her purse and get us inside and take her straight to bed. I pull off her chucks, leave on everything else and pull the covers over her. I sit beside her on the bed and brush her hair back from her face, letting the red gold satin caress the back of my hand. I watch her sleep and wonder just what the hell is going on in her head.

Carlisle Queen is beautiful and sexy and funny and

seriously fucked up. I should leave her alone but I can't. Somewhere in the middle of the sex and the drugs and the things that neither of us like to talk about, I started falling for her.

I stand and kick off my shoes and climb into bed beside her, tugging her over until her cheek rests against my chest and I can feel the steady rise and fall of her breathing, the warmth of her length pressed against mine.

I know better than anyone that I'm not the guy she's going to need. My track record for sticking when things go to shit is phenomenally bad. I couldn't do it for my sister. I don't know if I can do it for Carlisle.

But the truth is that when she needs me, even if she doesn't ask for it, I answer the bat signal. Every. Damn. Time.

And that has to mean something.

FOURTEEN
CARLISLE

"I know we call you Ariel but right now you look a lot like Sleeping Beauty."

I blink at the morning light streaming through my bedroom window and curl into the warm body pressed against me in my bed. I don't need to look up at his face to know that it's Teo. His smell, the muscles underneath his clothes, the way he holds me under the reassuring weight of his arm are well known to me, branded into my muscle memory.

I just don't know how he got here.

"How did you get here?" I ask, moving to the side as he stretches beside me. His dark hair is messed up in that sexy way I like and his stubble is dark on his jaw and makes his blue eyes stand out.

"Zane called me and told me that you were at Toot's having too much fun so I brought you home."

Last night is a blur of music and dancing and forgetting all about the phone call from my mom. I headed straight to Toot's. I knew Zane was playing so I was guaranteed a good show to provide a few hours of distraction. The crowd there is always a bit rough but friendly enough. I had a good time. Mission accomplished.

"Too much fun? No such thing." I wave him off, avoiding eye contact as I gingerly make my way out of the bed. I test the leg cooperation this morning and besides the stiffness that always is around in the morning I feel pretty good. I also feel Mateo's eyes on me and I stand, escaping to the shield of my bathroom.

He's not supposed to be here. I'm avoiding him for a very good reason and now I really don't need to drag him into all this mess. I need to get him out of my apartment.

I grab my toothbrush and squeeze out a generous dollop and begin the process of removing the nasty scum from my teeth. My reflection is nothing much to look at; my hair is in a tangled snarl, and the mascara smudged below my eyes makes me look like a deranged raccoon. Mateo appears in my side view, leaning against the doorframe, his sexy, lanky length tempting me to give him the slow once-over or to drag him back to bed and get all those clothes off of him.

He quirks an eyebrow at me as if he knows what I'm thinking and it pisses me off. I bend over, turn on the water and spit in the sink. I try to move past him but he stops me with an arm across the opening.

"Extra toothbrush?"

I lean back, pull open a drawer and locate a spare tooth-brush my dentist gave me at my last appointment and hand it over. He takes it with the hand stretched across the door and we stare at each other for a few moments before he finally lowers his arm and lets me pass.

"I take it back," he calls after me. "You're more like the princess and the pea. In a shitty ass mood after sleeping on a boulder all night."

I ignore him and head to the kitchen where I put on a

pot of coffee and stare at it while it begins to brew. I know Mateo isn't going to cooperate and just leave without talking about why I was at Toot's last night. If I talk about last night then everything will come out and I just can't handle it all if he knows. I care about what he thinks. I care about hurting him. I care about him.

He strides into the room and walks over to the coffee pot, pours a mug and settles back against the counter and stares at me. I can feel his eyes shoot laser beams into the back of my head and I resist the urge to actually flinch. I am so aware of him when he is in the room that it feels like a palpable touch. One more data point to prove that Mateo means too much to me.

"I get that we're done. You don't want me to call, you don't want me in your bed anymore. Fine. But you need to tell me why you were at Toot's last night. Alone. High," he demands, his voice low but angry.

"I wanted to go out."

"To *that* place? Alone?"

"I wanted to see Zane play and I've been to Toot's before. It was just another night out."

He lets out a frustrated sigh that tells me he's reaching the end of his patience with me. "Carlisle, you need to start talking because you're not stupid and you're not foolish so I don't understand why I found you in that bar high as a fucking kite."

I walk out of the kitchen and into my living room, taking a seat on the sofa. Mateo follows me, seating himself directly in my line of sight. He's gritting his teeth, pissed off and not even trying to hide it.

"I'm not trying to be a dick but I almost got my ass kicked last night by three very big guys who have likely done prison time. I get that something happened and you are done with me but I care about you and I need you to answer my question." He slams down his coffee and it splashes all over the table and his hand. It's still molten hot but he doesn't even flinch. "Do you have a death wish or something I don't know about?"

I freeze at his question, my blood and skin tingling with how close he's come to tapping into my brain. I am too slow to hide my reaction but I can see his clearly. I never understood it when books said that the blood drained from someone's face with shock but I do now.

"Carlisle." He swallows hard, his speech stilted as he chooses his words carefully. "Do you want to kill yourself?"

And then I realize that if I care about him at all, I need to tell him the truth.

"I need to explain—" I try to answer him but he cuts me off.

"What is there to explain? I cannot understand this at all." I put my coffee down on the table and move to sit closer to him. I reach out to touch him but he pulls away and I feel like I'm losing something vital. Elemental. "Don't touch me."

"Okay." I deserve his rejection and the venom in his voice and even though it kills me to see the pain and confusion in his eyes, I maintain eye contact. "You know that I have shrapnel in my back that surgeons could not remove. What you don't know is that if I leave it in my body it will paralyze or kill me."

"Jesus," he says, his shoulders slumping with the weight of my words. A burden I never wanted to give him.

"There is one guy in the whole world who can do the surgery that gets it all out and not kill me on the table but he refused to do it...until yesterday." Mateo's expression immediately lightens and the hope in his eyes makes my heart hurt. I can't let him think this is a viable option. "I don't want to have the surgery."

"What? Why?"

"If he does the surgery I will have some level of limited mobility. I could walk with crutches or I could be paralyzed from the waist down and be confined to a wheelchair."

"But if you don't have the surgery you could die," Mateo counters and I know the exact moment he understands what I have planned to do. Horror, stark and ugly, mixed with disbelief twists his lips into a grimace. He stands, his entire body shaking with his outrage. "You'd rather *die?*"

"I'd rather live...just not in a wheelchair."

"That's so selfish," he accuses. "What about your parents? Livvy?" He lifts his hand and pounds it against his chest, each hard thump punctuating his words. "*What about me?*"

I break eye contact with him but he's having none of it. Mateo drops to kneel in front of me and lifts my face to meet his gaze. He's in pain. I can feel it rolling off him in waves and I have to reach out and touch him, caressing his face with my open palm. He nuzzles into me and my breath catches, my heart squeezing painfully.

"Don't ask me that Mateo."

"You knew you were going to do this and you got involved with me anyway?"

"I didn't mean to. I kept thinking we were keeping it light or I was the only one getting in too deep." I lean my forehead against his and close my eyes. He leans into the touch like he always does, rubbing our noses together, lips brushing with the lightness of a butterfly. "I didn't know it would happen so fast and when I heard about Mari, I knew it had to end. I'm so sorry. I never meant to hurt you."

We sit like that for several long moments and I memorize his strength, his warmth, the pure pleasure of his touch.

"Mateo, I went too far. I was not fair to you when I began this or when I kept it going. And I want to tell myself to have the surgery so that we could have this for longer and see what it could be. It is enticing and you are the dream I didn't even know I wanted anymore. But I can't make this decision for you or my parents or my friends. It needs to be a decision I can live with no matter what happens in the end."

He pulls away from me and I have to sit on my hands to resist the urge to pull him back and wrap myself around him. I can't ask him to do this for me when I can't return the favor.

"Well, then you'll understand I can't sit around and watch you choose to die," his voice is wet with his emotion and it sparks the tears spilling down over my cheeks. "I did it before and I just can't do it again. I'm sorry Carlisle."

I watch as he walks to the door, opens it, and leaves.

He doesn't look back.

FIFTEEN
CARLISLE

"Dr. Shrieve, you have to tell me what to do."

"Carlisle, that's not how it works and you know it," she says from her usual chair. She's not dressed in her usual psychiatrist outfit but wearing jeans and a t-shirt from the last Miranda Lambert tour. I guess she doesn't bother to worry about her clothes when her patient calls after hours for an emergency appointment.

"I'm paying you double your rate and you're going to play shrink head games with me?"

"Carlisle, I can't make this decision for you. Nobody can." She puts down the notebooks and leans her arms on her elbows. "It is your body and your future and you are the one who has to live with the consequences. I'm here to help you make the decision for yourself."

"But, I don't know what I want. My parents want me to have the operation." I stand and pace the room, unable to sit while my gut is churning like an ice cream machine set on flash freeze. "Mateo wants me to have the operation. Livvy wants me to have the operation. If I make any other choice I let them all down."

"Okay, let's walk through your options. You already made the decision to take your life. If you don't have the operation you will have the same outcome. The only difference is that they know and will have to stand by and watch you do it and you will have to witness the impact your death would have on them. Correct?"

I nod and she's continues.

"If you have the operation, you live. Maybe in a wheelchair, maybe with crutches but you live. You'll have months of rehab and will need help and we both know how much you hate asking for help. But, you will have your whole like ahead of you to whatever you want. Stay in school. Drop out. Compete again. Move to Tasmania. The possibilities are endless."

And that is what terrifies me.

"I got used to only having to plan for a short period of time. Time where I could live like I wanted to live," I whisper, my mouth dry and throat sore.

"Carlisle, can I tell you what I think has you so scared?" I sit and nod at her, my entire focus on the woman I hop can make sense of all the threads tangled in my head. "I never thought I would see you even contemplate changing your mind. Your death, the timing, the way you were going to do it was all under your control. There were very few variables to surprise you." She takes off her glasses and places them on the table, for the first time in our entire relationship moving to sit next to me on the sofa. "When those people murdered Aaron and your friends they also took your control and that scared you. It would scare anyone. Suddenly, the world you had owned and ordered to your satisfaction was gone and it was at the whim of people you never met. Your perspective shifted and now the world was a big scary place where nothing was guaranteed, nothing was safe and there was nothing you could do about it."

Dr. Shrieve reaches over to the table and picks up the tissue box, handing it to me. I take one and wipe my face, surprised when it comes back wet.

"I've cried more in the last fucking week than I've cried since the bombing," I complain, swiping angrily at the tears.

"And I think your body is telling you that you need to so go with it. Let it happen. Stop holding on so tight." She pats my hand and asks. "Are you ready to hear more?"

"Yes, please."

"Hope is the belief that things in the future will work out for the best and they took that from you. So, for you there was nothing worth staying for, no reason to believe that the future would be any better than the past. But now you have things in your life that make you hope and taking your life isn't the only option. I think it's the reason why you didn't tell your mom no and I think it's why you called me."

I remember the moment my mom told me and the way that Mateo flashed in my mind. I

"But I can't make this decision based on people who may or may not be there. I lost Aaron and I don't know if I can live through that again. I don't want to love that way again. It's terrifying."

"Because they might leave or die?"

"Yes!"

"Well, welcome back to the human race, Carlisle. Join the terrifying adventure of love and life that the rest of have to endure. A journey that is only worth making because of the people we love along the way even though we know we could lose them." She reaches out and grabs my hand. "Embrace your hope again and decide if the future might be worth it no matter who comes or goes. There are so many things you will never be able to control but if you're the Carlisle Queen that *I know*, you'll wring out every ounce of adventure no matter what life throws at you."

And just like that, I know what I'm going to do.

SIXTEEN
MATEO

I went home.

College graduate. Grown ass man. I'd lasted one long, sleepless night in my house before I got in my car and headed home to my mom. My dad, actually. Carmela Montez Butler could be all kinds of sweetness, light and homemade cookies when necessary, but in this instance I knew what she would do. My mom would smack me upside the back of my head, tell me to get that exact body part out of my butt and head on back to Carlisle's house. She is the call-to-action part of our family, the one who believes that making lists and getting busy is the best way to get the shit in your head straight.

My dad, is the thinker. The listener. The one who patiently coaxes an answer out of you just like he gets every beat up car that rolls into his shop to purr like a kitten and shine brighter than a Victoria's Secret model on the runway.

And right now I need somebody to help me sort out all the crap in my head because I sure as hell can't do it myself. Maybe if I can get my brain straight, the ice in my veins will thaw and the shards of glass in my gut will disappear.

I pull into the gravel driveway tucked under the shade trees in the side yard and head for the garage tucked behind the barn on the back of our property. It is his place, his man cave long before there were TV shows about it. Instead of large flat screens and beer taps, my dad is happy with a set of hydraulic lifts and the smell of engine grease. I find him in his usual position, shoulders deep in the front end of an old car with an old-fashioned country station on the radio.

He looks up when I walk through the door, delivering his usual "Hey Son" in that deep, rumbling voice that can either soothe or strike terror in anyone within a five-mile radius. Something on my face makes him straighten up to his full height of six-feet three-inches and before I know it, he grabs me and pulls me into his arms. My dad isn't a hugger; more of the type to slap you on the back or place a heavy palm on your shoulder and I can count on two hands the number of times he's given me a hug since I hit puberty.

But he holds me now, letting my anger and grief and frustration leech out of me and dampen the front of his shirt.

"She's dying, Dad."

His arms tighten around me at my words and I burrow a little closer, grateful to hide my face against his shoulder as I give in to the panic and the teeth-chattering terror that squeezes me in its cruel grip. Gradually I calm down and pull out of his embrace, wiping my face with the hem of my t-shirt. I avoid meeting his eyes, embarrassed at the way I've completely fallen apart.

He says nothing, instead he does what he always does and walks back to the open hood of the car and reaches for a tool, handing it over to me. I take it from him, the wrench cool against the skin of my palm. I glance up at him and he barely makes eye contact before he gestures towards the engine. I know what he wants me to do, I've spent as much time in the garage as I have in school, or on the football field, or the backseat of my car with a naked girl.

I begin the methodical process of reconnecting wires and hoses, letting the familiar actions work their magic to settle my nerves and kick my brain back into the zone of normal. We work side-by-side for half an hour before he says anything.

"Why don't you tell me what's wrong with your girl?"

"There's shrapnel in her back from the bombing," I say, trying to quickly capture the basics of what Carlisle relayed to me last night. I hadn't caught it all. Not with the shock and the prior night's lack of sleep but the most important parts are cemented in my mind. "It's been in there causing more damage to her spinal cord and one day, very soon, it is going to paralyze her or... " I suck in a breath and force out the words that feel like razor blades in my throat, "... or it's going to kill her."

My dad stops what he is doing and looks at me, the steel gray in his eyes one of the things I know I inherited from him, along with my stubborn streak and hopefully his patience.

"They can't do anything for her?" he asks.

"There's an operation... nobody has been willing to do it until now... "

"But now somebody will do it. Yes?"

"Yes," I say, putting down the tools. My hands are shaking too hard to use them properly. I turn and lean against the side of the car, focusing on an ancient Miller Beer clock mounted on the wall.

My father puts down his tools and wipes off his hands, leaning against the side of the car next to me. "It sounds like she doesn't have much of a choice, though."

I pause. How do I explain what Carlisle told me? I'm not sure I fully understand it myself. And I'm... conflicted... about everything.

"She's not sure if she's going to have the surgery," I say.

"What?"

"She doesn't want to be... paralyzed... disabled. It's the most probable outcome for the surgery."

"That's terrible but the only alternative is... "

He stops talking and I can feel him turn to look at me. I swallow hard, suddenly unable to breathe even though my heart is fluttering like a hummingbird.

"Oh Matty," he says, using the nickname he abandoned when he gave me the speech about wet dreams and how to behave with real girls. The anguish in his voice tells me that he understands everything. His arm is a heavy weight across my shoulders and I appreciate the grounding it gives me when it feels like I'm going to fly apart.

"She's been planning to kill herself since before we even met. She doesn't want to live if it involves crutches or a wheelchair or anything like that." I turn to face him, hoping that I see some kind of answer in his gaze. "And this feels like it's Mari all over again. Karma, God, the fucking universe paying me back for not being there for her. For failing her."

He moves quickly, big hands around the back of my neck, forcing me to maintain eye contact.

"The God I know isn't going to dish out payback. Never." He is vehement, fierce in his tone even though his grip is gentle. "And you did not fail Mari. She made her choice and we all had to live with it because it was her decision to make. She didn't make it lightly or without considering all of us but she couldn't deny what she wanted, what she needed, just to live for us. I didn't like it then and I hate it now but I can't fault her for the choice she made."

I push him away, anger rising and eclipsing the hurt and the fear.

"How can you say that Dad? She gave up! She didn't fight!"

"If you think for one minute that your sister didn't fight then you weren't paying attention. She fought and got the chemo and puked her guts out for weeks. She lost weight and cried when her hair fell out and endured something no parent should ever have to watch their kid go through." He raises a fist, white knuckled and shaking and places it over his heart, his expression open and broken. I want to look away but I can't. "And when they gave her the options, she chose to go out on her terms. She knew she was giving up time but she wanted what time she had to be different. I didn't want her to make that choice but I understand that it was hers to make." He steps forward, lowering his voice and placing his hand on my shoulder. "And no matter how you or I feel about it, Carlisle will make her own choice and you will either be able to support her or not. *That* will be your choice."

I know he's right. Mari was right. Carlisle will be right with whatever she chooses to do. I just don't know what I can do.

"I failed Mari. I don't want to do the same with Carlisle," I whisper.

"I know you think you let your sister down, the family down, and all I can tell you is that none of us think you did. If Mari did, she never said one word about it."

I pace away from him and throw out there the one thing that has never been said between us. I can't even look at him.

"I wasn't there to say goodbye. I was drunk and fucking some girl whose name I still can't remember."

He closes his eyes and his fists grip at his side as he lets out a long, slow breath. When he makes eye contact with me I see disappointment in their depths but overwhelmingly I just see pity and love and something splits open deep inside me. I grab my abdomen, convinced that if I look down, I will see my guts and lifeblood spilling out and onto my feet.

"Zane never told me where he found you but I thought it was something like that."

I nod, bracing myself for what I have coming, what I deserve. "Don't you hate me? Hate my failure?"

"I could never hate you but I am disappointed in you," he says, honestly but with no heat. "But I know you've hated yourself for it enough for the whole world's judgment and I think you need to stop. Mari didn't hate you. She said there was nothing left unsaid between the two of you and she was at peace about it."

"I wish I'd been there," I say, choking on the bitterness of the truth. "Wish I'd had the guts to say goodbye."

"And that is something you'll have to put at rest for yourself. Give it time and you'll work it out," Dad says as he leans against the car, watching me closely. "All we can do is take what happened and try to make it into something that helps, that heals. Maybe that's medical school for you. Maybe it's loving Carlisle. I don't know."

"I don't know if I love Carlisle," I say, the words rough on my tongue. They taste of a bitter half-truth. I know how I feel about her—I just don't know if I can let myself follow everything that goes with it.

My dad shifts a look at me that says he doesn't believe what I just said but he lets it pass, instead saying, "I don't know if she's made up her mind or not but you've got to make up your mind to either be all in or all out. Whether she decides to go out on her own terms or spend the rest of her life in a wheelchair, if you don't love her enough to stand by her through all of it, then get out of the way so that she can find the man who will."

It isn't the answer I was hoping he'd give me, the solution to all my problems, but it's a direction. Something for me to consider along with everything else we talked about tonight.

I walk out of the garage, waving my mom off as I head to my car and climb inside. I pull out onto the road and make turn after turn, sticking to the two and one lane roads headed deeper into the country. The sun slides across the sky as I drive, stopping only to fill up the tank and grab a bottle of water. My phone is buzzing in the seat beside me but I ignore it. Zane. My mom. Zane again.

I need to figure out what I'm going to do.

One part of me wants to give in to the rage and crash this vehicle into the nearest tree, as if me giving up my life will somehow give Carlisle's back to her. The ultimate penance for being a shitty brother and a coward.

Can I learn from what I did wrong before and get it right this time? Can I be the man Carlisle will need? Can I be the man who will watch her struggle with whoever she'll be after the surgery? Can I be the man who will hold her hand as she passes on her own terms?

Can I actually give her up?

THE LIGHTS in Nashville shine like costume jewelry on a pretty girl when I head back into the city with the top down and the wind drowning out everything but my thoughts. My head is spinning, my heart catching with each thought of Carlisle, each memory.

I cannot get past the moment in my bed. Not the sex, not the way she controls me with a brush across my skin or the press of her lips on mine but the slide of our hands together. Fingers entwined in the perfect weave, stronger together than apart. The way she tightened her grip on mine when I whispered "*Tesoro*".

My treasure.

The one I was not looking for but found buried under the shit of all of our issues, our pasts, our pain. Carlisle shines like gold, warming me from the inside out. Repairing the broken bits and bringing the others back to life. *Mi Tesoro.*

I pull in to one of the empty spots on the street in front of her apartment, weighing what I'm going to say to her but knowing that it has to be tonight. It has to be right now. I look up and see the lights on in her living room and I take the stairs at a run, bypassing the elevator and power pulling off the railing to help me get there faster. I run down the hallway, banging on the door as soon as I get it within arm's reach.

I keep knocking even when I hear steps approaching and the murmurings from within that "they are coming as fast as they can". I hold my breath as the door swings open and I face an older woman with Carlisle's red-gold hair and freckles on her nose. Close behind her is a man whose intense stare I've seen leveled at me many times when his daughter is trying to figure me out. Carlisle is a fair blend of them both, stealing the best parts to mix into her own unique beauty.

Behind them both, Carlisle steps forward, her hair pulled up in a ponytail and she's wearing no make-up. She looks pale, the red around her eyes betraying her if she's trying to keep her tears a secret. I want to take her face in my hands, wipe every single one, and kiss her until she forgets her reasons to cry. Just for a little while.

"Mateo." Her father knows my name so I'm guessing that their daughter has brought them up to speed on the man she's been sleeping with. His face is rigid and I can tell by the way he's holding his hands at his side that he's itching to throw me out. "This isn't a good time."

I shake my head. "I think it's the perfect time for me to tell you that I love your daughter." Carlisle gasps and I turn to her, taking the several steps it takes for me to cover the distance to stand right in front of her. "I love you and I'm here. No matter what you decide to do I will stay with you, but I'm hoping you choose to stay with me because I love you. So much."

She reaches for me and I pull her into my arms, exhaling when she burrows in close and hangs on tight.

"I love you too," she whispers.

It's all the answer I need for right now.

"Do you two have enough towels, Mom?" I ask.

I look around the second bedroom in my apartment, making sure my parents have what they need. Tomorrow is my surgery and after a week of test, more tests, and invasively personal questions, I have the green light to jump off a cliff into the vast unknown.

That isn't entirely true.

I know these things: my chances of dying on the table are miniscule; my chances of using some form of crutches or a wheelchair for the rest of my life is at ninety percent. If there is a ten percent miracle out there for me, I might walk forever unaided but I have a sneaky suspicion that I used that miracle on surviving the bomb blast in the first place. I've heard over and over this week that I am a very lucky girl.

And this week I believe them.

Because Mateo is in the other room waiting for me.

My mom turns to look at me from her place at the desk and she's got "the face" on. Now I know why my dad is out on the balcony. He's not watching the city lights, he's avoiding the big emotional after-school special moment my mom clearly wants to have. I take two steps towards the door and she crooks her finger at me in the "come here" gesture and then points to the end of the bed.

I sit my ass down because what else am I supposed to do. Her baby is going under the knife tomorrow and she wants to say whatever it is she needs to say. I guess I should say some things too.

We are not an extraordinarily emotive family. My dad is a stoic rancher, fifth generation and a Texan to the core. Mom is an Alabama beauty who went to the University of Texas to get her teaching degree and ended up living on a ranch and raising two kids. Andrew, is a big, bad Marine and loves it. You hug him at your own risk.

"Emma Carlisle," she says, using my seldom-used first name. "I am so grateful you are having the surgery. I know you're bearing the burden for all of us. The physical therapy, the uncertain future. We love you for it."

I shake my head. She's got it wrong.

"Mom, I'm not doing it for you... "

She cuts me off with a wave of her hand. "For Mateo then. I don't care who it's for I just... " And then she starts to cry and I sit there feeling like a total asshole for making my mom cry. "You have no idea what it's like to watch someone you love die so young and so full of promise."

I gasp and she stutters a bit, her hands waving in front of her face like she's trying to suck the words back in. I know she didn't mean them the way they came out. I throw out all my usual hang-ups and rush to comfort her and gather her close in a hug. If there was ever at time for the Queens to get huggy, this is probably it.

"It's okay mom. I know you didn't mean Aaron." I rub her back as she cries on my shoulder and I remain strong, bearing her pain and letting her find her peace as I can. In an ideal world, she should be the one holding me as I weep and wail but I'm not built that way. I might look like my mom but I'm my daddy's girl where it counts. I can be strong for her and anyone who needs me to be. I've seen me do it. "It's okay. I'm going to be fine. Dr. Bertrand says so."

I hold her for a while longer, giving her time to pull herself together as I correct her assumption.

"I'm not doing this for you, or dad, or Mateo. I'm doing it for me."

She pulls away and looks at me, her eyes narrow with disbelief. "You told me you were planning on *killing* yourself. The only thing that changed since then is Mateo Butler arriving on the scene and while I'm beyond grateful, I do think it's a little fast."

Wait. What?

"What are you talking about mom?" I release her and scoot back on the bed not sure where this made such a weird turn.

"It's just that we've never heard about him and we get here and he comes running and declares his love and suddenly you're having the surgery. I just think it's a little soon for you to count on this working out between the two of you."

"Nice way to tell me you don't like my boyfriend, mom."

"It's not that I don't like him. He's wonderful, handsome and he can't keep his eyes off you. But what you're getting ready to do, all the hard work and the uncertainty would take its toll on a couple who had been together for years." She reaches out and grabs my hand, giving me a smile that tells me she's not trying to freak me out just hours before major surgery. "The kind of bond you need to get through this type of life-change takes time and you guys just haven't had that time."

I nod, completely understanding what she just said. She's not wrong. But Mateo and I aren't guaranteed to work even if we had been together twenty years. Nobody is.

"I get it mom. All I can tell you is that I love him and he loves me and we're going to ride this out together. Whatever happens will happen but I think we've got what it takes." I squeeze her hand and stand to go back to my room. "But I'm not doing this for Mateo. I am doing this because of how he makes me feel." She's obviously confused so I try my best to explain it better. "I loved Aaron and losing him killed off my ability to hope but Mateo gave it back to me. And as Dr. Shrieve reminded me hope is not a guarantee of the future but it's a reason to stick around. So I decided to stick and around see what life has in store for me. I hope it is with Mateo, I plan on it, but I know better than anyone that the best laid plans can be gone in the blink of an eye."

"I think I get that," she says as she rises and comes over to give me one more kiss. "But whatever the reason, I'm so glad you decided to do this. Your father and I will do whatever it is you need us to do. We love you Emma Carlisle."

"I know mom and I love you too."

I leave her room and pad silently across the living room where Livvy is crashed out on the sofa. I told her she didn't need to come but there was no stopping her and I'm so glad she came. She's the sister of my heart and since Andrew couldn't get leave to come home, she can help Mateo handle my parents. Dr. Bertrand already looks like he wants to run when my mom is around.

I slip into my room and hear the shower running in my bathroom. I kick off my flip flops, peel off my capri's, and sit on the edge of the bed in just a t-shirt and my underwear. I should probably try to go to sleep, take one of the pills Dr. Bertrand gave me and float off into oblivion. But I don't want to do that. Not tonight. I have plans.

The shower stops running and I listen as Mateo pulls a towel off the rack and closes the door. I close my eyes and try to track the sounds he makes as he completes the most mundane of tasks. Brushing his teeth. Opening the cabinet door and using his deodorant and then closing the door again. No shave tonight. He'll save it for tomorrow morning.

He's been here with me for the past week and we've quickly adopted our domestic routine. I will miss this nightly ritual, waiting for him to come to the bed we share together. I love sleeping with his big frame wrapped around me, the hair on his chest and legs tickling my skin, the soft puff of his even breaths on my neck, the possessive hand he splays across my belly. Tomorrow night I will stay in the hospital for the first of several nights and then they will move me a long-term rehabilitation facility affiliated with Vanderbilt University.

I'm keeping my apartment but I have no idea when I'll be back. I just can't give it up. It would seem too ... permanent.

Mateo emerges from the bathroom, the residual steam following him out as he fully opens the door. His dark hair is wet, one of my big, fluffy towels wrapped around his waist. He sees me and he smiles. That bright, gut-punching smile that makes me glad I'm sitting down because it reduces me to goo every single time.

He is so hot. His muscles. The washboard abs and those cut lines angling down like arrows pointing to the good stuff. His large hands that can do hard labor at his cousin's house and then touch me so gently that I fall apart like a broken window night after night.

But I don't want gentle tonight. I need to feel him.

"Hey," he says walking towards me and stopping just in front of where I sit. He looks down, tiny droplets of water trailing down his chest and just begging for me to lick them off. His lips twist in a carnal grin when he guesses what I'm thinking.

"How are your parents?" He asks.

He wants to talk about my mom and dad? I look at him more closely and I see the laughter twitching at the corner of his mouth. He's teasing me.

I reach out and grab the edge of the towel and tug, dropping it to the floor. He's only half hard but I know I can fix that.

"I don't want to talk about my parents or the surgery or any other fucking thing right now. All I want to do is have you fuck me so that for one last night I can feel like myself. A memory to last for a lifetime. Can you do that for me?"

He's starting down at me, all traces of humor gone from his face now and his dick is getting harder as the second pass. He licks his lips but his voice is still hoarse when he speaks. "I can do that for you."

"Good." I nod and swallow, thinking about what I crave most. "I want to suck you off first. Make me."

His eyes flare at my demand, his pupils now blown so that he looks like he's on something. I know he's only high on me and that turns me on even more. I feel powerful as my hand circles his cock, loving the feel of the hard length as it slides over my palm. Mateo grabs my hand and lowers it to my side, pressing it down on the bed.

"Keep your hands to yourself," he demands while taking my head in between his big hands and holding me still while he rubs my mouth with his dick.

We stare at each other, something primal and achingly

sensual suspended between us. I feel dirty and powerful in all the best ways and I moan when he rolls his hips and his cock presses against my lips. I lick them and open as he presses inside with his hard, hot thickness. The thick flare of his cockhead glides over my tongue leaving behind a salty, sexy taste of pre-come.

I open wider, looking forward to the ache I will have in my jaw tomorrow, and Mateo sets a rhythm. He's not gentle, sensing my mood and riding it out as he fucks my mouth and takes me out of my head and all the scary places its been lately. He pulls halfway out and then sinks back in again, bumping the back of my throat when I reach up and cup his ass, digging my fingers into the taut muscle there. My head starts to swim as he starts talking.

"Fuck Carlisle, that's so good baby. You're so wet and hot." He groans, his grip on my head tighter as his thrusts get faster. He's using me just like I want, the only thing I feel is the way my body responds to his, the wetness between my thighs and the ache in my breasts. I feel alive. Whole. Feminine.

"I'm close. If you don't want it down your throat let me know."

I don't. I want him inside me when he explodes. I pull off him and use my grip on his ass to maneuver him around and push him down on the bed. He lands with a bouncing thud and we both huff out a quick laugh of surprise. Mateo and Carlisle. Still laughing when we make love. I hope that part never ends.

I reach over to my side table and get a condom out of the drawer. I open the packet and crawl over him and roll it down his length, loving the way his body bucks up when I give I few leisurely strokes.

"How do you want me baby?" He asks, lying in a

submissive pose on the bed. "I'm yours however you want me. All I want to do is make you feel good. As many times as you want."

I run through the many ways I can have him take me. Mateo is an amazing lover and I'll come, over and over as he promises if I want. But tonight I want to be in charge, I need to have that control over our pleasure.

"Just like that. Hands on the headboard." He sucks in a breath but does as I direct him and moves around until his head is on the pillows, long body spread out. I lick my lips when he raises his arms and grips the wrought iron bars on my headboard.

I straddle him, resting my wet pussy against the hard length of him, undulating my hips just enough to cause sparks behind my eyelids and see his grip on the bars tighten. I trail my fingertips down his chest, tracing the cut of his abs, rubbing the hard pebbles of his nipples. His thighs are shaking, his feet digging into the mattress.

"I'm going to ride you, Mateo. Don't move until I tell you to."

He nods, jaw tight with his effort to remain still.

I position my body over his hard erection and I slide down, the glide so easy with how wet I am. Nobody gets me off like Mateo. Nobody. I suck in a huge breath as he fills me, stretching me, the first few moments walking that pleasure /pain path I love so much. I memorize all of it, committing it to memory and hoping this isn't the last time I feel this way.

I don't want to be in this alone so I keep my gaze on him. I could get drunk on the play of emotions across his face as I begin a slow up and down ride on his dick. I take my time, enjoying the moments as they pass by with us joined, suspended in our pleasure... together.

"You like that?" I ask and he nods, his grip making the muscle in his forearm go taut. "Do you want me to go faster?"

"I love being buried in your pussy. Fast, slow. I just want to stay inside you forever," he confesses. The naked honesty on his face making my chest hurt with just how loved I know I am.

I lean forward, placing my breasts at mouth level and whisper, "Suck on them."

Mateo lifts his head, capturing my right nipple in his mouth and he sucks on it hard and long. The pulse of lightening from his touch races across my belly and settles in my clit as it rubs against his abdominal muscles with each of my strokes. I let my ride speed up as he licks and sucks and lightly bites my nipples until they are sensitive to his every caress. I can feel the beginning of my orgasm low in my belly.

"Fuck me Mateo," I growl in his ear and it sets him free to move.

He bucks his hips up as I piston mine down and our bodies meet in a frantic press of hard cock and soft pussy. His hand remains on the headboard but I don't need them on me. I just need him inside me, filling me.

I want it to last longer but he returns his mouth to my breast and takes a nipple in his mouth and begins a fast flicker of his tongue against it. I explode. On him. All over him. My orgasm bows my back and forces me to lose my rhythm.

Mateo lets go of the headboard and grabs my hips, forcing me to follow his pace until he stiffens underneath me and yells with the force of his release.

We probably disturbed the neighbors or woke my

parents but I don't care. I needed this. What could be my last time to feel this way, to feel this, period.

I send up a silent prayer that this part of me will remain. That this next step will not strip me of what to me is so essential to my femininity, my enjoyment of life. I feel ashamed at my thoughts, knowing I should be grateful to be alive, to have this opportunity to reduce my pain and possible improve my mobility.

Sex should be the least of my worries but with this young, virile man panting under me, I wonder how I will make him happy. Will he ever look at me with his blue eyes filled with desire and want?

I knew all of this would hit me sometime.

I collapse against him as my emotions bowl me over like a freight train. I don't even realize I'm crying until Mateo pulls me in close and starts making those soothing noises against my ear. I cling to him, letting him tell me that everything is going to be fine.

That he's got me.

That we are in this together.

I listen to his words.

My lover's lullaby makes it bearable until I crash into a deep, dreamless sleep.

EIGHTEEN
CARLISLE

My mouth tastes like a wet swimsuit I left in my gym bag for two days, and people are talking about me.

I try to crack my eyes open, fighting the pull of whatever they have in my system to drag me back into oblivion. But this room is bright, I'm tired of sleeping, and I've got to stop my mom from telling everyone the story about how my swimsuit strap broke at one of my first competitions and I flashed the entire crowd when I pulled myself out of the pool and jumped around in victory.

I swallow a couple of times, my first attempt at speech producing nothing. I swallow some more and lift my hand in an attempt to make a gesture that will communicate "shut the hell up" most effectively. It works because the story stops and I hear chairs scraping and people gasping all around my bed.

"Carlisle," my mother is on my left, her voice loud in my ear. "Hold on baby, we're calling the nurse."

Fuck the nurse. I want a drink of water.

I crack my eyes open enough to see the pitcher of water

sitting on my bedside table and I point to it, clearing my throat.

My dad figures it out first and reaches for the pitcher and shakes out ice cubes into a cup with a spoon and hands it off to my mom. She scoops some up and feeds it to me and I sigh in ecstasy. Best ice cubes in the whole world. She spoons me another and I open my eyes, looking for Mateo.

He's there, on my right side, looking tired and stressed but also relieved and like he still loves me. He didn't change his mind about all this craziness and run for the hills while Dr. Bertrand was digging around in my back. Thank God.

"Hi," I croak out at him. I tell myself that I sound sexy but in truth it's more like I have a six-pack-a-day smoking habit. His smile and his hand closing over mine makes me not give a shit anymore.

"Hi." He puts my hand to his lips and presses a soft kiss against my knuckles and my heart does this jumpy thing that makes the monitor's bleepy sounds speed up and my parents start laughing as he leans over and kisses me gently. "*Tesoro.*"

"How do you feel baby?" my mom asks.

"We called for the doctor," my dad says, sneaking his large hand around my mom to squeeze my shoulder. "How do you feel?"

And that is the question, isn't it?

I begin to concentrate on my body under the covers, trying to detect anything from my waist down. I'm not sure what I'm supposed to be looking for at this point. It was fully explained to me that the meds for post-op pain might mask much of the sensation for a while.

"Yes, Carlisle, how do you feel?" Dr. Bertrand asks as he walks into the room, a nurse following close behind. My parents move away from my bedside, allowing the professionals access to the equipment and the patient. I can tell by the look on his face that he's seconds away from telling them all to leave and I feel panic building in my gut.

When Teo tries to pull back I grip his hand tightly and look at him. "Stay with me."

"Always," he answers, squeezing my fingers lightly before looking up at the doctor. "Don't make me break my promise, Doc."

Doctor Bertrand frowns, clearly displeased with not having me all to himself. He looks at Mateo and then at my parents and he relents.

"I can tell that I will lose whatever argument I try to start so I'll just cry uncle now." He taps on his tablet and pulls up what I can only presume is my record and reads for a few seconds before placing it on the side table and pulling a pen light out of his pocket. He shines it in my eyes. "Any nausea? Vertigo? Blurry vision?"

"No."

He looks at me, his gaze assessing for a few seconds before he grabs the edge of my blanket and pulls it down, exposing my lower body in the hideous hospital gown. From the slightly elevated position of my head and shoulders, I can see the bolster under my knees and I mentally tell my legs to flex against the cushion.

Nothing.

Doctor Bertrand glances up at me, clearly trying to gauge my reaction. "Carlisle, as I told your family, the surgery went very well. There was more shrapnel than anticipated and the scar tissue from your prior surgeries made removal difficult but we got it all." He pulls an instrument out of his pocket, a metal rod the size of a pen with a rounded tip on one end and a pointy tip on the other. "There will be significant swelling for at least a week and we will treat it with anti-inflammatories. The pain will be managed by narcotics for a couple of days but then we will switch you to higher dosages of non-narcotic medication. We don't want the drugs to inhibit your participation in your physical therapy."

I nod at this and he stares at me for two beats before moving to my feet. He lowers the instrument and uses it to press against the sole of my foot.

"Can you feel that?"

I shake my head. "No."

He moves his position and I can see his hands flex as he presses the instrument forward. I squeeze Teo's hand, willing myself to feel something. I close my eyes, searching for the sensation. Nothing. I open my eyes and shake my head. "No. Nothing."

I glance towards my parents and they both are as white as the bleach-scented sheets on my bed. My dad's arms are wrapped around my mom and I can see, even at this distance, that they are trembling. I'm glad I'm not the only one freaking out. I'm also glad I have Teo who is steady as rock next me, not even a flicker of worry across his face. I take his courage and inhale it, letting it soak into my body and calm me.

Dr. Bertrand places his hands, palms flat against the bottoms of my feet and looks at me, his expression determined and encouraging. It's as if he's willing me to pass this next test, as if it is the most important.

I ignore the icy tendril of fear chasing along my skin and the cold sweat that chills me in the cool hospital air. I hold my breath, waiting for his instructions.

"Press against my hands, as hard as you can."

I look down at my feet and I shiver because right now they feel like they belong to someone else. Or they are those fake feet that peek out from the end of the box in the magician's act when he tries to convince you that he's really sawing that chick in half.

"Carlisle. You can do it," he says, giving me an encouraging nod that reminds me of my swim coach. Sometimes only his gruff voice and that curt nod could get my ass off the starting block. Now, I'm standing on this new starting block and I have no idea if I will shoot through the water or sink like a stone. I almost wish I could stay in this moment and never know the answer but I never have been and I never will be that big of a coward.

I close my eyes and I concentrate, squeezing Teo's hand even tighter as I order my limbs to obey the command from my brain. The seconds seem to drag on forever and I feel tears welling up in my eyes as nothing happens. It's like the time I woke up in the hospital in Europe after the bombing and nothing worked the right way and the love of my life was dead.

"Okay, relax a minute," Dr. Bertrand says, removing his hands from the bottom of my feet.

"Let me try again," I blurt out, panic making my voice shake and quaver and giving away the fact that I'm on the verge of tears. "I can do this. Let me try again."

He flicks a glance at my parents and Mateo and then returns his focus back to me. He leans forward on my bed, placing his hands flat on the mattress on each side of my legs. When he speaks, it is the same calm, level tone he's had since my first meeting with him. No nonsense. Practical. Infuriatingly honest.

"I had two criteria for taking your case, Carlisle. The first was physical, the extent of damage to your nervous system and the likelihood that surgery would help you maintain the most mobility." He pauses, his eyes never leaving my own. "The second criteria was patient attitude and I believe is the most important of all. To get through all of the hard work that is coming your way, you need to be a hard worker who is also a fighter. Someone who doesn't let one small failure keep you from working until you achieve what you want. I knew that the young woman who endured years of grueling training and then won twelve gold medals had the attitude I was looking for. I knew you would fight and not let one little failure today stop you from getting up and doing it again tomorrow." He straightens, moving his hands back to the soles of my feet and keeps speaking. "So, I want you to try again and even if you don't succeed I know you'll try again tomorrow."

He nods and I blink back the emotion blurring my vision and take a deep breath. I'm shaking, scared to death, but I'm not ready to let go of the girl he was talking about. Once I made the decision to have this surgery, my course was set and now it is no different than making it to the summer games. No matter what, I'll be back tomorrow.

I concentrate. I squeeze Mateo's hand. I push.

Seconds pass by and nothing happens and then I feel it. It isn't much and his hands only move back a tiny amount but they move. I blink. Mateo yells. My mother cries.

Doctor Bertrand smiles.

I lean back on my pillows, exhausted from just that tiny bit of effort. My dad leans over and kisses my cheek and I kiss him back, loving the familiar rumble of his voice in my ear. "Love you baby. So proud of you."

Doctor Bertrand, embracing his role as chief buzz killer, holds his hands up and stops the party that has erupted in my room.

"That's excellent. I cannot predict how much mobility you will have in the end but that is a very good sign. You have months of hard work ahead of you. I know you can do it." He looks around the room at my parents and Mateo and his face sobers a bit. "Like we discussed in our pre-operative meetings, you need to figure out your schedules. Carlisle will need your help but you need to take care of yourselves, get out of here when she is in therapy, sleep in a real bed." He gives Mateo a meaningful glance, "Attend classes."

"Thank you Doctor Bertrand," I force out, quickly feeling all of the emotions crashing down on me. I don't know whether I want to cry or scream or laugh. I just know that I don't want do it with all these people in the room. I tug Mateo down to me and I hide my face in his shoulder, biting back the tears that I now know are coming. He sits down on the bed beside me and holds me as close as all the tubes, wires and my current condition will allow. He smells like coffee, sunshine, and Mateo and I drink him in and try to steal his strength.

"Doctor, let's talk out in the hallway," my mom says on the other side of the bed and I am grateful when she ushers everyone out of my room.

The silence isn't empty for long before I fill it with the sobs I can't hold back. Mateo holds me, silent but solid as I ugly cry all over his t-shirt. He doesn't try to get me to stop, doesn't tell me it will be all right. He just holds me. Lets me lose my shit with as much dignity as possible while sitting here in a gown with my ass hanging out of it and my hair in a walk-of-shame-without-the-fun-orgasm mess on the top of my head.

"That scared me," I admit, brushing some of the wetness off my cheeks as I feel the worst of it pass. "It was like the first time... when I woke up."

"I think that's a normal reaction, to remember that time." Mateo kisses the top of my head and squeezes me tighter. He pulls back and I'm surprised at the tracks of moisture on his cheeks. I raise an eyebrow and trace one of the tears. He shrugs. "I'm not even handing over my man card because even Chuck Norris would cry over the shit that just went down here."

"Oh really? You invoke the name of the great Chuck? I don't know... " I laugh at the death glare he gives me and tug him down to me so I can give him a kiss. It's a light one, tender and I hope he can feel all the gratitude I have for him in the touch. I decide not to take the chance and just tell him. "Thank you Teo. Thank you for being here, for loving me."

He smiles and brushes my hair back from my face, his warmth keeping away the chill of the room. "Loving you is the easiest thing... like breathing. No matter what, we'll do this together."

I snuggle against him, enjoying the moment and brushing aside any doubt or fear about what is to come. My mom's worries edge in but I push them away and focus on what I know: I'm going to beat this, and Mateo and I have what it takes to make it.

NINETEEN
MATEO

"Mr. Butler can I see you after class?"

I stop as I gather my things to leave the lab, turning to face my instructor, Dr. Steinberg. He doesn't look happy—he never looks happy—but the alarming part of his current look is that it is aimed at me. He is a hardass and he's been waiting to chew on mine since day one. My lab partners all give me pity glances but they aren't waiting around to be sucked into the vortex of fury that swirls around him.

"See you at group study later?" Adam asks as he slings his messenger bag across his body.

"Yeah. At your place?"

"Yep. See you later." He sneaks a peek at Steinberg and then runs away like the flying monkeys are after him.

"Mr. Butler, I'm afraid we must have an unpleasant conversation."

I sigh and put down my backpack, realizing this will not be a quick conversation. I sneak a look at my watch but I'm not sneaky enough because when I look back at him, he's glaring with renewed fire.

"Am I making you late for something?"

"My girlfriend is recovering from spinal surgery and she's in rehab and I haven't seen her all day... " I let my sentence trail off when I realize that he is uninterested.

"Maybe that explains your lack of focus and your poor attendance at lecture and group labs. I understand you slept through a lecture earlier this week and it's becoming a common occurrence."

"I know I've been preoccupied. I've got a lot to juggle right now but I'll figure it out," I answer, feeling the hot creep of embarrassment crawl up my neck. "I just need a little time."

"This course lasts three months. You have lecture and lab every day, five days per week. This was all in your materials."

"I know, Dr. Steinberg... "

"Mr. Butler you are exceptionally bright and you grasp even the most complex concepts quickly and thoroughly... " I think about thanking him but even I can hear the "but" coming. "... but that is only when you are here and actually present. I need to warn you that you are in danger of failing this course but as we are only three weeks in, you have time to turn your behavior around."

I'm stunned by his words. I know I've missed a few things and failed a couple of quizzes but I thought I could pull it out in the end. I always have before. It's just been a son-of-a-bitch to juggle school and Carlisle. She needs me and it's hard to focus on this place when she's battling it out on the other side of town.

I find my tongue and say the only thing I can say. "I'll fix it Dr. Steinberg. You have my word."

"I hope you will Mr. Butler. I think you have a bright future in this profession if you can focus on what needs to be done."

He hands me an envelope and walks away like he hasn't thrown a firebomb into the middle of my life. I open the envelope and pull out the paper, unfolding it and noting the medical school letterhead. I skim it, noting that it gives the same dire warning I just received in person. I refold it and shove it into my backpack. I'll deal with it later, right now I'll miss seeing Carlisle at all today if I don't get moving now.

I drive across town, irritated by the evening traffic but too distracted by my warning from Dr. Steinberg to really get worked up. I think about how I need to adjust my schedule and all of it adds up to seeing less of Carlisle. And that is the last thing I want to do.

She's wheelchair bound for now but they are working on moving her up to crutches in the near future. The therapy is grueling, physically exhausting and she is in a great deal of pain most of the time because she doesn't want to take the really good drugs because they make her loopy. So, she toughs it out, grinds her teeth and rolls around with dark circles under her eyes because she's not sleeping well. Her mom told me that she was the same when she was training, nothing was going to stop her except injury or collapse. She's that driven.

I want to be with her. I need to be with her. I promised her that I would be there and I refuse to break my promise. She is my world, more than this course, and that is the crux of my problem. It isn't the first time I've wondered if medical school is where I need to be right now.

I pull into the parking lot of the high-end rehabilitation facility where Carlisle will be living for at least the next nine months. She's lucky to have a single room and the place goes out of its way to not look like a hospital but I can tell she's already itching to leave and live independently.

I want her to move in with me when she gets out although I haven't brought it up yet. Her parents still give me the side-eye and I've overheard a couple of conversations between them that begin and end with "this has happened way too fast".

I jump out of my car, grabbing my backpack as I leave, hoping I can sneak in some study time before group tonight. The staff just wave me on as I enter, smiling as I practically run past. They love Carlisle and the rest of her entourage are included in the glow.

I knock and, hearing nothing, enter her room, throwing my bag on the loveseat under the window that overlooks the flower garden in the interior courtyard. Carlisle can afford a nice place and this one goes out of its way to not look like a hospital. She has a hospital type bed but the floors are warm oak laminate and there is real wood furniture instead of the melamine and pressboard stuff you usually see. Her mother brought in some of her artwork, a few blankets and her books from her apartment and the effect is cozy. As Carlisle says, "It's not home but it will do in a pinch."

No one is in here and I check my watch again. She should be done with her afternoon session and getting ready for dinner. The sound of the shower is faint through the closed door but I walk over and tap lightly. I get no response so I push the door open and I'm met with a wave of steam from the hot water running.

The first thing I see is Carlisle's wheelchair pulled up close to the rimless shower next to the location of the shower seat she needs to use.

The second thing I see is Carlisle. On the shower bench. Crying.

I am at her side in two steps, not caring that the shower spray is soaking me from head to toe.

"Carlisle, baby." I check her over, trying to see if she is hurt, if there is anything I can do. "What's wrong? Do you want me to call a nurse?"

She's crying so hard that I debate waiting for her reply. "Carlisle, you're scaring me. Are you hurt? Do I need... "

"It hurts all the time," she stammers out, her hands clutching the edge of the shower stall in a white-knuckle grip. She reaches out one hand to dig her fingers into her calf, pressing hard into the muscle. "It hurts all the fucking time but I can't feel anything! I work and I work. I practically kill myself to get out of that chair but nothing... " She breaks down in a deeper sob as she rakes her nails over her skin, raising angry red marks. "... nothing changes."

Aw fuck. My heart breaks. Shatters into a million pieces in my chest and I bite back the urge to rail against all the shit she has to bear. But she doesn't need me to scream alongside her, she needs me to be the wall of stone she can batter herself against. Her safe place.

"Hey, hey." I reach up to turn off the water and snag a towel from the peg nearby and wrap it around her shoulders. She's shivering a little in the air conditioning and I also feel the chill as my wet clothes stick to my body. I brush aside the discomfort and pat her down as she really begins to shiver. "It's okay. Let's get you warm and you can tell me about what happened."

Whatever fight she had went down the drain with water and she collapses against me and I hold her tight, willing my body heat into her. If I could give her the use of my legs, I would. I know she's frustrated at the pace of her recovery and this might be the culmination of days of frustration or it might be the result of a major setback.

Either way, I'll be here for her.

I stand, careful of the wet floor as I get to my feet and I

scoop her up in my arms. My memory immediately flashes back to the first time I did this for her, the day I think of as the time we really began. That day, when she trusted me with her weakness, was the beginning of this journey together.

I walk into her room trying to rub warmth into her skin and to soothe her when one of the night nurses, Susan, steps into the room. She takes one look at the two of us, soaking wet and shivering, and she rushes to my side.

"Did she have an accident in the shower?" I can feel her hands touching Carlisle, checking for any injury. "Where did you find her?"

"I'm fine," Carlisle says from where her head is lying on my shoulder. "I didn't fall."

"I found her in there seated on the bench. She was... " I consider what I will tell her when I feel Carlisle's fingers squeeze my arm. In spite of all she's been through, she's sensitive to anyone seeing her cry or anything less than the girl standing on the top of the tier with a medal around her neck. "She was upset."

Susan locks eyes with me over Carlisle's shoulder and nods, her eyes full of understanding. "I'll get more towels and I'll grab you some scrubs and throw your wet clothes in the dryer."

She leaves and I peel Carlisle off me enough to see her face. Her eyes are red, mascara smeared and her nose a bright pink. Her hair is starting to curl in those loose waves I love but her lips are tinged with blue. Susan returns with the towels and places a double layer on the bed so that I can sit Carlisle down and do what she needs me to do.

She is quiet while I help her dry off, taking over when I get to her hair and even accepting the comb when I snag it off her vanity.

"Do you want the Captain America pajamas or the ones Livvy sent you?" I hold up the sleep t-shirt that says "I've got 99 problems and liking men isn't one of them" for her inspection. "I vote for this one because it makes all the staff feel sorry for me since I have no chance with you at all."

She laughs a little at my joke and reaches out for it. "Yes, that one."

I bring it to her and she lifts her arms up, inviting me to slide it over her head. The move is sexy and I lean over to lightly kiss her, whispering against her mouth. "Have I told you how much I love that you hate underwear?"

I realize about two seconds too late that I've said the wrong thing when she pulls back from me and turns away. I'm not bothered by the fact that sex is off the table for recovery reasons, it's her refusal to talk to me about it at all. She can discuss any aspect of her recovery with me but she shuts me out whenever the topic of a future sex life comes up with her doctors if I'm around. I know that a sacral level spinal injury can cause issues with sexuality but I have no idea what's going on with her.

Sex is the least of our issues but it's one of the many that have created the tiniest gap between us. It's nothing we can't fix and I guess it's understandable but I hate it all the same. I just wish she would talk to me.

"Thank you, Teo," she says as I help her move her legs and slide under the covers.

"Hey, anything for you," I say, positioning her pillow behind her in the spot she likes it best. I perch on the side of the bed and lean down to kiss her temple, murmuring against her hair. "You want to tell me what happened?"

She pauses for the briefest second and I will her to answer me but she shakes her head in the end. "Not right now. I think I need to sleep for a bit."

I bite back my sigh and pull away to look into her eyes. Emerald green with flecks of gold look up at me and while I know she's holding back, I don't see anything that gives me a clue about what is going on.

"Okay, you sleep and when you wake up we can talk about what's going on. Sound good?" She nods and reaches out to cup my jaw and I grab her hand and press a kiss to it. "We're in this together. I'm not going anywhere."

She smiles at me, not a full-blown grin but the kind that accompanies the heavy droop of her eyelids. I kiss her palm again and tuck her in as she falls asleep.

I take the scrubs into the bathroom with me and change quickly, mouthing a silent thank you to Susan when she takes my pile of wet things from me. I watch her leave and close the door behind her and pull the recliner chair closer to Carlisle's bed so I can watch her sleep. I grab my backpack and pull out my textbook, opening it to the reading for tomorrow.

My phone buzzes and I pick it up, groaning at the text on the screen.

We are here for group. Where are you?

I stare at the gray box on my phone and glance at Carlisle. She's out cold and probably will be for hours if not the rest of the night. The PT sessions wear her out and today's reaction could just be the result of fatigue.

Or it could be something worse and I won't know until she wakes up and I can persuade her to talk to me. Her red-gold hair is drying on the pillow around her face. The freckles on her nose are visible in her too pale face. She's thinner now but not enough for me to be really worried, but it doesn't take a rocket scientist to figure out that she's carrying around a lot of shit in her head.

I start typing. *Can't make it tonight. Something came up. Sorry.*

I don't have to wait long for a reply. *I hope you know what you're doing. Don't miss lecture asshole.*

I toss my phone into my bag and settle back in the seat, my book unopened on my lap as I look at her. I know what I'm doing. Carlisle is my world and she needs me now. No matter how important school is, she has to come first.

TWENTY

CARLISLE

It is dark outside when I wake up and the digital clock by my bed says "2:15 am".

The room is quiet, the facility deep in collective REM as I blink the sleep away from my eyes. I stretch, flexing my arms, my torso and then it hits when my legs barely respond to my command. Like two heavy logs weighing me down into the mattress, the limbs that once propelled me through the water faster than anyone else on the planet have failed me again.

A snore, soft and low, draws my attention and I shift to the left and see Mateo sleeping in the recliner by the side of my bed. His head thrown back, long neck exposed and dark stubble on his chin. He looks delicious and I would love to walk over there and kiss all that exposed skin. I miss touching him, feeling all of his hot skin on mine.

I want him but I don't even feel like myself anymore.

"Hey baby. Why are you awake?"

His voice surprises me and I laugh in half surprise and half shock, smiling when his grin flashes me from across the room. I reach out my hand before I even know I'm doing it and he smiles even more, closing the book on his lap and unfolding his long, lean body from the chair. He crosses the gap in two steps and then he's there and I'm lifting the sheet and he slides in next to me. It's a tight fit but I love it.

He settles in beside me, placing his right arm under my head and looping the other around my waist. We are cocooned together underneath the thin, white, over-bleached sheets and it feels wonderful. He's hard and warm and every part of me fits with him. It's like we were meant to be together. In this moment, I almost feel... whole.

Mateo leans over and kisses me. Once on the right side of my mouth. Once on the left side of my mouth. And finally on my lips, soft and sweet but thorough with a deep sweep of his tongue. I kiss him back, my fingers tangling in his hair and pulling him closer until we have to break for air. We stare at each other for a while, enjoying the closeness. With all the people constantly surrounding me, we haven't had much time to just be together. This is beyond nice but I can't help but notice the fatigue sitting heavily on his shoulders. The slump matches the dark shadows under his eyes. My man looks good but tired, bone-deep tired.

"Why are you still here?" I ask, playing with the fabric of his scrubs. "Why are you wearing these?"

"My clothes got wet and Susan gave these to me." He glances down at himself and then grins back up at me. "I'm trying them on for size. Do you think I look like a doctor?"

I pretend to take my time answering but he looks hot. "You look fuckable-in-the-on-call-room hot."

"Yeah?"

"Oh, yeah." I poke him in the chest. "But you won't ever be 'Dr. Hottie' if you don't get decent sleep and study time. You are always here."

Mateo tenses next to me and I look closely at his face.

He avoids my eyes for a few seconds but when he looks back, I only see determination in them.

"I want to be here with you. I want to help you." He traces a finger down my cheek and I lean into it. "I need to be here."

"I have a posse of professionals who are here to help me." As soon as I say this I feel him stiffen again and I sigh, knowing I have hurt him even though I didn't mean to. He looks away and I have to pull his face back around to get him to look at me. "Teo, I want you here. I need you."

"I'm not so sure," he whispers and them almost immediately shakes his head. "Forget it. I shouldn't have said that." He stares at me, clearly thinking of what he wants to ask me. "What happened today?"

Now it's my turn to break eye contact but he doesn't let me get away with it. His finger under chin tips my face up for a quick, sweet kiss before he whispers, "Tell me. I need to know what's going on in your head."

I laugh. It's short and bitter and makes my throat hurt. Or maybe that's the emotion burning its way up from my gut.

"I work so hard and nothing is happening. I do everything they tell me to do. I follow every instruction to the letter and I don't feel any different than I did a month ago." I lean forward and bury my face in his neck, inhaling the comforting scent of my lover. "I'm scared Teo. Nothing works. I can't feel... anything."

I am not exaggerating. Nothing below my waist works right now. I have to empty my bladder and my bowels with enemas and catheters and my vagina and clitoris have gone the way of Elvis and left the building. I should be able to talk to Teo about this but I can't. Not yet. I'm not ready to admit that I might never be the woman he needs. The one he deserves.

"If I tell you everything, it will make it real," I murmur against his throat, pressing a kiss there to ease the sting of not telling him what he wants to hear. "It's just hard and I can't turn off the shit in my head."

"Have you called Dr. Shrieve?"

I shake my head.

"Not yet." I pause and pull back to look at him, willing him to understand and not run from the head case I am obviously morphing into. "But I will. I think I need to talk to her."

"I wish you would talk to me but I get it if you need to work it out with her first. All of this shit is scary."

"Are you scared?"

"Of you conquering this?" He shakes his head, his smile sweet. "No way. You'll kick its ass."

"No. About school. Tell me how it's going."

"It's fine," he says but his lack of eye contact makes me poke him in the side again. He sighs. "It's hard as shit but fascinating. I'm still waiting for it to feel real, though."

"I think it's because you're never there."

"Here we go," he says on a groan while he presses his forehead against mine. "I'm there plenty. I'm studying and doing fine."

We lie there in silence for a while and I can't pinpoint why I don't believe him. Medical school is hard. I know because I watched ER for all fifteen seasons and it was brutal in make-believe land. He cannot be doing what he needs to do and be here all the time.

"Teo, I can't worry about you messing up school because of me." I pause and then decide to tell him the truth that I can. "I'm going to be selfish and just put it out there that I can't handle one more thing on my plate. Besides the obvious question of whether my body will ever work again, I worry about my parents and Livvy and so many other things that I shouldn't but I do. I just can't worry about your school as well."

He stares down at me, his eyes searching my face in the semi-darkness.

"I need you to do this for me," I plead. "Take this thing off my mind. Please."

He sighs. "What do you need me to do?"

"Go to class. Don't come here every day. Sleep in your own bed and get rid of the dark circles under your eyes. Take time to study properly in a library. Come see me when you can on weekdays and then bug the shit out of me on weekends."

"I want to be *here*."

"And I love you for that but I need to focus on what I need to do and I can't do that if I don't know you're taking care of your business as well." I cup his face in my hand, running my thumb over his cheekbone. "I'm a control freak so give me one less thing to control. Please. Promise me you'll do this."

We have a stare off and I wonder if he'll fight me on it. I'm stubborn but he's just as bad. I release my breath when he nods, his voice low and resigned as he agrees.

"I'll do it."

"Thank you." I lean up and kiss him, letting our touches linger, enjoying the quiet and each other. My heart thuds in my chest, heavy and slightly elevated with the way he makes me feel. "I've missed you."

"*Tesoro.*" Teo hums against my lips and then traces a path across my cheek to nuzzle into my neck, inhaling deeply. I squirm when it tickles and he laughs softly against my skin. "I've missed you so much. Missed this."

I can't help the thought that passes through my mind. It isn't the first time it's been a visitor in the middle of the night: the question of how we will do this, whether he will want me when I finally have to accept a life of catheters, enemas. Countless trips to every kind of doctor imaginable. A partner confined to a wheelchair.

The definitive verdict of no children. No family.

I always resolve to talk to Mateo about this stuff in the morning but I chicken out. My mother isn't right about everything but she is accurate when she says we haven't had a lot of time to get to know the stuff about each other that comes with being together for a long time. The kind of time that makes you fearless to ask anything and the confidence to know that the answer will not change what exists between the two of you.

We do not have that confidence. We needed more time but we didn't get it and I'm not brave enough to ask.

So I let the moment pass as I lie in the dark and eventually fall asleep and dream of days when I will walk by his side.

"What do you want to talk about?" Dr. Shrieve asks from the sofa in my room.

The morning after the night with Mateo I called her and asked for her to come see me at the facility. It wasn't typical for her to leave her office to see a patient and I am grateful she is willing to help me out.

"I don't know." I twist the tie on my sweats and shrug. "Everything."

"Let's narrow it down a little bit, I've only got an hour," she teases before she pulls out the ever-present notebook and looks at me for a full thirty seconds. "You look good. Not great but good. I think you need more sleep."

"I fall asleep and then I'm up a few hours later."

"Maybe you need to take something," she muses as she writes something on the page. "Just to help you sleep better."

"I feel like I'm becoming one big pill. I don't want to shove another one in me."

She nods. "I can get you a prescription for medical marijuana. If I recall it was one of your favorites."

That makes me laugh and I slip her the bird as she answers me with a devious chuckle. It felt weird since she walked in but with this exchange, it feels normal. I spent the last year sharing more with her than with my own family and I think I missed it.

"Well, if you are turning down the chance for pot brownies, let's figure out what's keeping you up." She pauses and looks at me. "I'm presuming it isn't pain-related?" When I shake my head 'no', she continues. "How are you handling all of this? It's a huge change from where you planned to be and so much work."

I stop and think, rolling around what's been in my head since I woke up from the surgery. Should I have just taken the pill stash hidden in my apartment and avoided the whole mess? Saved people a lot of trouble? "I'm not sure that I picked the right choice."

"Okay. Do you plan on changing your mind?"

I think about it. Could I take all those pills now? "I've considered it...but no. I don't think I can now. I'm too invested, people are too invested."

"What do you think the outcome will be in the end? Will you walk? Wheelchair?"

I flinch at her words. They are too raw. Too direct. Everyone has been tiptoeing around me, even when my PT people are killing me, they are achingly polite. This stings but I lean into it. I need this, I think.

"I have no idea and it is making me fucking nuts." I smack the armrest on my wheelchair and the reverberating pain in my hand is sharp but I don't care. "Before I had this surgery I had pain, I hurt all the time and I thought I would do anything to have it gone." I grip my knee in my hand and it's the same light pressure I've felt for the last couple of weeks. "But this feeling nothing is killing me."

I start crying and Dr. Shrieve's eyebrows shoot up. In all our sessions I never cried, never broke down and now I can't seem to stop.

"My body is my enemy. The bombers were my besties compared to the shit my body puts me through on a daily basis. I can't walk. I barely have any feeling from the waist down and I can't even pee by myself." I suck in a huge breath and continue, saying the thing that wakes me and won't let me go. "Everyone keeps telling me that the girl who won all those medals can beat this but what they don't realize is that those goddam medals belong to a girl who should have died along with Aaron and everyone else."

The silence is profound but she keeps her gaze on mine as I gulp, and sniffle, and hiccup my way through the worst of it. And when I begin my descent, she gets up from her seat, walks over to the vanity and picks up the box of tissues. She returns to me and hands it over but instead of going back to her seat, she kneels down and takes my hand in hers.

"You are not that girl. A vital part of her did die that day right next to Aaron and that's okay. It's okay to be mad about it and to resent it and to wish like hell you could have her back." She squeezes my hand and I cling to her like she's a life raft because fuck knows I feel like I'm drowning. "But not all of her is gone. The part that makes you a fighter is there. I've read your medical records from that day and you should have been dead. There is no reason you are sitting here today except that you are a fighter, down deep in your overly competitive, pain-in-the-ass bones, you fight until you can't get up again." And then she smiles at me and pats my hand as she rises. "What I don't understand is why you think this should be easy or you should know the outcome. Learning to break every world record was not easy and every time you got on that block, you had no idea how the race would end. Get in position, wait for the buzzer and jump off the damn block. Be that girl."

She sits back down across from me and watches me as I process everything she said. I want to tell her to fuck off. To yell that she has no idea how hard this is but it doesn't matter. Nobody but me knew how hard every stroke through the water was. How difficult it was to get out of bed some mornings and spend hours in a chilly pool. Yes, they sympathized but they didn't know. It was my fight then and this is my fight now.

I've just got to decide to fight, to focus. I might win gold or I might not place. It's always a crapshoot after all the hard work is done. She's right, this is no different.

"You good?" She asks. I nod and she reopens the notebook. "Who are you talking to about this? What's your support like?"

I shrug. "My parents are here, hovering. I don't want to tell them everything because it freaks them out and they just hover more. I end up wasting energy being annoyed and not putting it into my PT."

"So, you're still trying to take care of everyone around you and not letting them take care of you."

This is well-covered territory for us. Apparently it is not uncommon for someone in an extreme health situation to want to take care of everyone around them by hiding how they are really doing and putting on a brave front. I am not unique in this but I am the poster child according to Dr. Shrieve.

"And Mateo?" she asks when it becomes clear that I'm not going to answer.

This is where it really gets hard. I let out a breath and get really honest.

"I love him but I can't talk to him about this. He's got so much going on and I don't want to burden him."

"Is that how you see yourself? A burden?"

I think about her question. Is that how I see myself?

"Yes. I do."

"Does he see you that way?"

I shake my head. "No. Not yet."

"But you think he will?"

"When we got together he knew nothing about all of this. It all happened so fast, before we really got the chance to know each other, to hash this out. It's like I lured him in under false pretenses and now he's stuck with me. He's too much of a gentleman to back out."

"Have you talked to him about this? How do you think he'd react if he heard this?" she asks.

"He'd deny it. He'd keep trying to do everything and be everywhere. I made him promise to not be here during the week so much, to go to class, to forget about me." I look down at my lap and twist the tie on my sweats again, facing my fear. The boogeyman under my bed. "I'm afraid that he'll mess this up and resent me when he finally gets the courage to leave one day."

Dr. Shrieve stares at me across the short distance. "You two need to talk about this."

"I know."

"Can you do that if I give you homework? Will you pick one thing and talk to him about it this weekend? You won't know each other better if you don't talk about it." She glances at the clock and closes the notebook. "Build the trust and let the rest follow. Even soul mates have to work at it. You wouldn't be worrying about this if you didn't love him but it's not the most important thing anyway."

"It isn't?"

"No, because even the biggest love won't survive if you don't have the foundation to support it. Work on that, forge that bond and you'll work it out."

She leaves and I sit there in my room, watching the birds and butterflies moving in the courtyard. It's a beautiful view and it helps me focus on what she said and what I have to do.

"Did you have a good session?" my mother asks as she enters the room, the ever-present knitting project in her hands. I have more scarves and mittens than I will ever need. She used to bring them along to my practices and competitions and I could always count on looking up in the stands and seeing my mom, the needles clicking away.

"I did. I like Dr. Shrieve better than the counselor here."

"I'm not surprised, you have a history with her." My mom stops and peers under the bed, squinting as she squats down to get a better look.

"What's up?" I turn my wheelchair, trying to see what she's looking at. I can't help her so I sit in place and watch her drop down on her hands and knees. She stretches her arm and sits up with a folded piece of paper in her hand. She opens it and glances at the top. "It's from Mateo's school."

I take it when she hands it out to me and I open it without thinking. The first couple of lines catch my attention. I know it's not my mail and I have no business reading the entire thing but I read every single word. It's like a car wreck on the side of the road, no matter how many times you tell yourself to get your eyes back on the road, the rubberneck is impossible to resist.

I read it again but the words don't change. Mateo is in danger of flunking out of school. Because he's here with me. At least he was. It's been a week.

"What is it?"

I look up and my mother is giving me the eyeball and I debate telling her the truth. I shake my head and refold the letter, rolling over to my desk and place it inside my planner.

"Nothing."

Nothing but another thing for me and Mateo not to talk about.

I walk into Carlisle's room exhausted after the week I just endured but excited to see her.

She's in her wheelchair, looking out the window into the courtyard and I sneak up behind her and bend down to kiss her on the cheek. She leans into me but doesn't respond in her usual way and I move around to her front and kneel down to get an eyeball-to-eyeball view of her face.

"*Tesoro*, you okay?" She looks fine but I quickly scan over her body to see if I can detect any injury, any change. We talk every night but its hard not seeing her everyday. I've got news she isn't going to like but Ill hold it if she's not up for it. "Rough day?"

"I'm fine. I had a good day. It was hard but good, I think," she says, reaching up a hand to stroke my jaw. I lean into like a cat, craving her touch like I've been without it for years instead of just five days.

"Good. I'm glad to hear it." I lean and kiss her mouth, delving in deep with my tongue. I capture her gasp and retreat, lightly biting her lower lip before I let it loose. When I pull back, her eyes are closed and she looks like the

Carlisle lying in the back seat of my car or on my bed that morning when this all really began. I am counting the days when we can be there again. "There you are. I've missed you Carlisle Queen."

She gazes at me, her green eyes dark and swirling with whatever has her mouth forced into a thin line. I know it's coming but I still clench my hand around the armrest of her wheelchair.

"We need to talk, Teo."

"The worst four words any man ever wants to hear," I try to joke but it sounds flat even to my own ears.

She reaches down and takes out a folded letter and I know what it is before she opens it. It must have fallen out of my backpack.

"Why didn't you tell me about this?"

"I didn't want you to worry. You have enough on your mind."

"You should have told me."

She pushes her chair away from me and I immediately feel the distance between us that has grown over the past few weeks. I would expect it to leave me feeling cold but what it creates is a burning sensation in my chest as if the link between the two of us stretched to its limits.

"I didn't want you to worry."

"You said that," her tone isn't ugly but it is unhappy and frustrated. "I'm not fragile Mateo. I'm broken and fucked up but I'm not a child that you have to protect from the hard things."

"Stop putting words in my mouth. I never said or thought any of those things about you."

"Really? Come on Mateo, you didn't tell me because you thought I couldn't handle it."

"You have enough on your mind," I'm firm on this point.

"I do not want to be one more thing you have to worry about."

She raises her voice for the first time, her cheeks pink from her high emotion. "I thought we were in this together. Isn't that what you're always saying?

I stand up and pace across the room, crumpling the paper in my hand and lobbing it at the trash can. I turn back to her and try to keep my voice calm. I feel like she's spoiling for a fight and I don't want to rise to the bait. It will get us nowhere to let this devolve into anger and hurtful words but she has to realize that it goes both ways.

"You can't throw that back in my face Carlisle. How many times have I asked you about what is going on, what you're feeling and you shut me out?" I slash my hand through the air and then rake my fingers through my hair. "There are so many topics you have declared off limits that I'm not sure we really have anything to discuss unless you want to stick to the weather. If we're talking about who's shutting who out, then let's take a good look at you too."

"Are you still in danger of being kicked out of a school?"

I stare at her, my mouth hanging open at the way she has completely ignored my comment.

"Just tell me how you are doing in school," she grinds out at me, it's dark and guttural and indicates just how upset she is with me.

"How was *your* day? " I ask, letting the sarcasm drip from every syllable. "And don't tell me it was fine."

She sighs and wipes a hand over her face and she takes a few seconds to bring it down a notch. When Carlisle looks at me again, her voice is softer, more controlled.

"I'm not sure I can do this right now."

I hear the fatigue in her voice and it stops my temper from rising any further. As much as she doesn't want to admit it, she is fragile and her focus can't be distracted by outside things.

"You're right." I agree, moving to sit down on the sofa near he. I reach out to take her hand in my own. "We can talk about this when we aren't both on edge."

She doesn't squeeze my hand back, in fact her grip is loose in mine. I search her eyes, not liking what I see.

"I think I need to go somewhere and just focus on getting better," she whispers and I think I didn't hear her right.

"Go somewhere? What are you talking about?" But I know. I know exactly what she's doing. I just need to hear it.

"I'm going to transfer to another facility for my rehab." The expression on her face looks pained but determined and my stomach sinks into my toes. "Not in Nashville."

"Where would you go?"

"I think I need a clean slate. Nothing on it but getting better. I feel like I've got too many things weighing on me and I can't concentrate." Her voice sounds dejected, flat. It's as if she has the weight of the world on her shoulders. "I'm going to go, Mateo."

"Carlisle," I say, swallowing hard to get around the boulder lodged in my chest. It's painful and I have trouble sucking in oxygen. My skin is clammy with fear. "Are you breaking up with me?"

She starts crying at my question. Big, fat tears rolling down her cheeks as she sobs quietly, little hiccups of emotion breaking out from between her lips. She has a death grip on my hand and I wonder why she is doing this if it is so damn painful.

"I think the biggest joke in the universe is finding the right person at the wrong time," she whispers and my blood runs cold with her meaning. "I love you but I can't stand the thought of you walking away from me one day." She lets go of my hand and scrubs the tears from her face with the back of her hand. "The only thing worse is that one day you're going to realize what a burden I am but you're going to stay anyway."

"I would never do that," I insist, angry that she is placing behavior and thoughts on me that are not mine. But clearly, they have been rolling around in her head. "I love you and I don't care if you are in a wheelchair or running marathons. I just want you."

"I want that to be true."

"It is true."

"You say that now because you're an honorable man but when you flunk out of med school and throw away this opportunity, you will resent me."

I stand, unable to sit and have this conversation one minute longer.

"Stop putting words in my mouth," I argue. "This isn't how I feel. You've got to stop this soundtrack of negativity going round and round in your head."

"It's how I feel Mateo. It's what keeps me up at night and keeps me from paying attention in physical therapy. It's real and it's hurting me."

"You think that I'm part of the reason you're not making physical progress?"

"I think worrying you and school and how my treatment is taking over everyone's lives and how I feel like I'll be double failure if I never get out of this chair is making me crazy. I'm a mess. It's eating me from the inside out and I just don't have it in me to fight it out on multiple fronts." She takes a deep breath and when she continues. "When I was training, everything else fell to the side. Things that took up too much headspace had to go and I was ruthless about making the hard call. I'm making it now. I need to go somewhere else and immerse myself in my recovery."

She's crying now and I know from her tones that she has her mind made up.

"I love you—"

"Then don't fucking do this," I say, the words like knives in my throat. "I love you too."

"I love you but I have to go and I'm not asking you to wait and I know if I come back, you may have moved on. I know this isn't fair."

"There is nothing about this situation where you make all the decisions about ending us is fair." I struggle to keep my voice down, everyone in this place does not need to witness the moment where my whole fucking world comes to an end. "You cannot do this."

"I'm sorry."

"You said that."

"I hate it but it's what I need to do," she looks up at me, her agony etched on her face but I don't have it in me to touch her, to comfort her. I'm in pain and contact at this point would bring me to my knees. "I'm not asking you to forgive me."

"Good, because I can't give it to you."

And even though I want to beg and plead for her to change her mind, I walk out of the room and leave. We need to time to cool off. Clearly things have come to a head and now that she's gotten this off her chest, we'll talk about calmly later. I'll come back tomorrow. This is not how we end.

Ten months later

I am late. Again.

My family and friends have gotten used to my constant state of incurable tardiness. I get caught up in the lab or my volunteer work at the clinic and the clock and little stuff like food and sleep become irrelevant. To my surprise the clinic is the most common culprit. The patients lined up in the waiting room, needy for free medical care grab me and it takes almost no effort to get me to work a few extra hours. Nobody is more shocked about this development than I am.

But the work keeps my mind off of the topic that is absolutely never discussed in my presence. Yeah, I know they spend hours hashing over how I'd buried myself in school when Carlisle left me. They'd given me my space, tip-toeing around the almost-mute asshole I'd been and then thrown about a dozen women at me in an effort to get me to move on. I'd finally caved, going out with a woman named Anne Price, a junior librarian at the Nashville Public Library my mother knew through some ESL class she helped coordinate.

I had intended for our first date to be our last but then she got me to laugh with her pitch perfect Monty Python quotes at dinner and we kept laughing when we tumbled onto her bed two hours later. That was three months ago and we're still together, seeing each other a couple of times per week and never letting our conversation venture past the here and now. But lately she's gotten this look in her eye after we both come; the look that tells me she wants me to say something other than "fuck, that was good" before we roll over and go to sleep.

Anne is shit out of luck. That isn't going to happen.

"Something more" has run me over like a fucking freight train once already and I'm not stupid enough to jump back on the tracks again.

Anne hasn't given me the ultimatum yet but I know it's coming sooner than later. I've never lied to her about what we are and what I can offer her, so she knows what my answer will be. But it hasn't happened yet and so tonight I'm running late for our mid-week dinner date with some of her friends and I still need to drop some stuff off for Kit from my mother.

I pull into the driveway of Max and Kit's house, nodding at the extra hands they have working on the old farmhouse and the large, landscaped yard. The nauseatingly happy couple will be married in the gardens later this summer when Kit returns from her tour and all the home improvements are on hyper speed. I lend a hand as often as I can but that isn't happening tonight.

I snag the box of invitations from the backseat and take the front steps two at a time, skidding to a stop on the doormat and hitting the doorbell. I glance around me, noticing for the first time the silver Volvo parked on the driveway to the left of the house. I don't recognize it or the license plate and I throw up a silent prayer they have company so that I have an excuse to keep my moonlighting as a UPS man as brief as possible.

Max opens the door and his usual smile does not appear. He doesn't even say hello. "Oh shit" is all he gets out before he glances over his shoulder towards the large family room off the main foyer and I see someone sitting on their sofa.

No. Not someone.

Carlisle.

"Oh shit" tumbles past my own lips as her gaze tracks to the door and locks with mine. Even at that distance I can see the widening of her eyes, the perfect "o" formed by her mouth.

I drop the box in my hands and grab the doorframe. I sway a little on my feet and wonder for a split second if I will be able to maintain the last shreds of my dignity and remain on my feet. Shocked. Gobsmacked. Blindsided. You pick the term you like best and that is me.

"Mateo... man, I am so sorry. If I'd known you were coming over, I would have warned you," Max says as he reaches out to catch me just in case I decide to take a header onto his newly refinished oak floors. "I'm sorry, man."

I just stare at her, soaking in every detail. Her hair is longer, still the same deep, rich red with the streaks of gold shining in the sunlight streaming through the huge windows I helped Max install. One look at her and I realize that the Carlisle that still haunted my dreams is a fucking poor imitation of the real thing. She is amazing. Gorgeous. Beautiful.

And my traitorous fucking heart keeps trying to jump out of my chest and get to the woman who'd taken it with her when she left the rest of me behind.

"Mateo. You okay?" Max's voice penetrates through the fog of "what-the-hell" that has taken over my brain and I drag my gaze back to his face.

"Yeah." I shake my head and bend down to pick up the box I dropped, keeping my eye on Carlisle in my peripheral vision. "My mom finished the calligraphy on the wedding invitations for Kit and..."

I barely register Max taking the box from my hands as Carlisle's movements catch my eye. She's rising from the couch, her actions careful, a little jerky but executed with purpose as she pulls over two forearm crutches and rises to her feet. Everything about her muscle tension, the way she bites her bottom lip, and the familiar bunching of her eyebrows testify to her concentration as she straightens and balances herself on her own two feet.

My breath catches in my throat and I know the sound that escapes from my mouth is harsh and wet with the emotion that threatens to break free.

I've never seen anything look so fucking good in my whole life.

At least I think so until she starts to walk towards me, her steps a little slower than her usual stride but strong and sure. I'd have to be a bigger asshole than I am to deny that the sight of her walking is like Christmas and my birthday and every fucking Fourth of July fireworks display I have ever seen or would ever see.

Carlisle's half smile is tentative, only her eyes giving away her doubt and all the emotion zinging back and forth between us. Somewhere in my head, I knew I would see her again and I knew it would be charged with everything we'd had between us at one time and all the things we would never have. But this actual moment is a million times crazier. Harder. Better. Worse. Amazing. Painful.

The ache starts in my gut and expands, sending out stinging tendrils pulsing out in time with the throbbing of my heart. After ten months I've gotten to the point where I can push it to the back of my mind and push on through. I get up in the morning. I go to work. The twinge is always there and I was reminded frequently enough to ensure that I never did feel "normal". It made sure I never forgot.

So, no matter how good she looks. No matter how glad I am that she is doing well, I can't afford to forget what she did to us. What she did to me.

She wrecked me. I went back to the rehab facility the next day and she was gone. All of her stuff packed. No forwarding address. Her phone turned off. And if I hadn't had my family and Zane to kick my ass, I might have stayed down on the ground where she'd left me.

Kit trails along behind her, stopping to stand next to Max with the best seats in the house to witness whatever this was going to be.

"Hello Mateo," Carlisle says, her voice soft but clear in the unnaturally hushed foyer. She glances down when she has to adjust her grip on her crutches but when she looks back up at me, her smile has more strength and purpose but doesn't disguise the nervous edge to her voice. "It's so good to see you. You were on my list of people to see now that I've moved back to Nashville."

"Well, it's nice to know I made the list." My tone is harsher than I intended, the effort it takes to push words past all the emotional shit clogging up my chest making the edges ragged. And I'm pissed. Fucking white-hot angry and it must have shown on my face because her upper body reels back a little bit, her emerald green eyes wide with her surprise.

"We'll leave you two alone for a few moments," Kit

murmurs as she tugs on Max's arm and leads him out of the room and back into the family room. I don't care if they stay or not. Anybody who has any doubt about how this is going down is a fool.

"Teo, I know you're angry..." Carlisle begins but I'm not having any of it.

"Wow. I'm allowed to have feelings or an opinion or anything with you around? I thought you had the monopoly on making decisions for both of us. I was ready to sit back and wait for you to tell me how to react when after *ten fucking months* of radio silence you show up at my cousin's house and tell me that I was on your list of goddam people to see when you prance your *royal highness* ass back into town."

My voice doesn't need the awesome acoustics of this old house to relay just how pissed off I am. Months of holding it in, sending emails to an account that bounces them back to me, and calls to a number that is never answered erupts in my speech. I regret nothing.

Not. One. Word.

Carlisle's cheeks turn a vivid shade of pink with her reaction, anger, embarrassment or something else, I have no idea. I don't trust my read on her anymore, not after she blindsided me with her one-sided decision for us to be over. Her grip on her crutches is white knuckle and her entire body vibrates with whatever is going on in her head.

"You were first on my list. The person I wanted to see the most."

"That explains you being *at Max and Kit's house.* I'm sure you got confused that I don't actually live here." I'm not giving an inch. No way am I making this easy on her. "Well, you can check me off the list and consider us caught up."

She steps forward, everything about her demeanor screaming how rattled she is but she pushes on in typical Carlisle fashion. I can't help the admiration and the spike of attraction that hits me in the gut. If I'd tried to kid myself that I was over her, it wasn't working.

"Teo, you were *first* on the list." Carlisle takes a deep breath and blurts out the rest in a voice barely above a whisper. "But I had to build up the nerve to come see you. I—"

"Did you think I was going to bite or something?" I walk towards her, close enough that she has to lift her face to look at me and close enough for me to smell her scent. The familiar smell of her gardenia soap envelopes me and I have to close my eyes for a moment, steeling myself against the rush of memories that accompanies it. I remember the day when I lost that scent on my sheets, in my car, on my clothes and realized she wasn't coming back to me. It was hell, whichever layer Dante reserved for fools. "Or were you afraid that I would lose my shit? Yell? Break something?"

She shakes her head, emerald eyes huge as she stares at me. I'm staring so hard right back that I don't even see her reaching out to touch me until her cool fingers brush against the skin on the back of my hand. My instinct is to extend my fingers and weave them together with hers, to pull her close and stop all this useless talk with the press of my lips against her own.

"No. I was afraid you wouldn't... " She stumbles on her words and I can hear the effort it takes for her to swallow down whatever is caught in her throat. "I was... " She corrects herself and starts over again. "I am afraid that you're going to tell me it's too late. That I'm too late and we're over."

I've spent nights, days, countless minutes praying for her to show up and say exactly what she just said. Longing, not just for her body or for sex, but the *need* for her to fill this Carlisle-shaped hole in my chest almost knocks me down. My mouth waters, my heart kicks into a beat that rivals a Red Hot Chili Peppers song, and sweat prickles between my shoulder blades. I'm a mess and I hate it. I hate that this is my reaction after all those fucking months, after she walked out and left me hanging with more questions than answers, after she acted so selfishly. I hate... her.

As much as I ever loved her, I hate her now. In this moment. Right fucking now.

"It's too late," I say and pull my hand away. I keep my eyes glued to hers because I want to see her reaction to my words. I want to see the pain I hope I'll inflict. It's not pretty and it's not nice but it's real. "I'm with someone else."

"Oh." She blinks rapidly and I can see the extra moisture filling them as she sucks in a ragged breath. "Are you... do you... ?"

"I love her." I answer the question she can't get out and I close my eyes against the pain that flares in her own and sends a flush of red heat over her porcelain skin. I immediately want to take it back, to rewind and delete the lie. Carlisle and I never lied to each other. Even when we said stuff that neither of us wanted to hear, we always told the truth. This is wrong. "Carlisle... "

My phone rings, the ringtone loud in the silence that has surrounded us. I fish it out of my pocket and glance at the screen. Anne.

"You take that. I'm sure it's important," Carlisle says as I swipe the screen to send the call to voicemail.

"Carlisle. Wait—" I shove the cell back in my pocket and try to capture her hand with my own but she's already stepping backwards and turning towards the family room.

"It was great to see you Teo... Mateo. I'm glad you're

doing so well." She pauses in her retreat and gives me one of those smiles you know is fake only because you know the person so well. It won't convince me and she knows it but this whole scene is now about saving face and acting like nothing between us ever happened. We aren't Carlisle and Mateo anymore. We're just people who used to fuck and share and tried to make each other happy. Strangers. "And I'm so glad you're happy. Really glad."

For a split second I think about following her but I don't. I might feel like an asshole for throwing out the whole "I love her" lie but nothing has changed. Carlisle is still the woman who makes me stop breathing but I can't forget what she did. Why would I do that to myself again? It's pride and ego and all that male bullshit but it's all I've got right now.

The hate I felt was real. As real as how much I still love her. I don't know how you get past that. I'm not sure I want to.

I turn and open the door, not even bothering to yell a goodbye towards Max and Kit. They'll figure out that I'm gone with one glance into the foyer. Besides, we're family and you can forget your manners with blood relatives and they have to take it. It's a rule.

I get to my car, slamming the door as I settle behind the wheel, my hands clenching at ten and two. I glance up at myself in the rearview mirror, my pupils are blown as if I'm high or aroused. Or angry. Emotional. Freaking the fuck out.

Where is the multiple choice answer for "all of the above"?

I pull out of the driveway and head towards downtown Nashville and the trendy, microbrew restaurant where I'm having dinner with Anne and her friends. Traffic is light and it's a good thing because I'm on autopilot, navigating the turns, the lane changes, and the speed limits with my mind very preoccupied with what just happened.

Carlisle is here and she's staying.

And while my head actually hurts with that mind-blowing truth another one pops in that threatens my ability to breathe.

She can walk.

Wherever she'd gone, whatever she'd done all these months, had worked. She was walking, with the aid of crutches, but she'd beaten the odds and made a comeback. It was all I wanted for her, no matter what happened between us.

As I pull into the parking area for the restaurant and hand over my keys to the attendant, the memory of Carlisle moving towards me would not banish itself to the background. I should not be thinking of her, should not linger over the details of how she looked: a little thinner but still strong, her hair longer and curlier, the same spatter of freckles along the bridge of her nose, the same cool fire in her emerald green eyes.

"Mateo." I am ripped out of my little fantasy by Anne striding towards me, her blonde curls framing her smiling face.

She walks straight to me and loops her arms around my waist, lifting her face for a kiss. This woman is openly affectionate, sweet, and uncomplicated. To fall for her would be easy and our relationship would be smooth and drama-free. I press my lips to hers, willing myself to forget what just happened, to keep Carlisle in my past where she belongs.

"Hey," I say when I end the kiss, hoping my voice sounds normal and not like the bottom just fell out from under me like those rides at the amusement park. "You look good."

She smiles at me but something in my expression makes it falter. "You all right?"

I nod, kissing the top of her head as we turn to walk into the restaurant. "I'm fine."

I look straight ahead as I try to forget the fact that for the first time in our relationship, I just lied to Anne.

TWENTY-FOUR
CARLISLE

"Why didn't we live in a place as nice as this when I was here?"

Livvy gives me a dirty look as she trails her gaze from the gorgeous view of the Nashville skyline to the modern interior of my new apartment. It is a lot nicer than the place we lived in.

"Because I hated you." I smile widely at the middle finger she is pointing in my direction. "I still do."

"Kiss my ass your majesty."

"I have no idea where that ass has been," I toss back at her as I roll myself across the hand-scraped floors to the sofa where I go through the movements necessary to transfer my body to the extra-wide cushions. Balance and strength earned through countless hours of training in a gym make it possible. Livvy watches from her place by the window, her eyebrow raised in the universal silent question of "do you need help?" but I wave her off. It's not the most graceful dismount but I make it there with minimal fuss and only a little breathless. "I loved our old place but this building has better accessibility for the wheelchair."

"How often are you in it these days?"

I settle against the armrest and reach out to snag my bottle of soda from the coffee table before I answer. "Lately, I've used the crutches more often but it really depends on what my body feels like doing that day. I still engage with my physical therapist and I work out every day but it varies along with my level of pain. I never know whether I will be in the chair or on the crutches."

She crosses the room and plops down beside me, her face full of concern. "I thought the pain was going to get better?"

"It's so much better than it was but it's never all gone." I tip the bottle back and take a sip. "I can handle it without drugs for the most part and on the occasions where it is elevated, I have a prescription."

"No more self-medicating then?" I shake my head and she gives me a teasing grin. "You single-handedly put an entire drug cartel out of business by going cold turkey."

I toss a pillow at her face. "Screw you." We settle back into comfortable silence and I get back to her original question. "This building has a place next to the elevator for my car and it's accessible no matter what my condition. I'd love to live in a funky loft with all kinds of weird levels but my independence is more important. From here I can get to school, my gym, my doctor. It works."

"So, school? What are you? The oldest sophomore in the history of Nashville U?"

"I think I might be," I say, thinking about the summer classes I will take to ease back into the life of a student. I'm nervous but not because of the academics or my classmates, it's more elemental. I look at my best friend and I confess. "This will be the first time I will live completely independently since the surgery. When you leave, I will be completely on my own."

"Scary shit," she muses.

"Terrifying but exciting too. I'm ready for it."

"I'm proud of you. I never told you but I am." She smiles but I can see the moisture making her eyes glassy. "And I'm really glad you're still here. I love you and I can't imagine anyone else standing up with me when I get married."

I reach across the couch and grab her hand, squeezing her fingers lightly while I also fight back the bawling that comes so often these days. The barriers I put up after the bombing, after Aaron died, are all gone. Taken away with the little bits of metal from my back and I feel things keenly these day. I'm not a walking/talking blubbering mess but the sensations of joy, sorrow, loss, and appreciation are sharp, clear and run very deep but are also just below the surface of my thin skin.

"I love you too Livvy."

We sniffle and laugh and give our eyes a very unlady-like swipe with our hands before we settle back on the sofa, enjoying the sunshine spilling in through the floor-to-ceiling windows and the view of downtown Nashville. I picked this condo for the view, even when I'm not in it I feel like I'm part of the life and bustle in the streets. Even rattling around in the large two bedroom, two and half bath unit won't feel so lonely when I can look below and see so much vitality and energy.

At least that is the plan.

"Have you seen Mateo yet?" Livvy asks and while the question is abrupt, I was expecting it so I didn't even flinch.

I nod. "I saw him yesterday when I went to Max and Kit's house."

"You went to see them before you went to see *Mateo*?"

"He had the same reaction," I laugh but it tastes and sounds bitter. "I felt like an ass when I saw him. I should have gone to see him right away but it wouldn't have made a difference."

"Why not? It would have shown him that you've been pining for the last ten months." I roll my eyes and she holds up a hand and gives me the "don't even try to deny it" finger wag and head toss. "I said it: pining. Don't you even try to deny it. You were a miserable bitch who took it out on everyone around her."

I wasn't going to deny it but I did have one objection. "I didn't take it out on anyone but I did channel it to make myself work harder."

"Miserable. Bitch." Her lips are in a thin line, telling me that I won't win this argument.

I let it go. Getting down to the heart of the matter... namely the new info I received from Mateo yesterday.

"Well, it doesn't matter anymore. He has a girlfriend and he's in love with her."

"He told you that?" she asks, her face incredulous. "I throw the bullshit flag."

"I can only believe that it's the truth." I take another sip from my bottle and consider my options. There aren't any. "I'm not a home wrecker so it's got to be the end. I'll see him around but it will have to be as friends."

"That's so wrong."

"I knew when I left that this might be the way it ended. I didn't ask him to wait for me and he didn't. I gambled and I lost."

"You weren't playing a game," she protests. "You did what you thought was right at the time. You guys weren't talking and had shit you needed to figure out."

"It was a gamble no matter what and I lost him." I gaze at the skyline outside the window and wonder where Mateo is out there. I wondered this a million times when I was in Texas but being here in the same city with him makes the longing almost painful. "I wouldn't change it, I wasn't in the right place to be with him but it doesn't make it suck any less."

Livvy scoots over to me on my big, new couch and cuddles up close and we hug, leaning back against the smooshy cushions. She brushes away my tears and kisses my cheek, holding me close as I let go of a dream I've carried around for ten months.

TWENTY-FIVE
MATEO

The party in the Veranda Room at the Hermitage Hotel is the last place I want to be but Anne is excited enough for both of us.

"I have always wanted to go to a music industry party and I can't believe my first one is here," she gushes and squeezes my hand. "I hope I'm dressed up enough for it."

I glance over her frame, admiring the pale blue cocktail dress that hugs her figure and sets off her blonde hair perfectly. Her cheeks are pink from makeup and her excitement and her smile makes me grin back at her. It is one of the things I like about her, her enthusiasm for life is infectious and she often pulls me out of my moods. I realize that I have been a shit boyfriend tonight and forgotten the most basic of moves.

"You look beautiful. Kit is gonna be pissed when everyone is looking at you and not her."

Anne blushes but leans in for a quick kiss, her "thank you" a little breathless. I'm glad I brought her with me. I've been distant since seeing Carlisle three days ago and Anne has noticed but she hasn't said anything. She wouldn't, it's not her style. So when Kit and Max invited me and a plus-one to her tour kickoff party, I jumped at the chance to make it up to my girlfriend.

"Mateo!" I turn and see Max waving me over from across the room. We make our way to him, entering the Veranda Room with its barrel vaulted ceiling painted to look like the blue sky and the floor-to-ceiling windows that open onto Sixth Avenue. My cousin is dressed similar to me: dark suit with unbuttoned white dress shirt underneath and dark cowboy boots. Nashville formalwear.

"Hey man." We give each other the one-armed bro hug and I watch as he gives Anne a full one and a kiss on the cheek. "Tell Kit thank you for not making us wear monkey suits to this thing."

"God forbid you have to get out of your scrubs for anything," Anne says, poking me in the side.

"You see me get out of scrubs quite often," I tease with a wink and dodge her poking me in the side again. I laugh and leer at Max.

"The less I know about your sex life the better," he says, leading us over to the open bar and placing our drink orders. "We've got a band later for dancing but Kit has a few things to do for the press here at the beginning."

He snags Anne's wine and my whiskey and hands them over and we all take a minute to look around the room. It's packed with band members, record executives, friends, family and the press. Anne spies a friend and leaves us to go and say hello at the same time I see Zane talking to a local magazine. I smile at how easily he rocks the bad boy guitarist thing with the dark hair, black leather pants and the tattoos. And if the way he's smiling down at the cute little reporter, there's probably a good chance I'll see her at breakfast tomorrow morning.

"Zane is so excited to go on tour with Kit. He's been driving me bat shit crazy."

"Those two are going to be trouble on tour because she thinks he's the greatest thing ever. She loves his playing and hopes they'll get to write a bunch of songs together," Max says. "I told him that if I have to bail them out of jail even once, that I will beat his ass and leave the parts for the buzzards to eat."

I laugh and take a sip of my whiskey, starting to relax and suddenly I'm glad I came. I don't see my cousin as often with school and I miss him. "Where is your bride-to-be? She didn't run off with some rock star and leave you hanging?"

"No, you ass." He points over to the side of the room where Kit is holding court with a group of people. "She's right there."

She's introducing a tall, leggy blonde around to the crowd but I don't recognize her, so I lean in to ask. "Who is that with her?"

Max levels a look at me and shakes his head. "That's Emory Cabell... Kit's half sister."

"What?" I don't even disguise my shock. As far as I know, Kit is an only child. "How did that happen?"

"Well, when two people love each other or just get really drunk, they kiss and take off their clothes... " He trails off when I punch him in the arm.

"Shut the fuck up and tell me how Kit suddenly has a sister."

"Daddy Landry couldn't keep it in his pants and he had a whole other family on one of his regular trucking routes. With Kit's mom gone or on drugs most of the time, nobody blames him but it's still a shock."

"Tell me you got a DNA test."

"We did and it's all legit." He nudges me with his elbow

and gives me a "but there's more" look. "She sings like an angel and plays guitar like nobody's business. Kit's taking her on tour as a backup singer."

"Of course she is." And I'm not surprised at all. Kit has the biggest heart and it would never occur to her to shut out family. Anybody who knows what she did for her mom knows what kind of person she is. "I hope Emory is ready for her big sister. Kit can be a little intense."

She's like a fucking hurricane of energy and we all just brace ourselves and go along for the ride.

"They are thick as thieves. It's like they've known each other forever."

I start to ask another question but I'm cut off by the sight of Kit's record label president heading to the small stage and tapping onto the microphone. He welcomes everyone to the party and goes on and on, telling us what we already know: Kit is amazing and this tour is going to make a shitload of money.

He doesn't use those words exactly but that's what we all know he means.

The suit finally gets off the stage and Kit jumps into his space and the room erupts into whistles, catcalls and applause and I join in, adding a loud whoop to the mix.

She rolls through her own speech, thanking her label and introducing her band, including Zane who looks like he's about to explode with excitement, pride or both. Anne joins me again as Kit says she has one more announcement and I slip my arm around her waist. I catch Max giving me a significant look but I was sleeping in the day they gave out instructions on how to read his mind so I have no fucking idea what he is trying to tell me.

I didn't have long to wonder.

Kit is talking so I give her my full attention. "I am really excited to partner with a very special friend of mine on a project that has become near and dear to my heart. I'm going to ask our newest Nashville neighbor and twelve-time gold medalist, Carlisle Queen to join me on stage."

I freeze on the spot, eyes glued to the auburn-haired woman slowly making her way onto the stage to stand next to Kit. She is using her crutches and dressed in a strapless gown the color of rubies and it matches her lipstick. She is fucking gorgeous.

"She really is," Anne agrees with me and I realize that I said it out loud. I bite back another curse at my stupidity. I need to be careful or I might hurt someone who has nothing to do with my history with Carlisle Queen. "I just want to cry when I think about all she's been through. She really loved Aaron Daniels. You could tell by the way they looked at each other that they adored each other."

I have nothing to say to that comment but I wondered if people thought that when we'd been together. I'd fucking worshipped the ground she walked on.

A t-shirt flashes up on the big screen. Black with stylized heart on the front, made of gold rectangles with words written on them: strength, community, hope. In the upper left of the heart is red block with the word "heart" written on it. The front of the tee flashes up and over the heart area is a familiar logo, the "A" and "D" interlocked with waves of water. It's the foundation Carlisle started to honor the memory of her dead lover.

"Carlisle and I designed this t-shirt and it will be on sale at every concert stop and every penny will go to support the Aaron Daniels Foundation and will provide financial support to athletes who wish to compete in the Paralympics." Kit joins the clapping that rises up from the audience. She gestures to Carlisle to step up to the microphone and at first she refuses but she finally gives in and takes the two forward steps necessary to be heard. Her voice is clear, that honey whiskey sound that I hear in my dreams sometimes. More often than I care to admit.

"I want to thank Kit for supporting this project." She pauses and I recognize the crease between her brows as a sign that she is gathering her thoughts. "As you can tell, my mobility has been impaired as a result of the bombing that injured me and ten more and killed twenty-two other athletes, including Aaron. I cannot express how much I have missed competitive athletics but I have wonderful memories of winning gold for my country. The pride I felt in that moment will stay with me the rest of my life. And so to have this opportunity to help other athletes to do the same thing is amazing. Thank you."

Applause rise up again and then dies down as people return to partying. I watch as Kit and Carlisle pose for photos and press the flesh but eventually they leave the stage and a local band takes their place and begins the first set. Many couples spill out on the dance floor as the party kicks up a notch but I can't take my eyes off Carlisle. Every inch of my skin is hyper-aware that she is in the same room and I have to fight the urge to walk across the room and haul her into my arms and kiss the living fuck out of her.

I TENSE when I notice Kit and Carlisle headed in our direction and I scramble to find a way to pull Anne away when she notices the same thing.

"Oh my God, Kit and Carlisle are coming over here. Max can you introduce me, I have always wanted to meet Carlisle," Anne gushes, her hand squeezing mine.

Max and I exchange a glance and I know he's thinking that I could introduce them. I won't... for obvious reasons.

"You bet," he replies and steps forward to kiss his wife and hug Carlisle. She hasn't noticed me yet but I know the second she does because her whole body stiffens and she bites the bottom of her lip. I almost miss what Max is saying.

"... introduce you to a friend of ours, Anne Price." He pauses just the tiniest second and I wonder how he's going to handle this. "She's Mateo's girlfriend."

Carlisle looks at me then, her green eyes widening with surprise and a tiny bit of hurt but she recovers quickly, her natural ability with people kicking in. She extends her hand to Anne with a warm smile.

"It's nice to meet you Anne. Mateo has told me wonderful things about you."

I haven't told her shit except the lie about loving Anne but I see what she's doing. Keeping it classy and ensuring that Anne isn't caught up in any awkward undertow pulsing between us. I am grateful for her kindness, the pit in my belly loosening a bit.

"I am so excited to meet you, Ms. Queen. I am a huge fan." She turns to look at me with a confused expression on her face. "But I had no idea you knew Mateo."

"I met him when I lived here last year." She glances at me, uncertainty with how much I've told Anne all over her face. I shake my head. I've told Anne nothing. What would be the point? "He was my teaching assistant for freshman Spanish."

I let out the breath I'd been holding. Excellent save Carlisle.

"Oh, Mateo didn't tell me he was a TA for that class but that's no surprise since he grew up in a bilingual household."

"He was a great TA." She twists her lips in a self-deprecating grin and laughs. "I was a terrible student."

"Is that true Mateo?" Anne places her hand on my chest and I watch Carlisle's gaze lock on the place she's touching. I'd have to be blind to miss the jealousy that skates across her features and the surge of adrenaline it gives me. "I don't believe it."

"She has the worst pronunciation I've ever heard." At my reply Carlisle's eyes snap up to meet mine and I realize that my comment was a mistake because now all I can think about is that first night in my house, in the laundry room, our bodies moving together and the look on her face when she came. I flash hot all over my body and my cock gets hard in my pants.

Fuck.

"Can I get a photo with you?" Anne's innocent question to Carlisle snaps us both back from the place we should not have been and I realize that my girlfriend is holding out her phone to me. "Baby, can you take it for us?"

I take the phone from her and tap the app to activate the camera, willing my body and my mind to get back under control. Carlisle and I are over. I moved on. I need to stay there.

"Say cheese," I tell them and snap a few for good measure before handing the phone back to Anne and accepting a kiss on the cheek in thanks.

Anne excuses herself to go freshen up and Carlisle and I are left staring at each other in a room that is quickly filling up with people. The crowd has pushed us closer to each other and I try not to flinch when her arm brushes my torso. Someone jars her crutches and she pitches forward, into and up against me and I automatically reach out to steady her, my lips brushing the soft curl of her hair as I lean in.

"I think I need to get to a place with fewer people," Carlisle says, her face tipped back to make eye contact with me. This close I can see the freckles on her nose, muted by the thin layer of powder on her skin. She still wears the same perfume; gardenias and sunshine. I'm not the only one feeling what is pulsing between us. Her pupils are large and dark, her neck flushed that pretty shade of pink that happens when she's aroused. I know that if I lean in and touch my lips to the blush, she will be warmer there.

I remember it all.

"Let me get you away from the bar. This area will be mobbed the rest of the night," I say, making sure she's steady on her crutches and waiting for her signal before placing my hand at the small of her back and leading her away. I hover over her, trying to block her from the worst of the crush as I lead her away from that scene and into the area just outside of the Veranda Room.

It's so much quieter here and the lights are dimmer. Along the hallway there are alcoves containing ornately leaded windows and built-in benches with cushions. I lead her over to the nearest one, releasing my hold on her body and giving her space to catch her breath.

The gold tone of the light here highlights the spun gold strands of her hair and the warm space amplifies her scent. I inhale deeply and clench my hands by my side. She's right here in front of me and I could reach out and touch her if I wanted to.

Carlisle's gaze is cast down when she says, "Anne is lovely. I'm very happy for you."

I want to throw back my head and howl at the game we are playing. I don't want her to be happy for me. I don't want her to praise my choice in her replacement. I want answers.

"Why did you come back here? Why didn't you just stay gone?" I ask, my voice gritty with anger and want. She hears it, I can tell by the way the muscles in her back and shoulders tense up but she refuses to make eye contact with me. She keeps her focus on her hands as they smooth out nonexistent wrinkles in her skirt. She ignores me.

"Kit tells me that she's a librarian. I think that's wonderful." Her voice falters and she clears her throat. "Wonderful."

"Why didn't you contact me? Would it have killed you to tell me where you were going?" I persist, determined to have the conversation I need to have.

We start the ping-pong of questions that only piss me off more and more.

"I love her hair. It's that honey gold that people pay a lot of money to get but I can totally tell she's a natural."

"I waited months for you to call or send an email. It was killing me not to know how you were doing."

"Kit says your mom introduced you two. Carmela has excellent taste."

"I waited and waited until it became clear that you weren't coming back, that you didn't give a shit about me or what I was going through."

"I'm feeling better now. I think I'll go back to the party."

She stands up and I move in closer, blocking her body with my own. I'm a mess of anger, hurt, and desire so poignant that it actually hurts to be in my skin. I reach out a hand and tip her face up to me and groan in pain with what I see there.

Tears. Tracks of wetness down her cheeks and agony in her eyes that takes my breath away.

"I waited and waited for you to come back to me. I missed you... " I swallow hard and try to breathe around the ache in my chest. "... I still miss you. Every second of every day and it's killing me. I'm carrying around all this pain because I'm drowning with the weight of needing you so damn much. I need to feel nothing for you. I love you so much I can't even hate you so I just need to be numb. But I can't." I tip her head back further, loving the feel of her fingers clutching my shirt, nails digging into my skin. We are so close, I feel the vibration of her soft moan against my lips. "So I want an answer to my question, why did you come back here?"

"I came back for you."

I can't lie, not about this. Even though every part of me is screaming for me to deny this truth, I can't. I barely get the words out of my mouth before Mateo is on me, his lips pressing against mine, his tongue pushing for entrance I freely give. It isn't the sweet, tender kiss you would imagine after months spent apart. No, this is rough and brutal and almost painful in its intensity.

I am on fire. My skin is burning, my blood running hot like lava in my veins. I move my hands from his shirt to around his neck, pulling him even closer when he groans like this contact just might kill him.

The slow burn in my belly is amazing, confirming that the sensations that had gradually returned were back and making me ache with need. My own experimentation with fingers and toys has produced orgasms and I am so relieved to experience them again. But they are nothing like his touch and I arch into it, barely registering the clatter of my crutches to the floor at our feet.

I'm not worried about falling. Mateo has me wrapped in his arms and he was holding me tight.

"I missed you so much, *Tesoro*." His words breathed against my cheek make me shiver and I blink back the tears of joy at hearing him call me "his treasure" once again. "I missed you."

"I missed you too."

Laughter erupts behind us as a group of people walk by, reminding me of where we are. Anyone can walk by and see us.

Anne can walk by and see us.

Mateo is not mine.

I lower my hand and push at his chest, ducking my face away when he leans back in for another kiss.

"Stop," I demand, emphasizing my point with a shove. He moves back and I lower myself to the bench behind me, running a hand over my heated cheeks. What had been fiery passion was now nothing but the ache of unfulfilled longing and burning shame. "We are not these people."

There are two beats of silence before he speaks and his voice is heavy and dark. "Fuck."

"We can't do this, Mateo. We shouldn't be doing this at all. What if Anne had seen us?" I raise my face to look at him and see what I know is reflected on my face. "She would be devastated, hurt. We *are not* the people who would do that to someone else."

"You're right Carlisle. You're absolutely right."

His voice breaks and he raises a hand to his face but I see his expression before he covers it up and what I see kills me.

Stricken. Devastated. Broken. Ashamed.

Those words are the first that come to my mind and I feel sick.

"I won't deny that I still have feelings for you Mateo but I don't want what we had to be spoiled by us making it ugly and hurtful."

"Neither do I." He finally looks at me and I can see the pain and confusion in his eyes and etched in the lines on his face. "Anne is a good person."

"She is and now is your time with her. We had our chance, yeah?" I nod and attempt a smile but my lips are too wobbly with the tears I am fighting to hold back. "I think we just need time. Time to adjust."

Time to avoid each other until I don't love him anymore.

"It's just... " He stops and considers his words and I hold my breath, wondering what he will say next. "We just need time."

We stare at each other for several long moments as the party is happening all around us. In another time we would have been out there with them, holding hands, dancing, kissing. Maybe we would have left the party and come to this very spot for deeper kisses and whispered promises for later. Our being together would have hurt no one and we wouldn't have hurt each other.

"I might have made a mistake coming back to Nashville," I say.

"Don't say that."

"I think it was selfish of me to expect for us to be able to start over or be friends. We have too many people in common to avoid each other and sooner or later this is going to ruin whatever we could hope to salvage."

"I will miss you too much if you go somewhere else," he says, before he kneels down in front of me so we can be eye level. "This is really fucked up right now and I have no clue what I'm doing or what I'm going to do but I don't want you to go. It's selfish and I have no right to ask you but I'm doing it."

My heart squeezes at his words and I feel something else in my chest and I recognize it for what it is: hope. Hope for him to come back to me. Hope that maybe I can learn to be content with just having him in my life. Hope is a bitch. She's the friend who swears to always be there and then ditches your ass when she gets a boyfriend. I hate hope.

I can't afford to have hope where Mateo is concerned because I will always yearn for the thing I cannot have. Somebody has to be the honest one in this crazy mess. It looks like it is me.

"I don't think I can promise you that, Mateo."

He opens his mouth to protest and I brace myself for his protest, but we are interrupted by Max appearing in the opening of the alcove.

"Mateo, Anne is looking... " He sees his cousin at my feet and his eyes grow wide with shock and so many questions. "Is there something wrong? Are you okay Carlisle?"

I muster a smile for him and even pat Mateo on the shoulder like he's a good dog who just obeyed my command to fetch or sit. "The crowd was too much with my crutches so Mateo brought me over here to rest for a bit, but now I think I really just want to get a cab and head home."

Mateo's eyes clash with mine and he frowns, shaking his head as he picks up my crutches and stands. "You don't have to go."

I break eye contact because if I keep looking at his gorgeous blue eyes, I will stay. "I think I've had enough excitement for tonight. It's time for me to go."

Mateo hands over my crutches and I hook them over my forearms and rise to my feet. I avoid touching him and smile at Max. "Can you take me to the lobby so that I can hail a cab?"

"I can take you," Mateo offers but I shake my head.

"I think I've kept you from Anne long enough." It's a borderline shitty thing to say and I know but I'm in full-on retreat mode and with the way he's looking at me, I'm not sure he'll just let me go. "It was good to see you Mateo. Thanks again."

He gives me a significant look but he goes, leaving me behind with Max who doesn't look like he's buying any of it.

"Just don't." I hold up my hand when he opens his mouth. "I can't talk about it. I'm all talked out."

"How do you know what I'm going to ask?"

I give him the same look Mateo just gave me. "It's what I would ask."

He nods. "Fair enough but if you need to talk... "

"I'll call Kit."

He laughs and offers his arm to me as we head to the elevators. "I like having you back in Nashville Carlisle Queen. I hope you decide to stay awhile."

"We'll see," is all I can answer.

"I thought you were staying with Anne," Zane says as I walk through the door at three in the morning.

I throw my keys on the table behind the sofa and walk to the fridge, opening it and snagging a beer from the shelf. I pop the top on the edge of the countertop and walk back to the couch where Zane is sitting and ease myself back on the cushions.

"What? You didn't bring one for me?" he asks, his hands open wide in the universal signal for "what-the-fuck-one-way"?

I flip him the bird and take a sip of my beer, dodging the pillow he throws at my face when he gets up to get his own beverage.

"If you're this much of an asshole, I bet Anne threw you out."

"I broke up with her," I say and take another sip while staring at the scuffed top of the coffee table we got for ten bucks at Goodwill the first week of sophomore year, when we moved out of the dorms and into our first apartment.

"This table is a piece of shit, Zane. We should get a new one. You're working now, buy us a new fucking table."

He sits down next to me and places his feet on the table in question. "I like this table. I had my first three-way on this table."

"Sentimental value for the win," I say and chug back the rest of the bottle.

Zane hands me his beer.

"I kissed Carlisle at the party so I broke up with Anne."

"Do you want to kiss Carlisle again?" he asks.

I nod. "More than I want to do anything else on the planet."

"Well, then breaking up with Anne was the right thing to do." I shift to look at him and he examines me, his expression twisted with his confusion. "What? What's going on?"

"I don't know if I can be with Carlisle. We've got a terrible track record, so much shit under the bridge."

"You guys weren't together long enough to have a track record. It will be like starting new." He shrugs. "It's probably better to start new."

"Just let all that shit go? Act like it never happened?" I lean back on the sofa and stare at the ceiling. The dart we threw up there about a year ago is still wedged in the drywall. "A fresh start."

"Brand new except that you two crazy kids are already in love. You never stopped. I know it. You know it. Max knows it. The only one who didn't know it was Anne."

"Well thanks for making me feel like a bigger dick," I grumble and pick at the label on my beer bottle. "I didn't mean to hurt her. I thought Carlisle and I were done."

He shakes his head and laughs. "You two are never going to be done. You've got epic love song written all over you. Trust me, I know it when I see it."

"I need to talk to her. She was talking about leaving Nashville." I reach for my phone and slide the screen to access my contacts, too late remembering that the number I had for Carlisle was disconnected when she left. "Fuck, I'll have to ask Kit for her number tomorrow and then figure out where to find Carlisle."

It blows my mind that I don't know where the person I love most in the world actually lives.

"I have her number and I also know where she'll be tomorrow," Zane says with a grin on his face that says I'm going to pay for the information.

I groan but I know that whatever the price, I'll pay it.

"I'm not wearing a dress or eating anything alive," I warn him and groan when all he does is laugh.

I've never seen Carlisle swim in person, only on TV.

I walk into the competition size pool at the University and nod at the lifeguard watching her closely as she shoots through the water like a bullet. Her long and lithe body moves in one flawlessly executed movement and the sheer power of it takes my breath away.

"She's amazing isn't she," the man standing next me says as she dives under the surface and executes a perfect flip turn. "She was born to be in the water."

"She's so fast," I say and I know my voice is full of awe.

The guy chuckles beside me and glances down at the stopwatch he's holding. "Not fast enough for her, I'm afraid."

"Is she tough on herself?"

"I won't be able to get word in edgewise with the ass chewing she'll deliver to the girl in the mirror." He picks up a clipboard and writes down something on the sheet and smiles. "Easiest coaching job I've ever had. So much talent and drive. I almost don't need to be here."

Carlisle stops swimming and looks over at us, her eyes

flaring wide with surprise at my presence. I wave and she waves back, a slight smile lifting her lips. She glides through the water, grips the edge and hauls herself out. A wheelchair is just behind her and I step forward to go help her but the guy next to puts a hand on my arm, stopping my progress.

"Unless you want to pull back a bloody stump, you need to let her do it. She'll ask for help if she needs it."

I stay where I am and watch her movements as she rolls the chair to her, sets the brake and lifts herself into the seat. She rolls over to a bench and removes her swim cap and grabs a towel, throwing it over her shoulders before joining us. She smiles at me but her focus is on her coach.

"How did I do, Joe?"

"You need to shave fifteen seconds off your time," he looks at me and grins when she mutters "fuck" under her breath, "And you need to work on keeping your hips from dipping down too low. It gives you too much drag. Use your weight work to strengthen your core and it should help a lot."

She nods and if the fierce determination on her face is any indication, she'll make it happen.

"Got it." Done with business, Carlisle makes the introductions. "Joe Griggs this is Mateo Butler."

We shake hands and then he moves off to gather their practice stuff.

"What are you training for?" I ask, suddenly nervous about my real reason to be there.

"I'm going to compete in the next Paralympics." She's running the towel over her body and squeezing the excess water out of her hair and delivers the news that she is going to compete on an international level again like it's something we all do.

"You've got a long way to go," Joe replies.

"And every time you tell me that, I am more and more determined to tell you to kiss my ass." She punctuates her words with a directly aimed glare.

I laugh at the exchange, enjoying the play between the two of them, the pink of her cheeks. Her eyes are like emerald fire and I know it's the joy of competing.

"I think you'll make it," I offer and she turns to Joe and gives him an "I told you so" look before returning back to me.

We stare at each other for a few minutes and I can see the big question of why I am here hanging over both of us.

I take a deep breath and decide to jump in with both feet. "I broke up with Anne."

She pauses, her lips parting on a silent "oh" at my disclosure.

"I'm sorry for that," she whispers, "She seemed to be a very nice person."

"She was and she deserved more than what I could give her. So I ended it."

My words fall into the silence as I watch Carlisle and she looks everywhere but at me. Her fingers twist the towel in her hands, the biggest clue that she's as nervous as I am.

I decide to put us both out of our misery.

"I was running errands today and you were on my list."

Her eyes snap to meet mine and her cheeks flush bright pink with her surprise. I can see her pulse pounding on her throat and she swallows before she answers.

"At least I made the list." Her lips twitch with the hint of a smile and it gives me the guts to continue.

"You were first on the list but I was trying to get the nerve to come see you." And then I keep going. "I wanted to see if you wanted to go out with me sometime. On a date." I press my luck when her smile gets wider. "If you have time for a coffee now, I can wait."

"Will my wheelchair fit in your trunk? I got a ride from Joe, so I'll need one home."

"I'll make room."

THE COFFEE HOUSE down the street from the University aquatic center is crowded and we opt for a table outside on the patio where it is quiet and almost deserted. Dusk has settled on the city and it's a little chilly in the air but the outdoor space heater and my excitement over being here with Carlisle keeps it at bay.

I come back to the table with our drinks and a couple of brownies and I settle into the chair next her wheelchair. I should probably give her some space but I don't know if I can stand to be even a table-length away from her. She doesn't seem to mind since she's leaning towards me, our arms brushing against each other as we move.

We both take a sip of our drinks but before it has a chance to get weird, I jump in.

"It was really great to see you swimming again."

She brushes a stray curl off her face and tucks it behind her ear and my fingers itch to do that for her. I grip my coffee tighter in an effort to keep them to myself.

"At the rehab place in Texas they really pushed me to get in the pool. Once I realized how much it helped my progress you couldn't keep me out of it."

"And the Paralympics?"

"That was me, being me. If there is someone to beat, I'm on it." She shrugs her shoulders. "Time will tell if I'll be successful or not."

"If I know you, you'll dominate the field as usual." She shrugs again and we stare at each other for several long moments before she begins, never breaking eye contact with me. I have no desire to look anywhere but at her so I'm good with it.

"And what about you and medical school?" She reaches over and touches my hand, letting her touch linger before she returns it to her cup. "Max and Kit told me you're doing great."

"I love it. It's hard and I'm tired all the time but I'm glad I went." I bump her with my shoulder and give credit where credit is due. "I'm glad you convinced me to go. I love working in the free clinic and I'm already planning to go into the General Practice track."

"So the Butler family practice will be a reality then?" she asks.

"I'm sure Mari is happy up there looking down on her big brother." I need to touch her so I reach over and take her hand, holding it between us. "Is this okay? I just can't sit next to you and not touch you."

"It's more than okay," she whispers and I lean over, brushing our lips against each other. Soft and gentle, the hint of coffee on our lips. I pull back and her eyes are closed so I move in again and take another until she sighs. "People are probably watching us."

"They're just jealous."

She laughs and moves away, just a little, enough for us to look at each other as we talk.

"How often are you in the wheelchair?"

"It depends on so many things. I use it far less than the crutches but if I have been on my feet a lot or if I my body decides to boycott, I'm usually in for a day or two. I've learned to read my body and the signals and I can stay out of it if I respect my limits and keep up my exercise."

"Do you still feel like you made the right decision?" I ask and I hold my breath not sure I'm ready to hear the answer. She seems to be happy but I know how hard the early days were for her and how much she doubted her choice.

"Yes, I do. It's not easy all the time but it's worth it." Her gaze is clear and sure. "I made the right call, I'm just sorry that I didn't know it soon enough to avoid hurting you."

And here we are at the crossroads and I know where I want to go. I just need to know if she is with me.

"Carlisle I understand better how it all went to hell. It's in the past and we are here now and I don't want to waste time going over and over what we could have done differently or better or whatever. I just want you."

"I want you too." She hesitates, her eyes cloudy with the uncertainty our past put there and I regret it. "Do you think we can just start over?"

"I don't want to start over. I want to begin again. Brand new as the people we are now, living with the choices we made in the past and choosing to be here together now."

A tear hovers on her lashes and splashes down her cheek and I lean forward, kissing it away.

"I'm not the same woman I was before Mateo. My body..."

"Carlisle, you can tell me anything. If we are going to be together we have to be honest with each other, shares our worries and our fears. I don't want what we had before, I want all of you sharing everything with me and I will do the same."

I think I know what she's worried about, the physical side of us after her injury. I've done my research and I'm sure I know what to expect but I want her to confide in me, to share. It's a huge step and the tightness in my chest releases when she takes it.

"My body needs help to function. It's getting better and the doctors think that I will eventually get beyond needing the assistance but I have to use enemas and catheters to maintain my health. Sex is completely on the table and I want it but I need help with lube and extra stimulation to have an orgasm. It's not a lot in my opinion but for some guys it might be too much. I don't know if it's too much for you."

Her hands are lying flat on the table in between us and it is the most natural thing in the world for me to put my hands in them and hold on tight.

"Carlisle, when I came back to you the night I found out about the surgery it was because it is impossible for me to be without you. I decided before I even got in the car that it didn't matter how it turned out, I was prepared to be by your side until one of takes our last breath. None of that has changed in all this time and it never will. It will never matter to me if you are on your own two feet or in a wheel-chair or if we have to buy out the adult toy store and a lube factory to make sure you have everything you want and need in bed. I love you, *Tesoro* and you are perfect to me."

She's crying full-on now and I release her hands to cup her face and kiss away the tears. Her eyelashes, her cheeks, and finally her mouth. Sweet, drugging kisses that leave both of us breathless and laughing.

"I love you, Teo."

And once again, that's all I need to hear.

I haven't been this nervous on a date since I was a teenager.

Carlisle's new place is really nice. The twenty-four hour guard had my name at the front desk and buzzed me into the elevator that shot straight to her floor. I clutch my gifts in my hands and second-guess myself yet another time. I think what I brought is okay considering the step we took yesterday and I hope it will help us have a new beginning. New memories. New understanding. New commitment.

The elevator doors open and I am facing the long hallway. I swallow down the nerves fluttering around in my belly and take one step and then the next until I find myself at her door. I press the button and wait. The lock turns, the handle moves, and the door sweeps open.

At first I see no one and then I look down. Carlisle looks up at me from her wheelchair and the smile she gives me is tentative, her eyes questioning.

"It's a wheelchair day," I observe, using her own words and I relax when relief crosses her features and her eyes sparkle. She wasn't sure how I would react and that makes my heart hurt a little.

We might have come so far but we still have a ways to go. Mateo and Carlisle are still a work-in-progress.

"I had a fundraiser this morning and I walked a lot. My legs are a little tired," she explains and then, "Come on in. Dinner is keeping warm in the oven. I hope you like lasagna," she says as she maneuvers her chair through the entryway and into her place. The living room is floor-to-ceiling windows and we've got the Nashville skyline lit up like a Christmas at our feet. I stop and stare.

"Oh my God. This is gorgeous." I look over at her and smile. "Quite a change from your last place. You stopped slumming."

She tosses her hair back over her shoulder and makes a face. "You sound like Livvy."

"And she's right." I hand her one of the packages I have in my hand. "A housewarming gift."

"You didn't have to but since I love presents, I'll take it." She snatches it out of my hand wheels over to the living space, motioning for me to take a seat next to her. The way she has her sofa arranged, with one side armless she can roll her chair up and its like we're sitting side-by-side.

I lower myself to the cushions and watch her as she rips off the paper. I know what's inside the wrapping paper, so I focus on her. The way her emerald eyes are glowing, her red-gold hair longer and draped around her shoulders like a veil. Yesterday when we kissed, the caress of it's silk on my skin was luxurious.

"You're gorgeous," I blurt out and she stops what's she's doing, meeting my eyes.

"What?"

"You're just the most fucking beautiful thing I have ever seen in my whole life and I can't stop looking at you." I grin, unapologetic in my adoration.

I could play it cool but I'm not. She's the one for me. I know it. She knows it.

"Teo... "

"Open your present," I urge and she watches me for a few seconds before looking back down and pulling off the rest of the wrapping paper.

She stares at it for a moment, confusion on her features and then her face lights up. She smiles as she runs her fingers over the framed t-shirt.

"It's from the concert... our first 'non date'."

"I bought it and forgot to give it to you. I kept it so... " I feel kind of stupid now that I've given it to her. "I thought you might want it."

"I love it," she says and holds it to her chest, her smile genuine. "That is an excellent memory."

"Yeah the show was great."

"I wasn't talking about the show," she says and my body reacts to the sultry lilt to her words.

We stare at each other. There's so much electricity pulsing between us that I fully expect the appliances in her kitchen to short out. I lean over and she leans in, the first brush of our mouths sparking with static. We pull back and look each other, laughing.

"I've never laughed with anyone like I do with you," I murmur, zooming back in for a new press of our lips.

She's still smiling when our lips meet and when I press forward to part her lips with my tongue, it is effortless. Natural. It's like there was never a gap.

I feel her hand reach out to grab my shirt and pull me closer, she tilts her head so I can have better access to her mouth. I take what she is offering to me, indulging my need to reconnect with her this way with sweeps of my tongue, nibbles on her lips.

I pull back and make eye contact with her, leaning forward to hook my arm under her legs and she loops her arms around my neck. I position her in my lap, the full body contact intensifying the kisses when I lean back in for more.

We make out on the couch like teenagers. Hands roaming over clothes at first and then she starts unbuttoning my shirt and caressing my chest with her cool fingers. I caress her back, rubbing circles downward until I each the hem of her blouse and burrow underneath, coasting my palm against the silken skin. The bra strap interrupts my journey so I open the clasp and expose her entire back to my exploration.

She's thinner but more muscular and I love the play of her muscles underneath my touch. Carlisle is raking her fingernails against my chest, over my nipples and I groan, releasing her from the kiss as I run my mouth over the place where her shirt has slipped off. A bite to the place where her shoulder meets her neck and she's gasping. Soft pants of desire against my hair as I continue my tasting tour along the column of her neck.

"You are perfect. A dream," I whisper when I reach the tender shell of her ear.

Carlisle reaches around and grabs my hand under her shirt and I pull back, thinking she is going to move it away but instead she drags it to the front and places it on her breast. I look up and meet her eyes, making sure we're on the same page.

"Mateo, touch me please. It's been too long," she whispers against my mouth, her tongue tracing my bottom lip before she dives in for another kiss.

I move my hand upward and cup the heavy weight of her breast in my palm. Skimming my thumb lightly over her nipple. Carlisle's fingernails dig into my bicep, my back, as she arches into my touch, begging me for more.

I want to give her whatever she wants but not on this couch.

"I'm not going to do this for the first time on your sofa. May I take you to bed?" I ask, staring down at her so that I can see every nuance of emotion on her face. "I know this is fast. We don't... "

"I want to try this with you, Teo. I want you in my bed and in my life. Please."

She doesn't have to ask me twice. I adjust my grip on her body and stand, at the last minute remembering my other gift. "Lean over and grab that please."

She does as I ask, her eyebrows drawn together in confusion. "What's this?"

"Something to help us navigate this new beginning."

"You bought me a GPS?" She teases and I grin back. Laughter and sex and Carlisle always seem to go together for me.

"In a way. You'll see."

I walk into the bedroom stopping just over the threshold to look around. It's a large room with the bold splashes of color on a dove gray background. The bed is set along one wall, the floor-to-ceiling windows covering another, a bathroom and closet taking up the rest of the space. I stare at the bed, doubt that this is the right time clouds my mind.

Carlisle's fingertips under my chin guide my gaze back to her own. It's like she can read my mind because she smiles at me and assures me, "I want this Mateo."

"Is there anything you need to do before we do this Carlisle? Can I help you?" I don't know how she'll react to my question; don't know if it will kill the mood blooming between us.

She shakes her head. "Not tonight. I took care of it earlier but I might need help later."

Her admission makes my chest hurt. I know how hard it is for her to ask for help, it was one of the things that brought us down before. But we both want this to work, we want to be together and that requires us to be different. To begin now.

I lower her to the bed and step back, watching her as I slowly unbutton the rest of my shirt. She leans back on her elbows, ogling me with a sexy, mischievous smile on her lips

"I like the view," she says, reaching over her head to grab the back of her shirt and pull it off, tossing it to the floor. I mimic her behavior and she leers with a sexy grin. "Keep going. It gets better and better by the minute."

"Pervert."

"But I'm *your* pervert," she says and throws off her bra.

That stops me with my jeans unbuttoned, my fly undone. I stare and then drop to my knees at her feet, diving in to take one of her rose-colored nipples in my mouth.

"You have gorgeous tits. I have always loved your tits," I mumble as I trace a path of kisses across her collarbone and take the other one in my mouth for lavish attention.

Carlisle's fingers are in my hair, holding me in place as I devour her. She starts the panting, the moaning that haunted my dreams for ten months. I'm so hard for her that I jump when her hand drops to my crotch and inserts itself inside my jeans to stroke me. I throw my head back enjoying the sensation, thrusting into her grip as my blood heats up.

It feels good and I want it continue but this first time has to be more about her than me. I need to show her that although we might have to find new ways of enjoying each other, we will still be combustible in bed. I need to show her that she is enough and will always be for me.

I pull back and move her hand away. "Get undressed. I want to make you feel good."

I shuck off my jeans and watch as she removes her skirt and them scoots back on the bed until she is naked and fully open to me in the middle. I reach down and open the package that I brought with me, handing the contents over to her with a smile.

"You told me that we might have to be creative and I took you at your word."

Carlisle

I LOOK down at what Mateo has placed in my hand and try to figure out what it is.

A wrist band, similar to the kind you use to strap your iPod to your arm when you run. From it's black material emerges two wires that lead to a set of pads that fit over the fingertips.

"Here let me show you," Mateo says, kneeling naked next me on the bed, his body distracting me from what he's doing. Ten months has not changed him at all. Skin still tan, hair dark, muscles everywhere a man is supposed to have them. If I wasn't really curious about what he brought me, I'd be exploring him up close and personal right now.

He fastens the wristband over his wrist and slips the pads over his fingers and presses a button on the band. A slight vibration sound fills the air between us and he reaches out to cup my breast.

"How does this feel?" He asks as he lightly runs his fingers over my skin. I react immediately, goosebumps running up and down my skin and then a jolt of electricity that runs straight to my sex when he glances it over a nipple.

"Holy hell," I gasp and clutch at his shoulder when he makes another pass at my nipple. "That's amazing."

"Can you feel it? I know you said that you needed more pressure more intense sensation. Is this enough?"

I open my eyes and look at the blue eyes of the most generous lover, the most perfect partner anybody could ask for.

"It's amazing," I say and cup his face in my hands, pressing our foreheads together, a replica of what he does that drives me crazy. "And *you* are amazing. I love you Mateo."

"I love you too. I'll do anything for you, *Tesoro*. All you have to do is ask."

"Come here and fuck me, Teo. It's been too long." I lean back on the bed and shift my legs, spreading them for him in invitation. I worry briefly that the heaviness in my limbs makes my movement more awkward than sexy but one look at Mateo's face erases that doubt from my mind. He's hungry for me and I can't wait for him to eat me up.

Mateo crawls up between my legs, leaning over to kiss me. Slow kisses, with deep tongue and tender nips that build our passion again. I run my hands over his back, down his chest, stroking his cock and reveling in the way his hips buck into my palm. He's leaking pre-come and it makes the glides slicker, my thumb rubbed over his head makes his whole body jump and we laugh softly.

"Two can play at that game," he growls against the sensitive skin just below my ear before he travels down my body. He presses soft kisses on my breasts, soft licks against nipples that make me squirm with the jolts of pleasure that shoot to my sex. I'm aroused, to a point more intense than where I've gotten on my own and watching Teo kissing down my belly spikes it even higher. I push the worry to the back of mind and just enjoy every moment with my lover.

He gives me one long look from his place between my legs before he dips his head and gives my entire sex a long lick that ends with a swirl on my clit. I arch off the bed a little, surprised by the amount of sensation I am feeling from such a gentle touch.

"Feel good?" He asks and when I nod he smirks. "Let's see how this is for you."

And then the pad on one of his fingers joins his mouth and I'm clutching at my comforter, twisting it in my grip as I cry out. Mateo groans and I reach down to cup the back of his head. It's intense, powerful and delicious. I'm too busy reveling in it to compare it whatever it was like before.

"Oh my God, don't stop. Please."

I look down to enjoy the view of this man pleasuring me with his mouth, His dark, sleek body writhing as he grinds his cock against the bed as I fuck up into his mouth. Its heaven and hell and I don't want to be anywhere else right now. An orgasm is building and I strain to reach it, a frustrated moan escaping my lips.

"Play with your nipples. Get your fingers real wet and play with them for me. I'll get you there Carlisle."

Mateo's eyes are a dark navy as he watches me follow his directions. Two fingers in my mouth, spit slick and twisting the sensitive tips before he finally resumes eating me out. He never takes his eyes off me and his eyes are the last things I see before I close my eyes when I come.

Fireworks. Shooting stars. An entire universe exploding behind my eyelids as I writhe against his mouth, against the vibrator before I even start to float back to Earth.

He crawls up my body, taking off the vibrator and

setting it to side of us on the bed before he leans down and kisses me. Thorough. Wet. Deep. Passionate. I throw my arms around his neck, keeping him close, pulling him down on top of me, relishing the weight of him on me, my taste in his mouth.

"Was it good?" he asks, his worry plain in the tone of his voice.

I grasp his face and force him to look at me. "It was amazing. Perfect."

"Thank God," he breathes and lowers his forehead to mine, his nose rubbing mine before leaning down to kiss me again.

"I want you inside of me, Teo. Please." I realize that I am going to have to ask, to guide him this time. New territory for both and too much opportunity to misstep if we aren't honest with one another. I nod when he asks if I am sure.

He turns and picks up the tube of lube from my side table and offers it to me.

"Get me ready, baby."

I take it and pour some in my palm, sliding it over his cock and enjoying the hiss and groans my touch pulls out of him. When he's slick enough, he settles in between my legs and pushes inside me.

I gasp at the fullness, the pressure that settles in my body when he is deep inside me. I've missed this. So much. I blink back the tears that in my eyes but I'm too late. Several roll down my face and Mateo stills. He watches me, waiting for my signal, his gaze patient and open. I can see the love pouring off him, the desire he has to make me happy.

"Are you okay?" He asks and I nod and he leans down, kissing me softly. "Good tears?"

"Yes," I whisper the word and it turns a moan when he moves deeper inside me.

We take it slow. This is not the time for hard and fast. We don't want to rush but the need for the physical connection has us both shaking. He pushes inside and I lift to meet each of his thrusts, the pressure creating a warm, sensual warmth rushing over my skin. I reach over and pull the vibrator to me, placing it on my hand like I saw him do it and I turn it on.

I run my hand over my collarbone, down between my breasts, across my belly, awakening the nerve endings under my skin. Mateo watches the entire time, his eyes tracking the path, a soft curse escaping his mouth when I detour back up to my nipples. The stimulation is direct, strong and Mateo stutters his strokes when my sex clenches around him.

"*Tesoro*," he says, his voice full of desire, want, and love. "I'm getting close. You feel too damn good."

"Come on Teo," I lift my head to capture his mouth in a carnal kiss that has his hips speeding up as he thrusts into me. He reaches down and grasps my legs, lifting them and opening me to him completely and he takes what he needs. I reach down between us and touch my clit with the finger pad and when he goes still above me with his release, a gentler orgasm from the one I had earlier races through my system.

Teo lowers himself to lie beside me, pulling me against his body as the little spoon to his larger one. I fit tight against him, the top of my head wedged underneath his chin, his arm lying possessively over my waist. We stare out of the windows, watching the lights of Nashville below us.

"*Tesoro*," Mateo says, his voice low and dark and tinged with the gravel of emotion. Soft kisses across my jaw, against my temple, my bare shoulder. "You *are* my treasure, you know."

I roll over to face him, the lights below nothing compared to his face. Nothing compared to his love.

"Teo, I have had fame and fortune. *Solo te necesito a ti.*" And it is true. All I need is him.

He smiles, leaning down to kiss my but veers off at the last, shaking his head. "Your accent is really terrible."

I grin back. "We've got lots of time for you to help me practice.

"Yes, we do."

EPILOGUE

CARLISLE

Four months later.

I never thought I would be here again.

I am standing on the block at the start of my first race at the Paralympics games. The stands are full of people and the press area is bursting with reporters anxious to get a shot of me as I compete again for the first time since the bombing. I am now, and I love it, an ambassador and spokesperson for disabled people and athletes around the world. It is fulfilling work and it takes the focus off the tragedy of that day and gives back a little hope because I, and all the other survivors, are proving that they could not destroy us.

And even though Aaron is gone, he lives on in his foundation and the good it is doing. There are several athletes here who trained and traveled with a grant from our fundraising efforts and I couldn't be more proud. I turned the day-to-day running of it to his parents and we are growing closer everyday. We spend more time laughing at memories of him than crying. It's a good thing.

I stare at the water below me. Blue, sparkling and probably too cool and I cannot wait to get in it. I am in the pool everyday as I push myself to do better, to be better. Today is the result of all my hard work and whether I take home another medal or if I just finish this heat, it will be worth it.

I look up in the stands and I find my parents and the Butlers waving to me. My mom has her knitting needles in her hand and an unfinished blanket on her lap as usual. Livvy and Sarah are here too and my best friend gives me the thumbs up when I catch her eye.

And there is Teo. My rock. My best friend. My love. I think we're getting it right this time. I lean on him more and he doesn't try to protect me from everything. We work. It isn't flawless but it is real.

He doesn't know it but I'm going to ask him to move in with me after the games are over. From the way he's smiling at me right now, I think he'll say yes.

Another step for us. Another new beginning.

The buzzer goes off signaling one minute until the race starts so I tear my gaze away from him and focus. I get into position, take a few deep breaths and close my eyes. Everything goes away except my heartbeat and the call of the water.

I take another deep breath.

The buzzer goes off.

I open my eyes and jump.

If you loved **SALVATION**, continue with the rest of the Nashville Nights series...

TEMPTATION

She needs to be good.

At sixteen, Kit ditched her crappy life and moved to Nashville with only $200, her guitar, and a notebook full of songs. She hit it big, but five years of living like a rock star plus a stint in rehab has killed any good will she had with her label. The suits have ordered Kit to shape up or ship out of the limelight. The last thing she needs is a hot, sexy distraction with a sinful smile.

He doesn't know the meaning of the word.

Max Butler is as far from a celebrity as you can get and he likes it that way. A Nashville firefighter, he's living the single life with a revolving door of parties, friends, and a different woman in his bed every night. When his normal life suddenly collides with the girl on his favorite Rolling Stone cover, he sees the perfect chance to fulfill his ultimate fantasy and see just how bad Kit can be.

Sometimes bad is so very good.

With three weeks until Kit leaves for her big tour, Max promises to give her a break from being the good girl--no strings attached. But when hot days lead to sultry nights, the lines get blurred and suddenly three weeks of bad might not be good enough.

Buy it on the TEMPTATION page.

REDEMPTION

Holding on never felt so good.

Emory Cabell is leaving the lies behind her.

Finding out that you're the half-sister to America's country music queen is game changer. Determined to meet the sibling she never knew and compelled to pursue the music career she's always wanted, Emory leaves her small town and heads to Nashville. Thrown by the bustle of Music City and the cutthroat dealing of the business, she finds unexpected shelter in a musical partnership with country music's notorious bad boy.

Zane has his eyes set on the prize.

Known as a man who never stays the night, Zane is reliable only when it comes to his music. Years of paying his dues has gained him the coveted lead guitarist spot on the hottest music tour of the year. Hoping this gig will lead to his own recording contract, he agrees to write a few songs with Emory but he's blown away by the sexual chemistry sizzling between them and leveled by his feelings for this quiet woman with the beautiful soul.

Can love be more than just a line in a song?

Darkness and light... they should not work. But one night in her bed proves they're hotter than the number one single they wrote together. Things get complicated when the spotlight sheds light on all of Zane's past sins and Emory struggles with trusting him with her heart. When the sought after recording contract stipulates they remain a duet, it threatens everything Zane has worked towards and challenges everything he thought he knew about himself. With his life at a crossroads, will he choose the music or the future with a woman whose love might just be his redemption?

Buy it on the REDEMPTION page.

ACKNOWLEDGMENTS

Huge, huge thanks to everyone who helped me get this book in your hands.

My best friends, Avery Flynn and Kimberly Kincaid, for keeping me on track and kicking my ass when necessary.

My editor, Nicole, for putting up with my crazy.

For Meredith and Anessa formatting — you always make it look so pretty!

For the Sizzlemongers... I couldn't ask for a better group of friends. Not just a street team, we have become a group who support each other and I love that so hard.

Nancy Weeks — thank you for opening up your story and your heart to me. I cherish your friendship. XXX

The Main Man, Little Man and Lulu. My reasons to keep going, you are the fulfillment of a dream I didn't even know I had. I am a very lucky woman.

A NOTE FROM ROBIN

Dear Reader —

Thanks so much for reading my book. If you enjoyed this novella you can find out latest info on my next release and enter for the monthly giveaway by signing up for my newsletter. You can also drop me a line at robin@robincovingtonromance.com. I'd love to hear from you.

And if you are so inclined, please leave a review on Amazon, Barnes & Noble, iBooks, or Goodreads.

I love to explore the theme of fooling around and falling in love in my books and I adore a hero who falls hard. When I'm not writing sexy, sizzling romance, I collect tasty man candy pics, indulge in a little comic book geek love, collect red nail polish, and obsess over Dean Winchester. Don't send chocolate . . . send eye-candy!

There are so many great books out there and I'm grateful that you spent your money and time to read my book.

Xx,

Robin

SOCIAL MEDIA LINKS:

Website
> Facebook Profile
> Facebook Page
> Twitter: @RobinCovington
> Pinterest
> Newsletter

If you enjoyed SALVATION, check out my other books:

REDEMPTION

BY

ROBIN COVINGTON

Holding On Never Felt So Good

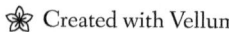

ONE

ZANE

I should have stayed at my place last night. I'm dangerously close to being late.

I slither out of bed, moving arms and legs gently out of my way, careful not to wake my bedmates. Angie mumbles in her sleep and rolls over, her movement jostling her husband and I freeze, hoping they will not wake up. I'm not worried about awkward moments and the walk of shame because I have nothing to be embarrassed about. I just don't have time to spend on any kind of goodbye.

Angela and Bobby Graves are a happily married couple who occasionally invite a third to their bed and lately that extra body has been me. As a rule, while I don't have many scruples about sleeping around, I draw the line at banging married women whose husbands are not part of the invitation. What arrangement they have between them is none of my business but I'm not interested in making some guy look like an asshole.

I'm also not interested in letting everyone in Nashville know where I sleep and how many people are in the bed at the time. The country music business puts up with my tattoos, my love of using the word "fuck" in as many ways as possible, and the sleeping around one woman at a time. A threesome would make their heads explode and I don't need any of the record label executive's brains spattering their office wall before they sign me to a solo record deal.

I worked my ass off for the last five years, hitting the pavement the second I got off the bus in Nashville to start college on a scholarship at Nashville University. I auditioned at record labels before I made sure I had the classes I needed and spent more time writing songs than doing my homework. My name as a guy who can write a Top Ten song is solid and I used it to build a name as a performer and to finally land the gig as Kit Landry's lead guitarist and opening act on her sold-out summer tour.

The tour I'm going to miss if I don't get my ass out of here and on the bus waiting for me in downtown Nashville.

I lean over to scoop my boxer briefs and jeans off the floor, balancing myself on one foot as I struggle to get dressed silently.

"Nice ass," Angie mumbles from where she lies nestled in the one thousand thread count sheets. She doesn't make a move to get up and I don't move towards her. This isn't about goodbye kisses or promises to call. We're friends but there are definite boundaries and we never cross them. I have no desire to.

"Well you can kiss it goodbye until September," I chuckle as I pull my jeans up and button the fly. She sticks her tongue out at me and I roll my eyes as tug my t-shirt over my head. "You guys are coming to one of the Nashville shows, right?"

"Bobby's company has a block of seats. We'll be there."

I nod and pull my shoulder-length hair back with an elastic I had in my pocket. Bobby's an executive at a big IT firm and like most successful Music City corporations they buy blocks of seats to wine and dine clients.

"I'll see you at the show," I back out of the room and give her a wave, not offering VIP passes or making any promises. With her job as a top pediatric surgeon at the largest area hospital and Bobby's high-profile career, they don't like to leave too many paper trails between us. That's fine with me.

I jog out to my car parked in the third garage slot of their gated-community mansion and back out once the door goes up. Nobody is up this early in the morning so I don't worry about raising too many eyebrows as I exceed the speed limit and make my way through the sleepy Nashville streets to the house I share with my best friend, Mateo Butler.

I used the terms "share" loosely now because he spends any time he's not in medical school or working at the free clinic with his girlfriend, Carlisle Queen. I see her exclusive building on the skyline as I drive by and offer a silent salute to the two of them. True love if I ever saw it. Just because I'm not looking for it doesn't mean I don't know it.

And it sure as fuck doesn't mean that I can't write a song about it. Thank God.

I pull into the cracked concrete driveway next to our rental house on the edge of the Nashville University campus, kill the engine and bolt into the house. I check the time. I've got enough time to take a shower and grab the duffle I packed last night.

With wet hair, a travel mug of coffee and a KIND bar in hand, I throw my bag into the trunk of the cab and pile into the back with my guitar and direct the cabbie to head to the parking lot near the rehearsal spaces of Kit's record label. When I pull into the lot, the buses are lined up and people are wandering around the lot like zombies looking for brains.

My blood pressure spikes as my feet hit the pavement and the familiar jolt of excitement builds up in my chest until I fully expect it to shoot out my fingertips. I love writing and performing, going on the road for several months and the prospect of playing in huge, sold-out arenas is giving me a boner that's making jeans tight. And on this tour in addition to the lead guitarist spot I get to be an opening act in many of the cities.

I can almost feel the pen in my hand as I sign the recording contract.

"Mac, are you ready my man?" I roll up beside the drummer, Mac Giles, and we fist bump both grinning ear-to-ear. Mac is a road junkie like me, loves the crowds and playing to a full house. We'll be riding together on the band bus along with the bassist, Aaron Rice, and the keyboardist, Mike Leonard. With these four guys I predict lots of X-box tournaments and jam sessions and I can't fucking wait.

"Zane, this shit is going to be awesome." He nudges me with one of his beefy arms and grins. "Sold out tour mother fucker."

I grin back. "Sold out tour mother fucker."

"Did you even roll out of your own bed this morning?" He eyeballs me as we make our way over to our bus. "What did you do? Give her a nine-inch wake-up call and make it home in time just to shower and grab coffee?"

"Something like that," I answer, refusing to kiss and tell my playmate's secrets. "I packed last night so it was all good."

"If you get as much tail as you did last summer, your dick is going to fall off," he warns, his smile evil as he continues. "And I'll be there to soothe all the sad "pick collectors."

"That was just that group of rabid fan club girls in Utah and I know better than to leave my stash lying around where they can get their hands on it." I lost an entire case of custom-made copper guitar picks when my hookup in Salt Lake City stole them and then sold them on E-bay. I will never make that mistake again. "Those picks aren't fucking cheap."

"Those Utah girls were freaky," Mac smiles as he shakes his head. We played three nights there and it was everything you hear about concert tours.

"Well, apparently what they say about the quiet ones is true," I say and stop when I bump into his large frame. "What the fuck, Mac?"

I turn my head to see what is causing his slack-jawed staring and when I do I understand completely. Emory Cabell. Backup singer. Exquisite guitarist. Honey blonde with legs that go on for miles and breasts that would fit perfectly in my palms.

And Kit Landry's new-found baby sister.

We both ogle as she bends over and tries to lift a heavy suitcase. Emory is wearing cutoff jean shorts, a little red t-shirt and flip-flops. Her legs are endless and the cutoffs are just short enough to give a hint of the sweet little curve of her ass.

"Oh my God," Mac says, his voice strained with the same tension I feel in my body.

"Fuckin-A." I shift slightly to redistribute the half-hard boner in my jeans and barely bite back the laugh that is bubbling in my chest. God was not kind when he put Emory Cabell on my path. She's a walking wet dream pulled right out my fantasy archive and she's so off-limits that she might as well live on Alcatraz but my dick is ignoring the memo.

We watch for a few moments longer as she struggles with the multiple pieces of luggage she's trying to get on the bus she will share with Kit and the other back-up singer, Sandra. I shove my own duffle at Mac, ignoring his grunt of pain as it plows into his abdomen.

"I should go help her," I say.

"No, you shouldn't."

"She needs my help. It's the right thing to do."

"Just remember that helping her does not require anyone to remove their clothes."

"And *that* is a fucking shame," I answer. I walk towards her, approaching from the side. The way she's heaving around the smaller bag it's become a dangerous weapon, so I reach out and grab it when I get within range. She pops her head up, eyes wide with surprise. We stare at each other for a few seconds longer than necessary and the all-to-familiar heat that simmers between us makes the emerald in her gaze catch fire. Yeah, there's something between me and this girl. "Let me help you with that before you put someone's eye out."

Emory hesitates for a second and then nods in relief and shoves the bag into my hand.

"I think I over packed," she grunts as she grasps the handle on her rolling case and positions it to move towards the door. I lean over and pick up a backpack and her guitar case but her hand on my arm stops me. She bypasses the backpack but takes the instrument from me. "I'll take this."

"I get it. I don't like anyone messing with my guitar either."

She smiles at me and I'm struck again with just how sweet she is. A nice girl. Not innocent; she's held her own with everyone during the rehearsal time, matching dirty joke for dirty joke and cussing like a sailor when it was required. No, she's fresh and open and completely unvarnished by this business. We all start out the same way and I regret that one day she'll be a cold bastard like me when it comes to non-musical side of this gig. Luckily, she has her sister to look out for her.

"I set my alarm super early and I still found myself scrambling to get here on time," she huffs out as she rolls the larger case towards the door.

I squeeze past her and grab the handle, hefting it up the steps into the bus and setting it just inside the opening. I place the backpack on the floor next to it before turning back to her. She's moved in behind me and now she's close enough for me to see the gold flecks in her eyes and smell whatever citrus scent she wears. She's even prettier up close and my mouth goes a little bit dry.

"I did the same thing," I confess. "This is my second time on this kind of tour and you'd think that I'd know better."

"If you started the morning out in your own bed you might not have been so strapped for time," Kit says, appearing in the doorway, smiling like the annoying sister who knows she just cock blocked you with her hot friend. I love her, I really do, but I want to throttle her right now.

Emory laugh and slaps her hand against her mouth. "Kit!"

"Now, that was just mean," I say, smiling and leaning up to kiss Kit on her cheek as Emory continues to laugh at us.

"But, you aren't denying it," Kit shoves me playfully and I stumble back, placing my hand over my heart in an action that mimics someone suffering from a shot to the gut.

"Kit, that was pretty harsh," Emory chastises her sister and leans over to pat me on the head with a smile. Her touch is supposed to be soothing but it is exactly the opposite. I would love to have her hands on me without so many other people around.

"Zane Wyatt you're a horny dog of the first order and you know it." Kit looks at her sister after winking at me. "Don't be fooled just because he's my favorite stray."

"Hey, I'm housebroken and I only bite on special occasions," I protest lightly.

I'm not offended by her words. Kit is engaged to one of my closest friends who is also the cousin of my best friend, so we've spent a lot of time together the last couple of years. If it wasn't for her and the Butlers, I wouldn't have any family where I can be myself. It's the main reason why I haven't really tried anything with Emory. That shit could get complicated really fast.

"It's a good thing I've got all my shots then," Emory interrupts my thoughts, her soft voice low and teasing with more than a hint of the suggestive. She gives me a lingering look before easing past Kit to enter the tour bus. I stare after her and it takes a few moments before I realize that Kit is still standing in the same place, her expression equal parts concerned and resigned.

"It won't do any good to remind you that she's my sister, would it?"

I swallow hard, deciding to go with honesty. "Probably not."

She nods. "I didn't think so."

I wait for the rest of the lecture to follow and I when I realize that it isn't coming I have to ask. "What? You aren't going to forbid me to hang out with your sister. Threaten to have Max break my legs if I touch her?"

"If I thought it would do any good, I would." She sighs and descends the steps to speak directly to me, her hand resting lightly on my arm. "I would have to be blind and stupid to miss the sparks between the two of you. I have no right to tell you guys what to do but I'm asking you to treat her right. Don't lead her on. Be straight with her."

"I am always honest with the women I'm with."

"I know and that's why I'm not putting a hit out on you right now. She's not some dumb kid from the sticks, she's smart and cautious and way more mature than I was when I came here but she's looking for something and that makes her vulnerable."

Alarm bells go off in my head. Depending on what she's looking for, I have no idea if I can deliver.

"What is she looking for, Kit?"

"I'm not even sure she knows what it is yet." Kit squeezes my arm before backing off and getting on the bus. "Just be careful Zane. You're both my family."

And right then I decide that if I'm smart, I'll never lay a finger on Emory Cabell.

TWO

EMORY

"I love Zane like a brother."

I stop unpacking my things and placing them in the storage compartment under my bed on the bus to look at my new half-sister. Kit is leaning against the outer wall of the bunk, her fingers twisting around each other. That outward demonstration of agitation matches the concern in her eyes and I sigh as I drop my clothes and straighten. I end up looking down on her since I'm a good five inches taller than her petite size but it doesn't faze her. She's in a full-on big sister mode and that makes her ten feet tall.

"Why do I know there's an unspoken 'but' at the end of that sentence?" I say.

"Because there is," she says, reaching out to lay a hand on my arm. "He's hands down one of the best songwriters in this town and I'd pit his guitar skills up against John Mayer or Keith Urban any day. He's funny and helpful and he is a dear friend but he sleeps with everything that moves."

"That's not news, Kit. It was one of the first pieces of information everyone offered up when rehearsals started.

The people in your band are bigger gossips than a bunch of high school girls."

"Tell me something I don't know." Kit slides onto the bunk and pats the mattress to invite me to sit next to her.

I hesitate, still not sure about where we are going with this relationship. Kit has been amazing ever since I contacted her manager, Paul Brandt, with the news that we shared a daddy six months ago. The realization that *her daddy* had a second, secret family and was *my daddy* when he was supposedly on "long trucking runs" served as the initial glue that bound us together. Whether we actually become a family of our own for the long-term is still up for anybody's guess but so far it's gone way better than it probably should. I grew up an only child and the prospect of having a sister is more appealing than I'd like to admit.

This tour is a way to help us grow closer and to allow me to see if the music business is what I really want. Up until six months ago I'd lived my entire life in Dutton, Tennessee, a small, podunk place outside of Memphis. My only visits to Nashville were with school trips and for special occasions. My dreams of making a life out of my music were secrets I only told myself until the realization that nothing in my past was true compelled me to find my own future.

Now I'm living in Kit's old loft in downtown and singing back-up on her sold out tour. The last time this much had changed so fast for a girl, Alice drank the wrong the bottle and ended up down a rabbit hole. There are days when I think the Mad Hatter is just around the corner.

"So, are you pulling the "big sister" card and telling me to stay away from him?" I ask as I slide into the bunk beside her. Our backs are against the wall and our feet are dangling off the edge. I wonder if this what we would have done if we'd grown up together.

"Oh, hell no," she laughs and looks at me. "I know better than to challenge your stubborn streak. You get that from daddy and I will not awaken that sleeping beast. I'm a firm believer that you need to make your own decisions, good or bad."

I wait. I know there's a "but". It's practically hanging over her head like a neon sign.

"I don't want to see you get hurt, Em. I know firsthand how a body blow like this can cloud your judgment and you already had one this year."

She isn't exaggerating. You can Google "Kit Landry" and get a front row seat for all the mistakes she made the year after a devastating break-up.

"It all ended up great for you in the end," I point out. "Your career is stellar and you have that big ass rock on your finger and a hot guy who adores you."

She smiles the goofy grin that always shows up when you bring up her man, Max Butler. At the end of this tour they're getting married and I swear that if you look up "happily ever after" in the dictionary, it points to them. I know that kind of love is real. I believe it's possible but I can't shake the thought that you never really know anybody and to put all your happiness in one person might not be a smart idea. The best acting isn't only done in Hollywood.

My daddy fooled us right up to the day he died and now I don't know whether to trust anybody, including myself.

Kit appears to read my thoughts and reaches down to squeeze my hand. "It will all work out for you too, Em. You wouldn't have found me and come to Nashville if you didn't have the guts to get the life you want."

I lean my head back on the wall of the bus and close my eyes. "What life do I want?"

"That's not a question I can answer for you little sister."

"I know what I *don't* want."

"That's a start. Give me the list."

"Lies. Insecurity. Doubt. My old boring life." I hear Kit suck in a quick breath and I realize that I might have over-shared. Dr. Phil would be all over me right now. I decide to lighten it up. "A minivan. I don't want a minivan. Or white heels. Nobody should wear white heels."

"Wow. That's a wide range of stuff. Your issues are like a Super-Walmart."

"Daddy and trust issues. Clean up on Aisle Three," I joke.

The silence that settles between us is comfortable. Kit doesn't feel like she needs to fill the silence or fix my life. She's cool just being here. I like thata lot. I didn't have lots of girlfriends growing up. Mom was too weird and I always felt like I had one foot out of the metaphorical door of that tiny little town. I didn't want to make attachments I'd have to give up.

"I know that I want the music. Thanks for the opportunity," I say.

"You didn't get here because you're my sister," she starts and then corrects herself with a laugh. "Okay, you got your ass in the door with zero experience because you're my sister but you wouldn't have gotten a back-up spot if you didn't have a voice that makes me want to kill you."

I nudge her with an elbow. "Whatever."

"You're also an amazing guitarist."

I motion in the air with my finger, giving her the "keep it coming" gesture. "Talk about my looks and my day will be complete."

She rolls her eyes. "You're gorgeous and you know it. I would kill for your legs."

"You have great legs." She really does. She's petite with dark curls with red streaks in it. There's a reason her cover of *Rolling Stone* is one of the most popular.

"I'm stumpy compared to you." She eyeballs me and shakes her head. "We look nothing alike. Did daddy contribute anything to our DNA at all?"

"The music. He gave us the music."

We stare at each other for several long seconds. The silent "thank God" remains unsaid but hovers between us.

"He did give us that." She leans over and kisses me on the cheek before moving to scoot out of the bunk. "Speaking of the music, I want you to work with Zane and see how you like songwriting. I think you two might have a good sound together."

"I thought I was supposed to avoid him?"

"Writing a song doesn't entail taking off any clothing."

"That's a shame." I mean it. I don't have a ton of experience with seeing men unclothed but I know enough to believe that seeing Zane Wyatt naked might just be the experience of a lifetime. He's hot and sexy and crazy talented. An irresistible combination. There's a reason that musicians get laid a lot.

"It's the hands. Women love the hands," I speculate.

"It's his hair. Women love his hair," she adds.

"His hair is pretty spectacular. Shoulder-length, dark and always messy like he just rolled out of bed."

"I think I should be worried that you've given it so much thought," she says her smile now dampened with a little bit of concern. "He's a great guy but he isn't the commitment type, so if you get involved with him just understand the law of the land."

I have no idea if I'm looking for a relationship or not. I'm in a new life and playing it all by ear. What comes my way will be considered and if I want to leap, I will. I've spent a lifetime living in a box constructed of other people's expectations and now I'm determined to stay out of that box. I'm open to anything and I really only have one, real hot button.

"Is he honest?"

Kit considers me for a long moment. She knows where I'm coming from. My showing up in her life just added another layer of suck to the memories of her already suck-tastic childhood. Neither of us relish the fact that our father lied to us our entire lives. So, there are a lot of things I can tolerate but lying isn't one of them.

"He is. He won't play games with you. Just remember, the only thing he really commits to is his career."

"Got it." I flop down on my bunk and watch her exit the bus.

Tired from a night of tossing and turning from excitement, I settle back against the covers, staring up at the ceiling and once again wondering just how the hell I ended up here. Six months ago I was living in Dutton and now I am here against the wishes of everyone in my life: mama, Eric, the entire town. Even the cashier at the Piggly Wiggly had an opinion about my decision to move to the big, bad city.

But I'm here.

Indulging in my passion for music. Traveling all over the country. Figuring out what the hell I want to do with my life.

Contemplating the delicious possibility of getting naked with a very sexy guitarist.

Life just got very, very interesting.

THREE

ZANE

"So, Kit wants us to try writing a song together."

I look up from where I sit on the floor of the stage, checking the strings on my guitar to find Emory smiling down at me. She's holding her guitar in one hand and wearing this tiny little dress that slips off one of her pale shoulders. I can see the light sprinkling of freckles along her collarbone and I bite back the urge to connect the dots with my tongue. Fuck, but she makes me want.

"Yes, she does." I cock my head at her, trying to gauge her reaction to the suggestion. "I think it might be a very cool thing to try. How about you?"

"I'd love it," she says, the pretty blush on her cheeks giving away her excitement. It's one of the things I like most about Emory; her enthusiasm for new things. She's brave and takes chances even when you can tell it scares her shitless.

"Are you doing anything right now?" I ask, standing up to be able to look at her in the eyes instead of putting a permanent kink in my neck. "We could find a spot, talk, get to know each other a little bit better."

"Do we need to know each other better to write a song?"

"No, but it doesn't hurt." I look around the stage tossing around the possible areas where we could work without interruptions. I shiver a little under the onslaught of air conditioning they are pouring into this place in preparation for the thousands of bodies that will be cram in here tonight and I know where I want to go. "You want to go outside? There's an area to the side of the stadium with picnic tables and shade trees. We can enjoy the sun."

"I like that idea."

We cut through the backstage area, making sure to avoid the guys working out the last minute electrical and sound kinks. We exit the building through the artist entrance and I lead her over to the little picnic area tucked along the back of the arena complex. It's empty and quiet. Perfect.

"Okay. Good choice," she hums in approval as she climbs on top of one of the tables and kicks off her flip flops. She places her guitar beside her on the flat surface and leans back, her face lifted to the sun. I stare. It's not a casual glance. I take my time and ogle the slender length of her neck and indulge in the fantasy of tasting her there. She looks up suddenly and busts me. Cold.

"I was staring," I confess, letting her see that I'm really not sorry.

"I noticed," she says, cocking her head to the side with her eyebrows raised in a question. The hint of a smile on her lips tells me that she's not offended by my behavior and isn't going to beat me over the head with the instrument siting within her arm's length. "Is your staring part of the 'getting to know you' thing we're supposed to be doing?"

"Yep. It is." I hop up on the table next to her, my guitar placed on the bench at my feet. "Writing music together is not just about notes and lyrics. It's about the dynamic between two people, the way you interact."

"And our dynamic involves you checking me out?"

"And *you* checking me out," I say and smile when she huffs out a sound of protest. "Come on, we're attracted to each other. We might as well just put it out there."

She laughs and nods, looking down at her feet as they swing off the edge of the table. I wait to see what her next move will be, anxious for a clue about where her head is. Emory looks up at me, her green eyes bright with curiosity that I want to pursue so badly my teeth ache.

"And what do we do with this attraction? Give into it?"

"We can." I reach out to brush her hair back off her face where the light breeze blocks my view of her expression. I need to see all of it. "Or we can do nothing. Either way, it will be powerful to channel it into a song."

"Do you sleep with everyone you write a song with?" Emory pauses for a moment and clarifies her question. "The women, I mean."

"First, there's no hard and fast rule. I sleep with people I'm attracted to when it feels right, no matter the gender." I pause to let that sink in and when I all get from her is an eyebrow raise and a smile, I continue with the rest of my theory. "Sometimes the attraction is just the music. All the emotion and heat all feeds into the song and then there's nothing left."

"And where do we fall into the spectrum?"

"Not sure yet but I know we've got enough going on that the music will probably be amazing."

She smiles and looks down, running her fingers over the strings of her guitar. "I like the honesty, Zane. Where I'm from there's a lot of talking around things."

"And you don't like that?"

"I hate it," she says and lifts her eyes to mine, her expression interested and open. "So, what is your grand plan, Zane? Lead guitarist and songwriter or world music domination?"

"Who told you?" I laugh and ease back to lean on my elbows across the table. "I want my own record deal and I'm so close to getting it I can almost smell the ink on the contract. My agent is talking to a couple of labels but they're waiting to see how my opening slot for this tour goes."

"Well, you've been amazing, getting great reviews. You'll get it."

"It all depends on the type of offer. I want a 360 deal with primary creative control. I've got the music; I just need their marketing money and reach to make me a global brand. These days there isn't much that a record label can do for you that you can't do for yourself if you work hard enough and use social media."

"Have you had an offer on the table before? Is that something a new artist could expect to get?" She pushes a blonde curl behind her ear and smiles in apology. "Sorry. I'm a total newbie and all of this fascinates me."

"No worries. Ask away. I had a deal last year from this smaller Indie label called Waterworld Media but they wanted more creative control than I wanted to give up. The owner, Maureen Richards, also wanted personal control over *me* but I didn't want to be the owner's toy of the moment even for a record deal."

"Is that how it usually works or is that just a thing I've seen on TV? Kit never told me about having to sleep with people to make it."

"Kit didn't and she was lucky to have Paul Brandt looking after her and protecting her when she was so young. Just remember that sex is a commodity that the majority of the people have no problem using." I pull a guitar pick out of my pocket and twist it between my fingers. "I'm also not talking about two people who both happen to be in this business who also want to hook-up. There's a difference between indulging in sex for pleasure and whoring around. Sex always complicate things but you don't want it to mess up your career."

"I hear ya. It's why I'm still a virgin."

I stare at her, not quite sure I heard what I heard.

"You're a what?"

She turns her head to look at me, squinting at the sun in her eyes. "A virgin. Untouched. Still holding my V-card."

"Umm. Now I feel like dirty old man." I take a good look at her and ask the question I'm not sure I want to know the answer to. It just never occurred to me to ask. "Wait. How old are you. Emory?"

THREE

EMORY

"Nineteen," I say and burst out laughing as he falls back on the table and with his fingers speared through his hair.

"I'm a dirty old man," He groans like he's in pain and I can't help but laugh louder.

"What are you? Twenty-three?" I roll over and prop myself up on my elbow to look at him lying next to me. "It's not that big of a difference."

He groans again, the sound muffled against his hands as he covers his face. When he finally looks at me, his expression is equal parts amused, intrigued, and horrified. It's really cute.

"Emory. You're fucking hot. How did you get out of Dutton Tennessee a virgin? Didn't you have a boyfriend?"

"I did have a boyfriend. A perfectly nice boyfriend named Eric who was the wide receiver on the football team," I say.

"And he never took you out to the river or the hill or a barn loft or wherever kids go in that town and talk you out of your clothes? Was it a religion thing?"

"We got naked plenty in the back seat of his car. There's

lots you can do to have a good time that isn't intercourse, you know."

"I'm aware," he smirks.

"I'm sure you are, smartass. I am *very certain* that there is no sexual activity you haven't tried."

"I draw the line at animals and anything that requires me to get tied up," he says and I can't help but snort with laughter.

"Thanks for over-sharing."

"Hey! We're discussing the fact that you're still a virgin at nineteen and that you used to give your boyfriend blow jobs after the game on Friday night but *my* aversion to rope is a problem?"

I stare at him and suddenly realize that this entire conversation is crazy. Zane apparently has the same realization and we bust out laughing like a couple of crazy people. I reach out and snag his hand, giving it a squeeze and taking his guitar pick with me when I retreat. I flip the small metal triangle over my fingers as I try to remember what we were talking about before it became all about my current status as the "Big V".

"To answer your question, it wasn't a religious thing and I'm not saving myself for marriage. I liked Eric and he was hot but I always felt like if I had sex with him then I'd never leave. And I *really needed* to get out of Dutton. I never fit in there." I sigh, feeling the heavy weight of being back in that town settling on my shoulders. I shake it off and let the glorious sun of this afternoon warm my skin instead. "And I was bored and that is *so much worse* than being unhappy."

"Amen" He nods in agreement, his grin making me smile even wider. I like talking to him. A lot. He's refreshinglyblunt.

"So, are you from Nashville?" I ask.

"Nope. Ivy, North Carolina," he says with a grin. "I left the day after high school graduation with a music scholarship to Nashville University and eight hundred dollars in my checking account. I completely get your exodus from Dutton."

"Did your parents freak out too?"

"Oh fuck. It was more like an explosion. I had a huge fight with my dad about my chasing a "dumbass dream" and not staying back in town to work the farm or take a shift at the Goodyear plant. It's the last time we really talked, actually. I don't go home much and they've never been to one of my shows."

He looks down and shrugs and I know that movement. It tries to cover up just how shitty the situation really is and how much it hurts. I am really good at that shrug and I know that it never really helps.

"My mama still cries every time I call home. It breaks my heart but I couldn't stay and I can't go back. Nothing about that place was right after I found out about my daddy." I reach over and touch my guitar, running my fingers lightly over the strings and try to focus on what he was to me before the lie was discovered. As much as he makes me mad, I need to remember my father as a good man. A man who was desperate to find some happiness.

I sit up, picking it up and lightly strumming with Zane's pick.

"How's that going? You and Kit doing okay with all of it?"

I nod, continuing my light strumming. "She's great. The best thing we did was not let what daddy did mess up what we can have together. It wasn't our fault."

"That sounds very healthy."

"Ha! Our joint therapist would disagree." I start playing

the chorus of one of my favorite Bob Marley songs and grin when Zane sits up, grabs his instrument and joins in. "We've still got lots of anger and shit but we're trying not to take it out on each other. Some days are easier than others. The close quarters on the tour bus make it interesting."

"How do you feel about your dad?"

"He was very unhappy. Tied to a wife who was mentally ill and a drug addict with a little girl to raise all by himself. He made hurtful, shitty choices but he was just trying to be happy. I have to believe that he didn't mean to hurt anyone."

"It still hurts though, right?"

"All the time."

We play for a few more minutes and then, as if on cue we both roll into a second chorus of "Three Little Birds" by Bob Marley and start to sing. Zane adds this really sweet finger picking thing to the end and we end laughing and singing with really awful Jamaican accents as the song concludes on a messy clash of chords. It isn't pretty but it's fun.

"Bob Marley? You like that song?" He asks, moving right into another tune that I don't know. I listen to the melody, closing my eyes to feel the rhythm. It pulses, a driving undercurrent keeps it edgy and off the pop song spectrum. Not traditional country either but the roots are there. I like it.

"'Three Little Birds' song is a favorite of mine. My daddy gave me this guitar when I was ten years old and he taught me how to play when he was home. That song was the first one I taught myself on my own. There was a book at the library that boasted you could teach yourself to play in ten days or something and I wore it out before I finally had to turn it back in. I surprised him the next time he was home."

"That's a great memory," Zane says. "You need to hold on to that one."

I smile as he firms up the new tune and really starts to play. It is even bolder now and I could see myself singing it at the top of lungs in my car.

"I like that," I say, tapping out the beat on the body of my guitar. "It would make a great chorus. Catchy. All you need is the hook of great lyric."

"So help me write one," he says with a smile and wink. "You know you want to."

The gesture is playful but it also has the heat that always seem to simmer between us. I consider him for a moment knowing that spending more time with Zane Wyatt will likely lead to naked time eventuallyeven it turns out to just be the music.

But he's right. I really want follow this thing wherever it goes. It's why I left Dutton.

I listen to him play for a few moments longer and then when he looks at me with his unanswered question in his eyes, I have the answer for him.

"How about this?" I sing as he plays lightly, adjusting his pacing to my words.

"When I met you, twenty-two /I knew it would be life or death/Love or lies/You and me for now or never."

Zane stops, stares at me and I hold my breath. Do I suck? Will he laugh?

"Well? What do you think?" I ask, unable to wait another second.

"Little Bird, I think it sounds like the start of a great fucking great song."

FOUR

ZANE

"Zane, I'm not old enough to get in this club."

I look at Emory standing in between me and Mac on the sidewalk staring at the huge bouncer standing at the entrance of the Javelin Club in St, Louis. We just finished the first of our two shows here and we're wired from the adrenaline of a night full of great music and an amazing audience. Emory and I have been working on new songs every spare minute but we need a night off.

And I wanted to do something with Emory away from the bus and the tour. A night so I can see whether this connection growing between us is a product of the tour fishbowl or something purely us.

"I'll get you in," I say with confidence when she gives me a skeptical look. "I know the owner and I called ahead. You can't come to St. Louis and miss music at the Javelin."

I grab her hand and tug her behind me as I head to the door. A quick word with the slab of meat impersonating a man at the door and we are inside. Emory gives me a look of surprise and I stop abruptly, my hand over my heart in mock hurt.

"You doubted me?"

She pokes at my chest and rolls her eyes. "You're a big talker. Sooner or later you're not going to be able to deliver."

I lean in close, bringing our faces nose-to-nose. I can see the flecks of gold in her emerald green eyes and the mischief buried in their depths. I want to close the distance even more and kiss her but I've promised myself that I'm not going to indulge in that particular vice. I'm pretty sure she's as addictive as heroin.

"Little Bird, you wound me with your disbelief."

"I can get you a band-aid," she says, her lips forming a sexy pout. She slides a look at the big guy standing next to us. "Mac will kiss it and make it better."

"You two lovebirds need to keep my lips and any of my shit out of this." Mac grumbles, his teeth flashing white in the dim light when he grins. "But you two should just go ahead and get it over with. I can practically feel the vibration between you."

I wave him off. "That's just the music, Mac."

"You keep telling yourself that asshole." He turns to Emory and taps her under the chin with his finger. "You can do better sweetheart. Just be strong."

She laughs in his face, reaching up on tiptoes to press a kiss to his cheek. "I should fall for you, Mac."

"But you won't. You'll fall for the tattoos and the long hair and he'll convince you that it really is nine inches." He gives her a pitiful look and a mournful shake of his head. His version of the sad puppy vibe that most girls fall for. "It's the story of my life."

Emory looks skeptical, biting her bottom lip looking like she really is considering her options. My chest tightens, just a little, at the thought that she might pick someone else.

Connection. We've got it.

"Come on Little Bird, I don't want you to miss Kirby Grace." I remove her hand from Mac's and lead her down the hallway towards the burble of the crowd.

"Why do you call her that?" Mac asks, as he helps us elbow through the growing mass of people.

I slide my glance over to Emory and smile. She grins back and it's like we share a secret. "She's a Bob Marley fan."

"Well, then you'll love Kirby, Emory," Mac says.

We both use our bodies to protect Emory from the drunks and the gropers that flock to the Javelin on the weekends. It's always busier when Kirby plays. Mac is a big guy so he gets us to the concert area and I scan the crowd for my buddy. I see him in the distance and nod at him. He points his fingers at a spot in the front and I give him a thumbs up.

I motion to the front to Mac and we push through the growing crowd until we reach the prime spot on the rail, right in front of the band. It's going to be standing room only and we have the best "seats" in the house.

"What's so great about this guy?" Emory asks, her voice raised to be heard over the crowd. Her eyes are roving over all the instruments placed on the stage, the traditional ones and the others Kirby has collected during his travels over the years. "I've never heard of him."

"Kirby is a half-Jamaican/half-Korean musician who has created this fusion of sound that is like a mix of George Clinton, the Red Hot Chili Peppers, and the Foo Fighters. I have never heard anyone play anything or arrange anything like he does. He will blow you away."

She looks excited and the spark of interest in her eyes tells me that this was a good idea. I've discovered that we have a lot in common with our backgrounds and personalities but our love of music is something I've never really found with anyone else.

She soaks it in, every type of sound, technique, style. Her iPod is the most schizophrenic blend of genre, era and type of music I've ever seen. There is nothing she won't try just to see if it will work. There is no sound she ignores because of "the rules". There is nothing she won't try to learn. Emory is fearless and it is such a fucking turn-on.

I love the music but I think I forgot how much since I got so wrapped up in the business stuff and my drive to get a contract. Emory has awakened the sleeping beast inside me again and that is dangerous because I can't separate one from another. And that ability to keep sex and music and life and career in their own swim lane is what has kept me on track, kept me sane.

And now I feel like I am certifiable.

The arrival of Kirby and his huge band on the stage interrupts our discussion. The crowd goes nuts and I know I'm going to be deaf because I've spent the entire night surrounded by ten decibel sound. Mac and will be yelling at each other on the bus for the next twenty-four hours. Occupational hazard.

Kirby wastes no time jumping right into the set and usually I end up watching his performance and soaking in all of his techniques but tonight, I can't stop looking at Em. Her eyes are riveted to the stage, her entire body pulsing to the driving beat of the drums. She's not only hearing it with her ears but I can see her absorbing the sound through her pores. Her eyes flutter closed and I have to swallow hard against the surge of longing that settles in my groin.

I ease up behind her and grip her hips with my hands, encouraging her to move with the music. She doesn't look at me but leans into my touch and soon we are one body moving together. The pace is frantic, Kirby isn't known for playing ballads, and soon we are part of the mass of bodies writhing together on the dance floor as the set rolls from one song to another.

Her skin is slick with sweat where my hands glide along her body, her hair a cloud of gold curls that tease me with every brush and sweep. Time screams by at the speed of an amazing set and when the band takes a break we are breathless and laughing and amped up on adrenaline more powerful than a Redbull high with a Mountain Dew chaser.

I look around for Mac but he's long gone, chasing some cute little brunette, no doubt.

Kirby catches my eye as he's heading off stage and motions towards the back. I nod and spin Emory around, putting my hands on her hips as I guide her through the crowd.

"You want to meet him? I ask.

She twists around to look up, her eyes huge. "You know him?"

"Little Bird, I know everybody worth knowing."

She rolls her eyes and makes the "let's go" motion with her hand and I steer her through the crowd. We get to the security guy at the entrance to backstage and he mumbles into his Bluetooth headset before stepping aside and letting us through. The sound level is about a million times lower and we both give a sigh of relief.

Kirby and his entire band is in the large dressing room used by the group and he comes over and pulls me into a huge hug. A big man, his multi-colored dread locks and pierced nose and lip give him an edgy look but his smile is warm and open.

"Zane Wyatt." He pulls back to look at me with an eyebrow raised. "You up to no good?"

I laugh. "Same shit, different day." I turn and introduce him. "Kirby, this is Emory Cabell."

She sticks her hand out but he waves it off and pulls her into a hug. "Nice to meet you Emory." He pauses when he releases her and gets a good look. "You look familiar. Aren't you Kit's long-lost little sister?"

She nods, her excitement from being recognized in the flash of her eyes. "I am. Do you know her?"

"I have met her twice. Very talented young woman." He smiles and grabs her hand, testing the fingertips for the tell-tale callouses. "You are a musician too?"

"She plays guitar like a dream but her voice" I say and bite my bottom lip in mock ecstasy. "her voice is like a sultry wet dream, K."

"Well hell, then I want to hear you."

"I hope you will someday," Emory says, the pink of her blush making her pink cheeks brighter than they were from the dancing. "How do you know Zane?"

I groan, knowing he's going to spill the beans. He loves to tell the story. She picks up on my distress and reaches out to grab Kirby's hand and squeeze.

"He looks like he's about to throw up. Now you've got to tell me."

He doesn't even hesitate. Bastard. "We were both playing a music festival in" He looks at me with a question. "Chicago?"

"Seattle," I correct him and settle back to wait for the bus he's driving to run over me.

"Right, Seattle. They had all of the acts staying at the same motel and at about three in the morning I hear someone knocking hard on my door. I get up to see what's going on and I get a full view of Zane Wyatt standing in the hallway with not a stitch of clothing on and his junk flying around like it was a free-range chicken."

"Are you kidding?" Emory chuckles, her hand coming up to cover her mouth when I glare at her for laughing at me.

"No, but that's not the best part of it." Kirby wheezes with the force of his own laughter and wipes at his eyes. "Apparently he'd had an overnight guest with him and had picked up condoms from one of the vendors at the festival."

"Glow-in-the-dark condoms," I mutter under my breath.

"Oh yeah. Day-glo orange, glow-in-the-dark condoms from some crunchy, tarot-card reading chick who also sold love potions and alien shaped butt plugs." He leans over and mock whispers to her. "I would never have bought anything from that chick. She was crazy."

"And cheap," I add.

"And cheap." He agrees with a firm nod of his head and continues. "Because whatever cut-rate rubber she bought was not colorfast and Zane's frank and beans were stained day-glo orange." He gave me a wink. "And while his cock is mighty impressive it looked like an inverted roadwork cone."

"Thank you," I say because you should always thank someone who complements your junk.

"You're welcome but that color was hideous. You looked like a exhibitionist Ooompa Loompa trying to escape from a porno," he says and then breaks down into fits of laughter that have him bowled over and trying to catch his breath.

Emory gives me a look of disbelief and then joins him as they snort, giggle, and crack-up for several minutes while I wait patiently for them to get control of themselves. When they wind down I flip Kirby the bird.

"Fuck you, man. Why do you always have to tell that stry?"

"I'm glad he spilled it," Emory says and gives him a high five.

"Of course you are."

"Oh baby," she croons and loops her arm around my neck and kisses my cheek. I tighten my hold on her and let my hands enjoy a little bit of exploration along her warm back. "Are your feelings hurt?"

"A little." I pout and try to gain some sympathy points and keep her pressed against me a little while longer. I am not above taking advantage to cop a feel. My cock is half-hard between us and when I shift out position to get a better grip on her, it presses into her belly. Her eyes flare for just a second and she grinds back. Just a little. If I wasn't so focused on her, I would have missed it.

"I'll make it up to you," Kirby says, his gaze telling me that he didn't miss anything that just happened. "You guys need to join me in a song during the next set."

"Really?" Emory gasps, her eyes wide. "I would love that."

Kirby laughs and points to a binder lying on the coffee table. "There's the set list. You go pick out which one you want to do with us."

She lets go of me and I suppress my disappointment. Kirby watches her for a moment as she flips the pages and then returns his gaze to me.

"So, what's with the kid? You never bring women to my show with you."

"She's nineteen, K," I say and note the defensiveness in my tone.

"I'm not going to arrest you, I'm only asking."

"We're writing songs together." Answering a question he never even asked.

"Is that what you're calling it these days?" He glances back over her where she is happily discussing songs with his drummer, Gonzo. "Does she know that you trade-in writing partners like some people switch their shoes? Because, I gotta tell that she's into you."

He isn't telling me anything I don't already know. But he doesn't know what I'm about to say.

"It's mutual."

He swings back to look at me, his dark brown eyes wide. "I know you want to fuck her but that sounded like something more than that."

"It is." I pause and gather my thoughts. "I don't know. It's never been like this for me. She fascinates me. Everything about her makes me sit up and take a gazillion notes. It's intense between us."

"It could just be the music," he says, his tone neutral.

"It could." And that is all I want to say or get to say because his break is over and Emory is back with her song choice.

On stage the crowd is incredible. In a place this small, you can see their faces, feel the body heat even more than the lights above us, and you can feel the vibration of people getting off on the music all over the place.

Unlike on stage with Kit, Emory and I are side-by-side and as we perform our bodies touch and glide against each other.

She chose *Cherry Bomb* by The Runaways and I am blown away as her sexy, raw voice just tears it up and has the crowd going wild. The song is perfect for her. Suggestive lyrics about a wild-eyed teenage sex kitten living next door in boring-ass suburbia. She slithers to the edge of the stage and entices all the men in the room to enter the fantasy of them popping her cherry and pissing off all the women who have reason to doubt their men.

It's the kind of performance most people would kill to deliver and she nails it. I don't know what Emory's plans are in the music business but if she wants to be huge, she only has to keep doing what she's doing.

Kirby catches my eye across the stage and mouths "wow" when she hits the first chorus on her knees, crotch open in mock invitation.

There isn't a man in a five-mile radius who wouldn't pop a boner like the one I have in my jeans right now, hidden behind my guitar. My mouth goes dry and I have to clear my throat to offer any kind of limited harmony as she stands up and dives into the second verse. I can't take my eyes off her or my mind from picturing her backstage, against a wall with my cock buried deep.

Fuck.

As if she can read my mind, Emory turns the heat on me and makes eye contact as she vibrates and gyrates to the beat. She inches closer, increasing the tension and the heat between us with each step. She gets close to me and slides up and down, using my body like a stripper pole and the crowd echoes the roar in my head by going fucking nuts at the show.

I watch her and she keeps her eyes on me so I don't see it coming when her hand sneaks to my package and gives it a squeeze to emphasize the same scenario in the lyrics. I buck up into her hand, involuntarily, and growl with my own frustration and need. She's playing with fire and from the slow blink she levels at me and the curl of her lips around the last chorus, she's not worried about getting burned.

Holy hell.

The song ends in a raucous avalanche of sound but I can barely hear it over the pounding of my own blood in my ears.

She's right there. Smiling. Laughing. Eyes full of emerald fire. Hair damp and her exposed skin glistening with her sweat.

I kiss her.

There is no way I'm not going to kiss her right now.

I wrap my arm around her waist, push my guitar to the side and pull her tight against me. I spear the fingers on my free hand into her hair and tug on it, forcing her face up so that I can take her mouth. I dive in, tongue thrusting inside her wet heat and it's only a matter of seconds before she's right there with me and it's nothing but mouths and tongues and wet, dark fire.

It goes on and on. Or maybe for just a few seconds. All I know is that time fucking stops.

I break it off and lick my lips, dipping my head down close enough to say in her ear. "That was *not* the fucking music."

FIVE

EMORY

Performing on stage is amazing but I think I love jamming with the guys even more.

Kit says that people are either born performers, like Zane, or someone who learns how to do it. I am definitely in the second group and I know how lucky I am to get to tour with this amazing group of people and watch them do it right, show after show. I'm getting the hang of it but I feel like I really hit my groove when it's just a bunch of people sitting around and playing our favorite songs, both old and new.

Like right now. We have a show tonight but we're packing up and leaving on the buses as soon as it's over in order to hit the road and make the next city. So, no hotel rooms for us but lots of downtime at the stadium in between the PR stuff, sound check, and show time. So Kit surprised us all with a cookout in the parking lot. Ribs, BBQ chicken and enough baked beans, coleslaw, and corn-on-the-cob to choke a horse, spread out before us by the catering company she hired.

Now the food is gone and we are all so full that all we

can do is sit around in a circle in the afternoon sunshine and play music. I grabbed a spot on a small hill of grass in between Zane and Mac and now I'm watching and learning from the more experienced musicians. I add my guitar and my voice to the mix when I can.

Country. Rock. Folk. You name and we've played it, jumping from Jerry Lee Lewis to Green Day to Miley Cyrus in the span of a few chord progressions. When the bass player, Aaron, starts to play *Freebird* everyone groans and throws empty soda and beer cans at him until he stops with a loud "fuck you" aimed at all of us.

"He's such an asshat," Mac says, his smile softening the blow in his words. These guys are like a family right down to the pranks and the constant taunts. "Nobody really likes that fucking song unless there are shots involved."

"Sometimes you guys make me glad that I'm an only child," I joke.

Zane nudges me with an elbow. "You *were* an only child. You've got a big sister now to boss you around, steal your diary and put Nair in your shampoo bottle."

"Do sisters really do that to each other?" I ask, shuddering when they both nod. Now I'm really thankful Kit and I didn't grow up together. "Well, then I better start locking up my make-up bag on the bus."

"You guys should play that song you were working on the other day. It is so ready primetime," Mac says, his abrupt change of subject catching me off guard.

I shake my head. "It really isn't."

I look at Zane for support and I'm not thrilled by the mischief in his dark eyes.

"I knew you'd say that. This is my 'not shocked' face," Mac says at the same time he signals to Kit and points at me and then Zane. "Zane and Emory have a new song they want to sing."

"We do not!" I punch Mac in the arm, the embarrassment from suddenly being the center of everyone's attention adding extra heat to my sun-drenched skin.

"Come on Little Bird. You did great at Kirby's show. This is just the same thing but with your own song." Zane's voice, low and husky tickles my ear as he leans in close. I lean into it, relishing the closeness and recalling last night and the kiss onstage. He's a touchy guy, unafraid to put his hands on me if he feels like it. I love it and I find myself wishing he would do it more often. He also uses it to shamelessly press his advantage. "Just say yes. This is what you left home to do."

I groan and dip my head as the crowd around us starts doing that chant thing, rounds of "sing, sing" punctuated by guitar strums and laughter.

"Em! Zane!" Kits yells out over the noise and I look up to meet her eyes. She gives us the "go ahead" gesture and I know I'm giving in. Apparently everyone else does too because the chant becomes cheers and Zane chuckles beside me. Bastard.

"This is gonna be so good," he says, his fingers poised over his guitar as he flashes me a triumphant smile. I let my eyes roam over his face for a moment, the memory of how soft his goatee was against my skin when he kissed me making me shiver a little. "You ready?"

I nod and listen for his soft count as we both launch into the driving beat and Zane takes the first half of the first verse.

When I met you, twenty-two, blown away by the fire in your eyes/You took my hand and led me into the night/the sparks between us the only light/I knew it would be life or death/Love or lies/You and me for now or never.

My turn comes and for a split second the butterflies have a free fall in my stomach but Zane's smile makes me bold. I open my mouth and I sing like my next breath depends on it.

When I met you/twenty-two/in love with the fire in your eyes/Your hand in mine was my lifeline, my spark/Your touch the kick start to my heart/ Reckless/Fearless/Love or lies/You and me now or never

By the time we hit the chorus the band is picking out their parts and playing along. When we get to the bridge the entire thing explodes in a wall of sound that makes me laugh with the pure joy of it. Zane is right, music is seductive and addictive. I could do this forever. I hope I will.

I look at him as we launch into the last chorus and the connection between us ignites, rivaling the summer sun in its intensity. Our voices blend in perfect, edgy harmony, sliding together as if they were made for each other. Zane's gaze is onyx, backlit with a copper fire and the "I-told-you-so" smile on his lips is pure seduction. I want nothing more to lean over and take his mouth as we drive through the last few notes.

My heart is pounding in my head and my chest so loudly that I don't notice that the entire area has gone silent for a few seconds. Zane reaches out and wraps his big hand around the back of my neck, drawing me to him with sexy intent in his eyes. Just like that, I'm back on the stage at the Javelin and I want him to kiss me again. I need him to kiss me. I lean in, licking my lips and ready to taste him again when the area around us erupts in applause. We both jerk at the sound but instead of pulling away immediately, he touches our foreheads together for the briefest second.

He holds me there long enough for him to growl in a voice just loud enough for me to hear, "That *wasn't* just the music." And then he's dragging me to my feet and I'm dazed, nodding thanks to everyone who clearly loved the song.

"Holy shit you guys!" Kit is on her feet, her face pink with her excitement. She makes her way over to us and crushes me in a hug as tight as a guitar still strapped to my body will allow. She lets me go and squeezes Zane too. "That was a crazy good song. You two are amazing together and I want you to play that one during my second costume change. I've been looking for something to put there to maintain the high energy of the set and that song would be perfect. You'll do it, yeah?"

I just blink at her, unable to process what she's saying to us. I know I sound as shell-shocked as I feel when I finally speak.

"On stage? During the show?"

"Yes, during the show. You've got to know how awesome that song really is." She turns to Zane and pokes him in the gut. "*You* know how good that song is."

He nods, smirking and not even trying to hide his ego. "It's a fucking Top Ten song, Kit. Too bad you can't sing it as a solo."

I expect her to balk at this but she nods in agreement. "It's absolutely a duet. It's like Johnny and June and Tammy and George and Faith and Tim all had an orgy and a song baby popped out of a cake at the end."

I laugh. She's right. I never would have thought to put it that way but she's right.

"You should find someone to cut the single with," I add, knowing she could have a huge hit on her hands with this one.

She looks us both over, her eyes betraying that she has some kind of calculation going on in her head. I know she won't share with the class until she's ready but I would bet money that she has plans for that song. I let my own head get a little bigger when I realize that I'm one-half of the team that wrote it.

"I really want you guys to perform it during the show. Not tonight. Tomorrow. You'll have time to rehearse it with the band. Will you do it?" She asks, giving me the wide-eyed look that tells me she will keep asking until I say yes. I may not have known her long, but Kit is like a terrier when she gets her mind set on something. It's one of the many reasons she is such a huge success.

I look at Zane and suddenly all of the elation I felt minutes before melts into a huge case of nerves.

"You can do this." Zane says, his hand reaching out to snag my own in a loose tangle of fingers. "I'll be right there with you the whole time."

"This is what I came here to do." I say in reply, feeling the truth of them down in my bones. It's leap-of-faith time, figuring out who I am by leaving no stone and no opportunity untaken. "Right?"

He nods. His eyes dark, solemn and intense on mine.

"Is that a yes?" Kit asks, bouncing up and down on her toes until I nod yes. She pumps her fist in the air and presses a kiss to my cheek. "Excellent. This is going to be great. I know it." Her phone rings and she fishes it out of her pocket, grimacing when she looks at the screen. "I've got an interview in an hour. Off to get all dolled up."

I watch her as she walks away, meeting her personal assistant in the middle of the scattering crowd and then jumping in a golf cart and taking off for the stadium. I feel a tug on my fingers and I shuffle to cover the two steps between me and Zane. He gazes down at me, his smirk less playful and more predatory. Just that one look and my skin flashes hot all over. The sounds around us fade into the background. We might as well be alone here in this parking lot.

He's right. It *isn't* just the music.

He stares at me for a few seconds longer, his expression shielding whatever decision tree he's scaling in his mind. But I don't need him to make this decision for me. I know what I want to do.

Look. Leap. Live.

"Come with me." I tug on his hand and weave my way through the crowd, making a beeline for what I hope is my empty tour bus. Kit is occupied with her makeup and I hope Sandra is busy doing something else for a while.

Zane follows behind me, his hand still clinging to mine and his smartass mouth unusually silent. We cross the lot and reach the bus without any interruption. I open the door and step inside, dragging him behind me. The interior is cool and darker with the window shades pulled shut against the harsh summer sun. I don't hear anyone else here but I need to make sure.

"Sandra?" When no one responds I turn to brush past Zane and lock the door.

I don't even get to turn around before he's pressed along my back, his hands reaching around to slip my guitar over my head. His warmth is gone for the briefest second and I spin around and catch him placing my instrument on the table alongside his own. Zane turns back to around, walks slowly towards me and stops far enough away for me to wish he was closer and near enough that I can feel the heat of afternoon pouring off his skin.

"I want to put my hands all over you," he says and my

mouth goes dry. He takes my silence as permission to close the distance between us and do exactly what he said. A whisper of a calloused finger over my collarbone and then the same shiver-inducing touch travels up my neck until his large hands are cradling my face."Em, you say the word and I'll let you go and walk out the door. We can just make great music together and that will be it. Otherwise, I'm not going to stop until I make you come."

I tense the tiniest bit at his words. I try to hide it but he senses it and smiles.

"I won't fuck you here. You deserve better for your first time than the couch on a tour bus. And just because we have some fun today doesn't mean that it ever has to lead to anything else, anything more. You're always in control of this ride, Little Bird."

His words soothe my only worry and I take my immediate future in my hands and close the distance between our mouths.

I gasp at the first touch. He's surprisingly gentle this time, completely different from the kiss in the club. Zane's tongue pushes past my lips and teases me, entices me to take what I want. So I do.

I grab his shirt and drag him closer, pressing our mouths together in a clash of teeth and tongues and hot, wet possession. He groans, his fingers twisting in my hair and setting off sparks of almost-pain behind my eyelids. I dig my nails into the hard muscle of his shoulders, hungry to have him all over me as soon as possible.

Zane maneuvers us around until the edge of the couch hits the back of my knees. He breaks off the kiss and lowers me to the cushioned seat. He remains standing, looking down at me with eyes dark and hot, his lips swollen from our kiss. Our breathing is harsh and heavy in the silence broken only by his voice, tinged dark with need.

"I've been hard for days." He rubs a hand over the bulge of his cock behind his jeans and my eyes are drawn to that spot and I can't look away. His long fingers trace the length of it, unfastening the top button, then two before dipping inside to shift his erection under the denim until I can see the fat, wet tip over the waistband. Suddenly my mouth is dry as sand. "You keep me hard all the time Emory. I want you so fucking much."

I look up at the edge of pain in his voice. I know it's the good kind of agony, the kind that has kept me up late in my bunk, my own hands touching me while I pretend it is him. But I don't have to pretend anymore. All I have to do is be bold. He's in front of me and he's mine for the taking.

I sit up and slide my palm against the hard length of him, my fingertips tracing the head. I smile when his hips push up against my touch, increasing the pressure on a long, deep groan. His long hair has fallen down, shielding his expression with the bowing of his head and I miss seeing the fire in his eyes. But his body, taut and trembling tells me everything I need to know.

His head snaps up when my fingers begin unbuttoning the rest of the buttons on the fly of his jeans. I'm staring back at him so I fumble as I release one button, then two, then a third until I feel his hot flesh against the palm of my hand. I break eye contact then and watch as I wrap my fingers around his fat, hard dick. I've not had the chance to see many penises up close and personal but I've seen enough to know that he is beautiful.

"Gorgeous, "I breathe out on a whisper as I stroke him from the silken-soft head down to the nest of dark hair around the root.

A flush of heat creeps across my skin, a hint of embarrassment but the look of pure want on his face makes me not care. There is nothing I can do or say in this moment that would be wrong. This is Zane. And while I don't understand our connection, it's there. So, I go for broke and tell him exactly what is on my mind because I know he'll give it to me.

"I want this in my mouth."

SIX

ZANE

There is a good chance I might not survive this.

I've had many women and men. All ages, sizes, hair color. We've used every kind of toy, costume, and mind-fuckery you can imagine. It was all hot, more than enough to get me off but sight of my sweet Emory with her long, slim fingers wrapped around my cock has me about to blow.

"Jesus," I huff out on a sharp exhale, shifting my hips forward to thrust into her grip. "Such dirty talk from a woman who looks like a fucking angel."

"I left my halo back at home," she answers and I chuckle at the stubborn tilt to her jaw. She thinks I'm going to back down from this, that my scruples will keep me from taking what she is offering. I'm a nice guy most of the time but never a saint.

I reach down and grab my dick, tracing the tip along the bottom lip she just licked in conscious or unconscious invitation. I'm not entirely sure if it's too much but she doesn't pull away. Her mouth opens on a moan and the moist heat of her breath along my tight skin makes me grit my teeth with the effort to hold back.

My experience with virgins ended when I popped my cherry in the hayloft with Becky Tanner. It had been a fun time; as much fun as two horny, clueless kids can have with a free afternoon and a stolen box of condoms. Emory says she's has experience in other things so I'll follow her lead until she tells me to stop.

"What does it say about me that I just want to dirty you up?" I drop to my knees in front of her spreading her thighs with my hands, letting my fingers wander over the silky skin on her inner thigh. I push her skirt up and the vision of the tiny panties barely covering her sex makes my balls tighten. I lift up until I can look in her eyes, loving the flash of gold-tinged desire in their depths. "A fucking angel, that's what you are and my idea of heaven is your lips wrapped around my cock."

She bites her lower lip, her hands sliding under my t-shirt to stroke my side, my abdomen. I arch into her touch at the same time I lean forward and kiss her. Slow and deep, coaxing and deliberate. I don't need to ravage her; she's right here with me and ready to explore how good this can be. Emory wants this, every touch, every sigh tells me loud and clear.

After weeks of slow burn we are ready to catch fire.

I pull back from the allure of her mouth and sit on my heels, my dick dragging along the exposed flesh of her thigh, enticing me to maintain the contact, to grind against her. But I want her to get off first. We don't have tons of time and I need to show her how good I can make her feel.

I hook fingers on the waistband of her panties and drag them down her legs and toss them somewhere behind me. She spreads her legs wider and it's my turn to groan at the display. Pale skin, the darker pink of her pussy, and blonde trimmed curls.

"You're gorgeous," I whisper, glancing to find her watching me. I smile at her and she gives one back to me, a little shy but full of anticipation. I won't make her wait. I run my palms against her inner thigh, spreading her wider to make room for my shoulders as I dip my head and take the first taste.

A long slow glide of tongue along her pussy lips, already slick with her own arousal. It is a sweet and sharp burst on my taste buds and I fight the urge to reach down and stroke myself. Instead I spread her open, allowing me to lick and suck and kiss every perfect inch of her.

Emory pushes against my face, her breathing harsh and staccato in the silence of the tour bus. This is going to go fast. We've been riding this edge of arousal for weeks and going over is a like a landslide: quick, dirty, and destructive. Whatever walls we put up between us will be rubble after today.

"Zane," she says on a gasp and I glance to see her squeezing her breasts, her tank top rucked up and exposing the tender expanse of her belly. She's biting her lip as her fingers slip inside of her bra and begin a slow rub against a nipple. I would give my right nut to get rid of her clothes and see her play with the taut flesh but I don't want to stop what we are doing for the time it would take to get everything off.

I lower my head and deliver a hungry kiss to her sex, finding her clit and passing the tip of my tongue over it in a rapid rhythm calculated to make her scream my name. Her body is hot and wet against my finger as I push it inside her, loving the way her muscles draw me in deeper. Her hips are bucking under me and I use my other hand to grasp her hip and hold her in place.

She makes a sound, something between a whine and a

plea when I add another finger and start pumping inside her. I finger fuck her, wishing that I could do it with my cock buried deep inside her.

Not today. Not here.

"Zane!" Her cry is rough and ragged as she shudders against me, her hand grabbing my shoulder and digging in with her nails as she comes all over my tongue. I continue my kiss, licking and caressing until she relaxes against me, her breathing rapid but deep.

I look up at her, her cheeks flushed a bright pink and her breasts heaving up and down with her gulping inhale and exhale. It's her eyes that capture me, dark forest green and open, soft, eager.

"Come here," she whispers as she tugs on my shoulder, encouraging me to join her on the couch.

I'm happy to oblige, lifting up with a plan to kiss her but I'm distracted by the nipple peeking over the edge of her bra cup. I lower my head and lick the flesh, loving her gasp and the way she arches into my touch, begging for more. I pull aside the soft fabric and continue my tongue lashing until the deep pink skin is shiny with my attention.

"God, that's pretty," I murmur as I reach around her back and under her top to unclasp the bra. With the tension gone, I pull down the other cup and bow my head to swirl my tongue around that nipple until it is hard and straining against my lips. That one is also pretty and I know I could spend hours feasting in the tips, the soft mounds of her breasts.

"Kiss me," Emory begs as she writhes under me, her fingers exploring every inch of me she can reach under my clothes. Her touch lights me up and them leaves me colder and hungrier when she moves to another spot. I reach over my head and pull my t-shirt off and then lean up to let my moan mingle with her own when my bare flesh connects with hers. "Kiss me, Zane. I want to know what I taste like on your mouth."

My plan to make the kiss slow and seductive goes out the window at her dirty plea. This meeting of our mouths is hard and bruising as I lose a little bit of my control. In the back of head I know we'll both bear marks from the ferocity of our kiss but I don't care. I plunge my tongue inside and make sure she can taste every drop of her passion.

"Your juice is sweet, salty. I could eat you all fucking day," I say against her lips, before I delve back in for another tour of her wet heat. Her hands are all over me and I jerk forward when the warmth of her palm wraps around my dick and squeezes. I pull away with a gasp.

"Come on, I want to taste you. Bring it up here," she asks while urging me up on the couch with the hand not driving me crazy.

I put a knee on each side of her body, hovering over her with the perfect angle to watch her lean forward and take my cock inside her perfect mouth.

"Fuck," I grind out, my eyes shut tight against the elec-trifyingly sensation of being covered by her hot, wet suction. Emory and her little high school boyfriend might not have gotten all the way to home base but she spent a lot of time practicing the art of polishing his nob at third. "Oh fuck."

My knees go a little weak, so I pitch forward and loom over her, my hands braced against the back of the couch. I pry my eyes open and I realize that this is the best fucking seat in the house. The scene before me is dirty and debauched and I will never get it out of my head, never.

My jeans are shoved down to mid-thigh, my dick sliding in between her lush, pink lips and her eyes are on mine, making sure I know how much she loves this. I throw out any worry that she can't handle me and I let my usual pervy, freak flag fly.

"Fucking gorgeous mouth all over me. Suck me off, baby." I gasp as I reach down and grip my shaft with hand, holding it out to her so she can take all of me. She moans deep in her throat and slides me all the way in and I can feel the vibration in my balls. It is so fucking sweet. I have to grit my teeth as I begin a slow pulse of my hips. "You feel so good, Em. So damn beautiful. Made for me."

I'm almost babbling and I know it but she loves it, her fingernails digging into my bare ass and hip as I speed up with my thrusts. I'm so close and I know there is no way I'm going to make it last. She's so amazing, so giving and I can't believe how she exceeds every single fantasy I ever had about this moment.

Emory Cabell is perfect and I know that this afternoon will not be enough. I hope she's ready for me because I don't think I'll be able to stay away from her.

She shudders underneath me and I glance down in time to see her lower her hand in between her own legs. Any direct view of what she's doing is blocked by my body and her skirt but the knowledge that going down on me has turned her on so much that she needs to touch herself sets me off like a firecracker.

"I'm going to come." I give her the warning and I ease back a little, giving her the choice on whether she wants to swallow or not. She chases my retreat and I have my answer and nothing stands between me and the pleasure pain of my orgasm. I grip the back of the couch tightly as it hits me like a tsunami, wave after wave making me shudder and twitch and writhe against the sensation.

I pull out of her mouth and slither down the couch until we are face-to-face and breathing like we both just ran a marathon. I kiss her, letting it linger and enjoying the heat of our bodies where we touch. Emory writhes against me, her hips moving in the unmistakable rhythm of someone who is still on the edge. I remember her hand under her skirt and I pull back just enough to murmur against her lips.

"You still need me, baby?" When she nods yes, I wedge my own hand between us and find her wet and swollen between her legs. I stroke her gently, somewhere between a tease and what she needs as I explore her soft skin with my lips. Nuzzling my nose along her cheek and behind her ear until I am surrounded by citrus spice of her shampoo. She comes against my hand, more gently than before and I return to her mouth, soaking in her gasp of pleasure.

Holy shit. She's perfect.

I tell her so and she just laughs at me. I do not have the strength to argue with her.

I wrap her up in my arms and maneuver us until we are able to lie together on the couch, legs woven in a complicated puzzle. We doze there for a while, enjoying the silence and each other until I can hear other people coming back to the tour buses to grab whatever shit they need to take to the dressing rooms to get ready for the show. I check my watch and groan.

"I don't want to move but we've got get moving or we'll be late," I say, lifting up to look down at her. Her hair is a wreck, her lips dark pink and swollen and her clothes look like she's been mauled by a bear. I grin. "You look amazing."

"I look like I just came twice on a couch during an afternoon booty call." She sits up, stretching her arms and reaching behind her to refasten her bra. I would offer to help but she looks so damn cute when her face screws up in frustration. When she finally gets it done, she catches me staring. "What?"

I shrug. "Is this a one-and-done or are you up another round on another afternoon?" I smile. "Or night?" I smile wider. "Or morning?"

She shoves against my shoulder and laughs but I can see the pink blush on her cheeks. There's the Emory I know and can't wait to get my hands on again.

"I could do that," she says and shoves off the couch, looking for her shoes. I can tell she's working hard to play it cool and I follow her lead.

"Well, you check your calendar and let me know," I tease, buttoning up my shorts and grabbing my shoes. "I had fun and I would love to do it again."

"Me too," she says and then pauses, concern looking very out of place on her face. "But we need to try to keep this quiet. I'm not embarrassed but I'm not sure I want everyone in my business."

"You got it."

"Kit won't be surprised."

"No one is going to be surprised, Emory." When she raises and eyebrow, I explain. "We've got heat between us. People already figured that out and they all assume that we'll do something about it. Half of the crew probably thought we were fucking instead writing songs until they heard the one today."

"Of course they did," she laughs and melts against me when I draw her closer. "You *are* Zane Wyatt."

"And you're hot." I press a soft kiss to her lips and then pull back with a sigh when I hear Mac yelling across the parking lot. "Gotta go, Little Bird."

I release her, grab my guitar and follow her to the door. We swing it open and both of us jump back when Billy, one of the roadies, is standing on the step, his big paw wrapped around the arm of a guy with broad shoulders, blonde hair, and a smile only for Emory.

"Eric?" She asks, her mouth hanging open in shock.

"You know this guy, Emory?" Billy inquires, his bored expression screaming just how much he doesn't want to have to deal with this situation. "He says he's your boyfriend."

SEVEN

EMORY

"Eric, why are you here?"

I'm beat from the show and the last thing I want to deal with is my ex-boyfriend trying to convince me to come home and back to him. Apparently my mom sent him. He's been at me about it since he arrived just before the show and followed me around backstage. Kit offered him a ticket and ignored my glare when he accepted. He seemed to have a good time but I couldn't care less.

All I can think about was the blank glance Zane gave me whenever we came in contact since Eric arrived. Yes, he was polite and friendly and welcomed Eric to the show. He gave him a short tour of the backstage when Kit requested so that I could sneak off and get dressed but I could tell that it was the last thing he wanted to do.

I can't tell if he's pissed or jealous. If I had to guess, it is the first one because there is no way Zane Wyatt is jealous of my old boyfriend. Yeah, our sex session on the couch was amazing but it wasn't a proposal for marriage. There is no reason for either of us to be jealous.

But I know that if I had one of Zane's old bed partners show up, I would definitely have a little green monster sitting on my shoulder.

It's stupid and childish but I know I have a little bit of a crush on him. He's hot and funny and a musician. He has long hair and tattoos and is sex-on-a-stick. I am obligated to have a crush on him. I'm sure there's a law somewhere.

He's also my friend and I love the way he makes me feel. Not just when his tongue is buried between my legs... but all the time. I feel special when he looks at me.

I know. It's stupid.

But what is dumber is the fact that Eric cannot get the memo and go home.

"Eric, I'm not going home and we are over," I say for the millionth time as we stand outside the door of my tour bus. We leave in fifteen minutes and I was hoping that I would get to see Zane before we get on the road but I can't get rid of my uninvited guest. "You need to go and move on. I'm not coming back to Dutton except to visit my mom."

"Your mom misses you," he says, walking forward until I have to back up and lean against the side of the bus to avoid him. He raises an arm and semi-brackets me in. I used to love this when he did it in high school but right now it's just irritating me with its creeper vibe.

"I miss her too but she'll learn to deal with it. Most parents have to get used to their kids moving out and having their own lives."

"But you left so quickly. One day you were there and the next you were headed to Nashville. It was very sudden."

I laugh and wonder how he knew me so little even with all the time we spent together.

"The only reason you were surprised about me leaving

is because you weren't listening. All I ever talked about was going to Nashville to pursue my music."

"That's just stuff people say, Emory." He chuckles and shakes his head and I want to smack him.

Suddenly I'm exhausted and disgusted with him and this conversation. I close my eyes and lean my head back against the cool, metal side of the bus which is why I don't see him make his move.

His mouth on mine isn't unpleasant. Eric is a good kisser and a generous lover. He made sure we both came and always paid for our dates. He's a nice guy, handsome and sexy. I liked him. I like him. I just don't want his tongue down my throat anymore.

I push against his chest and twist my face to the side. Eric pulls back, confusion all over his face as he tries to figure out why I stopped.

"Goodbye Eric. I hope you love college and that you are a huge success and I'll see you when I visit my mom." He opens his mouth to say something and I clarify my comment. "As a friend. We can grab a coffee or something." I pat his chest and duck under his arm to head into the bus. "Drive safely home."

I turn to add a smile to my goodbye when I see Zane standing a few feet away, near the door of his own bus. Mac is beside him, watching the scene closely. I raise my hand to wave Zane over, anxious to talk to him before we hit the road for the night but he just nods and mounts the steps to his bus and disappears. Mac looks at him and then back at me, eyes rolling in a "what the fuck" gesture before he follows in Zane's footsteps.

"Oh shit," I say, slumping against the doorframe. I know Zane saw Eric kiss me and I cringe. It's ridiculous but it

feels like cheating. I groan again, realizing just how complicated my life just got.

And then Eric chimes in with the understatement of the
century. "That Zane guy is nothing but trouble."

No shit.

EIGHT

ZANE

"You're ass hurt and you need to get over it."

I flip the bird to the general direction where Mac is standing in the dressing room we share backstage. It's a few minutes to show time and I really don't need him to psychoanalyze me right now.

"Fuck off, Dr. Phil." I pull on my boots and straighten up, rolling my shoulders to ease the tension. "Emory and I were just fooling around. I don't give a shit about this guy showing up. That's her problem to deal with."

"Except that you're a jealous motherfucker who has been a dick all day long to everyone," Mac says with a growl. "When I have to deal with your bullshit, then it becomes my problem."

I stop what I'm doing and sigh. I know he's right. I have been an asshole all day. Short-tempered and anxious.

"I don't like feeling this way." I offer as an explanation and an apology.

"Jealous? Welcome to the world the rest of us live in."

I sigh and sit down in the makeup chair in front of the vanity. I wish Mateo were here right now. He knows me so well that I wouldn't have to explain but he's across the country and he's got a huge set of medical school exams this week, so I'm not going to call him. He'd just try to fix it. He's hard-wired to save the world.

"I don't like the reason why I feel jealous. I like her, of course, I do. I try to like all the people I hook-up with but I've never felt like I wanted to jack-up some dude for kissing them."

"She wasn't kissing him back. You could tell that from a mile away."

"Yeah, I saw that too."

"It doesn't help?" He asks, wrapping tape around his drumsticks and testing the weight in his hands. "I saw how she looked at you. If you'd been the one with his tongue down her throat, Emory would have been climbing you like a tree."

I remember her under me on the couch, her lips wrapped around my cock. The look in her eyes when I kissed her as she came the second time. I think of that and I know he's right.

"I just need to talk to her," I grumble as we head to door as a roadie gives us the "ten minute" knock on the doorframe. "I hardly saw her all day between interviews and the fan club thing. I'll see if I can grab some time after the show."

"You'll need to make it quick. We're driving all night again."

"I know." I love the road but when we have several "in-and-outs" in a row like this, it becomes grueling. I have to check the calendar to see what city we are in since have no time to explore.

We round the corner and the entire band is there, huddled for the prayer before we hit the stage. Kit is in the middle, her smile lighting up the dim space. She's an incredible performer, a fantastic boss and everyone loves her. The road is hard but she tries to make it fun and feel like a family. Once again I throw up a thank you to the Big Guy for landing me this gig.

Emory and Sandra move up beside me and my eyes are immediately drawn to hers. The emerald green is cloudy with confusion and I hate the fact that I was the asshole that put it there. I reach out and brush my hand against hers, our fingers intertwining for the briefest few seconds before Kit breaks the huddle and we all start to hustle towards the stage.

I take two steps forward and then turn, dragging her to me for a quick but thorough kiss that leaves us both breathless and the taste of her lip gloss on my mouth.

"I'm a dick," I say and she bursts out laughing, leaning up to kiss my cheek before she heads out onto the stage. I follow with a grin on my face for the first time today.

The show goes quickly for me until the point where Emory and I perform *Lies and Love* during the costume change. Out there under the lights, flirting while we sing the words we wrote together, the entire world slows down to a crawl and we are the last two people on it for the final ride. I could have stayed on stage in that moment all night long.

The audience loved it and went nuts, as Kit predicted. The rest of the show was a blur of music, lights, people, and my fingers itching for the chance to touch Emory.

I make it just offstage before I catch up with her and pull her into my arms. This time the kiss is long and deep and borderline indecent. Our bodies, damp with sweat and juiced from the adrenaline of performance writhe against each other. My hands are in her hair, down her back, cupping her ass and hauling her higher against me until she wraps her legs around my waist.

She huffs out a muffled grunt when her back hits the wall but I don't care since it gives us more leverage to grind against each other. Her hands sneak past the waistband on my jeans and I feel her bare palms against the skin of my ass.

"I'm a dick. Sorry." I say when I finally release her mouth and we grin down at each other. She runs a finger across my lips and I kiss the tip.

"That's a shitty apology, Wyatt."

"I'll make it up to you later."

She opens her mouth to answer but the sound of her sister—my boss—behind us cuts off whatever she was going to say.

"Emory why do you have your hands down his pants?"

NINE

I can't sleep.

My body is still buzzing after the hot kiss after the show, adrenaline and arousal making it impossible for me relax. Kit and Sandra are wired too and we all sit on the couch in the common area of the tour bus ogling Ryan Reynolds in *The Proposal*, eating microwave popcorn and drinking.

I fidget, drawing my knees up to my chest as I munch mindlessly on the snack. I love this movie but I am barely following along as the memory of Zane's hands on my body refuse to let me go. It isn't like I've never had a guy touch me, Eric and I spent plenty of time figuring out what felt good. But, nothing he ever did turned me on like getting felt up by Zane Wyatt.

Tipping my bottle back, I realize that it's all gone. That will not do.

"Another round?" I ask as I lift myself off the couch, letting my body settle with the gentle sway of the bus under my feet.

"Emory are you even old enough to drink?" Sandra asks

as she eyeballs the beer I wave in her face, taking it with a nod of thanks.

I hand off the Orange Crush to Kit, admiring again how she sticks with her sobriety.

"And if I say no?" I inquire, taking another deep swallow of the pale ale as I lower myself back onto the cushions.

"Nothing. I'm not your mama but she's your big sister and I don't want the boss mad at me because I'm contributing to the delinquency of a minor."

"As long as she keeps it on the bus, I don't care," Kit says, reaching out for another handful of popcorn. "I'm more concerned with the kiss she laid on Zane after the show and what her hands were doing down his pants. They look like they'd been there before."

I quickly swallow my beer and wipe at my mouth when some dribbles down my chin.

"Oh, we're talking about that?' Sandra asks, her afro bouncing a little with her excited nod that matches her wide smile. "Excellent because I gotta tell you that I never believed you two were just writing songs together. Everybody knows that Zane Wyatt gets *all the* women horizontal *all the* time. He can't help it."

"I have not been *horizontal* with Zane," I protest, horrified and relieved that we are talking about this. I need advice and that's what big sisters and girlfriends are for. Right? "We have been writing songs and somewhere along the way...well, we ended up semi-horizontal."

"Do you want to sleep with him?" Kit inquires, her voice calm but her eyes wary.

"I know that's where this is headed if we keep up what we're doing," I hedge, not sure why when I know the answer. I want Zane to fuck me. But saying it out loud feels like I would be committing somehow.

"It's headed to him fucking you and from what I've hear it will be amazing and so worth it. But if you think he's the boyfriend-you-take-home-to-mama-type, then you need to keep walking," Sandra says.

"I know that. He's told me from the beginning what he is but I want more of it anyway." Kit groans and slumps back on the couch and I totally understand her reaction. If I were my big sister, I'd move my ass to Montana. "I know how stupid that is. Any smart girl would give him a wide berth unless they can spread their legs without opening their heart even just a little bit. I also know that I'm one big walking heart, ready and available to soak in all the good and vulnerable as well as all of the bad. I don't want to get hurt but I don't think I want to miss out either."

The room is quiet after my little speech and I wait for them to start with the "are you crazy?" talk.

"Just be careful Em," Kit sighs, leaning over to sling an arm over my shoulder. She squeezes me tight, my head automatically finds the perfect spot on her shoulder and we sit there for several long moments. I close my eyes, so grateful to have her in my life. Dad might not have been legit but I can't hate anything that brought her into my life. "I don't want you to get hurt but I don't want you to miss out on living either. Zane isn't a player, he's straight with the people in his bed and I don't think he would deliberately hurt you. But he's told you what he is and what this can be so the best advice I can give you is to believe him."

"You sound like Zane."

"I'm not sure how I feel about that but if it means he's being straight with you, that's all I can ask. You could do a lot worse than have a summer thing with Zane Wyatt."

"And if he does you wrong, Max Butler will kick his ass for you," Sandra adds her smirk telling me that she wouldn't mind a front-row seat at that event. She's a little blood-thirsty.

They settle down to keep watching the movie but I can't do it. I need to go and think and after the third glance from Sandra as I fidget, I excuse myself and go to my bunk.

I slide into bed and pull the long, dark privacy curtain. I'd heard nightmares about sleeping in a bus bunk but I love it. It's kind of like camping with climate control and no bugs. The motion of the bus lulls me to sleep most nights and I crash until my alarm goes off. I grab my phone and put in my earbuds, scrolling down my music until I find my Patty Griffith playlist. I hit play and settle back against my pillow to do some hard thinking.

I like Zane. I can admit that much and I think he likes me, at least as a friend. I know he wants me, would love to fuck me and that sensation is definitely reciprocated. He's sexy and exciting and adventurous. If I left Dutton looking for a wild ride, he would definitely fit the bill.

But I know that my feelings could very quickly slide into something deeper. I could be wrong. I've never had a fling with someone. Never been a fuck buddy. I could be great at it or I could fall...hard.

My phone rings in my earbuds and I jump at the sudden change to the ringtone. I glance at the number and see Zane's name across the screen. I bite my lip against the smile that blooms there and swipe the screen to accept the call.

"Hey," I say, wincing when a loud yell erupts in the background. "What is that?"

"Hang on, the guys are having a Playstation tournament."

I listen as he moves around on his end, the scrapes and grunts making me laugh as he stumbles over all the crap on the floor to get away from the noise. I've been on the bus and it looks like a frat house on meth. I never take my shoes off. Never.

"Okay, I'm back," he says as I hear the noise disappear. "I'm back in the rehearsal space."

Instead of master bedroom space in the back, their bus has a small room where you can go to get away from the noise of the kitchen and TV area and write some music or have a quiet conversation. We've worked back there a couple of times, both of us wedged onto the loveseat built-in across the width of the bus.

"What's going on?" I ask settling deeper into my bunk, trying to steady my pulse. It kicked up into overdrive the minute I heard his voice.

"I wanted to call you and tell you that I'm sorry I was such a dick."

I smile. "That's an excellent apology, Mr. Wyatt. No waffling. Straight to the point."

"Oh, you're going to give me shit about it, aren't you? I say I'm sorry real nice and you bust my ass."

"What are you sorry for exactly," I tease. "'Being a dick' covers a lot of territory."

It gets quiet on the other end of the phone and I hear him sigh and mutter "fuck me" under his breath. I should let him off the hook but I'm really curious about why he reacted the way he did. If I don't find out for sure, my hopeful romantic side will run wild. I've seen me do it.

"I didn't like that guy's hand being on you. I didn't like the thought that he'd *ever* had his hands on you." His breathing is harsh in my ears and my body reacts to the growl in his voice. "I still had your taste on my lips and the feel of them around my cock and he was there, looking like he had a right to be."

My mouth is suddenly dry, my nipples hard and my sex tightens. I swallow hard so that I can answer him.

"He has no right to touch me. Not anymore." I take a deep breath and take the plunge, offering up the way I see it. I might be wrong, I might be immature but I want Zane to know where my head and my heart are. "You're the only one that has the right to touch. You're the only one I *want* to touch."

The air in my bunk is stifling and I pull the blanket off me and shove it down to the bottom of the bed.

"Goddam Em. You're killing me over here," he says, his voice thick with what I now recognize is his arousal. "Is that what you want? Some kind of claim on me?"

"I don't know how this works, Zane. You enlighten me."

"What do *you* want? Tell me and I'll give it to you if I can."

What are we talking about? Our hearts? Our bodies? The orgasm I want so badly right now? I clench my thighs together to stem the ache that pulses there just from the sound of his voice over the phone.

"I don't know," I answer, too afraid to say what I'm thinking until I've had more time to think about it. At this point in time, my answer isn't a lie. "I don't know."

"What *do* you know?" His voice is deep and low, seductive. He's really good at keeping me tuned in to his every word.

"I know that I love how I feel when you touch me."

"God, so do I. I want your hands on me all the time."

"I want to do more with you." I take a breath and dive in and confess the one thing I know for sure. "I want you to fuck me, Zane." I feel the need to clarify. "With your cock."

He sucks in a breath and sputters. I can almost see him fighting off a cough on the other end of the phone. He wasn't expecting that answer. It would be funny if I wasn't so worried he'll say no.

"Em. You don't want" He clears his throat again. "you don't want me to take your virginity."

"I do." I launch into my explanation, my heart in my throat and wondering if I can convince him. "I told you it's not a religious thing and I'm not expecting champagne and rose petals and a big romantic gesture but if its going to be the sex I remember for the rest of my life, I want it to be a good memory."

"I can be memorable."

"I know you can."

He doesn't agree to do it but he doesn't say no, so I let it sit there between us. Suspended on the wireless threads out in the ether in the shape of a big fat question mark.

He breaks the silence like only Zane Wyatt can. Blunt and to the point.

"All this sex talk has made me horny."

I hum, letting my hand spread out across my belly. I let my fingers glide under my tank top, enjoying the warm glide of skin against skin. I let my hand drift lower and ease under the edge of my panties. I know where this is going: my first phone sex.

I gasp as my fingertip brushes my clit and I know Zane heard me because the next thing I hear across the line is him asking, "Em, are you wet? I'm so fucking hard, I hurt."

TEN

ZANE

I can hear her arousal over the phone and I make no effort to hide my own.

I'm jacked up on the amazing show tonight, the relief that Eric is long gone and my own reaction to the conversation I just had with Emory. It's not like I haven't had a partner try to claim me before. No matter how it starts, in a bathroom stall at a club or on a real date, eventually the time comes when they want to be more than a fuck buddy. Or they want to be the only fuck buddy. I'm used to it.

I've just never had a time when that thought didn't make me want to run.

Emory pretty much laid out that she wants it be just the two of us and I never had one thought of ending the call. No, my first thought was that I don't want her to want anybody else. I don't want her to let anyone else touch her.

That is some crazy shit in my world. I don't think those kinds of thoughts have ever crossed my mind. So I'm more than willing to let a little phone sex distract me.

"I'm wet, Zane. My panties are soaked," Emory whispers into the phone and I undo the buttons on my jeans and shove my hand in there and drag out my erection.

I am hard, aching and hot to the touch as I start the stroke. Not slow and calculated to last. Nope. I start babbling, letting her see every dirty, pervy thought that is going through my mind right now.

"Em, all I can think about you letting me fuck your mouth. It was so perfect. *You* were so perfect."

Silence echoes across the line for so long that I think we've lost connection. And then I hear her voice, small and unusually timid for her.

"I don't know how to do this. It's so much easier with you right here with me. I'm nervous for some reason."

She just asked me to take her v-card and now she's embarrassed to dirty talk over the phone? I smile and slow my stroke down as I settle back against the cushions and think of how to make her feel like I'm right there.

"Don't be nervous. It's just us. Em and Zane." I lower my voice and let it go low and easy, making sure my drawl coats every word. "You just listen to me and I'll get you there, baby. Okay?"

"Okay."

"Are you touching yourself?"

"Yes." She ends the word on a gasp so I know she's telling the truth.

"Good. I wish I was there, fingers along your pussy lips. You get so wet and it smells so good. Salty. Real. With a hint of that citrus shampoo you use. Pure heaven." I restart the slow stroke on my cock, letting my arousal spin out as I tease hers from her secret places. "I love getting inside you, the way your body clings to me. So pretty. So tight. I need all your sweet, juicy girl lube so when I fuck you its smooth and deep. You'd lift your hips to me and beg me with your body to put my mouth on you. You want me to suck your clit, don't you baby?"

"Yesoh." Her answer is more moan than words and a drop of slick pre-come rolls down my shaft in response.

"Baby, I'm so hard. My cock is leaking with how much I want to be inside you but I'll keep my fingers inside your heat. I'll touch you, stroke you to get you ready for me. Right now, I've got to have a taste of your hard, pink, pretty clit. Do you want that?"

"Yes."

"Beg me, Emory."

"Please, Zane," she whimpers across the line and I can hear her moving against the sheets of her bunk. I wish I was there with her, if only to see the desire in her eyes and on her face.

"You need to better than that, Em. Beg like you really want it." I put an edge of mean in my voice and I hold my breath to see if it will turn her off or dial her up to a higher level of burn.

"Please Zane. Suck my clit. Suck it hard and make me come."

Oh yeah. I've got her now and she's got me. I'm on the edge but I need to wait for her go first. I need to hear her moan my name.

"You going to come on my face if I do it? Or are you going to tease me? Make me want it until I beg?"

"No, I'll come for you. Please."

"Then do it, baby. Come for me. Touch your clit and let me hear it. Now."

One. Two. Three. Four. Five. Six seconds pass and I hear her suck in a breath and that momentary pause and whimper she does in the back of her throat when she flies apart. And then she growls out my name with a ferocity that aims right for my balls.

I come hard, spilling over my hand and my jeans like a teenager. I grit my teeth and then choke out a laugh as I keep coming, over and over.

All I hear on her end is rapid breathing and hums of pleasure as I try to catch my breath and say something with the two brain cells I have left.

"Damn, Zane." Emory finally says on her end and I laugh.

"I know. I know."

"That was my first phone sex," she confesses and I bite back my laugh. I don't want her to think I'm making fun of her. She just makes me happy with all her earnest honesty right after being such a white-hot sex kitten.

"I like being your first." It's the truth and it makes me think about another first I'd like to be. "I'll do it, Em. I'll fuck you if you want me to."

Big pause and I wonder if she's changed her mind. I try not to think to hard about the disappointment that builds up in me at that thought.

"I want you to."

"I'd love to be your first." I pause not really sure how to proceed. I've never been asked to be someone's first lover before. I go with my gut. "I'll work it out. Make it nice for you, okay?"

"You don't have to do that, Zane."

"I want to. Don't worry about it."

"I think down deep you're a nice guy and a closet romantic, Zane Wyatt," she teases as a yawn travels over the line.

"Shut up and go to sleep. Don't tell anybody that you think I'm a nice guy. It will ruin my reputation."

"Yeah, yeah," she says right before she hangs up the phone. "Your secret is safe with me."

ELEVEN

EMORY

"I can't believe that we just spent the last two days recording our songs."

Zane looks up at me and gives me a wild, happy grin as he leans over the shoulder of Leon, the sound engineer and talks about stuff that really doesn't make sense to me. All I know is that when they turn the sound back on and our song rolls like thunder out of the speakers, I can't breathe.

I have to thank Kit for this opportunity. Fans at her show videotaped our performance of *Lies and Love* and the footage went viral. Every media outlet you can think of started calling us and Kit sent us here to record a digital single to put up on iTunes and milk the notoriety for all its worth. Good for the tour and good us. Everybody wins.

But I still can't believe that I'm here. Six months has been an amazing game change for me and I feel the need to pinch myself every second of the day. I'm just glad I have Kit and Zane to walk with me. I'd be lost without them.

"That's not me," I say, backing up as if to emphasize my point. "There is no way I sound like that."

Leon, the sound guy shakes his head and adjusts a slide

on the board. "It's all you. I don't need to mix with of your voices. Pure gold in the pipes. You guys are lucky."

I look at Zane and just stare, unable to believe the whirlwind that has become my life. He straightens up and walks over to me, his hands cupping my face as he leans down to whisper a soft kiss against my lips and quick swipe of his nose along my cheek. He nuzzles into my hair and says into my ear, "Emory Cabell, your voice makes me hard and I want to cry every time I hear it. That is *all* you and don't you doubt it."

"You're crazy," I whisper back.

"Only about you," he says before pulling away, weaving our fingers together and leading me over to our guitars. I blink and think about what he just said and wonder if he even realizes it. Zane is an affectionate man, always touching and always making sure you know that you are the center of his attention. It's quite overwhelming and I have to work overtime to not read too much into it. This is just the honeymoon phase of any relationship, no matter how temporary.

He picks up his guitar and sits down on the sofa and I ease my but down on the coffee table in front of him. Our knees bump and I adjust my position so that one of my knees is between his and I scoot in closer. "Okay, listen to this and tell me if you think it needs to be change on the bridge."

He plays the notes, switching it up when it gets to point where the bridge flows into the resolution chorus. It sounds good but I'm not sure.

"Play it again," I ask and he does as I ask, making a slight adjustment that I like. It's darker and keeps the driving beat. I nod as he continues, urging him to go with that version. "I like it."

He smiles up at me and heads into the final chorus and starts to sing. I join in and we switch up the arrangement, shifting the harmonies and goofing around with the lyrics until we are both laughing. Leon snorts out a belly laugh over the system and we lose it again. I wipe tears away from my eyes and inhale deeply to catch my breath.

"I've never had so much fun in my life," I say and I mean it.

"The music is a good time, yeah?"

"And the company," I answer and feel the blush creep across my collarbone. What a cheeseball thing to say.

Zane leans over and gives me a swift hard kiss followed by a gentle rub of our noses together and then goes back to playing. It's new, a song that I don't know and I watch him as he works through the chords and the strum. It's sensual and slow and I start working on lyrics in my head. Ones that deal with the dark, mouths open, and bodies moving in a rhythm calculated to make it good.

It's hot and he's so sexy with his dark hair escaping the leather thong tying it off his face. I stare, taking advantage of his focus to ogle and memorize. The dark scruff of his goatee, the long fingers with callouses that feel so good against my skin, and his lush, full lips. Yummy goodness from the top of his head to the bottom of his very sexy, large feet.

Zane looks up and catches me in mid-drool.

"You can't look at me like that on stage," he says, leaning in close, our mouths almost touching.

"Why not?"

"Because this right here. . ." He plays the chords, making them rise at a slow, languid pace. "This is how you sound when you come. That little catch in the back of your throat right before you lose it."

"What? You're serious?" I lean in closer to catch his every word. I am mesmerized by him. And not just a little.

"Completely." He nods as he continues to play, smiling at me with his fallen angel smile that always convinces me to follow him into the dark. "Em, if you look at me like that when I play it everyone will know it's my favorite fucking sound in the world and that I spend all my time wondering when I can hear it again."

"Oh hell, how do you do that?" I lean in and brush a kiss across his mouth, sneaking a small taste with my tongue. "How do you say shit like that to me and make me so crazy?"

"I just speak the truth." Zane's eyes are dark and sultry and I don't know how I'm ever going to perform this song without having a spontaneous orgasm on the spot.

"Be careful. Your closet romantic is showing."

He grins at me and keeps playing.

"Isn't this just the cutest scene ever?" A woman's voice cuts into our little world and I look over my shoulder to see who it is.

A woman I do not know at all. Tall, auburn haired and wearing an outfit that can only be described as a "power suit". I look down at my jean capris and tank top and wonder which one of us didn't get the wardrobe memorandum.

"Zane, are you going to introduce me to your friend?" She walks towards us and throws her expensive looking purse on the table next to me. We both stand and I prepare to put out my hand to shake hers and she totally bypasses me for Zane.

She has perfect aim and hits the bulls-eye when she lands a kiss right on his mouth.

His mouth. The one that I want to claim.

I clench my hands into fists to resist the urge to smack her. He's not mine. Not even a little bit and he's never said he was.

He pulls back and looks at me, his expression mostly unreadable except for the embarrassment I see making the tips of his ears turn red. Zane rallies like the professional performer he is and begins the introductions, nice and smooth. No fuss.

"Maureen Richards. She's one of the A&R directors at Waterworld Media." He turns to me, tucking my hand into his and pulling me close. "This is Emory Cabell. Talented songwriter and singer and someone you'll be hearing more about."

I stick my hand out to her and smile. "It's nice to meet you."

"Now, *that's* an accent." She gives my hand a barely-there shake and returns all of her attention to Zane. "You like them fresh off the farm now?"

I want to kill her.

TWELVE

ZANE

Oh sweet baby Jesus.

Maureen is spoiling for a fight and Emory will give her one if I don't intervene. It's not that I don't think Em can hold her own but I'm not going to put her in the crossfire of a battle where I am the intended target. She would only be collateral damage.

"Okay Maureen, what are you doing here?"

Emory and Maureen are squared off like two prize-fighters in the ring, ignoring me so I step in between them, forcing the end of the stare off with my body.

"Maureen, we're kind of busy here so why don't you tell me why you're here?"

She blinks up at me and smiles. It isn't really friendly, in fact I would call it feral and at one time I would have called it sexy. Not so much anymore.

"I need to talk to you about your career."

"I'm going to grab a coffee," Emory says and cuts me a glance as she walks away. Her back is rigid and she's pissed. When I look at Maureen I let all of my irritation show.

"Why can't you be nice?" I ask, knowing that it's a

stupid question. Maureen isn't nice because she doesn't want to be. "You know what? Forget it. I know better than to expect the impossible."

"Did you check her ID, Zane? Did she actually graduate high school?"

"She's nineteen and that is not why you're here," I prod her on, hoping she gets to the point. "Emory and I have plans so"

"Right. She's probably got a curfew."

"Maureen," I say, making sure she hears the warning. "Leave Emory alone."

"Fine. I don't have time for toddlers anyway. I need you to get me an answer on the offer we made you."

"I told you that I'm not taking it." I cross my arms over chest and shake my head for emphasis. We've been around this block about a million times. "I'm not giving up creative control."

She smiles at me and this time she pours it all on and it is full of dirty promises. She reaches out and runs a fingernail over my forearm. There was a time when she got me hard and kept me that way. We never did get together no matter how hard she tried. We were always a failure to launch.

"You'll be working with me. I'll let you do whatever you want," she cajoles, her voice low and laced with sugar. Too sweet. Too syrupy. It has never sounded genuine to me and now is no different.

"Not good enough. You wouldn't agree to that and I don't know why you expect me to. Send me a better offer through my agent and we can talk."

She considers me, her teeth biting into her lower lip in either contemplation or seduction. I'm not entirely sure. I don't really care. I twist around to see if I can find Emory.

"Am I boring you, Zane?" Maureen's voice is laced with ice and the already chilly studio plummets into the arctic zone. I swallow, knowing I need to tread carefully. Nashville is a small town and Waterworld is a big label. I cannot afford to burn any bridge at this stage in my career.

I turn to her and smile, turning on a little bit of my charm. "No, but we only have this studio for a little while longer and we have more stuff to do before we can call it a night."

Emory comes back into the studio, a cup of coffee in her hand a frown on her face. She barely glances in our direction, concentrating on whatever Leon is telling her. I don't like the distance I feel between us. My fingers itch to touch the golden fall of hair that shields her expression from me, to sweep it back and let the silk of it caress my skin.

"Oh, you *like* this one." Maureen says from beside me and I look over to see her pick her purse up off the table. "I thought you were smart enough not to shit where you eat, Zane. At least that's what you told me when you turned me down."

I wince at the tone of hurt in her words but I can't deny the truth of them. I open my mouth to answer but I've got nothing. I'm not taking her offer and I'm not sleeping with her. We don't have much to talk about.

She laughs and the sound is bitter and sharp. "Don't freak out Zane. When you tired of playing Romper Room and you want to get serious about getting a record out, call me."

"Goodbye Maureen."

She takes another long look at me and then turns towards the door, her hand waving goodbye over her shoulder. "Take my offer."

I watch her leave and give a deep exhale.

"Is she pissed of that you won't be sleeping with her tonight?" Emory asks behind me.

I turn to see if *she's* pissed and I'm met with stormy green eyes and fierce emotion. Emory is a passionate person and I can see that it extends to all of her emotions and not just the ones in bed.

"I never slept with Maureen," I answer and decide that full disclosure is probably the best plan right now. "I thought about it. She wanted it."

"So, what stopped you?"

"I always figured that sleeping with Maureen would be a full contact sport, a cage match. I never want to work that hard in bed."

Her lips twitch with the hint of a smile and she dips her head to hide it from me. I could end it here but I figure she needs to know all of it.

"Her label offered me a deal but it wasn't what I wanted so I turned it down."

"And she doesn't want to take no for an answer?"

"Nope." I move close enough to pull Emory into my arms and get this day back on track and away from anymore talk about Maureen. "I don't want to talk about her. I want to talk about the surprise I have planned for you."

She curls her fingers in my t-shirt and yanks me close. "For me? What is it?"

"Yeah, no. I'm not going to tell you. That would spoil the fun."

"Will I like it?"

I lean down and kiss her, unable to resist the allure of Emory. Her arms twine around my neck and she curls into me, her lips open and her body soft. I could stay here and do this all night but I really want to show her the surprise.

"I hope you love it."

THIRTEEN

ZANE

"What did you do?" Emory asks, her eyes wide as I tug her into the suite at the Hermitage Hotel.

Everything I arranged is here: the champagne, the rose petals on the king-size bed.

Suddenly I'm really worried that this was the wrong thing to do. Too presumptuous. Too manipulative. I can't tell from her tone if this was a good move or a bad move. When she turns to look at me I scramble for another reason but my mind is a total blank. I go for the truth of it.

"Your first time should be special and I think you deserve more than my mattress sitting on a box spring on the floor."

She stares at me for so long that I really start to worry. It's clear that I might have completely misinterpreted what was going on here.

"If I got it wrong, we don't have to anything more than what we've been doing. We can just fool around, order some room service and pay-per-view. We can enjoy a big bed that isn't on wheels for a change."

Emory drops her bag on the floor and walks over to me,

her lips curving up in a sexy half-smile. She stops in front of me and lean up and kisses me. Not hot, not wet. It's almost chaste but the power of it rocks me on feet. I reach out and catch her face gently between my hands as she pulls away.

"This is perfect," she whispers. "Thank you."

I pull her close again and run my nose along the soft skin of her cheek. She closes her eyes and nuzzles back, a deep sigh escaping her lips and settling over me. Calming me. Suddenly, this feels right.

"Zane?" She asks, soft and sweet.

"Yeah?"

"Make love to me."

I look down at her and smile, watching as she slowly grins back. "I'd love to."

We lean towards each other again and I dive in for another kiss, licking at her lips until she parts them. Her hands settle on my shoulders, her fingers digging into the muscle there before sliding down my chest until they reach the hem. She tugs on the material at the same time I walk backwards and ease us both down on the bed. With a laugh I give in to her and help her lift the shirt over my head and toss it to the floor.

Emory dips her head and kisses the tattoo on my bicep, and then the one across my pectoral. She nips the flesh just below my collarbone and laughs when I jump.

"I love your ink. So sexy."

"You have too many clothes on," I say, easing my fingers under the hem of her top and quickly getting it off and out of the way. Her bra is a light pink and almost blends in with the pale blush of her skin. "Goddam, you're beautiful."

Emory slides her hands into my hair and tugs me to her and takes my mouth in a kiss full of longing and hot desire. I give in and lean us both back onto the coverlet, wrapping my arms around her and covering her with my body. She arches up into me, my jeans and her skirt an unwanted barrier between us.

"I've got to get these off you, baby. It's been too long since I got to touch you." I lean up on one elbow and brace myself, my other fingers unbuttoning and easing the zipper down on her skirt. I push it down to her thighs and she wriggles it off the rest of the way. I run my fingers down her arm, across her hip, the lightest touch between her legs. "You're so hot here already. Are you wet?"

"I'm always wet for you Zane. It's becoming a problem."

"Not for me it isn't." I laugh and grab her hand, kissing her finger, then her palm, and finally her wrist where her pulse is fluttering under the skin. "I want to see all of you, Em."

She nods and sits up, allowing me to unclasp her bra and slide it down and off her body. Her breasts are heavy, the nipples tight and my mouth waters to taste them but I postpone that in favor of getting her completely naked. I slide down beside her and reach up and slide her panties off. Emory lying back against the pristine white sheets with the rose petals sprinkled there is enough to steal my breath.

She's long and lean, her skin flawless and soft. The rose pink of her nipples and the deeper pink of her pussy entice me to taste and lick. I wedge my body in between her legs and crawl up her body until we are face-to-face. I look down at her and a wave of possessiveness grabs me and I take her mouth in a kiss.

This one is nothing like the others. It is deep, and fierce and sends sparks of fire under my skin. My cock is hard and heavy against my hip and I slowly grind it against the softer span of her belly. Her hands wedge between us and she distracts me from her mouth when she unzips me and starts shoving the denim over my hips and down my thighs. We keep kissing, laughing lightly when we both have to work at kicking the jeans entirely off.

When my erection settles against the slick heat of her sex, all laughter is lost in a bone deep groan from us both.

I reach down and grab her thigh, lifting until I can slide the entire length of my dick up and down, in between her wet folds. I kiss her lazily, taking my time and allowing us both the chance to taste and feel before we lose all control. We rock against each other, letting the pleasure build.

"You feel so good," Emory sighs breathlessly against my mouth.

"This is nothing compared to how good I'm going to make you feel."

I move down her body until I can suck on her nipples. I lick them both, alternating between the two, admiring the way they darken and glisten with my spit. I suck the right one into my mouth, covering the left with my hand when she arches up on a cry of pleasure. Her legs spread even wider and my cock is slippery with her arousal as she bucks up against me. Emory's fingers dig into my scalp as she tries to keep me in place and guides my mouth the skin I have neglected.

"Please Zane." She writhes underneath me, her body begging for something I'm not ready to give her yet. "Do it."

"Be patient, Emory. I'm not rushing this for you."

"I don't need all this foreplay," she complains but there's no heat in it.

"Too bad. I love foreplay and I want to lick you all over. Your nipples are sweet and I know you're pussy will be even sweeter." I run a finger along her lips, and spread the slick lube already there. "I'll eat you until your thighs are slippery and wet with it and then I'll slide into you with my cock and make you come all over again."

She curses at me under breath and I smile, relieved that she wants it as bad as I do.

I press a final kiss against her nipple and lift over my head to grab her hands and place them on her breasts. She lifts her head and looks at me, a question in her eyes.

"So, be a good girl and touch yourself while I make you come. I want you good and wet when I fuck you."

FOURTEEN

EMORY

I'll do anything he wants when he talks to me like that.

Eric never did. He was always careful, even when he was really horny but I never wanted to be on that pedestal. You can't let go when you're up that high.

Zane is making me crazy with the slow burn tonight. I'm on fire, crazy to have him inside me and he's taking his time.

"I want you inside me," I beg and I feel him shiver. Good, I don't want to be the only one on the edge.

He eases down my body and bows his head to press a kiss against my hip, then at the top of my curls, the inside of my thigh. I angle my head so that I can watch him and our eyes lock when he dips down with purpose. He stops and reaches up to lazily stroke my nipple.

"I thought I told you to touch yourself," he says and then licks once and only once across my clit. "Do it if you want more."

I don't have to be told twice when I need his mouth on me. I cup both my breasts in my hand and begin a slow, teasing swipe of my nipples with my thumbs. He gives me dark look and lowers his face to my sex.

His mouth is hot and wet as he kisses my pussy, sucking on me, licking. He uses his fingers to caress me, to tease me with shallow dips inside my body. I try to grind down on it, to force him deeper but he refuses, keeping me on the edge with it.

I ache with my need. My skin is hot and slick with sweat as I strain to come.

"Lift up baby, " he says and I follow his lead as he slips a pillow under my hips and raises me higher off the bed.

Zane settles back between my legs, his mouth tracing down my sex with light teasing kisses and then lower. I gasp in surprise and my legs spread even wider when his shoulders nudge them apart. I'm wide open to him, and anything he wants to do to me and I shiver in anticipation.

His thumb glides over my clit, spreading my lube and making me moan as I feel the orgasm building inside me. Zane laps at me as if he's starving for something he can only get by making me feel good. When he begins to fuck me with his tongue, I grab the coverlet and twist it between my fingers as the first wave hits me.

"Zane. Oh god." I hump against him as the hot, tingly glow of pleasure rips through me. It's amazing and awful in its intensity and I try to pull away from it, to distance myself from it but he doesn't let me. His hands grip my hips and he drags slow, lazy, wet, hot kisses along the tender skin of thighs, over my hip and across my belly until I'm relaxed and limp.

He reaches down to where his jeans are bunched at the bottom of the bed and produces a condom. I watch as he kneels between my legs and smooths the rubber down his length. He smiles, that's devil's own grin that makes me clench my thighs in anticipation as he strokes himself from tip to root.

Zane leans over and kisses me, his tongue stroking along my lower lip and I feel the head of his cock pressing against the entrance to my body and inside me. I gasp at the stretch, my hand reaching to grasp his hip and urge him on.

He drops his forehead against mine and groans, flexing his hips to push deeper. I can feel the strain of his muscles as he struggles to control himself as he slowly fills me up. He lifts his head and kisses me hungrily, sliding his fingers into my hair as he slowly rocks his hips against mine. Our tongues slide together as he continues the slow thrusts. All the way out and then back in. I can feel every inch of him.

I lift my leg higher and he slides in deeper and the fullness and pleasure interrupts the kiss. I slide my palms over the planes of his back, the bulge of his biceps until I can wrap them around his neck and keep him there with me. We are nothing but a slow glide, sloppy kisses, and gasping, aching breaths.

"Please baby, harder. I need you." The words out of my mouth before I even realize I've said them and it flips a switch in Zane.

He freezes for a moment and then the tension inside him snaps and he picks up the pace and pulls my leg up higher so that he can plunge in deep. His cock touches all of me on the inside while the hard plane of his pelvic bone rubs against my clit with every thrust. He kisses me, swallowing my louder moans and sighs as I release my hold around his neck and grip the bunched sheets under us.

"Oh Christ," Zane whispers against my throat and it feels like a prayer. His voice is broken and needy when he pleads. "Tell me that it's good. Tell me."

"So good. So fucking good," I answer in between the

deep lungfuls of air I try to inhale as a new, sharper tension coils in my belly. I've come before but this is different, the fullness making the pleasure almost unbearable. My skin is tight and hot and I don't know how it will keep me inside. I feel like I'm going to come apart. "Zane."

He must hear the fear and joy in my voice be cause he pulls back and all I can see is the copper rimmed onyx of his eyes focused on my He murmurs my name softly and then kisses me roughly, a quick thrust of tongue before he breaks it.

"Baby, just let go. I'm here with you. Right here. Let go and take me with you." His words are tinted with dark need and a gentle affection that makes my chest ache and my pussy clench around his cock. "Come on. All over me."

A drop of his sweat rolls down his nose and hits my breast, his movements sharper and focused as I lift my own hips to meet him each and every time.

"Yeah, fuck me. Emtake me. Take all of me," he growls and I close my eyes as the pleasure slams into me with his deep, hard thrust.

I claw at his back, my nails digging in like I'm afraid that he'll stop, that he leave me here alone in this intoxicating blend of sex and friendship and illusion.

Zane yells and bucks his hips, digging in his knees to get more leverage as he shoves his cock into me faster and in time with the beat of his orgasm. He slumps against me, his large, hard body covering mine as a final act of compassion from this man who is such a strange mix of elusive Peter Pan, loyal friend, and tender lover. His fingers shake as they cup my face and gently pull me to him for a soft kiss.

We lie there for a while, long past the time when his softening cock has left my body empty and aching. I have him wrapped in my arms, holding his full weight against me as his fingertips trace a hypnotic pattern on my shoulder.

"We need a shower," he whispers against my temple.

"I" I bite my lip and wonder if I should say what immediately came to mind. He senses my hesitation and huffs out a barely-there laugh.

"I've had my mouth on your pussy and you've had my cock in your mouth and inside you, just tell me. Embarrassment between us is pointless."

It's blunt and so totally Zane and it is completely, 100% right.

"I don't want to shower because I want your scent on me when I wake up tomorrow. I want to smell like us."

He groans and lifts up on one elbow to look down at me, the smirk on his face sexy and confident. "That is the hottest thing anyone has ever said to me."

"Yeah?"

"Yeah." He kisses me, gently as if he's sipping from my mouth. "You were so fucking good, Little Bird. I want to do it again. Please tell me it was so good you want to do it again."

"I want to do it again."

"Thank fuck," he murmurs and then kisses me deeply, his tongue exploring me slowly and thoroughly. When we pull apart we are both breathing hard and he swallows hard before speaking. "Thank you, Emory. Thank you for letting it be me."

"I'm glad it was you, Zane."

He pauses and I can see hesitation as it clouds his eyes and roots itself in the little furrow between his eyebrows. In spite of what he just said, a brief spark of panic lights up in my gut. I have no idea what he is thinking and right now I don't want the spell broken. I just want to hide here in this beautiful suite with the sexiest man I've ever met and pretend that this is my life. The one I came here to find.

"I've been thinking about what you said on the phone the other night."

I still have no idea what he is talking about so I just wait, my heart pounding.

"I think I want you to have a claim on me," he says and dips his head so I can't look him in the eye. He's hiding from me, from this and I'm going to let him because it scares the shit out me too. "I don't know what you call it but I want you to expect to be the one in my bed."

"Like a boyfriend?" I ask, stunned by where this conversation is gone.

He meets my eyes again and I see the struggle going on in his head. New territory for him but he's being honest with me, and right now, that's enough.

"You know what? We don't need a label. Not us." I say and push a curl of his dark hair from his face and smile. "Let's just write music and have more sex and see where this goes."

The relief on his face is clear and I tamp the tiny flare of disappointment in my gut because he's not ready to make some commitment that I'm not sure I'm ready for either. I like where this is going though.

A lot more than I'm ready to admit.

I'm glad when he lets it go with a sheepish smile and the second best suggestion I've heard all night.

"Are you hungry? This place makes the best grilled cheese you've ever tasted."

FIFTEEN

ZANE

"This is the best twenty-one dollar grilled cheese I have ever had," Emory says.

She sits on the other end of the window seat in the hotel room, wrapped in the complementary robe with one hand holding the sandwich and the other holding a french fry slathered in ketchup. Her hair is a mess and she has no makeup on but I think she looks gorgeous.

"What? You don't agree?" She asks, biting down on the french fry with a playful chomp. She watches me, pausing when I just keep staring at her. "Do I have ketchup in my hair or something?"

I laugh. "No. You just look really good."

"Better than this twenty-one dollar grilled cheese?"

"Way better." I lean over the distance between us and press a kiss to her mouth. It is short and salty and I while I take every opportunity to delve in and taste her, I pull back and smile down at her when it is done. "You okay?"

"Are you asking if I'm feeling any side effects from letting you take my v-card?"

"Smartass." I deliver another swift kiss to her lips and

lift my hand to glide my fingers along her cheek. She closes her eyes and leans into my touch. "I'm asking if it was good for you. Was it what you wanted?"

Two heartbeats pass and she opens her eyes, the green vivid and bright and something else that causes my breath to catch in my throat. Damn her, How does she do that?

"If it was the time I'm going to remember for the rest of my life, I'm glad it was you. You make good memories, Zane."

I blush and the heat of the sensation is foreign to me. It's insane the amount of pride and possession I feel right now knowing that we have shared this and no one else will ever have it with Emory. I let the sensation linger for a few more seconds before I push it away.

"I think it took two of us to make it something worth remembering," I say, dipping to press a quick kiss to the tip of her nose. It's her turn to blush when I pull back to look at her. I smile and get up, maneuvering us until I I'm sitting in her spot and she's leaning against me, the warm expanse of her body against me. The slow exhale we both make testifies to the fact that we are both where we want to be. We look out of the window and soak in the lights of the old capital building. "Tell me. First song you ever sang in public."

She thinks for a bit and then smiles. "*Jolene.* I launched into it at the Sunday School picnic and I thought my mama and all the ladies of the missionary society were going to die when I got to the verse where I'm crying because he calls her name in his sleep."

"Oh hell. How old were you?"

"Seven? Eight?" Emory giggles at the memory and I shift behind her as the movement vibrates against my semi-hard cock. It would only take a little bit for me to go for round two but I'm following her lead. I want to fall on her like a ravenous beast but this is her night. I want it to be what she wants. What she needs. "She told my daddy off all the way home but he just winked at me and showed me how to work the chord progression even smoother."

"I think I would have liked your dad," I say and nuzzle against the silk of her hair. I inhale deeply. She smells like citrus and sunshine and sex. I loop my arms around her waist, dipping my fingers inside the flap of her robe until I find the warm satin of the skin on her belly. She hums and rests her head in the crook of my shoulder, rubbing her cheek against me in a gentle sweep of affection.

"He was pretty great. I'm just sorry that he had to lie to be happy."

"You and Kit are okay with how that all went down?"

"We can't change it and it really wasn't up to us," she says, her voice soft. "She's got some anger for being left alone with her grandparents and her mom but she understands why he did it. I know for me I've decided that I need to just leave it in the past and embrace the fact that I have a sister now. To do anything else will make me nuts."

The silence stretches out between us again. Comfortable while also charged with the electricity that spans between us all the time. I've gotten used to feeling like I'm holding a live wire whenever she's around. It still feels dangerous but I'm starting to crave the edge of never knowing whether the spark is going to give me a thrill or kill me.

"Where did you grow up Zane?" Emory breaks into my thoughts and brings me to a topic I've had on my mind the last week.

"You'll see it tomorrow when we play at the PNC Arena in Raleigh. I grew up in a small town called Ivy, just outside of town."

She shifts to look at up at me, her eyes wide. "Really? How do you feel about going home? Happy? Nervous?"

"I guess I need to figure it out since my family is coming to the show," I offer with a tight smile and a shrug I know isn't convincing. "Mom, Dad, my brothers and their wives. The whole gang."

"Is this the first show of yours they'll see?"

"Yeah." I consider telling her the entire truth of it and decide to go for it when I look into her eyes and remember what a gift she gave me tonight. Our friendship is obviously the kind that can withstand a little bit of truth. "I finally feel like I've gotten to place where I can hold my head up to my old man. One of the opening acts for Kit's tour is proof that this music thing wasn't a waste of my time."

The words are still as bitter on my tongue as they were to hear them all those years ago.

"So this is a way to throw it in their faces?"

I shake my head and let it all out. The real truth.

"My dad wasn't the only one to draw a line in the sand all those years ago. I screwed up and so did he. It's time to try to leave it in the past like you and Kit have done." I take a deep breath but I fail to keep the emotion out of my voice. "I don't know how it's going to be but I miss my family and if there is a way to fix this mess, I need to take it. This is the first step, I think."

Emory shifts around even more to face me, her fingers trace along my lips and I press a kiss to them and do it again when she smiles.

"It will work out, Zane."

Oh hell. There's that simple honesty from her again. More seductive than any low-cut dress or come-on line. It's what makes her so unique, so real. Its what makes me want to stake my claim, to enter into that zone where promises are made. When I said it earlier, the words just tumbled out and once they were spoken I wasn't sure if I could back them up. I want her. I really like being with her but I'm not sure I'm ready yet and somehow she knew it and gave me the space to figure it out.

"Are you a fortune teller Little Bird?" I smile and lean down for a soft kiss. I linger, coaxing her into a series of progressively deeper kisses that leave us both panting for air. I tug aside the lapel of robe until I can stroke her skin, the taut pebble of her nipples, the tender underside of her breast and lower. She spreads her legs for my touch and I groan when I discover how wet she is. "Jesus, Em. I want to be inside you again. Please."

"I need to check my crystal ball," she teases, gasping when I enter her with one finger and stroke her clit with my thumb. I smile against her mouth when she moans.

"So, what does it say? Am I in or not?"

"Not yet" She pulls back and flashes me that dark angel grin that is quickly becoming my very favorite thing about her. "but you will be."

And that's all the future I need to know right now.

SIXTEEN

ZANE

The farm looks exactly the same.

I pull the rental car into the gravel area just to the right of the house under the crepe myrtles. They are in full bloom, the tiny white flowers sometimes raining down with the breeze and giving the illusion of summer snow.

"This is lovely, Zane," Emory says from the passenger seat, her big green eyes taking it all in. "What kind of farm is it?"

We unfasten our seatbelts and slide out of the car. I open the trunk and grab our overnight bags, hefting them over my shoulder. Voices drift up from the back of the house, kids squealing and the low rumble of adult conversation. I hold out my hand to her, relieved when she weaves her fingers with mine. Once again, I'm glad I asked her to come with me. Emory's gentle strength calms me and the cowardly part of me knows she'll be a great buffer between me and my dad.

"Cattle. Soybeans. Corn." I look around the land, noting the new barn behind the one I used to clean out when I was a kid. "I'm sure my brother David has changed some things. He runs the farm now and has an agricultural degree."

I follow the path around the house and duck under the lattice arbor covered in mom's roses and emerge into the bright sunshine of the back yard. Everybody is here and they all turn to look at me at the same time. It would be funny if I didn't have a million butterflies in my stomach. Emory squeezes my hand lightly and I look down at her and smile.

"I'm glad you came," I say.

"I'm glad you asked me." She smiles and nods towards my waiting family. "Introduce me Wyatt."

I laugh and tug her with me as I face the gauntlet of hugs and kisses from my brothers, their wives and kids. We are swarmed by the little ones, anxious to get a close look at the visitor.

"Emory, I would call out the names of all these brats but my brothers keep producing children faster than I can get the names memorized," I joke as she is engulfed in hugs from all the little Wyatts. They practically tackle her to the ground with their enthusiasm but I can see that she loves it.

"If I could just figure out how these babies are made I might be able to make it stop." David jokes as he picks up his youngest daughter, Ava. She reaches her chunky hand out to Emory, her face covered in what looks like watermelon.

"Well, what I heard is that when a mommy and a daddy love each other very much and share the same toothpaste, babies happen," I answer, keeping my voice deadpan and completely serious.

My seven year-old nephew, Stevie disagrees. "Uncle Zane, that's wrong. Babies are made when grown-ups kiss and the male puts his penis—"

David uses his free hand to cover up his son's mouth before he can spill the secrets of the universe.

"Stevie, I told you we weren't going to talk about that in front of the little kids," David warns and flashes an embarrassed smile at Emory. "He rides on the school bus with older kids who tell him *everything*."

"Do they get it right? Or are they passing on bad info?" Emory asks.

"It is scary how much they get right. I blame it on the internet." He lets go of Stevie and extends his hand to her. "I'm David. You were amazing last night. Best show I've ever seen."

"Thank you so much." She blushes and immediately tries to change the subject like she always does when it involves her talent. "I'm excited to meet all of you."

"I'll introduce you to the rest of the clan," I say and grab her hand again, leading her over to the brick patio covered in lounge chairs and tables. We spend a lot of time out here in the summer and my mom makes sure it's comfortable. I point to each person as I go around the crowd. "This is David's wife Susan. My other brother Sean and his wife Cathy."

She shakes hands and smiles at them all and I can see that they are already smitten. Emory has that gift on and off the stage, one look and most people are hooked. I know she intrigued me on first sight.

"This is my mom," I say and release Emory long enough to wrap my mother in a big hug. She squeezes me tight and I grunt under the pressure. "Mom, let go! I can't breathe."

"If you came home more often I wouldn't have to squeeze you so hard," She teases while she releases me only to give me a visual inspection from head to toe. "You need to eat."

"I eat fine. Ask Emory."

"If you count pizza as the only major food group, he eats all the time," Emory says and throws me under the bus with a look that says she's not sorry. My mom chuckles and pulls my guest into a fierce embrace that makes her squeak in surprise. I flash her a you-deserve-that look and lean against the picnic table. "Thank you for having me, Mrs. Wyatt."

"Call me Sylvia," my mom says as she lets her go. "You were really wonderful last night Emory. You have so much talent."

"So does Zane. Does he get it from your or Mr. Wyatt?" Emory asks, looking around my mom to my dad. He's standing by the grill and turning the burgers and when he looks up, his face has its usual stoic expression. Emory's smile dims and I know what she sees.

James Wyatt. Man of steel and granite. Every inch of him covered in sharp edges and thorns.

My father is not unkind man but he is not easy. He grew up poor, working a farm with his father and grandfather and sometimes taking on other jobs to pay the bills. He is solid and reliable and honest to a fault but he is not soft or welcoming. He is polite but never expressive.

If we were any more different, I'd be on Mars.

"He doesn't get it from me, I can assure you of that," he says and motions for Sean to come over and take his place by dinner. He wipes his hand on a towel tucked into his back pocket and extends it to Emory. "I'm James Wyatt. We are pleased to have you here with us."

"The pleasure is mine," she answers, her tone subdued but still warm. I don't think he scares her but she's treading carefully. "Thank you for having me."

I walk over and extend my own hand to him. We don't hug but the grip is firm and it lingers for a few moments.

"It's good to see you dad."

"You too Zane."

"Burgers are ready," Sean says and I could kiss him for the perfect timing.

The flurry of movement to get all the food on the table, the kids settled at their table and our plates filled sucks all the tension out of the situation. We tuck into the food and talk about the farm and the neighbors. A typical dinner conversation for the Wyatt family.

"You doing okay?" I lean over and murmur against Emory's ear, letting my cheek rub against the silk of her hair.

"I'm good."

"Still glad you came?" Her only answer is a smile and her hand landing on my knee under the table.

"The show last night was amazing," David says. "You two are really great together. And that song? You blew me away!"

"I'm just sorry that you couldn't have stayed and met all of the band," Emory says.

"We had to get back. Farm work starts early," my father answers from his seat at the other end of the table. "We aren't usually up that late and it took us an hour to get home."

"Zane, did I tell you we got a call from the Charlotte Observer?" My mom's eyes are full of excitement and mischief and I groan with all the possibilities. "They wanted to talk to us about your childhood and such. I even gave them some of your pictures."

"Oh my God. Which ones?"

"The one of you in your Little League uniform and the one with the purple hair."

I groan and drop my fork on my plate so that I can cover

my face. "You have a million pictures of me and you give him *that* one?"

"Purple hair?" Emory asks, her voice confused. I try to intervene but my brother David is happy to clear it up for her.

"Zane went through a period of time where he thought he was David Bowie or something."

"Iggy Pop," I mumble, the heat of my embarrassment crawling over my skin. "I went through a punk phase."

"Every time I would buy a tub of Kool-Aid, he'd use half of it to dye his hair," my mom says, her evil grin saying that she is happy to share all of my deep dark secrets with the world. "I finally had to hide it from him."

Emory starts laughing beside me, her belly laughs spurring all the others to join her and soon I'm surrounded by their snorts and useless attempts to get themselves under control. She looks at me, her eyelashes wet with her tears and I reach up to smooth them away with my thumb.

"You think that's funny?"

She inhales deeply, trying to stop the giggles. "I really do."

"So glad I could amuse you." I smile even though I don't think any of its funny. She's so pretty with her pink cheeks that I have to lean over and kiss her. I plan on it being short and sweet but she leans into my touch on her cheek and it lingers. Not porno or unsuitable for the kids sitting behind us but it is deep and filled with the longing for her that is always just under my skin.

We break apart and I realize that the laughing has stopped and everyone is eyeing us with curiosity. My sister-in-law, Cathy, looks ready to pounce with what I'm sure will be endless questions such as "How long have you been together?" and "Is it serious?" Topics I do not want to get into when I don't know the answer.

My mom saves me and I take back all the horrible things I was just thinking about her.

"The reporter wanted to know what we thought about your career. You know, as your parents."

My heart skips in my chest, a lead weight of crappy possibilities settles in my gut.

"And what did you say?"

"I didn't. Your father did."

My head swivels to the head of the table where my dad sits, quietly eating his potato salad and my stomach grabs that lead weight and does a dive into my toes. I can only imagine what he said and although I don't really want to know, I might have to do some damage control when the article hit the newsstands.

"What did you say dad?"

The table is silent because everyone wants to know. He's been so vocal about his opposition to my choice that I bet I can recite it without him saying a word.

"I told him that it takes a lot of guts to leave home against the advice of your parents and go to a city where you know no one and chase a dream that most people never achieve. I told him that as a father I couldn't be more proud."

My dad looks up and meets my eyes and what I see there is something I never thought I would see: respect. Not approval. Not understanding. But, I'll take it. It's more than I could have asked for.

I stare for several long moments before I finally find my voice. It takes a couple of short coughs but I eventually croak it out.

"Thanks dad."

"You're welcome."

He turns to Sean and asks about some fertilizer and gradually the conversation turns to topics that do not require me to contribute. Thank fuck, because I couldn't talk now if my life depended on it.

Emory's hand finds mine under the table and she leans over to whisper in my ear," That's good."

I hold on to her warmth and blink away the emotion pooling in my eyes, pulling myself together enough to nod and whisper back to her.

"The best."

SEVENTEEN

EMORY

I can't sleep.

I'm lying in Zane's childhood bed and staring up at the stars through the huge window just behind the headboard. The bed is a twin, made for a growing boy and young man, and surrounded by all of the paraphernalia from his childhood. Sports trophies, photos with his brothers at a lake and the beach and on the front porch. A letterman's jacket for baseball and a secret porn stash under a loose floorboard in his closet that his mom still hasn't found.

He's downstairs on the couch because he refused to sleep on the futon in the guestroom that doubles as Mrs. Wyatt's quilting room and I'm wide awake trying to sort through all the crazy stuff in my head and the even crazier stuff in my heart. It's like I have a constant lyric loop of the mushiest crap running through my head whenever Zane is around and even more when he isn't.

It isn't good. I'm falling for him and he's having a good time with a steady piece of ass on tour.

That's not fair. He's treated me well. He's invested in

our friendshiprelationshipas much as I have. But we have no labels and I think I might be a girl who needs them.

The stars above me are clear and bright. It's the kind of view you only get out in the country. I envy them their clarity. I could use a little bit of it right now.

The door opens on a sigh and I look over, pulling the covers up to my neck like some old lady in an old movie until I see who it is. I'd know that silhouette anywhere.

"Zane! You can't be in here," I whisper. "You're mom was pretty clear with that she doesn't want any funny stuff going on in her house."

He laughs and tugs his t-shirt off and tosses it on the floor. He's wearing only his boxer briefs and I can see the outline of his hard cock where it tents the fabric.

"Little Bird, my mom knows me. She expects me to get up to 'funny stuff' in her house. She'd be disappointed to find out that I didn't."

I shake my head and laugh even though I know I'm just encouraging him. I sneak a glance over his shoulder towards the door.

"I'm a guest here. I don't want to be disrespectful."

"Well, then we just can't get caught," he drawls, lifting the covers and sliding in beside me in the already too small bed.

He wraps his arms around me and pulls me close, so that I'm draped over his body, nose-to-nose. He grabs my chin and pulls me down into a soft kiss. I respond like I always do, eagerly and encouraging. I run my fingers over his chest, down to his waist where I dig my fingers in and pull him closer. Zane rolls over until I am under him and he starts a slow grind against me, clearly trying to be quiet.

He breaks the kiss, nipping gently at my bottom lip and I chase his tongue, hungry to have him inside me, somehow.

Anyway I can get it. I slide my hand down his back and across his ass, tracing the crack with my finger, brushing over his skin the way I know he likes it.

Zane groans and jerks against my touch and the bed squeaks. Loudly. We both freeze.

I let his mouth go but I can feel his hot puffs of air against the wetness on my mouth as we strain our ears for any sign of movement. Nothing.

I relax eventually but gasp when he growls in frustration and pushes himself up and off my body. The blanket goes flying off the bed and onto the floor, quickly followed by all the pillows and then us. A tightened arm around my waist and a flip and we both land in a heap on the pile of bedding.

"Much better," Zane says as he reclaims my kiss. It's hot and wet and dirty in the way that it can only be when you're afraid to get caught. His hand delves under my tank top and finds my nipple, rolling it between his fingers and making me shiver.

I pull out of the kiss and rest my forehead against his as I close my eyes and focus on the river of pleasure running between my breast and my sex. I'm already wet, burning up between my legs where I am rocking against his erection.

"I could come like this," I moan, grinding down harder when his hips buck up under me.

"Could you? You'd could come all over me with your clothes still on?" He asks, his other hand rubbing over the front of my panties. "Goddam, you're soaking wet, baby."

He spears his hands through my hair and pulls me back down to his mouth. This time the kiss is bruising and ferocious and desperate. It's like that first kiss in the Javelin Club but unlike any kiss we've had before. I'm not sure what's happening here but it feels important.

"This is different," he says, as if he can read my thoughts."

"In a bad way?"

He shakes his head. "No. Better. Like I belong here. Like you belong here with me."

"I do," I answer, pulling back to look into his eyes to gauge his reaction to my words.

"You belong *to* me," he says.

His emphasis is not lost on me and I can only imagine that the shock racing through my body is echoed on my face.

"You know it's true. Don't worry Little Bird" He puts two of his fingers in my mouth and presses against my tongue. I suck on them, getting them wet and becoming wetter in my sex with every suckling pull. "You've got a claim on me."

I struggle to wrap my head around what he just said but I stop analyzing the minute his hand glides under the back of my panties and his wet fingers press against my asshole. I arch up and against the pressure, panting with the extra adrenaline rush. Zane's head bobs down and I barely feel the rush of air over my bared nipple before it is replaced with the wet, scalding heat of his mouth at the same time his middle digit pushes up inside me.

I cry out and clamp a hand over my mouth as he penetrates me and sucks me to the sharp edge of my orgasm. The initial burn of his intrusion stings in the best way and I push down, encouraging him to continue fucking me with his slow push and retreat.

Another first for me.

Zane hums in approval against my chest as I rock back and forth, up and down. It feels amazing.

When he releases my breast, I look down and find him

staring at me. The twist of his lips is wicked, the twist of his fingers erotic.

"You like that, Em?"

I nod, biting my lip when eases the second one inside me. It stings a little and then it melts into the sweetest pulse of all good things.

"I like seeing your eyes go black, pupils so blown with your pleasure that I can't see any of the emerald. It's fucking hot."

"Come on and fuck me," I beg, lifting my hands to hang on to his shoulders for leverage. "I need it. Need you."

He looks at me like he's memorizing me and I hope he sees what he's doing to me, what he's made me into. A woman who begs her lover to take her whichever way he wants. A woman who is determined to make her own way, find her own path.

"I want to fuck you here," he says while flexing his fingers in my ass. I gasp and writhe against the penetration, wondering if his cock would feel as good. "But not on the floor when I can't let you scream." He nips my bottom lip. "Because I think you'd scream if I took your ass. I've got a feeling that you'd really love it."

"Too much talking, Zane. Just fuck me." I reach up and tug his hair to make him look me in the eye. "Now."

"You don't ever have to ask me twice."

I lift up far enough to slide my panties and top off and watch as he kicks off his briefs and grabs a condom from the pile of bedding. His cock is thick and hard and my mouth waters as he slides the rubber down and strokes his length as he finds the best position on floor and lies down.

I climb on top and ease myself down on him as he pushes up into me. It's the same as it always is for me. My heartbeat racing, my breathing ragged and my frantic nerves roiling in my gut and under my skin. When my ass touches his thighs I let out a slow breath and wait a moment while I get used to his thickness inside me.

Our eyes lock and I raise up on my knees and slowly lower my body back down. I watch his face in the shadows, the silver moonlight absorbed into the ebony of his hair. He's big and powerful under me but I want to feel that power over me, used against me.

EIGHTEEN

ZANE

She nudges my hip and I understand her unspoken request and flip us over.

She stretches out, her arms extended high over head, hands clasped together. I suck in a breath at what I think she's asking me to do.

"You want me to hold you down while I fuck you?"

She nods. "Yes. I want to feel you."

I get that. She wants to feel like she belongs to me. I know this because I want her to feel like she belongs to me. Possession. Primal.

"Fine." I lean over her and grasp her wrists with one of my hands. She arches underneath me and my cock slides in deeper with the movement. "Spread your legs wider."

She does, so sweetly that my eyes burn with the emotion that rises up in my chest. Goddam but I don't know what to do with her. She's fucking perfect.

I start to move my hips, thrusting into her and the soft, broken sounds she makes in the back of her throat make me insane. I know I'm not going to last very long.

"Why does it feel like it's been too long?" I whisper as I push into her, deeper and faster with each stroke.

"You just had me this morning," she half laughs and half moans, her fingers tight where they grip my hand locked around her wrists.

"Too. Fucking Long."

She giggles and then she's coming. The sight of her face in the moonlight, the joy and the pleasure that bubbles up from her chest and from between her lips is too much and I follow her over. The fire deep in my balls, throbbing and sharp as I let how good this feels take over every muscle, every brain cell.

I fall over her and take her own moan as mine with a kiss that is so desperate she must know how deep she's dug into me. My blood pounds in my ears as the last of my orgasm shoots through me and I whimper. I fucking whimper like a slave spread at her feet and begging for any little scrap. Fuck me.

I have never felt this way with a woman. This bone-deep, aching, twenty-four/seven desire to possess her and to let her own me.

It scares the shit out of me and in spite of my earlier semi-confession, I don't think I'm ready to let Emory know her power. It could be dangerous to more than just my sanity. It might be dangerous to my heart.

I fall to her side and drag her against me, letting my breaths even out with hers. Looking up I can see the same view I looked at every night my entire life. The dark sky shot through with thousands of stars. Every single one I made the same wish on: get me off this farm so I can make my music.

"Thank you for coming with me, Little Bird."

She nuzzles into my neck and I can feel her smile against my skin. "You're welcome."

"Was it terrible?" I'm almost afraid to ask because it matters to me that she like this crazy bunch that I have to claim as my family.

"It was" She pauses while she thinks about her answer and then she amps my curiosity with the "oh hell" she mumbles under her breath before answering. "It was great and awful and awkward and I'm glad I came. You're dad is scary but I think he loves you under all that gruff."

"I think so too." And for the first time in a long time, I do.

"And that's good, right?"

I repeat what I said earlier, "It's the best. It's a place to work on as we figure out the future."

We lie there a while longer and I let the warmth of her body and the citrus scent of her hair wash over me. We are both looking up at the sky when the shooting star falls across the view and out of sight. Freaking sign from somewhere but damn if I know what it means.

"Make a wish, Little Bird," I say, tightening my grip on her waist and drawing her even closer. "But don't tell me what it is or it won't come true."

Minutes pass and she asks, "Did you make a wish, Zane?"

"I did."

"So did I," she murmurs and sinks heavily against my chest, her breath evening out as she slips closer into the sleep.

"I hope we both get what we want."

I settle in to hold her for a while and to think about how I got to this place, full circle but so different and I wonder what tomorrow will bring.

NINETEEN

ZANE

The crowd in Atlanta is insane.

I make eye contact with Mac and we both shake our heads at the high energy that is pinging between the band and the audience tonight. I felt it when I opened earlier and it has just been building and building with every song. When Emory and I did our two-song set earlier in the show it was a head rush to actually hear the crowd sing the lyrics along with us. Between the video and the digital downloads, we've gained some fans and it is a bigger thrill than even I imagined.

We end the second encore on the drum and guitar avalanche of sound and then the lights go down for the last time and we all make our way off the stage to the chants of the audience for "one more song". I get off the stage first and grab a towel from a roadie and as soon as Emory is within arm's reach I tug her into the shadows of backstage and kiss her.

She wraps her arms around my neck and opens to my press. I'm sweaty and the hard-on I'm grinding against her could drill through concrete. I can't wait to get her back to the hotel and spend all night inside her. We head back to Nashville tomorrow for a three-show run and then a break for a couple of days. I want to spend the time off with Emory but I haven't found a minute to ask her.

Too many days on the road, too many early morning PR events and I've been in interviews all morning with the band or with Emory and I'm beat. But its nothing that a little one-on-one time with Emory can't fix.

It feels like forever since the night at my parent's house. She was so sweet as I fucked her on the floor, giving me everything she had and I realized as her wet heat squeezed me that I want it all. I want her. I want her in my bed and in my life. I want the labels.

My wish on that star was for her. Just her.

I'm looking forward to the time I will have to figure out exactly what that means for both of us. It won't be easy with my career and whatever she decides to do with her talent but I think we've got a better shot than most. Now, I just need to see if she's on the same page.

"Is that a guitar in your pocket or are you just happy to see me?" She jokes as we break apart.

"I can't help it. You plus the crowd and the music and I just want to get you naked and under me as soon as possible," I groan as I press a kiss against the sweaty skin on her neck. Her hands insinuate themselves under the hem of my shirt and I gasp at the sensation of her fingers gliding over my overly sensitized skin. She kisses along my jaw, nipping under my chin with little bites that make me shiver. I grab her ass, haul her closer and she raises her legs to climb me like a tree.

"As much as I like the porno encore you two have going on here, Kit wants you both in the green room," Mac's voice breaks through my haze of music–induced lust and I spin to shield Emory from his gaze. "Now."

"What the hell?" I ask and he just shrugs and gives me the "what-the-fuck-do-I-know" look.

"Come on," Emory grabs my hand and drags me through the backstage area. "The sooner we get this done, the sooner we can go back to the hotel."

I release her hand and grab her by the waist, dragging her back against me so I can still press kisses against her neck as we walk.

"I think I created a sex monster," I joke as she sneaks a hand back to grab my ass.

"Are you complaining?"

"Fuck no!" I laugh, letting her go when we reach the threshold of the green room. Everyone knows we're together but there is a place and time. Backstage after a show is always a yes. At a meeting called by your boss and your girl-friend's big sister is always a no.

We walk into the room and the wall of sound by thirty people screaming, "congratulations" makes us both stumble backwards. I reach for Emory and steady her on her high-heeled boots.

"What the hell?"

Kit is standing in the middle of the crowd with her manager, Paul Brandt and my agent, Andrew Locke. Mac stands beside her, his big hands holding a large framed item.

A gold album.

"Oh my God," Emory says and I look down to see her place her hand over her mouth, eyes wide with shock. "Oh my God."

Kit steps forward and everyone in the room gets quiet. "Emory and Zane. Congratulations, your single, *Lies and Love,* has gone gold!"

Flashes go off and I realize that the tour photographer is here capturing every moment. Everyone in the room starts yelling again and it takes a few moments for Kit to get them to shut up.

"This is an amazing accomplishment and the only thing that could possibly make it better is the fact that you have three offers on the table from three of the largest labels in the business." She gets choked up and fans her face with a hand as she takes a few second to pull herself together. "It is so well-deserved. Congratulations!"

The next minute the hoard of people rush towards us and we are hugged and kissed within an inch of our lives. Everyone is happy for us and many have tears in their eyes. They all get it. This business is hard and we just jumped a big hurdle. This is huge. I look for Emory but she's wrapped up in the arms of her big sister and Sandra. Our eyes meet across the crowd and I smile at her. She mouths "fuck yeah" and I laugh.

Emory gets me and I know just how lucky I am.

Mac looms in front of me and we fist bump before he hands over the framed record. I just stare at it, not quite believing what I am seeing.

"That's fucking awesome, man," he says. "You and Emory *killed* it."

I nod, a grin finally replacing the goofy look of shock I know I had on my face. "I can't believe it. This is...unbelievable."

"Well, *believe it* dumbass because you've got a decision to make about what label you're going to sign with so that you can start on your plan for world domination."

My plan. All that hard work. Years of writing songs for other people. Years of gigs in shitty bars and hand selling my stuff out of the back of my car. The plan worked. Halle-fucking-lujah.

"You are the luckiest bastard on the planet. You've got the hit, the contract and the girl," he says.

I look over at Emory and remember last night in my childhood bed. He's more right than he knows. "I should go buy a lottery ticket."

"You're not going anywhere until we talk about these contract offers." Andrew appears at my elbows and waves a leather binder full of papers in my face. "I got the first one about an hour after the news about the gold record hit the industry pipeline. By the time the third one rolled in, I booked a flight for Atlanta."

"Is this really happening?" I ask, wondering if I need to pinch myself.

"It's happening," Emory says as she wraps her arms around my neck and kisses me. Somebody takes the gold record out of my hand so I can hold her tight and kiss her back. She's happy and hungry and playful as she breaks it off with a tiny nip teeth on my bottom lip. "Can you believe it? This is crazy."

"It's about to get crazier," Kit says. "You guys want to take this into my dressing room and see what's on the table?"

I lean down and whisper against Emory's ear. "Come on Little Bird, let's get this over with and then I'll show you how I like to celebrate."

She shivers against me, her fingers digging into my side as we follow her sister down the hallway and into the quiet of her dressing room.

"Emory, I know you don't have an agent yet so Paul is here to advise you if that's okay," Kit says as soon as the door is closed. From her place at my side on the couch, Emory nods.

"That would be great. Thank you Paul."

"You bet kiddo," Paul smiles and lowers his big frame into a chair next to us.

"We have three offers on the table," Andrew begins and withdraws a pile of papers from his leather binder. "One from Tribeca Media, one from Roadtrip Records, and one from Radio 360. All are 360 offers with the difference being the amount of creative control."

He hands the papers to us and Emory and I take them. I look down and scan the first one and then the second and third. I look up at Andrew, confused.

"These deals are for a group. They aren't solo deals." Andrew looks at me like I have a third eye so I clarify. "We were looking for a solo deal, right?"

He glances at Emory and looks embarrassed. "Zane, the gold record was for the work you did together. Everyone loves the songs the two of you write. They want to see you perform *as a group*."

I stand up and drop the papers on the table. I'm shaking all over, vibrating with disappointment and anger. It's like whiplash when I was so high just few minutes earlier.

"Andrew, this thing was just for fun. Exposure. It was just fooling around." I just struggle with the words I need to express my outrage. It's hard to believe that I write songs for a living. "I did not work my ass off to *settle* for being part of a duo. Fuck that."

"Wow. I had no idea. I'm flattered you wasted your time with me at all." Emory fumes beside me, her green eyes on fire with her anger and her body rigid. I can also see the hurt but I don't know what she expected. This isn't anything we ever talked about. I never knew she wanted it.

"Godammit Emory, you knew what I wanted. I never hid it from you. We never talked about making this permanent. Don't act like I broke some big fucking pinky swear with you."

"I'm sorry. I thought we were building something together here."

"Sleeping together and my career are two very separate things. If you weren't nineteen you would have realized that."

Emory reels back from words and the look of hurt on her face. I replay what I said and too late I realize just how ugly they were.

"Wait. Wait. I didn't mean that. I'm sorry."

"The part about fucking me or the part about playing music with me?"

"Whoa. Time out." Kit jumps up and wedges in between us. "You guys are tired and there's a lot of shit to absorb here. Why don't you go back to the hotel, get a shower, food and we can regroup?'

She looks at Andrew and Paul and they both nod in agreement.

"It doesn't matter. I'm never going to sign those papers." I brush past Emory and head for the door. I put a hand on the doorknob and turn to direct my last comment to Andrew. "I hired you to get me a solo deal. I worked my ass off for a solo deal. Get me one."

I STILL CAN'T BELIEVE how fucked up this is.

I pace my room, head still wet from the shower, towel around my waist and a second beer in my hand. Over two hours to fume and think and I'm still pissed. Molten lava pissed. I can't believe that I worked for all that time and this is how I get a deal.

Three deals.

My gut clenches when I think of how it went down with Emory. I didn't mean to hurt her, I would never deliberately make her feel so shitty. I was pissed and the words just flew out before I even thought about them. I need to go find her and talk to her without a gazillion other people in the room and make her understand that our being together has nothing to do with business.

They are separate. At least they always were for me.

I reach for my cellphone to call her. She could be in her room or with Kit plotting the best way to string me up by my balls. I thumb across the screen to make the call when someone knocks at my door. I walk over to it, hoping that it's Emory and we can work this out. I open the door and the person standing in the hallway is not who I expected.

Not at all.

"Hey Zane. You busy?" Maureen Richards walks her ass right past me and into my hotel room. She always dresses to impress and to get you undressed and tonight is a stellar entry. Dark brown, form-fitting and very short. Her breasts are on partial display and her legs end in the kind of heels you usually see propped up on some guy's shoulder in a porno.

This isn't her office wear. This is what she puts on when she hits the club and wants to use all of her assets to get an artist to sign on the dotted line.

It almost worked on me.

"Not a good time Maureen," I say, turning to face her as she paces around my room. She picks up my beer and takes a sip and eye fucks me so hard that I wonder if I should get a condom. I'll have to adjust my towel if my dick notices anymore.

"I heard that it was a great day for you Zane. Congratulations."

"Thanks. I appreciate it." I wave my phone at her. "I was making a call when you showed up."

"You're not accepting those offers from Tribeca, Roadtrip, and Radio 360 are you?" She walks towards me but stops at the desk wedged behind the sofa. She places her bag on the tabletop and reaches inside, producing a folder full of papers. She holds it out to me and when I hesitate, she gives it an extra wave. "It's not going to bite you, Zane. Read it."

I watch her closely. Maureen never has only one agenda. It's why I avoided getting in her bed. She's always playing some angle and I didn't want a sex life that felt like a chess match. I take a step forward and put my phone down on the desk and take the papers. I open the folder and skim the pages, sighing heavily when I see what she's done.

"It's a 360 deal that gives you complete creative control. Solo. None of that duo shit the other ones tried to sell you," she says, her voice low with a hint of seduction on every single syllable. Maureen has me by the balls and she knows it. "You are going to be fucking huge and I want to be the one to help you get there."

"You or Waterworld Media?"

She shrugs and smiles, moving close enough to allow her to rub a fingertip over the edge of my towel. "I plan to take a personal interest in your career."

"Really? You weren't that interested in signing me before. Where was this deal six months ago?"

"That was six months ago." I feel her finger move inside the towel and stroke against the flesh of my hip. My cock perks up to applaud the additional offer that is obviously on the table. "Dump the teenager and take the career opportunity you worked your ass off for, Zane. All the rest of it extra perks for a job well done."

"Don't fucking talk about Emory."

"Oh, don't tell me its' gotten serious. Are you taking her to prom? Giving her your class ring?"

"Don't be a bitch."

"You want me to be a bitch, Zane, That's how I got you this amazing fucking deal." Maureen removes her hand from my crotch and trails it up my bare chest, resting the palm against my heart. Right now it is pounding like Mac's drum kit and I curse the fact that she knows she has my interest. "You don't want to throw this away because you're afraid to hurt the feelings of a girl you've been screwing for a few weeks. You really don't."

I don't agree with anything she said about Emory but it is an enticing offer.

All of my dreams laid out on a platter.

The Devil doesn't have to do anything but dress up as your wildest wish to get your soul.

"Fuck me," I breathe out on a sigh, my eyes closed tight.

"All you have to do is ask," she says and then her mouth is on mine.

I open my lips and she tastes of mint gum and the whisky she must have had down in the bar. Maureen is a gorgeous woman, experienced and she knows how to kiss a man to get a response so when she moves in and presses her body against me, I wrap my hand around the back of her neck to keep her in the place where I can control the kiss.

She immediately dives a hand underneath my towel and her fingers stroking my cock feels good. I'm a guy, so any hand on my dick that isn't mine feels good. But this doesn't feel right.

Maureen is not Emory. She doesn't smell like sunshine and citrus. She's not tall enough so our bodies don't fit together like a perfect puzzle. There's product in her hair so the strands do not feel like icy silk against my skin. She doesn't make the sound in the back of her throat that makes me shiver.

She's not Emory.

And I want Emory.

I pull away from the kiss so abruptly that Maureen stumbles and has to steady herself against the desk. She looks up at me confused and off balance, lipstick smeared until something behind me catches her eye and she transfers her focus to it.

I turn to see what she's looking at and I know.

I know just what a huge fucking mistake I've made.

Emory is there for a split second and if I thought the words I said earlier hurt her, the expression on her face right now tells me that was paper scratch compared to the knife I just put in her back.

TWENTY

Oh fuck no.

I back out of the room like my ass is on fire. There is no reason for me to stay since the image of Zane with his towel practically falling off his body and that bitches lipstick smeared all over his mouth is permanently burned on my brain. I take off down the hallway, digging my keycard out of my pocket and head to my room.

"Em, wait!"

I keep walking, refusing to look back at him. I blink my eyes, forcing back the tears I know are just waiting for the chance to roll down my cheeks. I will not cry in front of him or that woman. Never. I dig in my pocket for my keycard as I approach my room.

"Em. Stop. Let's talk about this."

Zane grabs my arm and I wrench it away, my own momentum bashing me into my door with a loud thud.

"Don't fucking touch me, Zane," I growl at him as the door across the hall opens and Kit comes out into the hall-way. I take a quick glance around and realize that half the band is witnessing my humiliation, my broken heart. "I am such a fucking idiot."

"No. No, you're not," he say, his voice gentle and pleading. It's like he thinks I won't make a scene if he talks sweet to me. I don't want to make a scene but he has lost his mind if he thinks I'm just going off quietly into the night.

I wave a hand over at where Maureen stands with smug look on her face. I hate her so much right now that I could do some damage if she got close enough.

"Yes, I am. I'm an idiot because I thought the problem was the contract for a duo when the real problem was your fear that you might have to pass up USDA primetime pussy somewhere else if you stayed with me."

"Emory!" Kit gasps, the shock in her voice clearly displayed on her face. "What the hell are you talking about?"

I laugh. It's broken and bitter and feels like glass in my throat. "I went to his room to talk this out and he's getting his new contract offer via the mouth-to-mouth method from this bitch. I shouldn't have been surprised. She's been chasing his tail forever and now she's going to get it."

"Emory, I think you need to think about this with your head and not your heart. Once you have more life experience, you'll understand that this is how business is sometimes. It's not personal," Maureen says, her tone so smooth, I wonder if she practices it in the mirror.

I ignore her and look at Zane. "It felt personal to me. Was I wrong?"

He has the good grace to look away, an embarrassed flush on his cheeks. When he finally returns my gaze, his eyes are sad and I fight the urge to make him feel better. Fuck him.

"I don't..." he stammers out his answer as his fingers run

through his hair in agitation. "I fucking don't know. I need to think..."

"Take all the time you need because I think I got my answer loud and clear. I'm not making records with you and I'm not fucking you. We're done. You can take your contract with Maureen and sell a gazillion records, see if I care."

But I do care and anyone who can hear how my voice is shaking knows it. Zane sure does and he moves to touch me but I flinch away.

"I don't want *us* to be over," he pleads.

"We. Are. Over." I say with conviction that is so hard it breaks what's left of my heart into a million pieces. "I got carried away and thought that what we had was *more* than the music. I was wrong."

We stare at each other for a several long moments. I break eye contact when I know that he's got nothing to offer me that will make this alright.

"Okay let's get this out of the hallway," Kit says and grabs me by the arm and shoves me in her room. She pauses on the threshold and barks out orders. "Maureen get the hell off my floor. I have the whole thing booked for tonight. Zane put some clothes on."

I flop down on the couch and lean over to open the mini-fridge. Grabbing a beer, I pop the top and take a deep gulp. When I look up, Kit is frowning at me.

"What?"

"Those were some pretty harsh words out there."

"I would have said more but I didn't want to lose my shit and cry in front of that awful woman." I put my beer down on the table and cover my face with my hands.

I can feel the tears seeping in between my fingers and dropping onto my knees. Kit's arms wrap around me and I let it all go. She sits there beside me and takes it like only big sister can and I am grateful for her.

"I'm so embarrassed," I say, in between my attempts to get my breathing under control.

"Don't ever be embarrassed because you fell in love. You can hurt and curse it and regret it but don't ever be ashamed," Kit murmurs against my hair. "He loves you. The stupid idiot just doesn't realize it."

I pull away from her, shaking my head as I dry my eyes. "No. No. You can't say stuff like that. I can't have hope about this. I need to see it for what it is and let it go."

"And what is it?"

"It's the end of an affair. A fling. Yes, it was intense and I invested more of myself in it than I should have but now it's over. I'm not what he wants on the stage with him or in his life. I need to accept it."

She looks mulish and like she wants to argue with me but she holds it in.

I understand the way it is. The entire situation is as clear to me as crystal and I can see that I have no place in it.

"Kit, he's worked hard for a solo deal and I think it's unrealistic for me to expect that I can come along and change that. He's a determined man and if he really wanted me, he would have fought harder but he didn't. In fact, he not only ran to another record deal but lined up another woman for his bed. To ignore that would make me either very stupid or crazy. " I sigh and face the rest of my truth. "For him the music and a relationship are two separate things. It's not for me. I wrote those lyrics for him, with him because I love him. For me it's the whole package. I can't just accept half of it and be happy."

"But will you be happy without any of it?"

"I think I have to be."

TWENTY ONE

ZANE

"You are such a dick."

I look up from my spot on the couch where I'm playing a ninja video game to see Mateo standing behind me. He drops his messenger bag to the floor and throws his keys on the table before going to the fridge to grab two beers. He hops the couch and lands with a thud, sloshing a little bit of the brew on his jeans before handing one over to me.

I take it and swallow down a mouthful of the cold beverage. It slides down smooth and then settles around the cold lump lying in the pit of my stomach. On the screen my character is getting his ass kicked all over the place. I don't really care. His beat down is the perfect demonstration of how I feel at the moment. It's the same thing I've felt since Emory left me in that hallway with my junk half hanging out of that stupid towel.

"You're getting killed, man," Mateo says, nodding towards the TV screen.

"I don't care." I throw the controller at the coffee table and watch as it bounces off and disappears. I hear a thump as it hits the floor and decide to leave it.

"For a guy who has an amazing contract just waiting for your signature, you sure are acting like an asshole." Mateo raises his palm and smacks himself on the forehead. "That's right! You haven't signed the fucking amazing contract sitting on the table yet. Instead you're lying on the couch and losing against imaginary characters in a stupid ninja game that only twelve year olds play."

"I can't sign it, Mateo. I just can't"

"Why? Because it isn't what you want? What does Andrew say about it?"

I take another sip of beer and settle back against the cushions. "He says it's a great deal because it is. They are all stellar deals and I would be crazy to turn any of them down."

"So, what's the problem?"

I know he knows the answer but he's going to bug me until I talk about it.

"I want to sign the one with Emory," I say for the first time out loud and it feels really good and shitty at the same time because I know it is too little , too late. I hurt her so badly. The look on her face in the hallway is etched on my aching heart with a burning coal. "I went to sign the deal from Waterworld. I had my pen on the fucking paper and I couldn't do it because I can't imagine doing this without her. I don't know when it happened but she became part of the plan...fuck, she's bigger than the plan." I stand and start to pace. This whole thing has me wired tighter than a newly tuned piano. "And she won't talk to me. She won't answer her phone. I even went to the loft and she's not there so I drove out to Max and Kit's place and they wouldn't even let me on the porch."

"I know. Max was torn between coming over here to

talk and jerking a knot in your ass. He is pissed and worried about you."

"I'm pissed at me too." I think back to the day in Atlanta when I screwed all this up. It was only a day ago but it feels like forever. "I panicked and said terrible things that I don't mean and then I kissed Maureen..." That thought makes me so angry at myself that I clench my fists to keep from punching the wall. "I can't stand the thought of never being with Emory again. It's got me by the balls, man. I love her and she hates me."

"Well then get her back." He looks at me like it's the easiest thing in the world. Like I can just snap my fingers and it will be like my stupidity never happened. I stare at him long enough that he says it again, slowly and with precise pronunciation. "Got. Get. Her. Back."

"I have no idea how to do that, Mateo. If I knew, I would be doing it."

"Who are you?' He plops the beer down on the table and stands cutting around the table to get within reach to poke my chest. "Seriously, who the fuck are you?"

"I don't know," I say, knowing that it is the truth.

"Where's the guy who ate mustard sandwiches when he used his scholarship money to buy a new guitar? Where's the asshole who dragged me to bars so dangerous that he had to perform behind a wire cage? Where's the man who wrote two top ten songs before he turned fucking twenty years old?" He throws his hands up in the air in disgust. "You'll do all of that for a dream but you won't fight for the woman you say you love? I ask it again: who the fuck are you?"

I stare at him as his words hit me in the gut like a sucker punch.

"You're right. But how do I do that when I can't get her to talk to me?"

"If you love her then there's only one real solution, Zane."

"Tell me. I'll do it." I am *this close* to begging and he knows it but he takes pity on me and doesn't make me wait too long.

"You need to grovel. On your knees and beg her to take you back. In public. You need to make a total ass of yourself." He smiles and delivers the singer like only a best friend can. "That should easy for you."

TWENTY TWO

EMORY

"Your Daddy would be so proud of you tonight," Mama says.

She glances at Kit standing over near the vanity in my dressing room of the Grand Ole Opry. Mama's expression turns to one of regret and apology when she realizes that references to our wayward, bigamist daddy might be a sore spot with my half-sister. But I can't even feel the full extent of the sympathy I should because I feel like I'm going blow chunks all over the "Cousin Minnie Pearl" dressing room.

"Kit" Mama reaches out a hand to the woman I now consider a sister and more importantly, a friend. "I'm sorry to bring up hard memories for you. Your daddywell he left us with a mess, didn't he?"

Kit glances at me and the look passing between us tells me that no matter how far we've come there's still a few bridges we need to cross. All I know is that if we want to do it then maybe we can become the family we both want. She nods at me like she understands what's rolling around in my head and then she reaches out and grabs Mama's hand before answering.

"Mrs. Cabell, I think we both loved him and I understand that he needed to find some happiness. He would want us to be family and share those memories."

Mama tears up immediately, her lashes blinking rapidly as she tries to force back the waterworks. Her voice is a little wobbly but strong. "Kit, I think you're right and I'd like that. Very much...but only if you call me Ruthanne."

Wow. What a difference a year makes. Even if everything else in my life went to hell, at least I've got this. A new beginning. A new family.

I step forward and we all mush into one of those sappy Hallmark movie group hugs where we all end up sniffling and awkwardly trying to maintain some sort of grip on the other two. Kit pulls out first and her eyebrows shoot up when she gets a look at my face. She shoves me towards my dressing table in the corner.

"Emory, you need to fix your eye makeup and stop bawling or you won't be able to sing."

I obey her instruction and balk when I see the damage our little moment caused. Frankenstein's Bride had more color in her cheeks than I do and fewer bags under eyes. Earlier, Kit had sent in her makeup artist to cover the evidence of all the crying I'd done over the last few days and while I can reapply the concealer, nothing will cover-up the hurt that swims in my eyes.

Wrecked. Ravaged. That pain is all my eyes and Maybelline hasn't made the stuff that can hide it. I pick up the case left by the makeup artist for touch-ups and start to fix the mess. I'm grateful to have something to do when Mama starts talking.

"Emory, I was hoping to meet Zane before your performance tonight."

I cut a glance at Kit and she winces at the question. I

haven't really filled my mother in on all of the details of what happened between us. I know there are some daughters who tell their mama everything but I'm not that girl. I'm built like my mama in that respect but where she bottles stuff up and lets it eat at her, I put it all in my music.

So tonight I'm the best damn performer in the universe and I should get an Oscar. As far as anyone knows, including mama, the only thing wrong with me is a rookie case of nerves.

I briefly lock eyes with Kit in the mirror before returning my gaze to my task. "Mama, you'll meet him tonight. He's just giving us some space to enjoy my first night at the Opry together."

"Emory got to pick her dressing room Ruthanne and she told me that you were a big Minnie Pearl fan," Kit says and turns the conversation over to a topic that doesn't make it hard for me to breathe.

Mama nods happily. "I just loved to watch her on Hee-Haw. I grew up listening to her on the old radio shows and I never in a million years thought my daughter would be playing on the same stage."

"When I played here for the first time, I thought I was going to fall down my knees were shaking so much," Kit says.

"Well, it must run in the family because if I don't fall down it will be a miracle," I say and send up a silent prayer that I don't end up on my knees in front of the live and television audience. It would memorable for all the wrong reasons.

Two quick raps on the door and just seconds after I tell whoever it is to come in, Max sticks his head inside and smiles. "Okay, they're giving you the ten minute signal so I thought I'd come get Mrs. Cabell and take her out to her seat."

"Max, that would be awesome," I walk over to Mama and pull her into a hug and kiss her cheek before pushing her towards my sister's fiancée. "I want you to clap really loud for me, okay?"

She nods and blows me a kiss as she walks away and I think I see her pull another one of the never-ending supply of tissues out of her purse and dab at her eyes as the door closes behind them. In the relative silence of the dressing room I close my eyes, take a deep breath, and slowly exhale, willing the tension that I feel creeping into my limbs to hit the road.

"You okay?" Kit asks and I open my eyes and look at her. What the hell am I supposed to say to that? It's like I'm split in two. One-half decimated by the ache in my heart and the other beyond excited that I am going to stand up in front of these people on the stage I dreamed about my whole life.

The rock and the hard place are looking really good right now.

I'm spared having to answer by another, sharper knock on the door and the voice of one of the assistants to some-body-who-makes-the-show-happen is loud and firm even through the heavy wood.

"Ms. Cabell, I need you stage right to get set-up with your monitor."

I walk over and open the door, smiling at the thirty-something woman holding an iPad and wearing a blue tooth headset. She grins back, clearly pleased that I'm ready to go.

"Excellent! I was hoping I wouldn't have to coax you out of the bathroom and slip you a barf bag like some other people I know," she jokes while sliding a look in Kit's direction.

"Hey, it was only that one time, Susan," Kit protests, walking over with my guitar in her hand. "And, for the record I didn't actually use the bag until *after* the show."

"Did you really throw up after your first-time performing at the Opry?" I ask Kit, unable to believe that my big sister, the consummate performer, ever had to deal with a case of the nerves.

"I confess to being a little green around the gills but I kept my dinner down before, during and after the show."

"I like my story better," Susan answers, giving me the "come on" gesture as she heads down the hallway. "We need to get moving."

I follow behind her trying to return the smiles of the people I pass as I make my way to backstage. My stomach is doing backflips and my heart is pounding but mingled equally with the nervousness is pure excitement. I dreamed about this moment and now it is here. Even heartache can't completely kill the moment

We turn a corner and there it is: the stage of the Grand Ole Opry. Bathed in lights I have a clear view of the performers and the full-house audience just beyond. The music is loud, the notes vibrating under my feet as the current band plays in perfect sync. It is exhilarating and terrifying at the same time, two sides of a coin.

"Wow," I say on a whoosh of an exhale, caught some-where between and laugh and gasp. "This is"

"I know. The Mother Church is an awesome sight isn't it?" Kit murmurs beside me, her hand at my back a steadying touchstone.

"Hey."

I hear his smooth, sexy-as-sin voice and curse that he still has the power to make my stomach flip-flop with excitement. I never thought I was one of those girls who go for the bad boy but when they wrap themselves up in a sweet candy coating, I'm a goner. Zane was a sugar rush and now all I'm left with is a bellyache.

I fell hard for Zane. I'm just glad I never told him. Just how big a fool I am remains my own little secret.

"Hey," I answer, proud that my voice remains steady as I turn to look at him.

He looks so good, white v-neck t-shirt, black leather pants and boots. His tats are on his muscled forearms and biceps, his dark hair down and brushing his shoulders. The cruelest part is the dark stubble in his goatee and the memory of how good it felt against my skin. He's staring right at me and I know he can see the heat that crawls over my skin. He knows me because I let him in. I hate it.

"You look beautiful," he says and the truth of it in his eyes makes me tear up. I can't answer him and just shake my head, grateful when the sound techs come over to hook us up with our in-ear monitors.

I know he cares about me. I know he thinks I'm beautiful. That's what makes this so hard; because I saw what we could have been and it felt real. I just can't get the sight of him in Miranda's arms out of my head where it replays like a marathon of grisly *Law and Order* episodes. He told me what he was about from the beginning and I just didn't believe him. My first hard lesson learned in this big city. It won't be my last heartbreak but the scar from this cut will be hard to ignore or forget. That's probably a good thing. It will serve as a warning to me in the future.

The techs finish their work and I look anywhere but at

him. I can feel his eyes on me and when I see him step forward in my peripheral vision I step back. I need to perform and if Zane touches me, I'll never get through it.

"Little Bird," he murmurs.

"Zane. Don't," I answer, my voice sharper than even I expected. I can feel his physical retreat.

"Hey, guys," Kit steps between us, her hands resting on our shoulders. "This is a big night, your first on the Opry stage. I know things aren't right between the two of you but you need to forget it for the next ten minutes. Three songs. One set. Your problems will be waiting for you when you get off the stage. You wrote an incredible song and the people in those seats want to hear you sing it. Don't disappoint them and don't steal this moment from yourselves."

I sneak a peek at Zane, we lock eyes and a lifetime of shit passes between us in those few seconds. What could have been. What we had. It all swirls in the space we can either leave gaping between us or close with one word. I don't have that word; I have no idea what he could say to make me believe him again. I have no idea what but Zane does.

"It's just the music Emory. Let it do the talking tonight." His dark eyes are intense, hot. It's like we're back in that club the first night we kissed and I feel the heat deep in my marrow. The music and this man are so tied up together for me and I have no hope of separating them right now in the wings of the Opry stage.

"Kit's right. Our shit will still be here when this is over and we can figure it out then. I don't want to miss this moment," I say as I place the strap of my guitar over my shoulders and turn away from him and face the stage. I'm a performer and that means that I will go out there and do what I need to do.

The band currently on stage finishes their set and bows to applause of the audience and then I watch as Kit is announced and walks out on the stage to introduce us. And then it is "go" time and I step out onto the stage, fighting the urge to look back at Zane.

TWENTY THREE

ZANE

The show must fucking go on.

I walk onto the Opry stage, close on Emory's heels with a smile plastered on my face. I've played when I was sick, hung over, and sleep-deprived. I can do this. Three songs. Ten minutes and the press junket after the show and then we get two days off.

Two days for me to initiate the plan get her back. I still have no idea what I'm going to do but I need to make it happen soon so I can sleep, so I can breathe again. We aren't done with the tour for six more weeks and if I fail, I don't know how I'm going to get through it with Emory so close but so far away.

The audience is still applauding and we both pause in front of the microphones to acknowledge the cheers and whistles. The lights are harsh but she shines under them, her golden hair in curls that form a halo around her beautiful face. The sweet slope of her shoulder, the spot I love to caress with my mouth, is exposed by her strapless top and the knowledge that I will never touch her there again forces me to take a sharp breath against the pain in my chest.

I step up and speak to the crowd, just like we rehearsed.

"Thanks so much for having us here tonight. What a crazy ride it has been for both of us. We never thought it would bring us here but we are so grateful. Thank you."

I look at Emory and she is poised, her hand hovering over the strings of her guitar as she waits for the drummer to count off. Our eyes meet for the briefest of moments before her clear voice spins out like gold with the melancholy song.

"Don't look back. There's nothing here for you to see. Whatever we had, whatever we made is lost. No rescue. No hope of revival. The unknown is the only thing worth hoping for since you walked away."

I close my eyes, cursing the day we wrote the lyrics. I thought I had some idea of what the words meant but I had no idea. It was like my subconscious saw the future and put the words on the page that night to torture me now.

I take up the song on the second half of the first verse.

"I saw you tonight and you looked right through me. You've moved on but I'm stuck in our past with no one to blame but myself. Foolish pride. Stupid weakness. Hoping you'll take pity on me."

A few bars and the chorus starts and I open my mouth to take up the harmony but I freeze, my throat tight. Emory continues on for two more bars, falters, and then turns to me, her eyes searching. Whatever she sees in my face makes her own voice waver, the words trailing off with the rest of the band as they realize that I have lost my mind.

The silence in such a large, packed place is complete and unsettling. Past the stage lights, I see the audience shift in their seats and the questioning looks passing between them as the moments stretch out.

"Zane," Emory says, stepping close to look at me. Everything about her stance is concerned but wary. I don't blame her. I don't know if I trust myself at this moment but I know what I need to do.

"Emory," I say, stopping when I realize don't really know how to start. I break eye contact with her and start to speak into the microphone again, unsure about what I'm going to say. Her blue eyes search my face and I ache to reach out and touch her but that won't fix this. Sex, kisses, attraction...that isn't the problem. I know what I need to do to get anywhere close to making this right. I turn from her and face the crowd.

"Ladies and gentlemen, I've spent most of my life hoping that I would be invited to play on this stage and this moment" I take a deep breath when my words catch in my throat. "this moment is a dream come true. Or it should be. But I realize that I'm standing here with everything I always thought I wanted and all I can think is that I did the wrong thing to the right girl."

I ignore the ripple of surprise that passes through the audience and turn to look at Emory. She's completely still, her eyes huge and the pale skin of her cheeks flushed with the blush that gives away her high emotion. Her long fingers grip the neck of her guitar with a white-knuckle ferocity.

"Little Bird, you have fascinated me since the first moment I met you because I knew you were special. Every second we've spent together has been the most amazing time of my life. It's never been just the music between us. The songs we've written are so good because of what we feel about each other."

She scoffs at my words, her eyes flashing with all the hurt and anger *I* put there.

"And how do we feel about each other Zane?"

"I love you and I know you love me."

I ignore the murmurings of the crowd listening to our every word and keep my focus on her.

"No. I don't."

"Yes. You do."

"I don't like you," she says, the stubborn tilt of her chin trembling a bit with her emotion.

"That's okay because I don't like me either." I reach out and grab her hand, tugging her closer. "Baby, I messed up. I was a coward and I hurt you because I was afraid to change my stupid plan for something different. Something better. But I *know* that you are the best thing that has ever happened to me or will ever happen to me. I want to live with you, love you, and make music together. Please give me another chance."

"Those are just words Zane," she says, her eyes glossy with her tears and her lip trembles but she forces out the next sentence and cuts me to the quick. "It's just the music. We got wrapped up in the music and now we just need to let it go."

There's a special kind of hell when you have your own words thrown back at you. I am there right now.

"We got wrapped up in *our* music. Not the notes we wrote down and recorded in the studio but the music that comes to life when you and I touch. When I kiss you it's like a damn symphony starts playing in my head. When we make love it's the universe's perfect melody." I take a deep breath, my own emotions choking me as I realize this might not work. I might have fucked this up beyond repair. "I love you and I need you. I need you in my bed, in my life and with me here on the stage. Nothing about this means anything if I don't have you."

"What about your plan?" She asks as a tear slides down her cheek and hangs like a perfect diamond on her chin.

I reach up and brush it away and when she doesn't reject my touch I walk forward as close I can get and cup her face in my hands.

"*You* are my plan. You've always been the plan. I just didn't know it yet."

Not a fucking sound fills the longest thirty seconds of my life as I wait to hear her answer. Her expression is full of pain and confusion and I have no idea what she's thinking. I can't wait. I give her all I've got.

"I love you Emory Cabell. When we saw that shooting star, *you* are what I wished for. Not contracts or big tours. Not even a new song. Just you."

Two big fat tears spill down her cheeks and my stomach falls into my boots because making a girl cry on the Grand Ole Opry stage can't be a good thing. But Emory surprises me. Like she always does.

"I love you too Zane."

The microphone picks up her whisper and the audience goes nuts. I ignore all of the applause and cheers and pull her to me, kissing her with relief and something that has to be joy.

Her lips are warm and soft and open to me at the first brush of my tongue against them. I dive in, wanting to claim her promise laden words before she can change her mind. My fingers slide into the silken fall of her hair and I pull her even closer, shoving our guitars to the side as we come together for our first kiss as lovers. The best kiss.

I can already hear the song I'm going to write about this. It will go fucking platinum.

I pull back from the kiss but Emory isn't done. She grabs my t-shirt in her fists and drags me back down to her mouth and the audience goes even crazier. Whistles. Hoots. Foot stomps. It is pandemonium. I get in a couple of quick swipes of my tongue before our laughter makes us break the kiss. I look beyond the footlights and everyone is on their feet as the band starts the beginning of *Lies and Love*, the opening beats fast and furious.

I turn back to look at Emory and she's grinning and giving me *those* eyes. The ones that tell me she's going to jump my bones the minute she can get me to a private, horizontal place. But this time there's something more in her gaze or maybe I'm finally recognizing what else was there all along.

"Never stop looking at me like that," I say, hoping she remembers when I said something similar but very different.

She does. Emory laughs and steps back, mimicking my movements as we get our guitars in position to play.

"Why?" She asks.

"Because I want *everyone* to know just how much I love you."

If you loved REDEMPTION, continue with the rest of the Nashville Nights series

TEMPTATION

She needs to be good.

At sixteen, Kit ditched her crappy life and moved to Nashville with only $200, her guitar, and a notebook full of songs. She hit it big, but five years of living like a rock star plus a stint in rehab has killed any good will she had with her label. The suits have ordered Kit to shape up or ship out of the limelight. The last thing she needs is a hot, sexy distraction with a sinful smile.

He doesn't know the meaning of the word.

Max Butler is as far from a celebrity as you can get and he likes it that way. A Nashville firefighter, he's living the single life with a revolving door of parties, friends, and a different woman in his bed every night. When his normal life suddenly collides with the girl on his favorite Rolling Stone cover, he sees the perfect chance to fulfill his ultimate fantasy and see just how bad Kit can be.

Sometimes bad is so very good.

With three weeks until Kit leaves for her big tour, Max promises to give her a break from being the good girl--no strings attached. But when hot days lead to sultry nights, the lines get blurred and suddenly three weeks of bad might not be good enough.

Buy it one the TEMPTATION page.

SALVATION

Letting go never felt so good.

Carlisle Queen is dying and no one knows it.

Burying the pain of losing her friends and her professional swimming career in a terrorist attack, America's former sweetheart dulls her pain with drugs, pills and parties. The bomb left her with more than nightmares; shrapnel is lodged in her back and inching closer to her spinal cord. When the doctors tell her paralysis is inevitable, she decides to take her own life rather than face a lifetime in a wheelchair.

Mateo Butler isn't anyone's hero.

Reeling from the death of his little sister and his own cowardice, he spends his nights partying and his days ignoring the medical school acceptance letters and his parents' concerned phone calls. Just a couple of months from graduation, he's facing a future filled with shame and regret. The last thing he needs is to meet the woman who compels him to be a better man.

Can they save each other?

When Carlisle and Mateo meet, the chemistry between them is combustible. They play, party and hide their true selves until one night turns their lust into something more . . . something real. As secrets are revealed and walls collapse, what they were and what they might become doesn't matter as much as who they are together. When the choice comes down to life or death, can love be their salvation?

Buy it on the SALVATION page.

ACKNOWLEDGMENTS

Huge, huge thanks to everyone who helped me get this book in your hands.

My best friends, Avery Flynn and Kimberly Kincaid, for keeping me on track and kicking my ass when necessary.

For the Sizzlemongers... I couldn't ask for a better group of friends. Not just a street team, we have become a group who support each other and I love that so hard.

The Main Man, Little Man and Lulu. My reasons to keep going, you are the fulfillment of a dream I didn't even know I had. I am a very lucky woman.

A NOTE FROM ROBIN

Dear Reader —

Thanks so much for reading my book. If you enjoyed this novella you can find out the latest info on my next release and enter for the monthly giveaway by signing up for my newsletter.

Newsletter sign up: http://bit.ly/1hde9GD

You can also drop me a line at robin@robincovingtonromance.com. I'd love to hear from you.

Xx,
   Robin

Social Media Links:

Website: http://bit.ly/1lewhMg
Facebook Profile: http://on.fb.me/YSW9n3
Facebook Page: http://on.fb.me/1fCyWuQ
Twitter: @RobinCovington
Tumblr: http://robincovingtonromance.tumblr.com
Instagram: https://instagram.com/robincovington/
Pinterest: http://bit.ly/1c1Tm5u
Amazon Follow: http://amzn.to/1L2PrAG
Reader Group: http://on.fb.me/1hZdeEu

If you enjoyed REDEMPTION, check out my other books:

A NIGHT OF SOUTHERN COMFORT
HIS SOUTHERN TEMPTATION
SWEET SOUTHERN BETRAYAL
PLAYING THE PART
SEX & THE SINGLE VAMP
PLAYING WITH THE DRUMMER
DARING THE PLAYER
TEMPTATION
SALVATION
THE PRINCE'S RUNAWAY LOVER
ONE LITTLE KISS
SECRET SANTA BABY
HER SECRET LOVER
RUSH